Mere

Carol Fenlon

TP

ThunderPoint Publishing Ltd.

First Published in Great Britain in 2018 by
ThunderPoint Publishing Limited
Summit House
4-5 Mitchell Street
Edinburgh
Scotland EH6 7BD

Copyright © Carol Fenlon 2018

The moral right of the author has been asserted.

All rights reserved.

Without limiting the rights under copyright reserved above, no part of this publication may be reproduced, stored in or introduced into a retrieval system, or transmitted in any form or by any means (electronic, mechanical, photocopying, recording or otherwise), without the prior written permission of both the copyright owner and the above publisher of the work.

This book is a work of fiction. Names, places, characters and locations are used fictitiously and any resemblance to actual persons, living or dead, is purely coincidental and a product of the author's creativity.

Various poetry quotes used in this book were taken by kind permission of the publisher from The Lake Poets (1980,1985) Dalesman Publishing Company Ltd

Cover Image © Margaret MacIsaac
Map Image © Jim Nicholson / Alamy Stock Photo
Cover Design © Huw Francis

ISBN: 978-1-910946-36-7 (Paperback)
ISBN: 978-1-910946-37-4 (eBook)

www.thunderpoint.scot

Printed and bound in Great Britain by Clays Ltd, St Ives plc

Acknowledgements

The author wishes to thank members of Edge Hill University's Narrative Research Group and Skelmersdale Writers' Group for their invaluable feedback and support during the writing of this book.

Dedication

To memories of Jo Powell

Mere

Map of Lancashire 1630

Exordium

Mere
German – meer – sea
Dutch – meer – lake

Once upon a time the great lake Martin Mere dominated the landscape of South West Lancashire and the lives of those who settled at its edges. It stretched almost to Tarleton in the north, to Aughton in the south, from Rufford in the east to Meols near Southport in the west and covered an area of some twelve square miles.

How could a body of water of such size disappear? If you look closely you will see ghostly traces in the lie of the land and the local place names: Mere Brow, Mere Sands, Merehey and Mere End. The water has been drained but human history is only a speck of time in the existence of Martin Mere.

It began long before that with the grinding of ice on rocks as the frozen wastes of the Ice Age retreated, leaving a great basin to fill with water. Polar bears and Arctic foxes roamed its fringes until tundra gave way to horsetail, duckweed, reeds and bulrush. Gradually peat formed from rotting vegetation at the lake edges, birch trees flourished and of course elders, the walking witch-trees of folklore, invisible feet sly-paddling underwater. Later came the great oak forest, gathering round the unstable boundaries of the Mere. Responsive to heat and rainfall, the Mere was forever shape-shifting.

Trees that grew on the banks in long dry years drowned and fell when rain prevailed and swelled the lake once more, sinking into the water's murky fringe. The Mere preserved its secrets in the anaerobic bog. Its edges wavered and wandered, as land gradually drifted to water.

Stone Age and Bronze Age men fished the lake in log boats made from the fallen oaks. These too in time were swallowed by the Mere along with their axes, tools and pottery shards.

Their storytelling seems to suggest they sensed the mysterious nature of the Mere. Tales of evil water spirits, boggarts and will o' the wisps were passed on through Roman and Viking settlers, through Medieval and early modern times to the stories still whispered by the older born and bred West Lancastrians over warm fires on winter nights. Celtic legends tell of water demons and the gifts and sacrifices necessary to appease them. In a number of British mosslands, ancient bog bodies have been found, almost perfectly preserved in the peat, the injuries still evident on their remains suggestive of some ritual sacrifice.

Perhaps there is worse evil in the meddling of men who try to go against nature in the pursuit of profit. In 1697 the great landowners of the district took the fateful decision to drain Martin Mere, in order to convert it to profitable arable land, destroying the old livelihoods of thatching, basketmaking, fishing and fowling and setting off a struggle that continues to this day.

Homes were built on the drained land and cereal farming attempted but implacably the water returned, flooding the whole area repeatedly during the next two hundred years. Despite ingenious drainage projects much of the land remained unworkable bog.

With the advent of modern pumping from 1850 the Mere was apparently vanquished. The old water-based industries are now virtually folk memories, although baskets were still being made in Holmeswood quite recently, but the peaty bed of the Mere is fruitful land if its acidity is carefully balanced. The area has been famous for its potatoes since 1700 when the crop was first introduced at Ormskirk.

And as agriculture has made the land give up its fertility, it has also torn out its secrets. Farm tractors have been turning up bog oaks and ancient log boats for centuries and finds of Stone Age and Bronze Age tools, Roman coins and Viking artefacts are not uncommon. The Mere keeps reminding us of those who have gone before us, of its own long history, of secrets still hidden in the depths of the peat.

To think man has conquered the Mere is human vanity. As water is drained and pumped from the land it dries and shrinks, creating the basin conditions ideal for more flooding. Even now in 2016, there is talk of withdrawing pumping from the area and farmers are throwing up their hands in horror. The Mere waits, hovering beneath the landscape, a ghostly presence under the veneer of 21st century civilisation. If you stand by the water's edge at Mere Sands nature reserve, when the day is sinking towards evening, when the mournful hoots of waterfowl flying to roost across the small lake pierce the silence, you may feel how the Mere simply bides its time. As you walk back to your car, when mist gathers, blurring the edges where land and water meet if you look up and out, you may not see the flat plain of cereal and potato fields dotted with white farmhouses; the Mere may show itself to you, mysterious and silent for as far as the eye can see.

Chapter One

June 2007

I will never leave here, no matter what they do or say. They've tried to get me to go in a home, but I put paid to that. I told them, the only way they'll get me out of here is in a box.

Oh, she's cute, that one. I'm not so daft that I can't tell when someone wants me out of the way. I can see it in her eyes, for all her syrupy words and little girl smiles. I can see her waiting, watching, when the cough starts, when I'm scrabbling for the inhaler. Well, I won't give her the satisfaction. I'm not ready to go yet, they'll see.

My ancestors fought for this land, but there were no human enemy. People die, the things they fight over are soon forgotten, but water's a creeping, seeping thing; it gathers together, puddles the land, forever trying to make itself a pond, a lake.

Happen it were a bad decision our forebears made to drain Martin Mere all those hundreds of years ago because we've had to fight it ever since with ditches and drains, hard labour, one eye cocked to the sky looking for clouds, our noses always in the air, testing for signs of rain. Yet it's grand land when it's well cared for. You get what you give and my family's give everything to New Cut farm – till now.

I can't believe our Con, wanting to sell up. There's been Askins on this land for over two hundred years. It's a good job Albert's not here to see things come to this. All our married life we slaved to keep on top of the farm and now, the fields are left to rack and ruin; strangers' horses grazing here and that Diane, leading our Con by the nose, spending the money Albert and me helped Con to save. A pond in the front garden, with a Chinese pagoda in it if you please, and fancy shrubs everywhere.

It doesn't bear thinking about; all that expense and she's still not satisfied. Now she's wanting Con to move away. What does she know of the way we worked? She's a townie, never got her hands dirty in her life. I were on the land from a very young girl, weeding, shovelling muck, bagging up spuds and all for no pay, neither.

'You'll get your reward when I'm gone,' Dad used to say and it were true, Bert and I did get the farm but not till Bert were in his forties and already struggling with his chest. I thought it best to let Con have the farm after Bert died. There weren't no one else to give it to and I couldn't manage it on my own. After all, he loves that land just the same as I do and while he were married to Christine, everything were fine, she were a good, sensible girl. Her family had Washway Farm across the moss. She knew the value of land, but like any woman she wanted a baby and no baby come.

It's like something in our family, that, because Lord knows I waited a long time for our Con to come along, thirteen years of marriage. Bert wanted to call him Thomas after his own father; he thought Conway were a daft name, after that pop star, Conway Twitty, what were popular around then, but there were something about it that I liked I don't know why. Coming so late he were so special, I wanted him to have a name that were special, different to the other local kids.

'Be patient, girl,' I said to Christine, 'it'll come.' She waited ten years before she went off. Con were in the fields spraying the barley and he seen her going up the road with Dad's old suitcase and when he got back to the house, there were a note on the mantelpiece, telling him she'd met someone else.

It turned out to be Snoakes, the butcher from Ormskirk and off she went to live in the town and before you could say boo her belly were up like a balloon. There were barely time for the divorce to come through and for her to get married before the baby arrived. I wanted to hate her for leaving Con like that but I know what it's like to hunger for a child and no child come. Sometimes I see her in the village, laughing with her little boy and I dream of how it might have been with a child here on the farm again to carry on the line, how Con would be happy and settled.

He turned silent and sour after she left, not that he'd ever been one to say much, bit like his grandfather. He were sullen even with me, so that I were glad at first, when Diane come along and made him smile again.

He met her in the British Legion. Oh she likes drinking and

dancing and gadding about all right and there's another thing. Our Con never used to touch a drop, only round Christmas time, but after Christine left he took to going into the village Saturday nights for a bit of company.

He didn't say nothing for a long time but I knew when I seen him sporting a new haircut, all stuck up in the latest fashion. I always cut his hair for him before, same as I used to cut Bert's.

Then Minnie Bickerstaffe told me at the church club as she'd seen him coming out of Diane's Den, the new hairdresser's on the High Street, but it were only when Bob Adams tipped me the wink that he'd seen the two of them spooning in the Indian restaurant that I found out it were Diane herself that he were stuck on.

I were right put out at first. Her family are in Liverpool, bog Irish I shouldn't wonder but she were sweet as a nut to me at first, taking me shopping in her car and out for trips to Southport and Blackpool, places I'd never been since I were a young lass courting Bert.

I were taken in. I'm not one to suffer fools gladly. I've always prided myself on being able to spot a rogue a mile off, but she's a smart one with a silver tongue when she wants something. I were so pleased to see our Con looking happy and it were true she brought sunshine with her, into my life too after Bert died. We'd always loved each other, me and Bert, good strong working love, not the sloppy romantic stuff you see on telly. The cottage seemed dark and empty after he'd gone, even though he got on my nerves when he were alive with his cough and his aches and pains. I'd got used to being on my own after eight years but all the upheaval of Christine going off and Con meeting Diane unsettled me and brought the old loneliness back. At first it were grand to have the company of another woman even though she weren't no help to Con with the farm work at all.

The good times didn't last. Soon as she'd wangled her way in to the farm, things started to change. First, the house. All the good furniture Dad and Mother had were thrown out and burned, then it were decorators, kitchen fitters, new bathroom, it went on for a year. I cringed at the thought of the expense but every time I tried to say owt, our Con cut me down.

Next it were the gardens, and after that holidays, her and Con going off together for weekends, now she's got Mary to run the shop on Saturdays. Half the time they're away and I'm left here, seventy-five years old, to look after myself. There's all kinds of people wandering around here at night. It used to be quiet and peaceful except for the odd poacher, but we knew who they were and we mostly let them be, they rid the land of vermin, but nowadays it's strangers with guns wandering the footpaths all hours of the night. There's kids coming down here in cars, drinking and taking drugs down by the canal. Fly-tippers in the middle of the night when they think no one can see them. If they'll come doing that who knows what else they might do, creeping about while we're all in bed? Annie Chapman told me there's a drugs baron gone and bought old Maitland's farm out at Roughlea but I can't credit that. Still, Con says it's true. Such terrible things you read in the papers too about old people being attacked by drug addicts desperate for cash. Our Con never thinks to ring and see if I'm all right. If I didn't have Blondie, I don't know what I'd do. Things come to a pretty pass when you got to rely on a dog for security.

Now, every time I do see them, she's looking at houses in the paper and our Con's grumbling that there's no money in farming any more. Oh, I can see the way the wind's blowing all right, but there's no way I'm budging. Let them go if they want. I'm staying. I've always been here.

***

'I don't know why you're so frightened of your mother.' Diane wiggled her bare toes and screwed the top back on her bottle of nail polish.

'I'm not.' Con stayed behind the evening paper.

'Yes, you are. You just won't tackle her about the farm. You know we can't stay here forever. It's just piling up debts. She doesn't understand. You can't go on growing crops that no one wants.'

'Can't you let me read the paper in peace?' Con rattled the sheets in front of his face. Milly, Diane's Yorkshire terrier, cocked an eye at him from her place beside Diane's armchair.

'But time's going by and nothing's settled. Look at that lovely place in Mawdesley we looked at last month. You know I set my heart on it. It would be ideal for the two of us and the dogs. It won't be on the market for long. You need to make your mind up, Con. Do you want to moulder away here for the rest of your life without a penny to bless yourself? Look at the way things are going. Money's getting tighter. Fuel's going up all the time, it's affecting everything.'

'Mum won't be here forever.'

'It seems like she will, Con. She'll do anything to spite me. You know how she talks about me in the village.'

'Oh, for Heaven's sake!' Con threw the paper down and glared at Diane. 'She's my mother, Di, it's her land.' Milly jumped up on Diane's knee in protective stance and snarled.

'But it isn't, is it? She signed it over to you. You just need to be firm with her. Old people are always cantankerous. We can't afford to wait. Everyone says the housing market's going to drop, it's already falling in other parts of the country.'

She pushed the dog down, got up and went over to the kitchen table. Moving behind Con, she leaned her head on top of his, letting her breasts lie against his shoulders while she massaged his chest with both hands.

'We could get a place with a granny flat, or better still, get her a cottage in the village. She'd be better off, Con. She'd be able to get to the shops and the doctor. She's got friends in the village. She just doesn't know what's best for her.'

'She won't go.'

'Don't ask her, Con. Just tell her. You're the man of the place, aren't you?'

Just as he was softening to her, to the touch of her body on his, as he always did, she pulled away and went to the kitchen window.

'Of course, if you want to rot away here, that's up to you.'

Con got up and slammed out of the kitchen. In the yard he whistled for Rolo and waited for the Border Collie to run to him from the barn before he made his way onto the footpath that skirted the edge of his land. Beyond the careful contours of the garden, the land ranged unbroken, seemingly endless, except for local landmarks and the lights of Burscough village to his left. He looked up at the wide sky lying on the flat fields. It was still light at nine o'clock but birds were flying urgently overhead as they headed for their roosting places. He gulped in air and felt his head clear in the open spaces of his home landscape.

When he reached the corner where the footpath branched off across the moss, he turned to look back at the farmhouse, Rolo standing at his side. Smoke curled from the chimney of his mother's cottage, despite the summer heat.

***

'I'm thinking of applying for another post.'

Lynn looked up from her marking. Dan had that hangdog look he wore when he knew she would disagree with him. He'd waited till supper was over and she was settled into her evening routine. This must be serious.

'Oh?' She put down her pen.

'It's in Lancashire; a new university; Head of Department.'

'Lancashire?' She pictured grimy terraced houses hunched against cold winds on steep hills. 'I thought you were happy here.'

'Yes, but Lynn, Head of Department. Think about it. I could wait years here for a chance like that. Phil Eckersley is there. He's on the interviewing panel. He reckons I'd be the ideal candidate.'

'But we'd have to move. My job. I like it at the college.'

'You can get another job. There will be colleges up there.'

Resentment rose in her, that her work was so unimportant in comparison to his.

'You can't spring this on me, Dan. I don't want to move to some dirty mill town. I don't think you've thought this out at all.' She took her reading glasses off, put them on the top of her head and gave Dan a straight look.

Dan's body pulled in tight. He took a step backwards. 'It's not a mill town, it's a market town, a nice little place in a rural area, but it's near the M6. You'd still be able to visit your family and it's not far from Liverpool. We'd be near my people. We'd soon make friends, settle in.'

'Is it near the Lakes?' Lynn softened, thinking of her beloved Wordsworth. Dove Cottage, Ambleside, Grasmere; she hadn't seen them since her student days although they came fresh to her mind every time she opened her poetry books. For a moment she recalled a long forgotten winter boat trip across Windermere, grey sky and grey water – that serene expanse, its shores blurred with mist. She'd felt strangely at home there.

'An hour or so's drive.' Dan visibly relaxed. 'Come on Lynn, you know you hate Birmingham.'

She looked out of the apartment window at the rain-sodden street below. The traffic lights smeared red in the dark. It was true she'd hated the traffic, the fumes, the busyness of the city when they'd first arrived, but now she'd got used to it. She rubbed the space between her eyes.

'I need a drink.'

Dan rushed to fetch the bottle of Merlot they'd opened with their meal. He clinked the glasses as he sat down beside her at the dining table. She could see his enthusiasm. It made her feel tired.

The wine was soft and sweet with a little peppery kick. She could have drained the whole glass in one glug but she swilled a sip round her mouth, savouring the taste while she watched Dan. His sureness was returning already. He thought he had won her over. Was she really so easy?

'You've made your mind up about this haven't you?' She made her voice sound accusing.

'It's got to be a joint decision,' Dan said, but his tone was uneasy. 'Think about it. Head of Department before I'm thirty-five. That's a great career move.'

'Dan, you've moved jobs four times in seven years.'

'Always for the better. I didn't hear you complaining about the money.'

'Yes, but we've stayed in the area since we came to Birmingham. Now you want to up sticks to the other end of the country.'

'It's not that far away.'

'But it means starting all over again for me. I'm settled at the college.'

'If I make Head of Department we'll be miles better off. House prices are cheaper in the north. We'd be able to afford something really nice with a big garden. You've always wanted that, haven't you? In fact, you probably wouldn't have to work at all, if you didn't want to. You've always had a hankering for green fingers and the good life.'

The wine warmed Lynn's stomach, softened her mind. She

thought back to her Somerset childhood, the warm red bricks of the old vicarage her parents had bought. She remembered how potatoes tumbled out of the rich soil as her father forked the bed, the smell of apples in the loft. It was true she had a secret longing for growing things, a more natural way of life, but the way he was dismissing her own career rankled.

'Oh, so I can stay at home playing housewife while you're out being the breadwinner?'

'You could take it easier, that's all. Work part-time if you preferred, have some time out for gardening, hobbies. Write more poetry. You never write poetry any more. It's a loss. You've got talent, even a prosaic sociologist like myself can see that.'

He was handling her, manipulating her. This was his skill; he was used to arguing his way through debates, seminars, meetings. He looked for his opponents' strengths and weaknesses and he knew her inside out, every crevice of her body as well as the pathways of her thoughts. He was sure of her, of himself. She could see that and she resented it. What about her? What did she really want? Those kids in her classes needed her; kids who'd left school with no qualifications, spent a year or two bumming about unemployed or in low paid jobs. She got them into university, into careers, made them believe in themselves. Not just kids either, but single mums, unemployed dads. Still, that dream of her childhood garden, the longing to get close to the land, see the lakes once more and find her poetry again was tempting. She wavered, smiled up at Dan but his face was a mask, he was hiding himself from her and something cold peeped from the corners of his eyes.

Suddenly she knew that this was all a sop to her pride. The move was a fait accompli.

'You've already put the application in.' It was a statement. The confidence slipped off his face.

'Lynn – there was so little time. The deadline was yesterday. Phil only rang me last Thursday. I wanted to tell you but I had to be sure myself first, to find out what the place was like.'

'You've been there.' The ground seemed to waver under her feet. How could he go this far without consulting her? 'When? When did you go?'

'Last Friday. It was really short notice. You were working. You were having your supervision, remember?'

'I could have cancelled.' She felt winded, couldn't even be angry.

'It was just a quick visit to the campus, a chat with the Dean. There was only an hour to look round the town.'

'You didn't think I ought to be there?'

'It wasn't that, I needed a clear head. I just wanted to see it by myself first.'

'And you kept quiet about it all over the weekend.'

He coloured slightly, looked away from her stare, down at his glass.

'I needed to think about it. I wanted to be certain.'

'Then why are you talking to me like this? You're not consulting me, you're telling me.' She waved her hands at him and knocked over her glass. The red wine spilled on the blond wood creeping towards Dan like an accusation.

'Lynn.' He reached out and trapped her hands between his on the table, the wine staining them both like blood. 'I want this, I really want this.'

She pulled away, fetched a cloth and mopped up the wine. Her action seemed to signal an uneasy truce. She went back to her marking, while Dan was clearing up in the kitchen but she couldn't settle. When he'd gone into the spare room that doubled as his study, she picked up the phone and rang her mother.

'How nice, Lynn. Your dad's out at a dinner in Taunton. He'll be sorry to have missed you. I cried off, I'm afraid, bit of a cold, but you know your dad, work before everything. You wouldn't think he's supposed to be retired would you? What about this weather? Is it raining there? These terrible floods; we haven't been too bad, but Gloucestershire – Did you see Tewkesbury on the news? It's so odd to see water where it shouldn't be – swans actually swimming down the streets.'

Lynn listened, waiting for the flow of chatter to slow down.

'You're quiet tonight, is everything all right?'

Lynn leaned back in her chair. She wanted to cry, to be hugged. 'Dan wants us to move. He's after a new job up north.'

'North? Where?'

'Lancashire, near Liverpool somewhere. It's a small market town, he says, nice area but...'

'You don't want to go?'

'It's so sudden. I'm settled here and it's not too far from you and Dad.'

'Liverpool's not the other side of the world. Your dad often goes there and back in a day for meetings.'

'I know, but he didn't even ask me, went up there and applied for the job without telling me.' She bit her lip to stop herself whining.

'Dan's like your dad, his career means a lot to him. I've always supported your father and he's given me a good life in return.' She was making her voice gentle, trying not to be critical.

Lynn's face burned. She twined her fingers in the telephone cord. 'But you stayed in one place.'

'Life was more stable then. Everyone moves about now, it's something we have to live with. Look at Debra, and even Fiona wouldn't think twice about moving to another country, never mind another town.'

Lynn thought about her sisters, but they were single, they didn't need to consult partners or think about anybody else. Still, maybe her mother had a point. 'We would be better off; Dan's going for Head of Department.'

'You can't blame him, Lynn, he's ambitious. That's all to the good, isn't it? Houses are cheaper up there; you'll be able to get something decent with a garden instead of that scrappy apartment. What's the name of the town?'

'Ormskirk. It sounds Viking, doesn't it? It's not far from the Lakes.' She thought again of the expanse of Windermere and brightened.

'There you are. Inspiration for your poetry. It sounds perfect for you. You know, there's someone in our family came from somewhere round there, the name sounds familiar, anyway it was definitely Lancashire. I'll have a look in the family Bible and see what I can find out.'

Lynn wasn't interested. She wanted commiseration and comfort but with her mother supporting Dan she felt beleaguered. Maybe her mother was right, maybe the benefits of the move would outweigh Dan's duplicity.

In bed that night she lay awake, listening to Dan's easy breathing. Anger was beginning to make itself felt through the shock and hurt. He'd showed her a new side, it marked a new point in their relationship, which she'd always thought of as open and trusting.

Now she came to think about it, didn't Dan always get what he wanted, when it came to the big things like changing jobs or moving house? That first post in Bristol when she'd just qualified had suited her fine, they could have stayed in Somerset. She'd let him have his way because she loved him so, as a free choice, but now she wondered, if she'd refused, what would he have done?

She looked at his profile in the dark and saw a stranger but she could feel his warmth, and the familiar musk of his body disarmed her, softened her towards him. She turned her back and fitted her body against his. Dan moved behind her and murmured.

She thought of herself in a warm, walled garden, vegetables growing abundantly round her. Fat, juicy raspberries glistened on the bowed canes and when she picked one it fell into her hand with perfect ripe readiness, the skin so thin that juice stained her fingers. The sun beat down on her head and she could feel the soil, soft and warm between her toes. A child squatted at her feet, playing in the earth, looking up at her, face screwed up against the sunshine, with a halo of wispy fair curls. Her stomach knotted with yearning. She opened her eyes, let the image dissolve. Dan muttered and moved against her. His arms snaked round her, pulling her close and he snuggled into her neck. She felt the in-out of his breath then she was striding across bare moorland, the smooth rounded slopes shaping and containing the lake that glittered in the distance, where a small figure waited on the shore.

Chapter Two

August 2007

Rolo was waiting at the gate when they came back after the funeral. Tears pricked Con's eyes at the sight of the dog sitting there. Diane got out while he opened the gate and by the time he'd parked the Shogun she'd opened up the house and Milly was dashing round the yard in circles, yapping furiously.

Con refilled Rolo's water bowl and watched the dog pad back to his place in the barn. Rolo had a relaxed air now that his master was home and everything was back to normal, though he was quieter than usual, as if he sensed how Con felt numb all over.

Con looked up at the leaden sky. At least the rain had held off till his mother was decently buried. Everything seemed meaningless. The straw bales he'd stacked in the barn only last week, the red of the tractor, the wooden sheds, the metal struts of the barn all suddenly looked unfamiliar. Last week seemed like a million years ago. Only three weeks earlier his mother had turned seventy-six. They'd had a celebratory meal at the Haywain, the best restaurant in the district. How quickly she'd slipped away. He looked round again but still nothing seemed real. Even the concrete felt alien under his feet but then he was wearing his best shoes, not his comfortable old work boots.

He kept his head turned to the left, away from the sight of his mother's cottage. Right now, he couldn't bear to see the smokeless chimney.

The smell of coffee came from the back door of the house. In the kitchen, Diane was fussing with the new machine she'd bought the day before. She was humming brightly, but stopped when she caught Con's look. He dropped into a chair at the table. Diane spooned tea into the small brown pot kept just for Con's use. He remembered his mother buying it at Ormskirk market when he was about twelve-years-old.

He watched Diane as she moved around, reaching into cupboards, stretching up, bending down, getting out mugs, milk, sugar. She looked good in black, it showed off her fair hair. He wanted to catch her hair in his hands, to feel how soft it was sliding through his fingers as he clutched the shape of her skull and pulled her mouth to his. His gaze slid over her tailored black suit, the slight sheen on her black stockings, the definition of her calf muscles sloping down to her spike-heeled shoes.

His penis stiffened, then he remembered his mother and everything died in him except shame. Milly raced into the room barking as she chased a fly round the table. Con put his head in his hands.

'It was a good send off, wasn't it?' Diane put the pot of tea in front of him. 'She would have been delighted.' She turned back to the coffee machine and its hissing noises. 'Did you see Minnie Bickerstaffe and Elsie Langham? Like two old vultures. You should have heard them in the salon this morning. Had the whole family trees of half the village off by heart, arguing over whose relatives had lived the longest.' She set her froth-topped mug on the table and giggled, then sobered, putting a hand on Con's arm. She sat down, leaning close to him.

'She had a good innings, Con, good health till the last couple of years. There's nothing to reproach yourself with.'

Con lifted his head and looked at her. Milly jumped up, begging for a biscuit. She rested her paws on Diane's knees.

'Milly get down. Oh, look, you've snagged my stockings.' She held her leg out for inspection, but Con was looking at her face. Her clear blue eyes showed no emotion, but she was different somehow. There was a lightness about her, as if something had lifted from her shoulders.

Con drank his tea in silence, struggling against desire. He should be consoling himself with memories of his mother's life but Diane's breasts peeped at him from her suit jacket. She petted Milly, all the while sneaking little glances at him. She was leading up to something.

She sipped her coffee, looked at him over the mug. 'I thought, maybe, we could take a walk over to the cottage later, just have a look, there's a lot to do there, a lot of stuff…'

'To get rid of?' The words rushed out bitterly.

'Well, yes.' She ducked her head, stroked the dog. 'It'll have to be done and doing something practical will, you know, help us get used to it.'

He wanted to scream at her. Rage rushed up in him. He daren't let it out. Anger, frustration, fired his blood. He opened his mouth. A croak came out.

'No, not yet.'

If she mentions selling the farm, I'll kill her, he thought.

She tossed her head and for a second he saw something alien on her face, so unlike her that he didn't know who she was, then she caught herself and smiled.

'Okay, if you're not feeling up to it. It's early days yet, isn't it?'

She finished her coffee, put the dog down and stretched her arms above her head.

'Think I'll walk into the village to see Mary about the hair convention next month. The sky looks like it's clearing. I'll take Milly. She's been cooped up in here all day.'

She was withdrawing from him, punishing him for not doing what she wanted but it was for the best. He needed to be alone.

As soon as she'd gone, he went into the bedroom, tore off the despised tie and shirt, lay down on the bed and masturbated, eyes squeezed shut while behind them he visualised his penis sliding purple between Diane's white breasts, the black jacket pulled open, her pink mouth making round Os with each shove as the tip pushed up towards it.

He wiped the cum off his belly with a tissue from the box on Diane's side of the bed, making sure not to get marks on the satin duvet. The anger was gone but he felt worse than ever, wanking like a schoolboy after his own mother's funeral.

He got dressed and went outside. In the barn he felt better. This was his world: Rolo, the colours of grass and sky, the dusty smell of straw and the damp air that promised rain before long.

Rolo ran ahead, his tail waving as Con crossed the lawn to reach the footpath. The grass squelched under his feet, the ground still holding last night's downpour. At the edge of the garden, Con looked carefully around the fields and went out onto the empty road. There was no sign of Diane. He whistled Rolo to come back, told him to sit by the bed of hollyhocks at the gate to his mother's cottage. The dog seemed restless, whining and looking round the garden.

'What's up with you boy?' Con patted Rolo's head, took the

keys from his pocket and opened the cottage door.

***

Here's Con with time to visit at last and looking like the whole world's on his shoulders. There's no need for sad faces and tears because after all, I'm still here.

I suppose it's good to see he's some respect left for his mother though what he was thinking of letting Barney Dougan take Blondie, I don't know. Poor Blondie, she were used to the cottage and sitting by a nice warm fire, not being parked outside the Turk's Head all day and night. It'll be her taking him home at the end of it not t'other way round. I thought Con'd have kept her, that would have been the proper thing to do, but I suppose that fancy one of his wouldn't hear of it, she never had much time for poor Blondie ever since Blondie took a bite out of that yapping thing of hers.

It's strange to see someone touching your things, even the things on show, never mind your secret possessions, the things no one ever knew about, but then he's my son, my baby. He lived inside of me and touched places even I don't know about. If only I could reach out or talk to him. It takes some getting used to, this helplessness. I swear Rolo saw me though. Look, Con, I'm here, over here.

Ah, the shoebox, all our photographs, though there's precious few of them. We worked so hard there weren't time for taking pictures but there's you, Con with Dad on old Jessie. How you used to love that carthorse when you were a tiny chap and she loved you right back, no matter how much you pulled her mane and she could have tossed you to kingdom come.

Lord, how we skivvied in those days, when your granddad still had the farm. He were like a sergeant-major, and me and Albert was his foot soldiers, even though we was a married couple with a baby to look after.

Dawn to dusk, even when I were a young girl, me and our Joan did the same work as the men. Dad wouldn't get in paid workers, only a few paddies in the summer. There weren't any farmhands anyway, only land girls once the war got going and it weren't much better after, when the men come back, what were left of them. My brother Thomas were never the same after the war and he died in 1947. I were a slip of a girl then, just seventeen. I don't remember much of Thomas as a young man. He were a boy one minute, showing me and Joan where the skylarks nested, the next he come back from the war an old man though he were only twenty-two. At first he seemed happy to be home but it were like the light had gone out of him after a while and somehow it never got kindled again. When he took sick it were like he just give up, like life weren't worth fighting for.

Sometimes I think Dad blamed us girls, because we never had to go to the war. He were always cold and angry before, but after Thomas come home he were terrible with us and even Mother didn't dare defy him. He never said much, your grandfather, but he didn't need to; a look were enough. They say still waters run deep and it were true of him. No one ever knew what he were thinking but you could tell it weren't nothing pleasant. My grandma must have known him when she named him Douglas, dark water it means, but then maybe she didn't know that. Douglas is a name that's traditional in our family, passed down through generations. I used to be so tired at night I'd fall asleep sitting at supper and me and Albert'd be in bed by ten with no thought of loving. We'd be asleep soon as our heads touched the pillows. Even in winter, the only time we'd be idle were when the snow stopped us or when the rain flooded the fields so bad we was all afeart the Mere were coming back to claim its own.

Think on, Con. Remember why this place means so much to us. The land this farm stands on were under water on and off for centuries. There's them as says it were a foolish thing, draining the Mere, that it should have been left the way nature meant it to be, but moss land is fertile and when it's well drained, it grows the best spuds in the world.

We've beaten it, made it yield, but nature don't give up, it's a constant fight. You know how the water's always trying to creep back and you know if you relax for a moment it could rush in and sweep away everything you've worked for. And sometimes even with all the watching and looking after the ditches and drains, it's not enough. You don't have control of the weather and you live with the thought that the pumping stations might fail.

I remember the floods in the fifties, before you were born.

Three years in a row, all the crops destroyed and Dad raging like a storm and us all creeping about keeping out of his way. 1957's harvest were the worst and a hard winter after it. It were a poor Christmas that year, no photos then.

But it were me dad made this farm what it is today. In my granddad's time the land were still flooding every winter, most of it only fit for poor pasture, not that my granddad had it long, he were killed in the war in 1917, way before I were born. He only had the farm three years afore he volunteered. A fine healthy man he would have been, no more than thirty-four and it weren't as if he wouldn't be needed on the farm, but just like in the next war, everyone thought it were their duty to go. I don't suppose they ever thought they would be the ones to be killed. He died bravely, Dad used to say, but didn't they say that about them all? Who knows a man's heart when he suddenly faces death?

Best if you don't know about it beforehand, I think, but then you don't get the chance to put things in order. It crept up on me like, I knew it were coming, but I just kept thinking it wouldn't be, not yet. When it did come, it weren't so bad, but then I've had a good, long life, I never got cut down in my prime.

That's my grandmother Mary there Con, you won't remember her, she died in 1965, you were only three. Oh, she made you welcome all right. Sight for sore eyes, she used to say when you were toddling up the path to the farmhouse. It were a long time since there'd been a child at the farm, with our Joan going to Canada. All we ever had were photos of her kids and now and then strange voices on the phone. I kept thinking one day I'd go and see her but I never got further than Blackpool in my whole life.

Dad took over the farm in 1928. His brother Philip had inherited it from my grandfather but he died young and all, caught in a threshing machine on the far field. Our Thomas would be about five and Will just a tiny baby, there's a photo of him somewhere in your gran's arms, with Dad standing proud behind her. Maybe Dad only turned so bitter after the scarlet fever took Will, I don't know. I never knowed him to be any different.

There's no photos of me as a baby. I come right after Will's funeral. Maybe that's why Dad flung himself into building up the farm. The land gets under your skin. It's called husbandry, Dad used to say and yes, he were married to the land as much as he ever were to my mother, and it were the same for me but the other way around. I don't know how I would have gone on if me and Bert had had to leave the farm and make our living somewhere else. I thought it were the same for you too, Con.

Sometimes when dusk is spreading and mist is creeping up, the line of the land blurs. You must know those moments, Con, when the geese and ducks fly over to the nature reserve. Among the honks and quacks you think you can hear the water lapping the reeds and you can see it, see the lake coming back, glimmering as the moon starts to show in the sky. I were born under the sign of the moon and all my life I felt the pull of it in my blood. At school they told us we was made of water and when you stand still and silent in these misty twilights you can feel the ebb and flow even though the land under your feet is solid. You're an Askin, Con; you can't deny your nature.

She knows nothing of this. She's all show and throwing things away when she tires of them. I can see what she's plotting, see you like a lamb to the slaughter, turning away from your own.

Think on, how we fought for this land. It's in your bones, same as it's in mine and no good'll come of it if you leave.

***

'Never mind that. Get your glad-rags on, we're eating out.'

Lynn's heart sank. She put down the spoon and turned away from the sauce she'd been stirring on the stove.

'You got the job then?' She smiled.

'Absolute doddle.' Dan put his arms round her, kissed her and lifted her off her feet. 'Jesus, Lynn, you're putting on weight.' He set her back down. 'There were five candidates but as soon as I walked in there I knew they didn't stand a chance. You can just tell the way it's going. I clicked right away with the rest of the team.'

'The team – already?' Lynn raised her eyebrows. Dan's jubilance tugged at her. She was drawn into his excitement, away from her alarm at what this would mean for her.

'I need a drink.' He went to the wine rack, pulled out a bottle of South African Shiraz. 'Loved the place, Lynn. Not too big, still got character, not like Birmingham.'

'The town or the uni?' His movements were quick and jerky as he opened the bottle. He was still on a high.

'Both, both, just fantastic, and the landscape, flat like the Fens, huge blue skies, and the location, right by the M6, Manchester, Liverpool, just a stone's throw away.'

'Sounds great.' Lynn stared at the spoonful of congealing sauce on the worktop.

'Come on, get ready. I've booked a table at Pierotti's. Shove that stuff in the freezer.' He looked at his watch.

She turned off the gas, went into the bathroom and took off her jeans and tee shirt. It was true, she was getting heavier. She examined herself in the wall mirror. If she wasn't careful she could end up like her mother. Would Dan still want her then, tipping the scales at thirteen stone? She would go on a diet tomorrow she decided, pinching the flesh round her waist as she soaped herself in the shower, but then she remembered that tomorrow she would have to start planning a whole new life.

Pierotti's was still quiet this early in the evening. Lynn caught her reflection in the mirror by the entrance. The dim light suited her, making her mouth soft and vulnerable, highlighting the sheen of her hair. She stood for a second, admiring how it hung straight to her shoulders. The dark red dress and high heels made her look slim. She strode ahead of Dan who was telling Frank the head waiter all about his success.

There was iced champagne waiting in a bucket on the table.

'Pushing the boat out?'

'Head of Department. It calls for a celebration.'

She felt guilty. Was there a note of reproach in his voice? Had he noticed her lack of enthusiasm? Her mother's voice echoed in her head, urging her to support her husband.

'It's a fantastic achievement. I'm so proud of you, darling.' She half-rose and leaned across the table to kiss him.

He was still in his dark suit, the white cuffs of his shirt contrasting sharply with the black hairs on his wrists and hands. Desire twisted through her as she thought of his hands on her body and for a moment she was naked as she looked up at his face. He caught her glance and grinned triumphantly, dropping his eyes to her breasts.

'You look amazing tonight.'

As soon as the wine was poured, he launched into plans for the move.

'They want me to start in January, but the sooner we get up there the better, give me time to familiarise myself with the faculty. Time for you to look round for something else.'

She pretended to be reading the menu but she felt bewildered, thinking how this had suddenly crept up on her, even though she'd known since June. She'd kept pushing it away, clinging to the hope that he wouldn't get the job in the end. It wasn't all selfishness. Even though her mother had urged her to go, her parents weren't getting any younger. She was the only one living reasonably near. Fee could never pry herself away from her column on the Daily Mail for long enough to visit and Debra had been nursing in Dubai for the last three years.

'You'd better give your notice in right away.' Dan poured two more glasses of champagne. 'We'll have to get the flat up for sale too. I'll see to that tomorrow. We could start looking for a property up there now, or we could rent something for the time being and take our time finding exactly what we want. What do you think?'

Lynn looked up. She wanted to say, 'You're asking me?' but couldn't burst his bubble. He was so excited. 'Couldn't we just order some food? I'm starving.' She could feel a flush on the skin of her neck and chest from the effects of the red wine and champagne drunk too quickly.

'I'm going to have the mussels and the seafood linguine.' Dan refilled his glass yet again.

Lynn pulled a face. 'Garlic mushrooms and spaghetti bolognaise for me.'

'God, you're so boring with your food. Why don't you experiment a little, live dangerously?' He raised his glass boisterously so that champagne spilled out on the tablecloth. 'A toast to our new future.'

Later, in bed, his grip on her was firm, sure. How she loved that, her choice to yield, her gift of herself to him. He lay behind her, pressed skin to skin, against the hollows of her back, the spaces behind her knees. Warmth flowed between them, a contrast to the cool air on the rest of their bodies. In the faint light of the alarm clock, she could see the dark heap of the cast off bedclothes, and in the wardrobe mirror, the pale gleams of their arms and legs, blurred dark patches of body hair. His face was invisible, buried in the deep curtain of her hair. She watched his hands on her breasts, on the curve of her belly. His lips burned along her neck and she saw her toes wriggle, the involuntary movements of her thighs, then she turned to him, reaching out to cross the barriers of skin between them. He met her, matching her closeness, pulling her in. His mouth trailed across her throat, traced her jawbone up to her ear and whispered there, 'What do you say we go up there next weekend and take a look?'

Chapter Three

September 2007

Con came in hungry from repairing fences at twelve-thirty. In the old days, the Christine days, the smell of a hot stew would churn his stomach juices as he came through the door, but those days were gone. Everything was cold. Diane was at the salon. In earlier years the range would have been pushing out welcome heat but the new kitchen, for all its smartness, was cold and clinical.

Con unlaced his boots and switched the kettle on, rubbing his stockinged feet against the quarry tiles. The hunger was in him as usual, not for food, but for her, that hunger that made him want to suck and bite, gobble up the juiciness of her.

She had a maddening scent that he couldn't quite identify. It clung to her flesh even over the smells of the salon that she carried around with her and then there was the way she looked at him. Just thinking about her made the hunger worse. It was like the grabbing of young plants for life in the soil, an ecstatic fusion of air, water, land, that produced the wonder of fruits, foods, even flowers, though he'd never had much time for flowers.

Flowers were like words. He couldn't speak the things he felt. He might say, 'Fine crop of carrots this year,' while the sensuous joy of the carrots, their round bodies, their flaunting leaves, bound him to them, satisfied something in him that he could never express.

He got some bread and cheese and made himself a sandwich, conscious all the time of her absence. He wanted her now, on the kitchen table even, in a way he never had wanted Christine for all her cosy hearths and hot stews. Christine had been at the funeral, she'd looked old and dowdy compared to Diane. At least she'd had the decency not to bring Snoakes and the child with her. She'd cried when the coffin went into the ground. She'd always got on well with his mother. He looked out of the window across at the empty cottage. It was hard to get used to his mother not being there, to not seeing the smoke rising lazily from the chimney.

He turned back and glanced at the calendar on the door. Diane had been prompting him about her birthday coming up next week. She would expect flowers, red roses on top of the money he would give her to buy jewellery. He would order them when he went to Ramsbottom's for new fence posts, even though he would feel a fool, tongue-tied in the female, pretty world of Myrtle Pilling's florist's shop. Christine would never have expected such things of him.

He jumped as the back door suddenly opened and Diane bustled in with Milly under her arm. She was wearing her overall and the familiar salon smell of hair dye and heated air invaded the room.

'Come in, come in.' She turned to the man behind her. He was young, smart in a grey suit and bright striped shirt, his hair freshly styled. Diane turned a smile on Con.

'Con – Mr Aspinwall, from Village Estates. He was in the salon for a haircut. We got chatting, you know how it is. He offered to take a look.' She glanced quickly at Con, then put Milly down. 'I didn't think you'd be in. Coffee, Mr Aspinwall?'

'Yes. Lovely.' Aspinwall smiled at Con. 'Pleased to meet you, Mr Worrall.' He put out his hand but Con ignored it.

'Lovely property this, at least what I can see so far.' Aspinwall tucked his hand behind his back. 'So many of these old farmhouses need a lot of renovation.'

His face had a look of earnest honesty. Con stared. The bread in his mouth stuck like wet newspaper. The boy looked familiar.

'Don't be rude, Con,' Diane said. 'Please have a seat, Mr Aspinwall.' Aspinwall wriggled nervously as he sat down, Milly sniffing at his ankles.

'So what kind of property are you thinking of moving to? Smaller or something a bit grander?' He looked round the room as he spoke, assessing the kitchen fittings, peering through the windows at the garden.

'We'd want to stay in the area, wouldn't we, Con? Something a bit smaller maybe, more modern, less isolated, just a nice house, with a reasonable garden, no land.'

Con swallowed. The lump of bread went down. 'Your dad had the chicken farm on Sykes Lane,' he said.

'Yes, that's right.' Aspinwall beamed. 'He's retired now, bought a seafront flat in Lytham St Annes. My mother always loved it there. I managed to get them a good deal on it.'

'It were a smallholding before that. When you were a little lad. I remember you. I used to help your dad with the harvester.'

'Yes, well, even then there wasn't any money in agriculture. Dad had enough sense to see that and invest in poultry. There's always a market for eggs. It was either that or growing tomatoes and there's less work in poultry.'

'You didn't want to follow him then?'

'God, no, afraid not,' Aspinwall giggled. 'Not my type of thing at all. Anyway, they needed the money for their retirement.'

'There's no money in anything to do with farming nowadays.' Diane carried the tray of mugs to the table.

'But it's our life!' Anger burst out of Con.

'It's not my life.' Diane stared at him across the table.

'I'll take a look upstairs, shall I?' Aspinwall got to his feet, startling Milly so that she nipped his trouser leg. 'Good dog.' He pulled his leg away and hurriedly backed out of the room.

Con drank his tea in silence, watching Diane as she petted Milly. He could hear Aspinwall pacing the rooms upstairs, imagined him putting a price on everything. He struggled to equate the image of the little blond boy in dungarees, sitting on his father's tractor, with this dark, good-looking young businessman. He remembered Aspinwall's father, brown and leathery, and thought of his own father in his blue boiler suit.

'You're being rude, Con,' Diane sighed. 'Why don't you go and show him round?'

'You brought him. You show him.'

'Con, we talked about this. It was just a good moment. He was in the salon and I thought, why not? It's only to give us an idea.'

'You talked about it.'

She reached across the table and stroked his face. Her hand rasped on the slight stubble there. 'You know we can't afford to stay here. Look at the price you got for the barley, and last winter's potatoes.'

'It's the rain. It's been a bad season.'

'There've been too many bad seasons. But it's not just that, is it? The markets aren't there any more. If it wasn't for the salon, I don't know how we'd manage.'

Con tried to look away from her but she held his chin in her hand, forcing him to meet her gaze.

'Maybe we could rent out some of the land.' It tore his heart to think of someone else working his fields but it was better than giving up the house.

'This place is too big for us. Justin doesn't want to be here, now he's sharing a student house and Simone has her own life. They spend more time with their father than with me anyway. Something smaller would be easier to manage and we'd have money left over to enjoy ourselves. You deserve a bit of time to have fun. You could get a job, get rid of all that worry and responsibility. We don't need the room. It's not as if we're going to have a family is it?'

Now she wounded him with his sterility, just like Christine. He'd thought she didn't want more children anyway, now that Justin and Simone were grown and gone. He'd thought she'd done her stint at motherhood and was enjoying her career, but there'd been a flash of bitterness in the look she'd thrown at him. He looked again and thought he was mistaken. She was smiling softly.

'All done.' Aspinwall appeared round the kitchen door, setting Milly barking again. 'Very nice, tastefully decorated. It'll be a pleasure to handle this sale.'

'We haven't actually decided to sell yet,' Diane shot him a warning look, then flicked a guilty glance at Con. Con knew he had lost the battle already. 'Why don't you show Mr Aspinwall round outside. There's the cottage as well.'

'I've got work to do.' Con got up and blundered out, accidentally kicking Milly as he went.

He strode along the footpath, not thinking where he was going, not even whistling for Rolo. He was just mapping the landscape, marking his territory. Water rippled in the ditch but the level was low, nothing to worry about. A breeze had blown up and he pushed his face into it, enjoying the resistance.

'I know how you must be feeling.' The words blew past him before Aspinwall arrived at his side. 'My dad felt the same.'

'We've always been here.' Con tramped on, forcing Aspinwall to trot to keep up.

'I know, but life's not like that any more, is it?' Aspinwall tripped over a root and swore.

'What's it to you anyway?' Con stopped suddenly and turned to face him. The wind ripped across the flat land and tore at their hair.

'So many farming people are struggling to keep going when it's just not working any more. It's never going to work again. Farming's had it in this country.'

Con walked away. Aspinwall followed.

'Why put yourself through misery? You're sitting on a small fortune. You'll get nothing for the land, but the house, very desirable. Easily fetch four-and-a-half-hundred thou, maybe five.'

'As much as that?' Con stopped and turned his head to look at the farmhouse sitting on the reaped fields. He was standing directly in front of his mother's cottage.

***

In a week, the new term would begin. It was a bad time to give notice. Lynn's new students would only be settling in by Christmas, then would have to get used to a new tutor.

It was no good thinking like that, she had to concentrate on her own future. The last fortnight spent with her parents had helped. The excitement of discovering the family connection had pushed her misgivings about the move to one side. Poring over the family Bible with her mother, they'd come across a handwritten note in rusty black ink on the fly leaf. 'Presented to Lavinia Askin for good conduct. Miss Johnson's Sunday School, Aughton 1875.'

Her mother had been apologetic. 'Well it does sound a bit like Ormskirk.' But when they'd looked on the map, it was so close, practically next door to the town of Ormskirk.

Lavinia Askin was Lynn's great-great-grandmother. The whole family tree was recorded in the back of the Bible, down to Lynn herself and her sisters, their names in her mother's careful script. Since she'd returned home, Lynn had done more research on the internet. Aughton, once a separate village, now lay on the outskirts of Ormskirk, mostly a rural agricultural area close to Dan's new university. How had her family come to migrate to Somerset? Her mother had no explanation; her people had been in the south-west for as long as she could remember.

Lynn couldn't wait to find out more. Maybe the next day when she went up to meet Dan, she might be able to persuade him to take a look round the local graveyards. When they moved, she would be able to search properly, through parish records, local libraries. By then it would be spring, the best time to visit the Lakes, when they would be washed in cold thin sunshine and decked out with primroses and of course the ubiquitous daffodils. She longed to see the clean, clear waters of rushing streams dashing over rocks, stopping to well in deep pools. The vista changed to the great smooth meres, backed by distant mountains with snow on their peaks, crisp frost crunching underfoot. She began to scribble words on the notepad in front of her – ice – crushing – crested – cracks – crags – light – listing – lemon – broken – bracken –

Syllables melted and re-formed. When the phone rang she surfaced to find two pages of phrases, disjointed but teasing, ready for further play.

'Dan?' She felt disoriented. 'How's Manchester?'

'Smoggy.' Someone was laughing in the background.

'Worse than Brum?'

'Maybe just different. Are you ready for tomorrow? Got your tickets?'

'I'll be there by lunchtime. I'm looking forward to it.'

'I'm glad you're feeling better about it.' The edge of anxiety disappeared from his voice.

'I'm excited about finding this relation.'

'Oh, yeah. Well there'll be plenty of time for that once we move. Pack a few extra clothes for me would you? I might stay here a bit longer.'

'But I thought we were coming back together. I have to be in college on Monday.'

'I know. I just thought I'd have some more time with the family. You know it's ages since I've been here, and it'll give me a chance to look round. I'll be too busy once term starts.'

Another week to be spent alone. Lynn put the phone back on its rest and stared at her pages of notes. Things would be different once they moved. A change, a fresh start would bring them closer together, they would be caught up in making a new home. She picked up her pen and began to link the words on the pages into lines and clusters.

***

I can't believe it. I knew, oh yes I knew she wanted it, but I hoped our Con'd stand up to her, stand up for the family. She couldn't wait, couldn't even wait a decent time after the funeral.

I knew, soon as I seen Aspinwall's lad here in his fancy clothes. I could see Con thinking of the money, thinking of the unsold potatoes rotting in the ground last winter and I wanted to scream and shout at him but nothing come out and then I tried hard as I could to throw something, to make him see that I were there. That blue bowl I always kept on the kitchen table, if I could just have moved it, but no matter how I tried, it wouldn't budge.

There were an old newspaper still on my chair by the fireplace and I wore myself out trying to lift it and in the end I did manage to rustle the pages but they took no notice. Aspinwall's lad were too busy peering everywhere, adding up what he were going to make out of selling my home, but for all he looked at everything, he never seen me. Yet this place is me, every stick and stone of it and the farmhouse too, all the days of my life soaked into it. I could tell by our Con's face that it were all over, the lad had talked him round and though I couldn't see her, I knew that bitch would be gloating in the farmhouse, counting our family's money in her scheming head.

You'd think that death meant the end of pain but it isn't true. Such a lost feeling come on me, worse even than when my mother died. I wanted to sink into the flags on the floor, be hard like them and after that come a rage like I would do for the lot of them but though I tried to come at Con with all my might, screaming for him to put this stranger out, it made no difference. 'That wind's getting chilly,' were all he said and went and shut the cottage door.

I couldn't stay there no longer. I went out and up along the ditch. The black water were creeping up after all the rain we've had, but not high enough to fret over. Everything looked the same as always, like the whole world weren't falling apart. She come out of the house with that yapping thing in her arms and I flew across the fields at her. I were surprised how fast I went, with the red madness in my thoughts but for all that I couldn't touch her and she never knew I were there for all that excuse for a dog were barking and going crazy.

She got in the car and picked up Con and Aspinwall's lad from the cottage and they went off towards the village, leaving me here free to wander where I please, but I couldn't settle anywhere for fear of what's to happen. It come to me that if Con goes, I'll be all alone, there'll only be me standing up for what is right. I always were a stubborn one. I've fought for this land my whole life and it'll take more than a snotty-nosed estate agent to get rid of me.

***

Lynn stared out of the train window. People's back gardens rushed past, filled with barbecues, children's swings, ornamental ponds, then open fields and farmhouses.

Everything was going too quickly. She felt the weekend, the events rushing past her like the landscape. On Friday she'd been full of dreams, but the reality had shattered her. After being cramped in Dan's parents' terraced house for the night, the open flat fields of West Lancashire had been a delight, but instead of exploring the countryside, Dan had rushed her round a series of boxy homes on executive estates in the town of Ormskirk. It was a nice enough place but her dreams had been of Lakeland villages built of weathered stone. When she'd asked about looking at country places Dan had treated her to a well-rehearsed lecture about the perils of buying a tumbledown property in the middle of nowhere. He'd already made a list of homes he thought suitable, garnered from property pages on the internet and from local agents and he was spending the week investigating them while she had been sent home to begin cutting the threads of their life in Birmingham. Without warning tears began to run down her face and once started she was unable to stop them.

The train thundered into a tunnel. She rummaged in her bag for a tissue and the sleeping boy next to her woke up. He looked round in confusion for a few seconds till he realised where he was. She could feel him watching her as she sniffled into the paper hanky, trying to look as if she just had a cold.

'Are ye all right?' He fidgeted as he asked, not looking at her directly. She smiled even as she went on crying. It was a silly question.

'Yes – it's okay. I'll be fine.' But the awkward kindness in his voice just made the tears come even faster. She tried to choke back a sob.

Other passengers were looking. The train was crowded.

'I'm going to get some coffee. Would ye no like some?' He stood up, unfolding a long skinny body, and fished some coins from a pocket somewhere round the knees of his trousers.

Lynn looked up, surprised by the Scots accent coming from this boy who was obviously Afro-Caribbean.

'Thank you. Yes, that's very kind of you.' she gasped, the tears beginning to dry up now.

While he was away she managed to compose herself. It wasn't as if the area hadn't appealed to her. At first sight of the vast fields of cabbages and potatoes, she'd fallen in love with the open sky, the unbroken expanses of land. She'd felt the smallness of herself, placed in this world, yet part of the whole. That effect had been lost in the town, where every corner was built on, except for the parks. Excitement had blossomed in her when Dan drove to Aughton but it hadn't been the way she'd imagined. Instead it was all leafy suburbs and sprawling Victorian villas hiding in shady gardens, home to Ormskirk's more affluent residents. Was this where her ancestors had lived? She'd peered round, looking for churchyards or schools as Dan pulled up in front of yet another mini-mansion. At one time she would have loved such a place but those glimpses of the open land had called to her as if she'd always known them. Dan preferred the town, he felt safer with walls around him.

Over the weekend, she'd gradually realised that he'd planned it all his own way, letting her fall into her dream of the good life in the country, while all the time he'd been ringing up estate agents, picking out properties that suited him.

She began to cry again, because Dan's deceit and the distrust she now felt as a result were spoiling her picture of their marriage, not just the relationship she presented to the outside world but the one she kept for herself. The tears stung hotly and she wiped them away, turning her face to the window in the hope that no one would see but the boy came back with the coffee and she was forced to face him.

'Thanks. What do I owe you?'

'It's okay.' He watched her mop her face and take the lid off the cardboard cup. There was a silence as they both drank.

'I didnae see you get on the train. Was it at Crewe?'

'Wigan. You were asleep.' She focussed on the tattoo on his left arm, half-hidden by his tee shirt sleeve. It was a stern figure, half-familiar to her, some character from a film or TV show. Darth Vader? Someone he wanted to be like, maybe? Thinking about it dried her tears.

'Wigan?' He looked at her like she'd said Betelgeuse. 'You live there?'

'No. We live in Birmingham.' She sighed. 'But we're going to move into the area. My husband has a new job. We've been up to have a look round. I needed to get home but he's stayed there to try and find us a house. I really wanted a place out in the country.'

'Are ye used to the country? I'm a townie, myself.'

'I'm from Somerset originally. My family still live there in a little village, so yes I've a country background, but Dan and I have lived in Birmingham for years and he's from Manchester, so he's a townie too. Of course Wigan's an industrial place, really built up, but we're going to a small town called Ormskirk, it's quite rural. Dan's really keen.'

'But you're not?'

Lynn looked up. He couldn't be more than eighteen or nineteen but he was looking at her like he could see right through her.

'It wouldn't have been my choice, but it's his job. And it's been so sudden. One minute we were settled, I was enjoying my work, expecting promotion, then Dan applied for this post up here. It's a good move for him, he's done so well, but it was as if I had no choice in it. He'd already applied for it before he even told me and then once he'd got the job, it was only three weeks ago, we had to rush up here. He said it was just to look round but we spent the whole time viewing houses he'd already picked out. I just feel so – manipulated. I've always thought we were together in everything but now it's like he's ridden roughshod over me to get what he wants. You don't do that to someone you love, do you?'

Her tears had stopped. It was anger that flowed through her now.

'Ah well, shite happens.' There was a despondency in his tone that made her aware of him as a person with a life and concerns of his own.

'I shouldn't be telling you all this.' She smiled. 'It's funny how you can talk to a perfect stranger sometimes.'

'Well, we're not strangers now, are we?' He was trying to reassure her.

Lynn noticed his fingernails, bitten to the quick. She'd been so wrapped up in her own problems that she'd hardly given him a thought. He'd just been someone to bounce her thoughts, her feelings off, as if just talking about it would help her think it through.

'Ye've practically told me your life story.' His voice was solemn but the brown eyes looking at her were friendly.

'I'm sorry. I've been very selfish. You must have been bored stiff.'

The chains on his trousers rattled as he shifted in his seat. She looked at his skull-and-crossbones tee shirt and wondered if he were still a virgin. His arms were light brown, the developing muscles retaining a childish roundness.

'No, I wasnae bored.' He seemed embarrassed, as if he knew what she'd been thinking . 'It sounds like a nice place to live. No ma type o thing but better than a council flat in Glasgow, yeah?'

'You've always lived in Glasgow then?' What she really wanted to ask was what he thought about Dan, about the way Dan had railroaded her into the whole idea of the house, the move. She wanted to hear a male viewpoint. Was it her just being silly, or was there a disregard, a putting down, a malevolence even, in Dan's attitude? At the same time she was curious about this kid opposite her, no older than the students she taught every day.

'Aye, ma maw's family are from Birmingham. That's where I'm going now, to see ma Aunty Violet. Ma maw married a Scot, a long-distance lorry driver. She wouldna go to Scotland at first so she went on living in Birmingham and he lived in Glasgow and visited her twice a week till I was born, then he made her move up there. I dinna think she's ever been happy there, away from her family, you know?'

'And you?'

He shrugged, avoided her eyes. 'Your man shoulda been straight up with you. If ye dinna want to go you should tell him.'

For that moment she loved him just for saying that, and for a second he was an older, wiser man. She wanted to lean her head on his shoulder but she stopped herself, looking at the soft curve of his neck as he bent forward to pick at something on his trousers.

'I wouldn't mind if we could get a place in the country. I found out I had a relation who lived in the district a long time ago. Dan pretended to be interested but I didn't get a chance to try and find out anything. I think I'd be happy to move, if we could just find the right place.'

'Stick up for what ye want then. Stand up to him. I don't let no-one walk over me. I got bullied for long enough when I was a kid, till I decided I wasna going to take it no more.'

The train pulled into Wolverhampton. People got off and on.

'I hate it,' he muttered suddenly, bending his head even further forward so she couldn't see his face at all. 'I fucking hate Glasgow. I don't fit in.' His fingers picked furiously at the zips on his knees. 'How could I fit in – a black Jock? I was the only one at our school. And having a stupid tart's name on top of that.'

'Tart's name?'

'Imogen. Fucking Imogen. That's ma name.'

Lynn sighed. Parents could be very thoughtless. 'It's unusual.'

'Yeah.'

'They must have had a good reason for calling you that?'

'It's the name of some stupid computer game my dad was nuts about at the time. All about this dragon-slaying wizard called Imogen.'

'Sounds like a powerful character; it must have been what he wished for you.'

'Yeah, I had to learn to slay a few fucking dragons in the playground.' He laughed bitterly.

'Boys your age don't usually go visiting their aunties,' Lynn probed gently.

'Yeah, well. So what you gonna do?' He sat up, and looked her in the eye.

'About the house? You're right. I'm going to ring Dan and tell him as soon as I get home. I'm not budging unless I get the kind of house I want. You've done me a favour. I appreciate it. I feel much better about it already. I can get another job, I'll be able to do my family research and it's near the Lake District.

Wordsworth's one of my favourites, you know.'

He looked blank. 'Favourite what?'

'Poet. You must have heard of him.'

He stared for a few moments then recognition appeared. 'Somethin to do wi daffodils?'

'Yes,' she said. 'But much, much more.'

'I wasna much at that sort o thing at school.' He squinted out of the window again.

'So what do you do now?'

'I'm a cooper's apprentice.'

'What?' She'd expected him to work in a factory or a fast food place.

'A cooper. You know, makes barrels.'

'Barrels?'

'Aye, for the whisky. Ma dad wanted me to have a trade.'

'You like it?'

'S'okay. I liked woodwork at school.'

'I don't know much about woodwork.'

'Makes us even then. I don't know much about Wordsworth.'

She smiled. 'You're not really going to visit your aunty are you?'

'It's just somewhere to stay. I'm no going back there. I'll get a job.'

'There may not be much call for coopers' apprentices in Birmingham.'

'I'll find something.'

His neck was so vulnerable. She wanted to touch it. Instead she wrote her mobile number down on a page torn from her diary.

'Here, ring me if you need to.'

The train pulled into New Street station. He pushed past her without speaking but he took the sheet from her hand. As soon as he'd gone she regretted doing it. She didn't know him from Adam.

***

It was no use putting it off. Con stared at the phone. It sat there like a menacing toad. Picking it up would change his life permanently. He'd make himself a cup of tea first. Diane had gone to work. She'd put no pressure on him over the weekend but she'd been unusually quiet.

The row they'd had on Friday afternoon after Aspinwall left had been the worst ever. Con hated to fight, he'd held back while Diane shouted abuse but in the end rage took over and choked him so that he couldn't speak and he'd forced her up against the wall, found his hands round her throat, frightening himself with his own violence.

Suddenly it had turned to sex. His fury had rushed out as he pulled at her clothes, making her do it his way. He'd showed her who was the boss and she'd loved it. She'd been with him all the way, pushing her arse back at him as he took her from behind; bracing herself on the mahogany dining table that had been in his family for generations, yelling as her orgasm ripped through her. He'd held on, held back for her, though it nearly killed him, then everything had blotted out as he let go, spurted into her, shouting his throat raw till it was all gone and his legs had buckled.

He could still hear her screams echoing round his mind. The kettle was boiling, steam clouding the kitchen. He was disoriented, still in that wonderful moment, lying spent on her back with his face buried in her hair. He wanted her now but he could wait. Tonight he would be tender. It was her birthday. She'd been happy with the card and the money. He'd got a quick kiss but she'd dodged out of the way when he'd tried to hold her. Myrtle Pilling would deliver the roses to the salon and then, when she came home at dinnertime...

He eyed the phone. He would do it now, then he could tell her when she came in for lunch. She would know then, how much he loved her, that he would do anything for her.

Sharon Burney answered his call. 'I'm afraid Mr Aspinwall is out at the moment. May I take a message?'

Snooty bitch, Con thought. He remembered her as a girl with scarcely a rag to her back. Her grandparents had kept pigs out at Lathom.

'It's Con Worrall here. Aspinwall were here on Friday to value the farm. Tell him we've definitely decided to sell. Tell him to put it on the market right away.'

***

The phone was ringing when Lynn came into the flat at four o'clock but by the time she reached it the answering service had cut in. She put the ready meal she'd bought for her supper in the fridge and made herself a coffee before playing the message.

'It's a message for Dan Waters. Graham Aspinwall here from Village Estates. I've got a property you might be interested in; it's only come in today. I've not advertised it yet, so give me a ring as soon as possible.'

Lynn sighed. Another boring house. He sounded young, enthusiastic. Why had he phoned the flat instead of ringing Dan's mobile? She was tempted to ignore the message, sit down with her new term timetable and pretend that she was planning the year's projects instead of preparing to hand over her precious students to someone else. Maybe she'd better see what he wanted, at least she might get a say in what was going on. She sipped her drink as she keyed the redial button, thinking of all the dull places she'd seen over the weekend.

'Hi, thanks for ringing back. I've been trying to get Mr Waters on his mobile but it's switched off.' He had the cheery open manner of a good salesman.

'He's still in Manchester. He won't be home till Friday but I'm sure he'll ring me later.'

'It's just that a fantastic house has come up, only this morning, an excellent property and great value. Thought I'd let you know right away. I know Mr Waters is keen to find something in the area quickly.'

'We don't want a town house.' Lynn made her voice decisive.

'Actually it's a farm. New Cut Farm. I wasn't sure if it would be the kind of thing you'd want, but the house is perfect for a professional couple and the land, well you could sell that on. There are three bedrooms and the whole property is thoroughly modernised, not like some of these old places. And it's close to local amenities on Askin's Moss, just a few miles from Ormskirk. Burscough village is within walking distance on the main Preston road with bus and rail links, and it's only a few miles to the univ –'

'Where did you say?' Lynn set her mug down almost spilling her coffee. All her attention was focussed on the phone.

'Burscough, it's a village about four miles from – '

'No, no, before that. Askin – did you say Askin?'

39

'That's right. Askin's Moss, it's just a name for an area of land behind the village and the canal, it spreads over towards Martin Mere bird sanctuary. Askin's quite a common name round these parts.'

***

'A farm? Is he out of his mind? What would we do with a farm?'

'He says we can sell the land. He says the house is perfect for us.'

'He would say that, wouldn't he? It's no good going after some place out in the sticks. Some of those areas are really remote, even nowadays.'

'It's on a main road, Dan. The estate agent said it's only a few miles from Ormskirk.' There was a moment's silence but she sensed his irritation.

'Lynn, there are plenty of perfectly good houses in Ormskirk. The market's falling. We can get a good deal. You saw what a nice little town it is.'

'I told you last night, I want a place in the country. I mean it, Dan.' She tried to put steel in her voice.

'You're a hopeless romantic and I love you for it, but you've got to take a practical perspective when it comes to real life. You know how I have to move around. I need good transport links.'

'There are transport links.' Lynn stopped herself from shouting. 'I looked on the map. There's a railway station in the village and the M58's only ten minutes' drive. You're asking me to change my whole life. You have to meet me part-way. I'm determined Dan, if you try to make me live in that town, I won't go. You can go on your own.'

She waited through the ensuing silence. Dan would be pursing his lips and frowning as he thought his way round the problem. She twisted a lock of her hair in her fingers.

'Okay, we'll think about it. I'll get Aspinwall to email the details. We'll discuss it when I get home.'

'No! I'll come up. Tomorrow. I can be there by lunchtime.'

'Don't be silly. What's the big rush? You're in work tomorrow.'

'I'll take the time off. I'm under notice anyway. I've got a feeling about this place, Dan, I need to see it.'

'You're being emotional, you've no details, no photographs. I'm suspicious. Why's he offering it to us before anybody else?'

'He thinks it would suit us.'

'What's the asking price?'

'I don't know.'

'Oh, for heaven's sake, didn't you think to ask?'

'I was too excited. Dan, it's in a place called Askin's Moss.'

'So?'

'Don't you see? Askin? It's got some connection to my family. It's like it was meant for me.'

'Jesus Lynn, there are probably hundreds of Askins up there. You know how common some of these local names are.'

'Dan, I want to see it. Tomorrow. I'll catch the ten o'clock train. You can meet me at the station.' There was another silence, then at last an aggravated sigh.

'Okay, we'll do it your way.'

As soon as she realised she'd won she felt guilty. She could tell he was put out but he covered it well, chatting about his parents before hanging up. Once he'd gone a triumphant joy overcame her guilt. She was too excited to eat, spent the evening looking up information about Burscough on the internet and went to bed hugging herself over her victory.

***

Dan met her at Oxford Road. One look told her that he was furious, but trying to put a good face on it. They had a quick lunch at a coffee bar outside the station, covering the dissent between them with stilted chit-chat about their respective journeys. Manchester was bathed in autumn sunshine that heated the traffic fumes. Lynn's breath caught in her throat as she followed Dan to the multi-storey car park.

She watched with relief as the racing traffic thinned and the city landscape gave way to suburban greenery and eventually to occasional tracts of open countryside. The silence became uncomfortable. Dan barely spoke as he drove, staring straight ahead, a smile stretched over his jaw as if pinned there. His hands gripped the wheel, tension evident in the set of his forearms. She set her own jaw, abandoned the attempts at conversation and concentrated on the landscape as it flattened. The vast fields already seemed familiar, some reaped, bare or stubbled, others green and woolly with vegetables and there was the occasional surprise of dying sunflowers, faces turned to the sun, or spiky sweetcorn stretching acre after acre against the blazing sky.

'This is Burscough,' Dan said grimly, following the SatNav directions. They passed through a single street of shops and the entrance to a supermarket. They turned left through a maze of industrial buildings and redbrick terraced houses. Lynn's heart dropped but a moment later they were out in open fields of unrelieved flatness with the shining snake of a canal away to their left.

'This must be it.' Dan slowed the car. The farmhouse sat in the sunshine, its bricks mellowed to a soft rust colour, surrounded by empty fields. There was a tiny cottage to one side and surprisingly, a formal oriental-style front garden that didn't belong there. Lynn re-populated it with foxgloves and delphiniums, lupins and marigolds, roses round the door. A white painted board proclaimed NEW CUT FARM in black lettering. Close by a man in a suit lounged against the side of a yellow Volkswagen Beetle, waiting. He started towards them as they got out of the car. Lynn turned to Dan. 'Yes, this is it.' She smiled.

***

Before it even had time to sink in that they would go and leave the farm and strangers would come here, there were a great kerfuffle and young Aspinwall come back again bringing these two that's interested in buying and there's Diane showing them round, acting the lady of the manor, and Con straggling behind like he were going to his own funeral.

I couldn't help laughing to myself when I seen this pair, even though I were sick as a dog at the thought of the farm being sold. There's no chance either of them could handle this land. She were pretty enough, but soft like a slug and as for him, you could tell he thinks spuds grow in plastic bags on supermarket shelves, if he thinks about them at all, probably eats foreign muck in fancy restaurants and looks down on folks like me.

Soon as she opened her mouth I knew they weren't from round

here, but I forgot about that when I heard what she had to say. Right off, she says to Aspinwall's lad, 'You said this place is called Askin's Moss, do you know why?' Aspinwall's lad said as how he thought it were an Askin that built the farmhouse and he called Con over from where he were showing her husband the outhouses.

Con told them the story of how we've been on this land for a hundred and fifty years, but he couldn't even remember his own great-grandfather's name. I were trying to tell him but it all flew out of my head when she says, 'There was an Askin in my family, a long time ago. I've been trying to find out about them. That's why I was so interested, when you told me about the farm.'

You could have knocked me down with a feather. I went up and looked right in her face but I couldn't see owt of our family in her and yet – and yet there were something. I could feel it in my water; but I didn't want to feel it, didn't want no strangers here. I told myself I were mistaken. It's a common enough name and so far as I know there's none of our family ever went travelling off down south or wherever she's come from. I kept praying they wouldn't like the place and they'd go away. I could tell he weren't keen and that give me hope but she were walking round with that dreamy look that a woman gets when she's got her heart set on something.

I followed them everywhere. Right across the fields they went as well as round the farm and the cottage. He were another Diane, only in trousers, kept putting her down every time she said something and I almost felt sorry for her till we were in the cottage and she said, 'Mum and Dad could stay here when they visit.' I were mad then, so I could have choked her but I couldn't get hold on her no matter how I tried. She shivered and looked right at me. 'It's cold in here,' she said and moved closer to her husband, not that he took any notice of her. 'Damp,' he said and sniffed like the place weren't good enough for him.

'It's been empty for a while,' that witch Diane said. 'Con's mother was in hospital for some time before she died. It'll be all right once it gets some heat and air. She always had a big fire going, even in summer.'

I wanted to go out then, out of the way, but I couldn't. I had to stay and see it all, the betrayal, the satisfaction on that smug bitch's face when she saw how keen the woman were. I could have knocked her down, and our Con too for being so nesh, but I couldn't do a thing, not a thing.

When they'd gone, I followed Con and Diane back to the farm and listened to them arguing in the kitchen but it were a lost cause. She's bewitched our Con and I could see he were thinking of the money and then she pulled him up the stairs to the bedroom and I didn't want to see no more.

Darkness were falling and it started to rain. I went all around the fields trying to calm myself down but a terror took hold of me and I were shaking for fear of what were coming. I stopped on the edge of the far field, where the land drops down, what were once the edge of Martin Mere, and looked back at the lights in the farmhouse windows.

I could feel the water in the ground under my feet. It were slow, always seeping, filling empty spaces, moving towards the ditches Dad had made so many years ago, ditches that would soon be blocked if these townies bought the place.

I turned and the Mere were before me, ghost trees waving, thickets of reeds rattling and beyond, the black water receiving the rain, whispering, stretching to mix with the dark sky in the distance.

I looked at the water, almost invisible in the night. It were blank, holding its secrets.

I looked my fill and the Mere never wavered. It wants to come back, I thought and the ground quivered under me. The water were bubbling, I seen the farmhouse dissolving, like it were built of sugar, the cottage too crumbling, the fields, all sliding into the lake. I put my hands over my eyes, I couldn't bear to look but when I took them away there were only the water, silent, endlessly moving, no sign of house or field or human hand. It were like none of us had ever been.

Chapter Four

January 2008

Rolo lay sulking in his new quarters. Even when he saw Con coming down the path he kept his head on his paws. Only his eyes moved, rolling at Con, filled with all the sadness in the world.

It's not fair, Con thought. Rolo was used to freedom, acres of land to roam. He had spent his whole life guarding the farm.

Con stopped himself from thinking about the farm. He thought about Cuba instead, about the warm sea and the heat, a miracle in January after the post-Christmas cold snap. He remembered Diane's golden skin turning deeper brown each day, how smooth it was when he rubbed her with oil. He'd never had holidays before meeting Diane. They had always been too busy on the farm for more than an occasional day out to Blackpool. He'd never felt the lack of them, the farm was their way of life, always had been and Christine had felt the same way too.

Diane had made him change his way of seeing things with her hunger for novelty and rewards. She was always booking weekends in hotels down south and although he'd grumbled at the expense and felt out of place in those artificial environments, he'd come to enjoy the chance to forget about the worries of the farm and to revel in being alone with her. They'd managed a couple of winter weeks in Spain over the last two years, but nothing like Cuba. He'd been more interested in the tobacco farms and sugar plantations than in the history and politics of the island, but it was the sensual heat, the superb beaches, the constant music and dancing, together with the endless white rum cocktails, that had made it a strange and magical fortnight. He'd managed to forget the nightmare of packing up and leaving the farm that had ruined Christmas, and he'd pushed away the thoughts of the horrid sterility of the new house and its strangeness that waited for his return.

Now he had to get used to this way of life. He looked at Rolo and knew how he felt but then maybe Rolo was still feeling miserable after being in the kennels while they'd been abroad or maybe he was missing the barn, finding it hard to get used to his new, purpose-built kennel and enclosure.

But as soon as he touched the bar on the door, Rolo leaped up, barking and flinging himself against the wire enclosure.

'Steady on, mate.' Con couldn't help laughing as Rolo rushed out, his tail whacking Con on the leg as he flew past and began to race round and round the garden.

Con went back to the house and stood in the back doorway, watching Rolo's joy. After a few seconds he shouted, 'Here!' It had rained all weekend, ever since they'd got back on Friday and Rolo's flying feet were tearing up the grass. This garden couldn't cope with exuberance. The dog came at once to sit attentively, eyes fixed on Con's face. Only his tail escaped control, waving and thumping on the concrete path.

'Good boy.' Con snapped the lead on his collar, still fumbling slightly with the unfamiliar catch. He'd rarely used a lead on Rolo in the past. He remembered to lock the back door, reaching inside to get the key. The smell of the house filled his nostrils, a mixed odour of fresh paint and new carpets. Packing cases still waited in the hall. Even though they'd moved in over Christmas, there was still so much to do. Upstairs needed decorating. Tomorrow was a new working week but as yet he had no work. He would start on the bedrooms in the morning.

It was good to be outside. The house was all right when Diane was there but she'd gone to the wholesaler's to re-stock the salon. Con felt uncomfortable there by himself, as if he was in a stranger's home. They'd brought some furniture from the farm but everything was in a different place, and the sounds, echoes, smells and textures were new and constantly disturbing. Even the views from the windows were unfamiliar. The sight of other houses, even though they were not close, unnerved him after his lifelong landscape of empty fields.

Rolo trotted sedately alongside as they walked through the village. There weren't many people on foot, it being Sunday, but the main road was busy as usual, full of families driving back from lunches at country pubs, or from browsing the shops at the retail park.

Con said hello to Peter Simonson, the local butcher who was coming out of the Spar with a carrier bag of clanking wine bottles.

'How are you settling in? Bit of a change from the farm?'

'Oh, fine, fine. Busy time, you know.' Con carried on walking. He knew the ripples their move must have made among the old village families and he didn't want to feed the gossip.

At the canal towpath, he looked to the right, towards the farm that was hidden by the bend in the distance, then turned the other way and walked briskly along, not looking at anything. He was thinking of all the days he had walked home along the towpath, knowing the exact spot where the farm would come into view, the sight fixed in his mind in every detail.

Gradually he became aware of Rolo's irregular gait at his side. Every few steps the dog was slowing, looking up at him, eager for freedom.

'Sorry, old chap.' Con released him and the dog bounded off to urinate on the nearby bushes.

It had begun to rain and Con pulled the hood of his waxed jacket up. Two ducks skittered on the water and he remembered how the canal had still carried occasional working boats when he was a child playing pirates with the other village boys. Even then, they had been a rarity. It had been more usual to see leisure narrowboats, beautifully restored and decorated, their owners trim in shorts and summer shirts, looking relaxed and happy as they sailed through Con's world, waving as they passed. Con had wondered where they came from and where they were going but he'd forgotten them as soon as they'd gone out of sight. He'd lived in a fixed circle with the farm and his parents at the centre. Now he too was on the move without really knowing where he was going. He looked up and saw Blondie tied to the rail in the porch of the Turk's Head.

In summer the place was a honeypot, crowded with day trippers, the waterside tables a riot of colour and noise but today the bare benches dripped gloomily in the drizzle. The bright umbrellas were all in winter storage.

Blondie stood up as he approached, wagging her tail and squirming with excitement.

'How are you, old girl?' He squatted to stroke her head and feel her body. She had lost a little weight, but otherwise seemed healthy and happy. Rolo ran up and the two dogs began to exchange greetings, sniffing each other's smells, both new and familiar.

Barney Dougan was in full flow at the bar, gabbling garbled poetry as always. Con never knew which poets he was quoting and most of it went over his head. Barney had been doing it so long that hardly anyone listened to him.

'All nature stands aghast,
Suspended by the viewless power of cold.
Their wintry garment of unsullied snow
The mountains have put on, the heavens are clear
And yon dark lake spreads silently below.'

'There's no snow here, you silly bugger.' Jack Atherton looked up as Con came in. 'Nor no mountains neither, only Parbold Hill. What'll it be, Con, half of bitter?'

'Make it a pint. And one for Barney.' Con was conscious of his status as Barney's former employer.

'You're a good lad, Con.' Barney drained his glass and handed it to Jack.

'Ah but the dark lake, boys, the dark lake, it'll be coming back and no mistake if this rain keeps up.

When the chill rain begins at shut of eve
The Heaven itself is blinded throughout night.
The memory of the world is gone
And time and space seem living only here.'

'Ah, shut your noise. Here.' Jack pushed a pint of Guinness across the bar. 'How's it going at the new place, Con?'

'Great.' Con took a gulp from his bitter. 'Lot of work to do, decorating and stuff.'

'Must be wonderful to be living in a new modern place like that,' Barney piped up, 'but sure you must miss the old farm now, your mammy must be turning in her grave, so she must.'

'That's enough now, Barney.' Jack wiped the bar with a towel and looked uneasily at Con.

'Sure, I didn't mean no harm now, I got such fond memories of the place.

'How soft those fields of pastoral beauty melt.'

'Rubbish, man, you well know, farming's bloody hard work and no return for it nowadays.'

Con stood silent as they waited for him to respond. There was nothing to say. Both arguments were valid. He sipped his beer and looked round the bar. There were still a few couples and families eating in the dining area as Jack's wife and daughters glided around with plates and cutlery. The smell of hot food tugged at Con's stomach, but he and Diane were going for a curry later. He was looking forward to it. The food in Cuba had been awful. He couldn't wait to get a good Madras down him.

'Ah well, what you done was for the best, I suppose. The new people now, will they be working the land, do you know?'

Con thought about the Waters, about Mrs Waters – Lynn, with her shining eyes, her delight in the farm. She had no idea that she was turning him out of his own place. And how was she ever going to manage the farm? Con had seen at a glance that she hadn't a clue, she couldn't even stand up to her own husband, never mind master the land the way his mother had done. She had worked like the devil, and Christine too, putting in the hours alongside him to keep the land productive. He'd had to work twice as hard since Diane moved in, because she had her own career, she'd refused to help with the farming, but he didn't mind. Diane lit up his life, she made him feel like he could work forever, like he had something worth working for, she was a goddess of fire and strength, not like the Waters woman who was soft, pale, overweight, weak.

Still, her eyes had burned when she told him the story about being related to an Askin. Couldn't be one of his family though, he'd never heard his mother mention a Lavinia Askin, but it had made him warm to her. Not like the husband, he could never take to him, a sly, arrogant bugger. You could see he thought nothing of the land, the district, or even of his own woman. What a couple! God knew what would become of the place in their hands. It was no longer his problem. He came out of his reverie. Barney was watching him, still waiting for his answer.

'How should I know?' He shrugged and supped his beer.

Harry Ramsbottom came up to the bar to pay his tab. Con hadn't noticed him in the corner of the restaurant with his family.

'Con, how are you? How are you settling in? Bet you miss the farm.'

'Things have to change.' Con wished they would all stop going on. It had been a mistake to come in here.

'What are you doing with yourself now, then? Must be a bit of a culture shock, no land to look after.'

'There's a lot to do with the new place; decorating and so on.' Con looked at his glass, it was nearly empty. The beer was going to his head. 'I'll have to think about work, once it's done.'

'Got anything lined up?'

Con felt like a butterfly on a pin.

'Not yet, we only just got back from Cuba.'

'Cuba, eh? Well, it's good to take a winter break. Mary keeps going on at me to winter in Spain, but I can't leave the business. One advantage you've got now, not being tied to the land.'

He took his change from Jack, turned his back to Barney and lowered his voice.

'Look Con, I know what a hard worker you are. There's a job for you at the woodyard if you want it. Could do with someone reliable in the office as well as some help on the general side. Know it's a bit of a comedown after the farm but the offer's there if you want it.'

'Thanks.' Con swallowed the last of his beer. 'I appreciate it Harry.'

'Come over and see me if you're interested. Have to go, she who must be obeyed is waiting.' He grinned and slapped Con on the back.

Barney and Jack were both waiting to find out what Harry had been saying but Con ignored them and picked up his empty glass. He wanted another pint but he couldn't face their inquisitiveness any longer.

'Same again?' Jack took the glass.

'Sorry, have to get back. Diane will be home. We're going for a curry.'

On the way back, he stopped off at the village shop and bought four cans of Stella.

***

'Hey, Rasheed, another Kingfisher please. What about you?' Con turned back to Diane.

'I'm okay.' Diane put her hand over her white wine spritzer.

'You look as if you've had enough already.' She broke a piece off her poppadum and spooned raita on it. 'You must have been drinking in the pub all afternoon.'

'Only had a pint with Barney.' Con thought about the four empty beer cans in the bin back at the new house.

'I don't know what you're thinking of, going in there and hanging round that Barney Dougan. You're just feeding their wagging tongues.' She crunched the poppadum. Con admired her even teeth, the way her jawbone moved, but he was alarmed to see the flinty look in her eyes. He looked round to see if the waiter was coming with some real food. His stomach was awash with beer.

'I grew up with Barney Dougan around.'

'And it shows.'

She was wearing her hair down, the way he liked it. Had she done it that way especially for him? She'd straightened the natural waves so it fell from the crown of her head like a pale yellow waterfall, paler than the primroses he'd picked in Mere Sands wood as a child, but brighter, shining like a sunlit stream. He wanted to touch it but she wouldn't let him, she was angry and he would have to placate her. He smiled at her and swigged at the new bottle of beer. When he set it down it was half-empty.

'Con!' Red spots appeared on Diane's cheeks. She glared at him.

'Aw c'mon Di.' He nudged her knee under the table with his own. 'Loosen up. It's the weekend.'

'I have to go to work in the morning.' Her voice was ice. She pulled her knee away from him and glanced round the restaurant. 'And don't think you're going to sit around just because you've no work. Justin's coming home for half-term. I want those bedrooms painted before then.'

Con thought about the new house. It wouldn't quite take shape before his eyes. He kept seeing the farm yard and Rolo by the barn.

'S'one good thing about that house. It's close to the village, means no driving, more drinking.'

He looked away. Across the restaurant something familiar caught his eye. That old woman with her back to him, something about the shape of her shoulders, the movement of her head. Was it his mother? His stomach lurched. The woman turned, glanced at him. She was a complete stranger.

'Beef Madras?' Rasheed set the plate in front of him with a flourish. Con forgot about his mother and about Diane.

The food sobered him and Diane mellowed as she relaxed. The cold crisp night was a shock after the heat of the restaurant. He held Diane's hand as they walked through the village, feeling the sure delicacy of her fingers, the hardness of the wedding and engagement rings he'd placed there.

'Let's go to the Legion.' He was ready for another drink.

'Oh, I don't know, Con. I have to get up early.'

'Not that early,' he squeezed her hand. 'The salon's not open till ten.'

'No, but I've cleaning, stocking, ordering, lots of stuff to do.'

'Just for a quickie. I want to show you off. I can't stop showing everyone how lucky I am.'

'You're drunk.' This time she laughed, till they turned the corner and saw Blondie tied up outside the Legion.

'Oh no,' Diane said. 'No way. We're not going in there while he's there.'

Con stopped outside the doorway as Blondie rose to greet him.

'Come on, Con.' Diane moved in close and reached inside his jacket. Her hands were cold on the back of his neck. Under her light perfume, he could smell her and juices flowed into his mouth. She kissed him and her tongue made him forget about the camaraderie and the Sunday quiz, the warm fire and dark beery smells inside the club.

She pulled back. 'Let's go home. We can have a drink there. We'll play some music, light a few candles, relax and be comfortable.'

But the house unnerved him with its quiet central heating and sterile smells so that his mood evaporated as soon as they walked in. He fetched a bottle of brandy from the drinks cupboard, poured himself a large glass and lay down on the couch while Diane lit candles and made coffee. He could hear her talking to Milly in the kitchen and he wondered how Rolo felt out in the new compound. He emptied his glass and poured another small one just as she came in.

'Just a little for me.' She came to the couch, sat down facing him and held out her coffee mug. He set the bottle back on the coffee table. She was stunning in the candle light. Her skirt had ridden up showing the stocking top on her left leg, with a glimpse of scarlet suspender against the golden flesh of her thigh. There was a dark space where the short skirt shadowed her crotch. Con drained his glass and reached for the bottle.

'Don't drink too much,' Diane said. 'Drink makes for droop.'

He didn't hear her. He was still thinking about Rolo, how the barn had always been home to him, how it had been home to Barney Dougan and other itinerant farmhands in his father's time.

'Wonder how the Waters are settling in?'

'Who cares?' Diane put a hand on his leg, rubbed his knee. 'Stop worrying about them.'

'I'm not worried about them. It's the farm. I bet they let it go to rack and ruin.'

'So what? It's not our problem. You have to let it go. Forget about it Con.'

She pouted and moved up close to him, her knees poking his ribs, her skirt hiking even higher. She leaned over him and her hair showered over his face. He thought of the pale yellow barley swirling the fields in summer, turning darker and brighter while they all waited anxiously for the right moment of ripeness, fearfully watching the sky and the clouds, feeling for the dampness in the air that might herald rain and the dreaded mildew. He reached out to touch her hair but his hands didn't seem to be working properly and Diane got up and began rummaging through the CD tower.

He watched the muscles in her calves tighten as she reached up to feed the disc player. He thought of his mother, young and lithe, helping with the planting in a short flowery dress, her legs bare and brown. He thought of the old woman in the restaurant with his mother's shoulders, thought of Blondie tied to the post outside the Legion, then turned his head into the sofa cushion and closed his eyes.

***

'I'm sorry to bother you, I'm Annie, Anne Chapman. We have Holmes Farm at the bottom of the lane.'

'It's no bother.' Lynn smiled. In the three weeks they'd been at the farm, their only visitors had been Dan's parents. 'Won't you come in? I'm Lynn. You're my first local visitor.' She led the way to the kitchen.

'Well, I didn't want to call too soon, thought you'd like time to settle in.' The woman looked round the kitchen, stared at the mixing bowls full of dough and the floury table and burst out laughing. 'My God, you've been busy!'

Lynn washed the flour from her hands. She was conscious of Annie's incredulous stare. She was much older than Lynn, probably in her fifties with ice-blue eyes in a red face that seemed to have been perpetually exposed to a cruel wind. She looked as if she'd never worn make-up or been to a hairdresser in her life. Not at all like Diane Worrall. Lynn wondered if they'd been friends.

'I expect you've been here before.' Lynn put the kettle on.

'Not for years. Not since Christine were here.'

'Christine?'

'Con's first wife. We came to be good friends, but I don't see much of her now.'

'Oh. I didn't know he'd been married before.'

'Well, you wouldn't, would you? No, Con's only been married to Diane for two years. She's not from round here.'

'Oh.' Lynn waited but Annie didn't explain further and she didn't want to appear nosey. 'Please, sit down, would you like tea or coffee?' She cleared a space on the table.

'Coffee'd be grand, though I can't stay long. Jim'll be back for dinner. They're out clearing the ditches.'

'In this rain?' Lynn looked out of the window. She'd planned to spend the morning working in the garden, but because of the weather she'd decided to bake instead.

'Aye, well, if we waited for the rain to stop we'd never get owt done. Ditches has to be kept clear or the fields'll flood.'

'Oh.' Lynn thought this over. 'Do you think we need to get ours done?'

Annie laughed. 'Haven't you looked at them?'

Lynn couldn't say that she wouldn't know what needed doing if she did look. 'I'm sure Mr Worrall's left them in good order.'

'Aye, I dare say. Best get your husband to check them out anyway.'

Lynn swallowed a giggle and turned back to the kettle.

'Must be nice to have time for all this.' Annie nodded at the bowls of dough.

'You don't make your own bread then?' Lynn set the coffee mugs down.

'Good God no.' Annie looked at her as if she were crazy. 'I've the farm shop to run and the fruit and veg shop in Ormskirk to see to. My daughter Penny runs the shop but I've to see to the deliveries for her and do the accounts. Where do you buy your vegetables?'

'We're planning to grow our own, organic of course, but for now we usually go to Sainsbury's in Southport. Do you sell organic?'

'That's a lot of old rubbish, all that organic nonsense. It's no different to the stuff we grow. Organic – it's just an excuse to rip you off, charge you the earth. And how do you know it's really organic? They only get inspected once in a blue moon. I've heard tales, let me tell you, how they hide the sprays and the bagmuck when the inspector's coming round. And most of it gets dragged halfway round the world before it gets here, so how can it be better for you than good, fresh local produce?' Her blue eyes blazed at Lynn for a moment then she ducked her head and sipped her coffee.

'Oh, I didn't mean –' Lynn was mortified. 'I'm sure you're right. I hadn't really thought about it like that. There must be arguments on both sides.' She floundered, desperate to avoid alienating her neighbour at their first meeting. She imagined Annie gossiping to all the shopkeepers in the village about the daft townies out at New Cut Farm. 'I'll certainly buy some vegetables from your shop now that I know about it, at least until I grow some of my own.'

Annie seemed mollified. Her smile lit up her blue eyes. 'Anyway, that's not what I come to talk about. I wanted to ask you about the cottage. Whether you got a tenant for it?'

'The cottage? We haven't planned anything. I thought it might do for when relatives come to stay. My parents could come for holidays.' Lynn felt disappointed. She'd thought Annie Chapman had come to see her out of friendliness.

'Place like that'll get damp if it's not used all the time. 'Course it's up to you, it's your property.' Annie looked down at her mug.

'Thing is, I'm looking for a place for my son, Andrew. He was in Iraq, got caught in a bomb blast, lost the use of both legs. He's been in hospital the last two months but they're discharging him soon. We need somewhere nearby.'

Lynn didn't know what to say. She reached a hand out to the other woman but stopped halfway. 'How awful, I'm so sorry.'

Annie shrugged. 'He took the Queen's shilling. He were unlucky.' There was an unfathomable expression on her face but her eyes seemed softer than before. 'He could stay with us at the farm. His old room's still there but he wants to be independent. He's a grown man — twenty-five in May. He thinks he can look after himself but...' she shrugged. 'I just thought the cottage would be ideal, but if you got other plans — you don't mind my asking?'

'No, no of course not.' Lynn was in a quandary. She was overwhelmed with pity for the young man and full of admiration for Annie's stoic acceptance of the catastrophe, but she didn't want strangers invading the farm even before she and Dan had had time to get used to it. She was already beginning to love the peace and isolation, the huge empty spaces, the joy of being able to walk for miles along the bare land without meeting anybody.

'I'll see what Dan thinks.' This would get her off the hook for the moment. She smiled at Annie. 'We haven't actually decided anything. He's away at a conference at the moment, but he'll be home tomorrow night.'

'He's not going to be taking up farming then?'

'I don't think so. He's a lecturer at the university.' Lynn wriggled under Annie's gaze but she smiled inwardly at the thought of Dan sitting astride a tractor. 'We're planning a big garden though. I think that's as far as we'll get. Maybe a few chickens.'

'What about the land?' Annie looked out of the window at the bleached-straw colours of the winter fields.

'I think we'll be looking to rent it out for now. We haven't decided whether to sell it or keep hold of it.'

'There's a lot of vacant land hereabouts already, too many crops not fetching their price. Farmers are up to their necks in debt, trying to keep afloat. Lots are selling up, or getting jobs and leaving the land idle. That's why Con gave up you know. No one can believe he did it. His mother's family had that farm for donkey's years. She must be turning in her grave. She lived in that cottage you know, and here in the farmhouse, when she were younger and her husband were alive.'

Lynn remembered how cold she had felt, the last time she'd been in the cottage. Maybe Annie Chapman was right, maybe it needed a permanent tenant.

'I think I may be related to her family. There was a Lavinia Askin on my mother's side, who lived in Aughton. She was my great-great-grandmother.'

'You're originally from round here then? Is that why you've come back?'

'No, my people are from Somerset, but I'm sure there must be a connection. I know it seems a coincidence but when I heard this place was called Askin's Moss, well it seemed like fate.'

'I don't recall any Askins out at Aughton. Have you checked the library, parish records and such?'

'I've made a start. I've traced some of the family tree from Mr Worrall's parents, but there are so many Askins. I can't find a connection and I've so much to do here with the house, it's difficult to find the time.'

'Well you won't, moidering round like this.' Annie waved at the mixing bowls. 'And you'll have no time at all, once spring comes, even if you're just growing a few vegetables. Fertile soil this, loves to grow weeds.'

'We were thinking about putting the land up for auction.'

'I wouldn't do that. Gypsies are buying up land like that. It happened to my cousin at Aughton, now he's got a permanent traveller site next to his house. It's no joke, I can tell you.

'Pilling might rent it from you. I know he's got a contract for leeks to fill this year with one of the big supermarkets. I'll have a word with him for you if you like.'

'Would you?' Lynn didn't know who Pilling was but she knew Dan was keen to get rid of the land. For some reason she didn't want it to be sold, to be separated from the farmhouse. Maybe her ancestors had trodden the footpaths, worked on these very fields. The Askin who had built the farmhouse had built it for this land.

'I'll let you know about the cottage, soon as I've talked to Dan.'

'Thanks.' Annie smiled at her and Lynn felt a bond between them. She liked this raw-boned woman, even though she had come with an ulterior motive.

'Come up to the farm one day and have a coffee with me. I'm nearly always in the shop.' She got up and Lynn followed her outside. The rain had stopped.

'See you soon then.' Annie gave a little wave as she climbed into the rusting white van by the gate. Lynn looked up the lane. A small man with a yellow Labrador was ambling towards them.

The dog ran to the gate as Annie drove away but stopped short when it saw Lynn and bared its teeth at her, all its body tensing. The man was still some distance away. She kept very still.

'Good dog.' She made her voice sound confident. 'Come on, I won't hurt you.'

The dog growled. Lynn badly wanted to run inside the gate and swing it shut but she knew she wouldn't get there quickly enough if the dog decided to attack her and she didn't want to startle it.

'Here, you silly bugger, here!' the man ran up and grabbed the dog's collar. 'I'm sorry missus. She's gentle as a lamb as a rule. It's because she used to live here and she doesn't know you. She's Mrs Worrall's old dog. Sure she'll be fine once she gets used to you. Come on now, Blondie, stop that growling and make friends.'

The dog whined. It looked at the man and then back at Lynn. It still seemed suspicious but its body relaxed and Lynn felt safer.

'I'm Barney. Barney Dougan. I used to work for Con and for his father before him. A fine man so he was. You'll be the new owner then?'

'Lynn Waters. My husband's name is Dan.'

'Children?' He peered across the garden.

'Not at the moment.'

'Ah well, there's plenty of time so there is, young woman like yourself. Your husband, will he be looking for farmworkers now?'

'I shouldn't think so, Mr Dougan.'

'Ah call me Barney now, everybody else does.'

'We're not sure what our plans are yet, but if you'd like to leave your number, Dan could give you a ring later.'

'Well there's no need for that now. Everyone in the village knows me. I'm easy to find.' He laughed and patted the dog's head.

'You've always lived here, have you?'

'Ah no, well see I came over in the seventies to Liverpool and

I worked my way around for a few years and it got so every summer I'd come back here to work for old Douglas Askin, that were Con's grandfather, or down at Holmes and in the end I just stayed on and settled down here. I used to live in the cottage there, until Con took over the farm. 'Tis a beautiful place in summer.'

'I like it now,' Lynn said. 'It's so wide open and clean after living in the city.'

'O! 'Tis quiet spirit healing nook!
Which all methinks would love.'

Lynn's mouth dropped open. 'Coleridge!' she gasped.

'A soft eye music of slow waving boughs.'

'But that's Wordsworth.' She stared at the wizened Irishman as she struggled to locate the quotation. 'Aira Force.'

'Aye,' Barney's dark eyes twinkled at her. 'They're poems my mammy used to read to me.'

'The Lake Poets. They're my speciality. I'm an English teacher.'

'The lake once covered all this land.' Barney swept his arms out to the horizon. 'This very land we stand on, all under water.'

'Lake?' Lynn stared at him.

'As I live and die. Do you not know the story of Martin Mere? Three miles long and two miles wide.'

'I've read a bit about it, I've been researching my family history, but I thought it was only small. Isn't it a nature reserve now?'

'Sure that's all that's left of it. Imagine it as it once was.

Now view the lake whose placid bosom shows
The smallest twig that on her margin grows.'

'But that's Windermere,' Lynn cried. 'Joseph Budworth.'

'Ah but think of it,' Barney ignored her. 'Glittering as far as the eye could see, since time immemorial. Cave men camped here, they've found their boats, dug one up on Pilling's farm years and years ago, 'tis in the museum at Churchtown so they say, though I've never seen it meself. They say Merlin was born on the shore and they say it's the lake where Excalibur was thrown.'

'But what happened to it?' Lynn couldn't understand what Barney was talking about. He seemed harmless but she was suddenly aware that she was alone here and the man's conversation was becoming increasingly bizarre. She comforted herself with the thought that anyone who was so familiar with

Wordsworth couldn't be that bad.

'It was first drained in the seventeenth century but it came back. They drained it away to the sea but the flood gates burst and ever after they was trying to keep the land dry for making money out of it with crops instead of being content with the fishing and the fowling of it. All the natural life of the place gone with it, the water birds, the fishing livings, the people living on the margins, among the reeds, cutting peat, making baskets. They all went and the land was rented out to tenant farmers. But the lake came back. It kept coming back.'

'It's solid land.' Lynn stared round the fields, felt the firm ground under her feet.

'If it wasn't for the pumping station at Crossens, you'd soon see it return. If you'd lived here long enough, you'd know how we worry when it rains. This land loves to flood. You've got to keep them ditches clear or all you'll be growing is whin for all your efforts.'

It was the same as Annie Chapman's warning. She and Barney were harbingers of doom. Her visions of soft friable soil, rewarding, freely fruiting, was turning to a nightmare of constant struggle with encroaching water, with mud and rain. How silly she must seem to these people. Her heart faltered. How was she going to cope here? What had she done? She would never succeed. She would look a fool in front of Dan and everyone else here.

'Look at the soil in your garden, missus. Rub it through your fingers, feel how damp it is. Black peat, made from trees and vegetation, rotted in water over centuries. You can't get more fertile soil, when it's drained right and the acid's took out with lime.'

She brightened for a moment, but his next words knocked her down again.

'We're only caretakers here, nature lets us live, but it's constant work. We drain the land to get crops but the more we drain, the more the peat dries and the land shrinks and drops. Makes it all the more likely to flood.'

Drops of rain began to fall. He looked up at the sky. 'It'll be back,' he crooned to himself.

Lynn shivered. Barney leaned towards her.

'You'll wake up, look out your window,
Towards a crystal Mere, to sight restored and glittering in the sun.'

'Grasmere,' Lynn muttered. The dampness in the air seemed to envelop her. For a moment she felt unsteady, as if the land was softening, liquefying. She remembered the dream she'd had of the glittering lake and the child on its shore. Suddenly a cold wind tangled her hair and made her shiver.

Barney looked keenly at her, 'The lady of the lake,' he murmured almost to himself, his head on one side, eyes bird-bright, examining her.

'What do you mean?' Lynn stammered.

'Your name – Lynn – it means lake.'

'Oh,' she tried to laugh, 'I'd forgotten.'

'Happen it be meant,' he said.

The dog jumped up and ran through the gate to the farmhouse door. It sat for a moment with its head cocked, its eyes fixed firmly on a spot somewhere above the door handle, then began to whine loudly, its claws scrabbling furiously at the bottom of the uPVC door.

***

I remember Barney Dougan coming because it were just before Mam died in the summer of 1974.

As a rule, Dad didn't take on labourers, but he weren't thinking straight with Mam so sick and even me and Bert could see how he were distraught underneath his stern front. He liked to have power, Dad did and this were something he had no control over, he couldn't make Mam get up and go about her business and he couldn't make the cancer stop eating her from the inside out.

I were wore out with nursing her at the end and doing the cooking and cleaning for them both and I still had Bert and little Con to see to. I weren't much help around the farm so when Barney come whistling down the lane, Dad took him on, even though we all thought he were drunk or crazy with his jabbering of his poems. I'll say this for him though, he's a damned hard worker in the fields, and with animals. And for all his blarney about how we've stolen the land, changed it from what nature intended, he has a respect for it and the things that grow on it, gentling it like he would a horse.

Me and Bert were still in the cottage then and Barney used to sleep in a corner of the old barn while the harvest were on and then he'd be off round the district picking tomatoes or packing cabbage. Where he went in winter nobody knew. I always thought he went back to Ireland to his family, but he never mentioned no relatives. All that talking in riddles and it always come back to poetry about lakes and mountains.

Bert and Dad used to scoff, sometimes get narked with him, especially Dad who had no laughter in him, nor interest in books or owt of that sort. He couldn't be doing with anything fanciful. But Barney has a beguiling way with him, I like to hear the poetry, especially with that Irish lilt of his. It says things as I never could say, strikes a memory here and there of resting from work, looking at the fields, the sky, and feeling happy, like you belong.

All foolery of course but everyone had a soft spot for Barney, even Dad, though sometimes I think Dad were a bit afeart of him, when he would start coming out with all that stuff about nature taking her revenge. There were a strange side to him for all his comic ways. I used to think maybe he had second sight. After Dad died we kept him on, or at least Barney kept us on, for as long as he were willing to stay. We moved into the farmhouse and let him have the cottage. It were only two year after Mam died when Dad went. He never used to say much but her death broke him. I never thought I'd see the day Dad lost interest in the farm, but that's what happened. He carried on but he just didn't have the heart any more.

But the biggest shock were to find out that he'd left the farm to Bert instead of to me. After all the work I done, year in, year out for nothing but my keep, to be passed over, to see what should have been mine given to my husband, as if I weren't capable of looking after it. I always felt as Dad disliked me but I couldn't believe he had done this to me. A cold lump of hate settled inside me and it's been there ever since. Every time I think of him I can feel its weight.

'It doesn't matter,' Bert said. 'If owt happens to me, it'll go to you and our Con.'

I held my peace because I knew he were right but oh how it hurt. Albert never knew how much it hurt.

It's a good while since I saw Barney Dougan down here. He don't stray far from the pubs now he's supposed to be retired but it's done me good to see Blondie and she run right to the back door like she could see me. Lord, how I longed to stroke her but my hand just slid over her.

Strange too, to see bread dough rising on the old kitchen table – took me right back to the forties. Me and Mam used to bake for the week every Friday. We had to put spuds in the dough when the war were on and the snotty-nosed Liverpool kids we had billeted on us used to stand watching with their fingers in their mouths. They'd only ever seen a loaf in a shop before though half of them looked like they'd never seen a loaf at all.

If she weren't in my place, I might quite like this girl, Lynn. Her's got no airs and graces, not like that Diane. I were here watching when Annie Chapman come. Eh up, I thought when I seen her coming up the path, she's not one to come visiting for no reason. I were glad when the girl stood up to her about the cottage because if the cottage goes there'll be no place left for me. All the time now it's one crisis after another and I'm helpless as a new born babe. A curse on you Diane Dawson, I'll never call you Worrall, and a curse on you too Con, for bringing me to this.

***

'Come on Dan.' It was the third time Lynn had called him for supper and he was still fiddling with his laptop. 'No, you're not bringing it to the table.' She took it out of his hands and set it back down on the coffee table, then pulled him by his tie so he had no choice but to follow her to the kitchen.

For a moment, she thought she smelled perfume but then a cold draught at her back distracted her. The house was full of cold spots, despite the double glazing. They would have to get someone in to check it.

She turned back but there was only Dan behind her, his arms slipping familiarly round her waist. 'Something smells good.' He nuzzled her neck.

The fragrance of the rabbit stew filled the kitchen. She'd felt silly asking the village butcher to skin and joint it for her but it had been worth it. Next time, she would learn how to do it herself. Maybe she could get a book, or maybe Annie Chapman might show her if she asked.

She'd opened a bottle of Chilean Cabernet Sauvignon earlier and now it was just right. Dan poured the wine while she lifted the casserole out of the oven.

'How was the conference?' She admired the dumplings as she spooned them onto their plates. They were just as fluffy as the ones in the picture in the recipe book.

'Oh, fantastic, fantastic.' Dan put his glass down. 'You know this department is so dynamic, the whole university is just buzzing with new development. It's so exciting Lynn, I'm so glad we came here.'

'What was the conference about?' She lifted rabbit pieces on to Dan's plate. The meat was falling off the bones, it was so tender.

'Ethics, at all levels, undergraduate to research. There are some real forward thinkers in these regional universities and I think ours is one of the best. You know, I think the North is going to be the new place to be; Manchester, Liverpool. There's a regeneration under way. My department's getting a new state-of-the-art building and we're extending the courses for health and nursing students.'

For a moment Lynn thought about her college work in Birmingham. Already it seemed like a lifetime ago that she had talked like Dan, discussing student needs and course structures. She looked out of the window at the empty yard. In spring she would fill it with stone troughs and sinks full of flowers.

Dan was wolfing the stew down without comment.

'You must be hungry.' She tasted the food herself, savouring the flavours. The rabbit had simmered all day in a red wine sauce.

'Need to get back to work,' Dan said between mouthfuls. 'Got to have this presentation ready for tomorrow.'

'I thought I might make a start on the garden tomorrow, if the weather keeps dry.'

Dan looked up. 'What's wrong with it the way it is?'

'It's not the way we planned it, is it? Remember we talked about a vegetable patch. I'd maybe like a few chickens.'

He stared at her for a moment. 'Yeah right, well whatever you want.' He tore off a piece of bread and wiped his plate with it. 'This bread's good.'

'I made it myself,' Lynn beamed.

Dan burst out laughing with his mouth full..

'What?' Lynn laughed too but she felt uneasy.

'Nothing.' Dan swallowed the bread. 'You're not thinking of going back to work then?'

'Well, later maybe. There's so much to do here at the moment.'

'Maybe I could put in a word for you in the English Department, be a step up for you, but I told you, you don't have to work unless you want to.'

'I'd rather wait a bit. This family research just spreads wider and wider, there are so many angles to follow, different records to look up. I've found Con Worrall's mother Alice and her father, Douglas Askin.'

'Yeah, well, it's like all research, you need to stay focussed. Don't go off at tangents. Might be a better idea to start with this relative of yours. You've got some dates for her?'

'Mmm, but it's dry work, sifting through records and microfilm. I thought now I've got the car, I'd like to explore the area a bit as well, visit this Martin Mere nature place, have a run up to the Lakes. Maybe we could have a day out together; we haven't done that since we got here.'

'In the Easter break maybe.' Dan's glance flickered away. 'I'm really busy right now.' He pushed his plate away. 'Jesus, that was good. I'm stuffed. I'll be putting on weight if I'm not careful.' She caught him looking critically at her, changed the subject before he could say anything.

'There was a funny little Irishman here yesterday. I think he was looking for work.'

'Yeah? Well we can afford someone to help with the gardening if you like. But I think it's better to be careful, get someone with proper references.'

'He seems to be well known round the village.' Lynn relaxed now Dan was off the subjects of work and weight. The wine and food had made her warm and lazy. She laughed softly, pushing her foot against Dan's under the table.

'Funny thing is, he talks in poetry – and it's all Wordsworth and the Lake poets, but jumbled up.'

'You're kidding?' Dan sat back and drank his wine, letting her foot play over his.

'Honestly. He just came walking along, he's got the old lady's dog, the one who used to live in the cottage, and right off he started spouting lines about lakes and fields. I couldn't believe it.'

'That's incredible. He must be meant for you.' Dan fidgeted with his glass and pulled his foot away. She could tell his mind was already sliding back to his laptop.

'He said I was meant to be here, I was the lady of the lake.'

Dan laughed. 'What?'

'He said there used to be a lake here, a big one.'

'You don't believe that sort of guff?' Dan pulled his chair back.

Lynn's face clouded. There was something strange about Barney, the things he had said. She didn't know what to think but she felt something hovering at the edge of her mind.

'Come on Lynn. I think you need to spend less time on all this. Think seriously about getting back to work.'

'Someone else came. A woman called Annie Chapman from the next farm. She wanted to rent the cottage.'

'Oh?' Dan's interest snapped back.

'She's got a disabled son, injured in Iraq. It makes you think. When you see it on TV it's not real but when it's someone local, even someone you don't know, it's terrible. A young, strong man, fit, full of life, coming home disabled, no way of changing it, no putting the clock back. And what's it all for? It doesn't stop it happening again and again, does it?'

Her relaxed mood had disappeared, tears pricked her eyes. For some reason she felt annoyed with Dan, as if it were his fault. Don't start your sociological diatribes, she thought but he just stared at her and drained his glass.

'Poor bastard,' was all he said.

Lynn tried to concentrate on practicalities, to stop the tears spilling out onto her cheeks. 'She's looking for somewhere nearby, where he can have some independence yet be near enough for her to help him.'

'That narrows things down.' Dan refilled their glasses. 'There isn't anywhere else till you get to the village. What did you say?'

'I said we weren't interested, but I did say I'd ask you. I don't want to let it Dan, at least not yet. It's nice having the place to ourselves. I thought it would be good to keep it for our relatives, for when they come to stay, give them a bit of space.'

'But we've got two spare bedrooms.'

Lynn flinched; she'd thought the smaller one would make a perfect nursery. Dan was giving her that calculating look she knew meant he intended getting his own way. 'It might be a good idea, as a temporary thing, bring in some extra money.'

'But you just said – '

'Oh, I know, but it doesn't hurt to watch the pennies a bit, everything's getting dearer with the way fuel's shooting up. You don't need to be an economics expert to see there are hard times ahead, and we're not using the cottage at the minute are we? If mortgage repayments jump, we might have to tighten our belts, especially if you don't want to work. It'll have to be done up anyway, we could let it in the short term while we're thinking what to do with it, just tart it up a bit for the time being. You heard what the Worralls said about it getting damp when it's unoccupied.'

'Mmm.' Lynn hadn't expected this reaction, but she decided not to argue. She would just let sleeping dogs lie and hope Annie Chapman wouldn't ask again. She got up and turned the thermostat up a notch, pulling her cardigan round her shoulders. Since the oven heat had dissipated, the kitchen felt much colder. 'We need to sort something about the land, too.'

Dan got up and put on the kettle. He measured coffee into the cafetière. 'You're right. We can't let it lie, it'll get out of hand, then no one will want it. We need to shift it before Spring. I'll get on to Aspinwall about putting it up for sale or auction.'

'No!' Lynn shivered as a blast of cold air came from nowhere. 'Annie Chapman says travellers will buy it if we do that. We don't want a caravan site on our doorstep.'

'Yeah?' Dan poured hot water into the cafetière. Fragrant coffee steam displaced the lingering smell of their supper. 'She could be right. I hadn't thought of that. You know, some interesting studies of travellers have been done recently. Greaves and Pollock is the best one. I'm thinking of introducing a module on the BA course, 'The Alternative Side of Contemporary Mobility' or something.'

'I don't think it's a good idea, selling it.' Lynn made her voice authoritative. She was determined to hold on to the land somehow. 'We could just let it. Annie says there's a local farmer who's looking for land to rent.'

'Yeah? I suppose that might solve the problem for now, at least it would give us some breathing space till I'm settled into the new job a bit more.' She could see his attention slipping. He was itching to get back to his paper. 'Tell her to see Aspinwall, I'll ring him when I've got a minute to instruct him.'

Lynn cleared the kitchen and washed the dishes. She'd meant to ask Dan about getting someone in to sort out the draughts but maybe she'd just do it herself, ask Annie Chapman if she knew someone. Or maybe she could find Barney Dougan and ask him. She felt safer with these people than she would ringing some anonymous firm in the Yellow Pages.

Dan was soon busy working in the room he'd already appropriated for his den. Lynn went into the dark lounge. She felt too restless to watch television. She stared out of the front window at the garden which was lit by the single lamp outside the front door and pictured how it would look when she'd remodelled it in cottage style.

Across and beyond the lane, the land was a solid dark mass, in contrast to the sky where a crescent moon rode, lightening the shades of night. She half-closed her eyes and the black land seemed streaked with silver, as if it were rippling. She thought of Wordsworth striding his beloved moors, climbing the nooks and crannies of the hills, seeking out the secret silences of mossy tarns, the freshness of rushing streams that poured over smoothed rock. This land wasn't like that, wasn't clean and clear, open and confident in itself. It seemed a caricature of something else, hiding secrets behind a bland landscape of flattened shapes. There was an aura of deceit about it and yet she'd loved it at first sight. Could Barney Dougan be right, that she was meant to be here? But for what purpose? She thought of the Lady of Shalott floating down the river, hair like weeds in the water and without thinking she stroked her own long dark locks.

The room seemed colder, icy, as if the heating wasn't working at all. She felt a terrible sense of foreboding and she turned and hurried to Dan's study, where the familiar books, the bluish light of the laptop, the rosy tones of Dan's face in the soft lamplight, all reassured her. She looked at the pale wooden shelves, already laden with sociology paperbacks, the Bokhara rug, Dan's CD and his expensive stereo.

He glanced up at her impatiently. 'Won't be long, just got to finish this.'

She nodded and went upstairs to the bedroom. It was warmer there, the heat rising up from the ground floor to collect under the roof. She undressed in the dark, not bothering to draw the curtains, thinking that she would make a deal with Dan. She would agree to letting the cottage, providing that they didn't sell the fields.

Maybe she should talk to Annie Chapman after all. If she just let things lie, Dan might tell Aspinwall to put the cottage on the market without consulting her. She felt she couldn't trust him to consider her viewpoint any more.

She got into bed quickly; it was more chilly than she had at first thought. Tomorrow, she would mark out the vegetable plot. The hum of the central heating cut out as the boiler shut down for the night. She lay listening to the creaks of the house for a long time, waiting for Dan to come to bed. Through the square panes of the window, she could see the moon, but not the outline of the land. Her mind played on themes of darkness and waves, hair fronds and glinting lights. She wanted to write down the words floating through her mind but her notebook was downstairs and the thought of moving, of getting up again dismayed her. There were dark shadows by the folds of the curtains, in the spaces between the furniture that seemed to move and take on a human shape. She closed her eyes and turned her back, reaching out to the empty space where Dan should be. She pulled his pillow into her arms and held it tight, smelling him as she drifted off to sleep.

Something, someone was pulling her hand. It was incredibly cold. She opened her eyes. Something was bending over her. She blinked, trying to make the shifting shadows solidify but the shape was like smoke, forming and reforming in the dark. Was it just her imagination? But no, the grip on her arm was firm.

The shape elongated, stretched away towards the bedroom door, pulling her with it and she couldn't detach herself no matter how she tried, so that she had no choice but to follow. Its strength seemed superhuman though it had no substance and Lynn's brain was too numb to resist further as she was dragged down the stairs and through the house to the back door.

The door swung open and Lynn stepped out, staring at the full moon that dominated the landscape. She screamed in shock as she plunged up to her thighs into icy water, her nightdress ballooning out round her to float on the surface.

Her mind locked, trying to deal with the flood of information and fear. She stared at the great lake that stretched as far as she could see, its blank surface silent under the moon, except for the faint lapping against the reed beds that smudged its margins.

The dark shape capered. Lynn could sense its laughter. 'What? What do you want?' she cried at last, as she tried to struggle back out of the water but her legs would not obey her, she couldn't feel them at all, couldn't even feel her feet on the lake bed, and she couldn't tell if it were the reeds or the shape that hissed, 'Do you think you belong here?'

The thing pointed at the water while its other hand still gripped Lynn's arm, forcing her to bend closer. Something was down there, maybe a foot under the surface, something black and shapeless, its boundaries indistinct in the dark water that surrounded it. Lynn peered fascinated as it came closer to the surface, trying to make out what it was, until she saw its blackened teeth, prominent in a lipless mouth, its charcoal fingers reaching stiffly up towards her and then at last she opened her mouth and screamed.

'Jesus! Lynn!' Dan was shaking her. 'What is it, for Christ's sake?'

'My nightie,' she sobbed, 'my nightie. I'm so cold, so cold.'

She grabbed Dan, her teeth chattering and his heat burned her, shocked her awake.

'What nightie?' Dan said, pulling her into his arms and cuddling her close. 'You're not wearing one.'

Chapter Five

February 2008

Con was in the Farmers' Arms. It was handy for a lunch break, just across the road from Ramsbottom's yard. Smells of polish and air freshener overlaid the ingrained perfume of beer.

'First customer of the day.' Jackie Mack passed over a pint of bitter and flashed him a lipsticky smile.

'I'm on early lunch.'

'Having a sandwich with that? Or there's a nice hotpot, but it's not quite ready yet.'

'Ham and mustard please.' Con wasn't hungry but he thought he'd better eat in order to stay sober. The dusty woodyard made him thirsty and half the pint went down his throat in one go, while Jackie gave his order to the cook.

'How's Di?' She folded her arms on the bar and leaned her bosom on top of them. 'Haven't seen her for ages.' Her gold bangle earrings swung lazily as she leaned her head closer. 'You used to come in here a lot – together.'

'She's fine,' Con said. Jackie waited. 'We've been working late,' he said at last.

'Hairdressing doing well then? And you must be settling in at Ramsbottom's. Bit of a change for you, eh?'

'Yes.' Con wished someone else would come in. He knew that Jackie knew he wasn't working overtime like he'd been telling Diane, but that he was stopping off for a drink after work: that one drink became three or four so that often he didn't get home till ten. She knew this because she sometimes worked the evening shift and served him herself. Thankfully the sandwich arrived and saved him from further explanation. Barney Dougan came in as he took his first bite.

'Ah Con, 'tis good to see you and it's a beautiful day, so it is. *The lambs are bleating out now May is near.*'

'It's February you silly sod.' Jackie Mack pulled him a pint.

'Ah, but it's coming, it's coming,' said Barney.

*'Land and sea
Give themselves up to jollity,
And with the heat of May
Doth every beast keep holiday.'*

Sure the catkins are out on the branches, the snowdrops nearly finished. You can feel it, feel the earth awaking.'

Jackie Mack rolled her eyes, then went off to serve another customer.

'So how's it going Con, how are you doing down at the yard?'

'It's different,' Con said, thinking how the stock in the wood yard was the same all year round. There was nothing to indicate the approach of spring except an increase in the sales figures on the computer screens.

He longed to walk round his fields, assessing the sky and feeling the texture of the soil, waiting for just the right time for ploughing. He wanted to feel that excitement of starting each year afresh, like a new love affair, except that the land was such a hard mistress, just like Diane. For a moment the old desire burned up in him. He remembered a night on the beach in Cuba, where the sky lay on the sea like dark velvet, how he had gone into her, with the water crashing over them, oblivious to other people, other lovers walking along a few yards away on the crescent of sand.

'Got any plans for Valentine's Day?' Jackie was back, wiping the bar with a towel. 'Wayne's taking me to Paris.'

'Ah, a young man's fancy turns to love.' Barney leaned his drinking arm on the bar and winked at her.

'Get on with you, Wayne's nearly forty.' She looked at Con, waiting for him to speak.

'I'd forgotten about it.' Con put his glass down. He thought with dread of the fuss with flowers and a card again. He would have to take her out for dinner or something, but maybe it would be a chance to recapture the magic. Somehow things weren't the same since they'd moved.

At first she'd been all over him, treating him like he was really special but not long after they got back from the holiday she'd started badgering and pushing him to do the decorating, to get a job. There was always something he should be doing that he wasn't. He'd begun to dread going back to the house at night.

The desire she always provoked in him was overpowered by the way she acted towards him.

'Thanks for reminding me.' He smiled at Jackie and gave her his empty glass to be refilled.

'You want to take Diane away somewhere nice, give yourselves a break. We're going to see all the sights, the Eiffel Tower, Notre Dame. I want to see Montmartre, you know where all the artists used to live and then we're going to Disney. Diane would love that.'

'We've not long come back from Cuba.' Con drifted away again to the beach, the sea and the heat of the Caribbean sun.

'That must have been so romantic,' Jackie's eyes took on a faraway look.

'Ah, you should take a trip to the old country if it's romance you're wanting.' Barney supped his pint.

'We'll probably go to Raj's for a curry.' Con looked at his watch and gulped his beer.

'Oh Con, come on, you can push the boat out a bit more than that. Show her what she's worth.' Jackie pouted. 'At least take her somewhere decent, like the Haywain.'

The name pierced Con with that last memory of his mother enjoying her chicken roast but he knew Diane would like it, would enjoy the opportunity to show herself off.

'That's not a bad idea.' He finished his beer and paid his tab. A romantic dinner might be just the opportunity to get them back the way they used to be. He pictured Diane, mellow from being spoiled and petted, opening her legs for him under the restaurant table. His hand prickled with the remembered sensation of sliding up her stockings to the warm flesh of her thigh.

He stood stupidly on the threshold of the street for a moment, lost in his physical sensations, the harsh winter sun blinding him after the darkness inside. Across the street he saw a dark-haired woman waving at him but she had moved on by the time he realised it was that man's wife, the one who had bought the farm. What was their name now, Rivers? No, Waters, that was it.

He stared at her back, resenting her for being on his farm. Diane in the new house wasn't the same as Diane at the farm. He couldn't make love to her in that house the way he could at the farm where he knew every creak of the floorboards, where he was the master of all he could see. He wanted to go down to the salon, drag Diane out and take her to the farm right now. He wanted to fuck her in the barn or in the fields where there were no windows with prying eyes, no sterile smells.

There was a great black space opening up in him, like a dark lake, but he pushed it away, making himself angry at Mrs Waters, balling his fists in his jeans pockets. Tonight after work, he told himself, he would walk Rolo round the farm fields and just let them have anything to say. He turned away and walked back towards Ramsbottom's yard. Halfway there he came to Myrtle Pilling's shop and went inside.

***

Lynn saw the yellow Labrador tied up outside the Farmers' Arms and made a mental note to pop in and see Barney Dougan about the gardening on her way back. Con Worrall came out of the pub and stood screwing his face up against the light. She waved, thinking he looked a bit the worse for wear, but he ignored her and she went on her way. Maybe he hadn't recognised her. She'd only seen him once or twice; most of their negotiations had been done through Aspinwall with occasional appearances by Diane.

She stopped outside Diane's Den, then plucked up her courage and went inside.

'Do you think you could fit me in for a cut and blow dry?'

'I'll just see.' The girl on the reception desk went into the back of the salon, although there were no other customers except an elderly man getting a very sparse trim.

Diane Worrall came bustling out, looking slim and sexy in a white overall and black trousers. Her hair fell in perfect blonde sheets on either side of her face.

'Oh, it's you, Mrs Waters. Let's get you a gown. What did you want to have done?'

'A cut and blow dry if you can.' Lynn was conscious of her tangled hair, of the way her flesh bulged over the waistband of her jeans as Diane fussed about tying the bow of the gown round her middle.

'Just a straight trim? You don't fancy something a bit more stylish?' Diane held up a limp lock of Lynn's hair and looked at her in the mirror.

'Not today,' Lynn stammered. 'I'll think about it. Maybe next time.'

'Some highlights would look good. Give it some lift.' Diane riffled through her hair as if searching for something.

'Yes, I'll think about it.'

'How are you settling down at the farm?' She collected brushes and scissors in the tray next to Lynn's seat.

'Oh, I – we love it. I can't wait to grow some vegetables, get a few hens.'

Diane's pencilled eyebrows rose.

'Not that I didn't like the garden the way it was –' Lynn's voice tailed off.

'Everyone's got different tastes,' Diane motioned her over to the sinks. 'We've had to completely redecorate the new house.'

'But you like it?' Lynn said anxiously. She would feel awful if she thought the Worralls weren't happy in their new place.

'Oh, it's marvellous.' Diane rubbed energetically at Lynn's wet hair. 'Much easier for me to look after. I'm so busy here you know, and it's much more convenient for the village. And then Con's got a new job at the woodyard, regular money, no more worries about weather and the price of barley.'

'Must be a big change for him though, he's lived there all his life, hasn't he?'

'Well, it's not as if we've left the district, is it?' Diane's fingers seemed to rub harder as if she was angry at the question. Lynn could smell the fresh woody scent of the conditioner she was massaging in.

'Have you always lived here?'

'Me?' Diane's voice held laughter. 'I'm from Liverpool. My first husband was a builder. We got divorced and I bought the salon up here with the settlement money. That's how I met Con. First in the British Legion one night, then he came in for a haircut and that was that.'

'I've only passed through Liverpool on the train. I must go and have a look round one day.'

'There are some good shops but Manchester's trendier really. There are museums and stuff if you like that kind of thing. I'm from Great Homer Street, what's left of the Scottie Road area.

The heart of the city's gone now, all rebuilt years ago and now they're at it again with this Capital of Culture. It's like a building site. I'd wait till it's finished if I were you, there's going to be lots of new shops then. People grumble about the old city going, but it was a dump. You've got to keep up with the times, and retail's so competitive these days.

'Of course, it was me got Con to modernise the farmhouse.' She wrapped Lynn's head in a towel and led her back to the chair by the mirror. 'It was in a terrible state, I don't think it had been touched since the war and after Christine went, that's his first wife, she ran off with a butcher from Ormskirk, I don't think it even got cleaned and she left in 2001.' She expertly combed and clipped sections of Lynn's hair.

'But you didn't want to stay there after doing all that work?'

Diane's scissors snipped sharply. 'It wasn't for me. I enjoyed doing it up, but it was too big for us and there was all the worry of the land and trying to make a living out of it. Of course we couldn't sell while Con's mother was alive. She wouldn't hear of it.'

'You didn't find anything strange about it?'

'What do you mean?' Lynn flinched as the comb dug into her scalp.

'I don't know. It feels sort of spooky sometimes.'

'Spooky? Like ghosts you mean? You think there's a ghost?'

'No, no.' Lynn felt stupid. She supposed Diane was laughing at her. 'I don't know. It's just so cold sometimes – and I've had strange dreams.'

'All these old places feel a bit creepy, creaking doors and all that,' Diane shouted over the noise of the dryer. 'There's no ghost as I know of, unless it's Con's old mother, God knows she haunted me enough when she was alive.' She laughed and Lynn looked up at the brittle sound.

'Barney Dougan told me it used to be a lake.' She shivered despite the stream of hot air being directed at her head.

'That old sot!' Diane tugged at her hair with a styling brush, trained the dryer so close Lynn could feel her scalp burning. 'Don't let him scare you with his nonsense, old blarney tales and stupid poems.'

'But there was a lake?'

'Oh yes, they say so, but that was ages ago. All that's left is the bird sanctuary outside the village and there's a lake up at Mere Sands. You'll be all right once you settle down.' She fetched a hand mirror, showed Lynn the back of her head.

'It's just different coming out from the city and getting used to country life. I know. I was born and bred in the inner city.'

'But you didn't settle.' Lynn bit her lip as she counted out notes from her purse.

'Different for me.' Diane tucked the money away in the till. 'You've got a genuine love for it, I could tell when you came to look round. Didn't you say you thought you might be related to Con's family? Have you found out anything about that?'

'A bit, but I've not found a connection. I haven't had much time to look yet, what with moving in and I want to get started on the garden.'

'You're interested in growing things aren't you? I'm afraid I'm not.'

'Yes.' Lynn brightened. It was true she was thrilled with the marked out vegetable patch and the excitement of poring over seed catalogues. 'And I just love the open space.'

'Ugh, I hated it,' Diane shuddered. 'I used to feel lost with no houses round me and no one to talk to. Thank God I had the salon and Milly.' She looked down at the little dog asleep in her basket.

'I'm sure I'll be fine,' Lynn said. She'd been about to say how she wished Dan was at home more often but something made her cautious. Diane seemed the type to gossip and she didn't want to feed her information for the amusement of the whole village.

'There seem to be a lot of draughts. Did you find that?'

'Draughts? There shouldn't be after all the money we spent on double glazing and central heating. Ramsbottom did the work. Not Harry, the one Con works for. It was his cousin Peter, up at Rufford. Get him to check it over. I'll give you the number.'

Outside, Lynn saw the yellow Labrador was no longer outside the pub. She felt slightly disappointed. She would have to catch Barney another day. She stood irresolute for a moment, watching a young woman with a pushchair coming towards her. The little blonde girl in the chair lifted her arms to Lynn and giggled, showing tiny milk teeth. She wanted to reach down and touch the child's soft velvety skin, feel the little hands clasp her neck, but she smiled at the mother and walked on by.

Maybe here, now in this new life, it would happen. After all, the tests they had taken had revealed nothing wrong. Dan had been so defensive about getting tested that it had been a relief to find they were both okay. Why was he still so prickly about the fact that she'd never conceived? Gradually they'd stopped talking about it. In her heart she believed that Dan was secretly glad; a child would interfere with his career. She turned onto the canal towpath to take the scenic way back to the farm but before she reached the first bend her mobile rang.

'Lynn? Mrs Waters?'

She didn't recognise the voice.

'It's me. Imogen.'

'Imogen?'

'Do ye no remember me? On the train? You said if I needed help – well I do.'

***

The cottage looks bigger now. Strange, I've never seen it empty before, even though so many people have lived in it. 1928, Dad built it, before I were born. It were for Aunty Dot to live in, after Dad's brother died and Dad inherited the farm.

These white walls make it look bigger. We used to whitewash it outside, when me and Albert first lived there, but we never had it white inside, I like a nice bit of wallpaper. It does look clean now, but bare. I'll say this for her, this Lynn, she's made a good job of the decorating without a scrap of help from that husband of hers. I could see he were like that the first time I set eyes on him.

I were excited when me and Albert got the cottage. Well, I were sad that Aunty Dot died but it made it easier for us, we'd only been married two year and houses were hard to get after the war. We'd been renting a tumbledown place right at the far end of the village, which meant having to walk to the farm every day for work, so it were a godsend that the cottage come empty and we didn't have to pay Dad no rent.

She's coming now, Lynn. She's looking right smart. Don't tell me she's been to that witch to get her hair done. Looks worried though. For all I never wanted them to come there's something about her that draws me. I got no time for him though, if it's up to him they won't be here long. I were mad as hell when I seen them shifting all my things out. The best were already gone, the good Welsh dresser and the pine table out of the kitchen. That Diane couldn't wait to send them to the auction in Southport and I bet they fetched a pretty penny. They belonged to Aunty Dot.

I couldn't believe it when I seen our Con burning the bed where me and Bert slept all our married life. Then Diane come with a load of plastic bags and boxes, rummaging through my clothes, my china, and all the papers and things in the sideboard. All the time I were dancing round her, trying to get my hands on her but it were useless and she never so much as turned a hair.

I followed her all the way to the car and that were the last I seen of my possessions. She'll have taken them to the charity shop in the village. Elsie Langham's probably walking round now in my good tweed skirt and eating off my plates.

They left the other stuff, though, the bits and pieces we got in for Barney Dougan after Dad died. Albert said it weren't right to leave Barney living in the barn after we moved in to the farmhouse. I remember him coming in with his cheeks red from the wind that were blowing that day.

'That bloody barn'll have to come down, it's got more holes in it than a sieve and poor Barney's half clemmed to death in there,' Albert said.

Then before I knew it, the old barn were gone and a new tin affair put up in its place. Albert never even asked me what I thought, and that's how it went. I could see how his confidence grew, once the farm were in his name and I used to look in the fire and picture me dad burning in the hobs of Hell and I'd comfort myself with the thought that I wouldn't lift a finger to help him.

She's mooning about the place like a lost dog. Looks like curtains she's got in that bag. At least I know the rest of my furniture's safe. They stored it in one of the outhouses so they must be going to put it back. I'll feel better then, more at home.

That old furniture's good stuff, even though it were shabby by the time Barney Dougan finished with it. When I moved back in after I let Con take over the farm, I never bothered replacing it.

I brought our bed over from the farm but I just went on using Barney's three piece suite and such. I've had that armchair so long that I don't think I could get used to new stuff. Lord, look at them curtains. What's she thinking of, white curtains on white walls? The place'll look like a flaming hospital.

***

Lynn got the folding steps from the kitchen where she'd left all the decorating things and started hanging the new curtains. Doing something practical helped her to concentrate, stopped her mind running over the conversation with Imogen. She should have said no, she should have just cut him off but he sounded so desperate. The window looked out on to the back field now that the grime had been washed away. Funny how soap and water and a lick of paint could transform a place. She switched on the electric heater they'd installed to supplement the open fire. Maybe it would take off the chill.

When they'd come it had looked as if it had never been cleaned for years, but then the old lady had been in her seventies and in poor health.

It was the first time she'd thought about the old woman. Diane didn't seem to have cared for her. Lynn wondered what she'd been like. She imagined spending all her time looking out of these windows at that flat, blank landscape. It wasn't the sort of land that invited you in with dells and streams and copses; it presented bleak emptiness, as if humans were just some alien things that crawled across it from time to time. It didn't ask to be explored. It lay there, looking open and exposed, yet seemed to be hugging ancient secrets. Lynn's skin puckered into goose-pimples. The cottage was freezing. Tomorrow she would light a fire, get the boiler going before she got Dan to put the furniture back at the weekend, ready for the new tenant.

She counted out curtain hooks and spaced them methodically along the header tape. What was she to do about Imogen? Her promise had been made in a careless moment of pity. Now it was being called in and she couldn't let him down could she?

If only he'd rung a couple of weeks earlier, she could have put him in the cottage for a few days, but Andrew Chapman was moving in on Monday.

She'd tried to talk Imogen round on the phone but he'd been almost hysterical.

'I'm no going back to Scotland and I canna stay here.'

'What happened? You were going to your aunty's.'

'I lost my job and I couldna get more work and her man threw me out.'

'Threw you out?'

'He didna want me there in the first place, neither of them did, but she would hae let me stay.'

'Couldn't you go to Social Services? Maybe you could get a hostel place, till you sort something out.'

'I'm no going there. I did go to a day centre help place and they sent me to a hostel yesterday. I had to share a room with this older guy and he started coming on to me. He was bigger than me and- and – '

It sounded like he was crying. Lynn was horrified.

'He didn't? He didn't – '

'No. I got away, but I couldna stay there after that.'

'Didn't you tell someone?'

'Tell someone? No, I couldna do that. I just left. I slept in a doorway. I wouldna bother you, but I don't know what to do.'

Lynn had wanted to put her arms round him. His childishness, his vulnerability would be a magnet to any predator. He needed protection. The thought of him wandering the streets of Birmingham alone was intolerable.

'Have you got any money? Enough to get to Liverpool?'

'Aye, I think so, but Liverpool?'

'Get the train and ring me when you get to Lime Street. I'll come and pick you up. You can stay with us for a bit till you sort yourself out.'

She finished hanging the first curtain and started on the second. Maybe she wouldn't hear from him again. Maybe he would have made it up with his aunt and gone back to her.

Lynn really hoped so. How would she cope with him? It was one thing dealing with teenage problems from the safety of her college office, but quite another bringing him into her own home, and he was really a complete stranger. Dan was going to have a fit but it was too late now, if he turned up she would have to take him in, just for a few days. She looked at the fields outside, they seemed steady, calming. She would deal with it, everything would be okay.

She got down from the stepladder and admired the curtains. The room looked so cool and fresh. She wondered about getting some covers for the three piece suite which was pretty grotty although it had a shabby chic look that went well with the style of the cottage. Maybe just some cushions and a throw or two, white throws, but some colour for the cushions. She wondered if Andrew Chapman would like it. She had no idea what he was like or how he would manage in the cottage with his disabilities. What if he started asking them to make all sorts of adaptations? Before she could worry about this, her phone rang and adrenaline ran through her blood, drying her mouth. She turned to fetch her handbag and saw an old woman standing by the kitchen door. She stared as she reached for the phone, her heart jumping in her chest, then looked at the unfamiliar number on the mobile's screen. She looked up again. The doorway was empty. The room was freezing despite the heater. Imogen's voice was breaking up, something was interfering with the signal. She hurried outside.

All the way to the station as she walked through throngs of children coming out of the village high school, the picture of the old woman played in her head. She'd looked real, she must have been real, someone local maybe; the back door of the cottage had been left open. But no one had been there when she'd gone out to look. Her legs felt wobbly. She remembered the dream, the feeling of being pulled out of her bed, the dark capering shape. Diane Worrall had laughed about her mother-in-law haunting the place.

She sat on the train, staring out of the window as the fields gave way to new housing estates and then streets of terraced houses, shops and small factories. It was crazy, she didn't believe in ghosts and yet something about the woman, the way she had looked at her, as if she wanted something from her, had turned Lynn's blood to ice. She was shivering now, despite the stuffy heat in the carriage. She was being a fool, all this was nonsense. What was wrong with her, getting so oversensitive? The train began to fill up as it drew nearer to the city. People were reading books, newspapers. Two women sat opposite her, discussing the problems of their central heating boilers in loud voices. By the time the train began to glide along the Mersey estuary, slipping past the idle docks, Lynn had convinced herself she'd imagined the old woman.

When she got to Lime Street station, Imogen was sitting on the steps outside while people went up and down, passing him without a second glance.

'Hi,' she said awkwardly. 'Let's get a coffee.'

She didn't know the city at all so steered him round the corner to the café outside the station. It was just that time of day when people were coming out of work and doing a bit of shopping before going home and the afternoon shoppers hadn't yet departed, so the town centre was crowded, but the café was quiet. Across the road, Lynn could see a huge Georgian style building and a great banner proclaiming the city as the Capital of Culture 2008. It looked interesting but she would have to save it for another time.

'This is really good of you.' He didn't meet her gaze. 'I thought maybe you didna really mean it. People say these things. I wouldn't hae minded. I was ages trying to make up my mind whether to ring or no.'

'You did the right thing. I wouldn't leave anyone roaming the streets, especially not at your age.'

'I dinna want to be a nuisance.' He glanced up at her and dipped his head again. He looked like a schoolboy.

'Shh now. Drink your coffee. You can stay with us for a few days while we sort out what you're going to do.'

She'd already decided on this, picked out one of the spare rooms at the farm for him. They hadn't got round to giving it a makeover yet, but there was nothing wrong with it. It would only be until she talked him into going home, getting in touch with his family.

'Your husband doesna mind?'

'Dan? Oh, no.' Lynn bit back the fact that she hadn't told Dan. He didn't like to be disturbed at work with phone calls and it would be better to present him with a fait accompli.

Thinking about calling Dan reminded her of the old woman in the doorway when her phone rang. It had only been the blink of an eye, then there had been nothing there. It must have been a shadow, something in her mind. She was more able to dismiss it now, but the raw horror of the moment had been like a bucket of water thrown in her face. Maybe it would be good to have some company for a few days.

'But I don't know how to pay you back. I've no money.'

'We'll sort something out. Maybe you can help me with the garden or something. Don't worry for now. You must be tired out. Let's just get back to the house and we'll take it from there.'

Travelling back on the train reminded Lynn of the first time they'd met, how heavy-hearted she had been about moving. Did she feel better now? She loved the farm but she didn't yet feel that she belonged there and with Dan always so busy with his work she felt alone with the responsibility of it. Then there'd been that awful dream the other week, no doubt brought on by that Irishman and his creepy stories and now she was seeing things. It wasn't a ghost. She wouldn't believe that. She thought about how silly it had seemed, talking about ghosts in the bright modern hairdressing salon with Diane laughing. She couldn't imagine any ghost daring to appear to Diane Worrall.

Imogen fell asleep beside her and again she saw the sweep of his eyelashes, how his face still contained traces of childhood, his skin young and soft. She felt old suddenly and tired. She still had to face Dan when they got back.

***

Someone else here now. It's one change after another. She's put him in Con's old room, the one he had when he were a boy. Diane took everything of Con out of it. She decorated it all modern with vases of them paper flowers and pictures of Yorkshire terriers on the walls.

This one's no more than a boy himself but he's one of those coloureds. Never see many of them round here. They like living in the cities where they can all stick together.

Skinny-looking thing, but some good muscles in his arms. He must be used to a bit of labour. I remember Con at that age, still with a touch of innocence but you could see by the muscles of his back and shoulders, by the depth of his chest, the promise of the man coming to the fore.

A beautiful man Con were, until those women got hold on him. I were still young enough then to see that beauty in him, even though he were my own child, yes, even though I were coming up for fifty. I were still a woman then, not a dried up old stick. My hair were long and dark with only the odd strand of grey and I were always quick and slim, what with all the hard work and plain food.

What's he doing here, I wonder? Maybe she's going to get him working on the farm but then it seems funny she's got him staying in the house. Maybe he's some relation but there's no sign of colour in her or her husband.

She looked right at me before, in the cottage, when she were hanging the curtains. Right at me, and the look on her face, I could swear she seen me, but that couldn't be, could it?

I weren't trying to get her attention. I didn't want her to see me, but she must have seen something, she run out of the cottage like she'd seen the Devil himself. She were on the phone though, maybe she got an urgent message. I followed her for a bit and she kept looking round but I don't think she saw me then.

No one else seems to see me. I wonder how it works. Can I control it? I wouldn't mind popping up in front of that Diane. That'd show her she can't get rid of me so easy and if this Lynn can see me, maybe she really is some relation to me, maybe there's some reason why we're both here.

***

'You brought him back here? Are you out of your mind? He's probably a drug addict with a criminal record.'

Dan banged his glass down on the kitchen worktop. Lynn flinched but it was worth seeing a straight reaction from Dan instead of his usual smooth front.

'He's not like that, Dan. I can tell. I've worked a long time with young people, remember? He was desperate. I couldn't refuse to help him, not after offering.'

'I can't understand why you gave him your number in the first place.'

'I felt sorry for him. It was a spur of the moment thing. He had so many problems. I didn't think he really would ring me.' Lynn lowered her voice. Imogen might be awake, listening at the bedroom door.

'You're such a sucker for a sob story.'

'Dan, he was terrified.'

'Yes, but bringing him here – and not just a boy, a lad from the rough end of Glasgow – it's not like the stray kitten you brought home in Birmingham.'

She could tell he was still angry but his voice had softened. Lynn bit her lip. The kitten had only lasted a week before Dan had insisted on taking it to the pet rescue centre.

'You should have advised him, yes, talked him into going home, or getting some help, Social Services, a hostel place or something, but to bring him here – ' he reached for the bottle and poured more wine.

Lynn placed her glass next to his. She needed a drink herself. 'Don't you think enough people have done that already? And when he was in a hostel, someone tried to rape him.'

'You should have asked me first.'

He pointed an accusing finger at her. He was treating her like a naughty child.

'You didn't ask me about the job, about moving here.'

A muscle twitched in Dan's face. He stared out of the window. Rain slanted down outside, misting the fields. He turned and sipped his wine, studying her face.

She set her jaw and bit back all the inflammatory things she wanted to say.

'You could have rung me.'

'You don't like being rung at work. Anyway, I was in a hurry.'

'You knew I wouldn't agree to it. That's why you didn't ring me. You just went ahead and did it.' He looked at her, waiting for her to acknowledge her guilt.

She stared right back at him. After a moment he dropped his eyes.

'Well, he's here now.' Lynn drained her glass and set it down. She turned to the oven to check on the lasagne she was cooking.

'Not for long.' Dan lifted a warning finger. 'I've got a lot of meetings next week, I shan't be around much in the evenings. I may even have to go to London for a couple of days.'

What's new? Lynn thought. 'I'll talk to him,' she said, 'see if I can get him to phone his mother.'

'I don't like leaving you here alone with him. It's inappropriate. He could have mental health problems. You don't know anything about him.'

'Dan, it seems like I'm on my own all the time lately. Anybody could wander in here; it's not exactly Fort Knox is it? It's so isolated. You don't worry about that.'

'Well, I can't help it, can I?' He gestured irritably. 'I've got to set myself up, establish myself in the department. There's such a lot to do. Surely you realise that?'

'But when we talked about moving – ' Lynn broke off. Something horrid and cold fingered her brain, something about Dan that she hadn't fully grasped before. His gaze held contempt. Suddenly she saw that her plans for their life together meant nothing to him. All he cared about was his career.

'Don't forget the faculty social next Thursday. Make sure you get your hair done and get a new dress.'

'But it's Valentine's Day.' Lynn was still numb from that look in his eyes; she barely registered that Dan hadn't noticed she'd had her hair done that day.

'All the better. Two special occasions in one, then we can come back here and celebrate it properly.' He pulled her to him and ran a hand down her spine to the cleft of her buttocks. There was a flare of desire but she pulled away from it.

'I'd better call Imogen down for supper.'

The spare room door was open. Imogen was sitting on the bed, staring at the floor. He looked up warily as Lynn knocked and entered. He had changed his clothes and his hair was damp from the shower.

'It's okay,' she said, sitting down beside him. 'Supper's ready, won't you come down?'

'Is everything all right?' His hands twisted in his lap.

'It's fine,' she said brightly. 'Come on, you must be hungry. Dan's waiting to meet you.'

'Who else is here?'

'Nobody.'

'Then who's that lady? She came up the stairs before.'

'Was she an old lady?' Lynn's mouth dried. She could barely get the words out.

Imogen considered. 'Well, older than you, but not old like my great-gran. Fiftyish, I'd say, long dark hair. I thought she was your sister.'

***

Lynn lay in bed, waiting for Dan to come up. It was after one and he was still working. She had left the bedroom door ajar, to admit enough light to chase away the shadows.

She'd thought the old lady in the cottage was a trick of her imagination but now Imogen had seen something, here in the house and it was someone different.

Was he imagining things too, maybe overtired, or half asleep and dreaming? She tried to remember if she'd gone up the stairs herself. Maybe he'd caught a glimpse of her and thought it was someone else.

How was she going to live here if the place was full of ghosts? She went over the conversation she'd had with Diane Worrall. Diane had been genuinely surprised, she'd insisted she'd never seen anything, so if there were ghosts, they must be something to do with herself and Dan. Maybe they resented them coming here.

Had Dan seen anything? She ought to ask him but she knew he would only laugh at her. If he did see a ghost, Dan would never admit it even to himself. He was so self-confident he couldn't possibly believe in such things. With her eyes closed, the room felt oppressive, as if shades were gathering round her bed, closing in on her. To look or not to look? There was no sound, just a feeling of expectation. She realised she was holding her breath and exhaled sharply, opening her eyes. She could see nothing out of the ordinary in the dim light yet there was a brooding presence, as if everything in the room were alive and watching her. Diane Worrall had joked about Con's mother haunting her.

'But I've done nothing to you,' Lynn whispered. 'I'm an Askin too.' She waited, but there was no response.

She was being stupid, ghosts didn't exist. They were just tales you read in books or laughed about in silly films on TV. She'd been distracted with Imogen's phone call, caught a glimpse of someone passing, and it had been herself that Imogen had seen climbing the stairs, half hidden in the shadows. Maybe Dan was right, she'd been listening to too many of Barney Dougan's old wives' tales. She snuggled down under the covers, wishing Dan would hurry up but all was silent. Perhaps he was punishing her because she had brought Imogen here without consulting him. He had seemed okay at supper, chatting away to the boy, reassuring him with a sympathetic attitude, but Lynn knew he was like a chameleon, able to assume any personality without compunction in order to achieve what he wanted.

In that moment of revelation earlier in the kitchen, as Dan talked about his work, she'd seen that he had no intention of getting involved in the farm, the land, growing food, any of the things she had planned. She realised that he'd never actually said a single word to suggest that he was remotely interested in the country. He'd let her think he was keen. Yes, she could have her garden, her farmhouse, her proximity to the Lakes. These things would keep her occupied while he got on with what he wanted to do and the family connection had been a bonus for him, making her more receptive to the idea of moving here.

Dan's dream was radically different from hers and it was the first time she'd faced up to it. Was it a betrayal or was it her own fault? Had she idealised Dan, made him appear to be as she wanted him to be? She began to cry quietly, conscious of Imogen in the room just across the landing.

She would be left alone here with her ghosts, to try and make a home, a space for herself and the work that needed doing would all be left to her, while Dan was away pursuing his ambitions. For a moment she lost her bearings. She felt the heavy responsibility of the land and knew she was out of her depth. Something seemed to shift in the room but she closed her mind to it, grabbed on to the thought that the old Dan was there too, wasn't he? The Dan she loved; the Dan who loved her? She heard his light footfall as he ran up the stairs to her and she pushed her fears away to join the muddy shadows in the corners.

***

It weren't love at first sight for me and Bert, we'd known each other since we were kids at elementary school, not that we took much notice of each other in them days.

Me and our Joan weren't allowed to play much, there were always work to be done on the farm and when there weren't Mother would collar us to help round the house.

I were fifteen when the war ended but by then Albert were away doing his military service and it were when he come back in 1947 that we started going together.

I'd had my eye on him before then, when he were home on leave after VE Day. There were a dance at the village hall and he looked so smart and handsome in his uniform. I couldn't keep my eyes off him but he never even noticed me. He danced all night with Jennifer Winrow. He knew all the latest dances and so did she, the jitterbug and everything. Me, I didn't know any, well, just the waltz and the foxtrot and then only backwards because our Joan always made me take the man's part. We used to practise to the radio, when Dad were out at the pub on Sunday evenings.

It's a sad thing to say but it were our Thomas's death that brought me and Albert together. It were after the funeral that he first asked me out. Not that I had any thought of romance with our Thomas took so sudden. He survived all through the war and we all relaxed when he come home but he weren't right. He'd almost drowned in a flooded shell hole.

He were always having nightmares about it, running in the dark, the flash of fire, the drone of planes, deafening explosions, the screaming and shouting. Something hit him in the leg, he never seen the hole, he fell right in and he'd never learned to swim. If it weren't for another couple of Tommies pulling him out, that would have been the end of him, but it all were the end of him anyway.

When he come home he could never work proper on the farm. The war done something to his mind and every time he seen water, he'd shake till his teeth chattered. He were useless on the fields with all their ditches, even in summer there were always water about. He could feed the chickens and such like, but he knew that were work for children and that made him miserable. He were always moping about so it were as if when the pneumonia come along, he just let it right in, as if he couldn't be bothered to fight it, as if he'd fought enough and realised it were all for nothing anyway.

It were good then to have Bert's friendship because if Dad were cold and angry before Thomas died, he were ten times worse after and by then I were the only one left to pick on because our Joan couldn't wait to get married and skip to Canada in 1946. Bert were kind to me but even more than that he made me laugh. He were always ready with a joke even in the worst times and that were precious to me because there weren't much of laughter and joking in our family.

It were a secret romance at first. We were both too frickened to tell Dad. I were allowed out till ten-thirty on Saturday nights if there were a dance in the village or I could go to the pictures and Bert used to walk me back along the canal bank as far as the bend, where you couldn't be seen from the farm. That winter of nineteen-forty-seven were bitter, the worst I ever knew. There were ice and snow on the ground for months on end as if the land itself were mourning our Thomas. I used to push away the thought of him lying frozen in his grave, trying instead to remember the brother who tamed a field mouse and kept it in his pocket. The only comfort I had were the warmth of Bert's body in our clumsy first embraces. When he kissed me it took away the pain and the grief; all I could feel were his lips hot on mine and my ears burning in the frosted air.

Later, I started sneaking out in the summer evenings and me and Bert did our courting under the bridge where the main road runs through the village. My heart nearly stopped the night we were strolling back arm in arm and I looked up and there stood Dad on the towpath with the dogs, leaning on his stick like nothing in the world would move him.

There were the devil to pay after I were dragged home and called all the sluts and whores going. I shook so much I could scarce keep standing and I knew Dad were itching to take his belt to me, but I seen in his eyes that he realised that I were a woman now not a child and then Mother put her tuppence-worth in.

'Stop it, Doug. It's not right, calling her names like that, you know she's a good girl, we've raised her right.'

It were true, I never let Albert get his hand past my stocking top. Lord knows, sometimes I wanted to but all the tales I'd heard in the village about girls dying or getting infections and never being able to have babies, after going for secret abortions frickened the life out of me. Then there were Maisie Burton who got pregnant to a Yank from the aerodrome in Burscough but he went and left her with a handful of promises. She disappeared and come back a year later crying she were a widow with little Christopher to look after but everybody knew she'd been in one of them mother-and-baby homes and the gossip stuck to her like goose-grass till in the end she moved away. Dad would have killed me if I let that happen to me.

The next day at dinnertime, Bert come round cap in hand to declare his intentions. Mother let him in, so when me and Dad come in from the fields, he were already sitting at the table with a cup of tea and a slice of apple pie in front of him.

I were sent to the scullery to wash the smell of muck shovelling off myself and I trembled as the sound of Dad shouting carried through the thick walls. My eyes were still swollen half-shut from crying the night before, and didn't look no better for all the splashing with cold water I done, trying to make myself look a bit nicer for Bert. Suddenly it went quiet and then Mother come and called me in.

'Come on love. It's going to be all right.'

When I went in, Bert were sitting there all dressed up and straight as a ramrod like he were waiting to have his photograph taken and Dad were pouring him a glass of beer.

'Mr Worrall, Albert here, has come to ask for your hand,' Dad said, not sounding angry at all now.

I didn't know what to say. I just stood there like a great lummox but the fear knotted inside me started to melt into something warm.

'I can't afford to lose you Alice. I need help on the farm.'

I were stricken with the thought I weren't going to be allowed to escape. I looked at Mother but she just smiled and nodded at me.

'Albert's agreed to come and work here if I'm agreeable to the wedding, so that's what we've decided.'

Dad weren't daft. He knew Albert had a reputation for hard work and that he were one of the best ploughmen in the district. I could see him mentally calculating the profits he would get out of us, but I didn't care, I were so happy.

It weren't until later that I realised nobody had actually asked me if I wanted to get married. That evening, me and Albert sat in the parlour for the two hours Dad had allotted us for courting. We were playing rummy and Albert looked over his cards and said, 'You do want to marry me, don't you Alice?' and that were as near a proposal as I got.

***

It was almost eleven when Con returned to the house. He'd meant to come straight back after walking Rolo round the farm but the welcoming lights of the Turk's Head had pulled him in from the eerie quiet of the canal bank. He staggered a little as he came up the path, went round to the back and tried the wrought-iron gate. It was bolted on the inside. He tried to climb up to reach over but his legs didn't want to obey. The back door suddenly opened and Diane stood in the wedge of light coming from the kitchen.

'Is that you, Con?'

'Open the gate.' His voice came out angrier than he felt. 'I've got Rolo.'

'For God's sake stop shouting.' She let him in. 'It's almost eleven o'clock. Where have you been? You're drunk!'

He grinned at the disgust in her voice. Milly's shrill barking sounded from beyond the kitchen door.

He shut Rolo in his compound, took a last look up at the stars, a last breath of fresh air. Spots of rain fell on his upturned face.

He followed Diane into the kitchen. She was dressed in a fluffy bathrobe and she smelled damply scented. He wanted to put his face against the skin of her neck but he didn't dare. Every line of her body showed her anger. Milly had stopped barking but was whining behind the lounge door.

'Is there anything to eat?' He opened the fridge and pulled out a can of Stella, a packet of cheese.

'You are joking?' Her eyebrows disappeared into her fringe and her eyes had turned from the soft blue that he loved to a greyish steel. 'What are you playing at Con?'

'Playing?'

'This is nearly every night. Ever since you started at Ramsbottom's. And don't think I haven't seen you coming out of the Farmers' Arms at lunchtime. Is it Jackie Mack that's the big attraction? I'm sure it's not Barney Dougan that's keeping you busy all night. I'm not working all the hours God sends at the salon for you to chat up barmaids and piss all our money up against the wall.'

'Jackie Mack? Don't be daft.' Con sat down. He pulled the tab on the can and drank.

'Well who'd look at you anyway? You haven't even had a wash have you? You stink of the woodyard. You must have come back here to get the dog after work; you didn't even bother to change.'

Con looked down at himself. It was true, but his work jeans were still fairly clean and he couldn't smell anything.

He laughed. 'Come here Di.' He held out his arms. She moved away, opened the lounge door and caught up Milly as she rushed in, hugging the dog against her chest.

'Do you think I'm coming anywhere near you, smelling like that?' She wrinkled her nose. 'You stink of beer too.'

She put Milly down and wrapped her arms round her chest. 'It's not funny Con. I don't know what's got into you.'

'I love you Di.' He shook his head helplessly.

'You've got a funny way of showing it. First it was six or seven o'clock, now it's nine, ten, even eleven. I'm not standing for it. You're not leaving me alone here night after night.'

'You wanted to come here.'

'Oh, is that it? I'm to be punished for getting you out of that muck heap? I thought that was what you wanted, to get rid of that responsibility.'

He shrugged. 'It's so different, Di. I lived on that farm all my life. It *was* my life.'

'Well, it's not your life any more.' She stood in the doorway like a stranger. 'Forget it Con. The farm's gone. It's gone. Stop being a stick-in-the-mud.'

He didn't move. Her words tolled like a bell in his head.

'Oh, I'm going to bed. I have to get up early in the morning and so do you, so don't be sitting here half the night. I'm warning you, this isn't good enough. You'd just better get your act together.' She swept out of the room and up the stairs.

'Or what?' Con thought, crushing the empty can in his hand. He got up and looked in the fridge. There was no more beer. In the drinks cupboard there was only a half-empty bottle of whisky left over from Christmas. He poured a large glassful.

The lights of the farmhouse had pulled at him, a physical tug in the gut as he walked the edges of the fields in the darkness, Rolo padding quietly alongside. Both of them were sure-footed on the uneven ground, imprinted memory taking them safely over the ruts and banks. He had turned away from the dark hulk of his mother's cottage.

The blackness opened up inside him again and he poured the whisky in. It softened to a brown, peaty murk that he could just sink into. He felt it spread. There were no margins to it, no ledges to clamber out on to.

He thought of the new people at the farm, cosy inside, wondered how they could live there, somewhere they did not belong, then looked round at the kitchen he sat in, that was like someone else's world. The fridge hummed, the clock ticked, the surfaces shone. He looked at his own blurred reflection in the high gloss cupboard doors; at the bright picture of chickens and eggs on the chopping board. The clock said one-fifteen. An hour-and-three-quarters had gone by somehow since Diane went to bed and there was less than an inch of whisky left in the bottle.

He got up and switched off the light. He lifted the kitchen blind and peered out. The glow of the street lights behind the garden fence illuminated the shapes of the sleeping houses in the next cul-de-sac.

Chapter Six

Thursday February 14th 2008

The ground wasn't really dry enough to work but Lynn was desperate to get started. She'd marked the veg patch out a couple of weeks ago but it seemed to have rained on and off ever since they had come to the farm. The last three days had been clear and the morning's mild sunshine heralded spring and thoughts of new life.

She had measured the first bed. She would begin at one end and Imogen would start at the other. When they met in the middle they would stop for coffee. Someone from Ramsbottom's was coming to start on fencing off the patch from the rest of the garden.

'You've never done any digging, have you?' Lynn suppressed a smile as she watched Imogen's first efforts. 'Look, you have to hold the spade up straight. Drive it in with your foot.' She demonstrated, delighted that even though she hadn't done it for a long time, the mechanical skill was still second nature to her. For a moment she was transported back to the red Somerset soil of her childhood then she looked down and saw the rich black peaty loam, looked up at the huge open landscape.

'That's it.' She stayed close, encouraging him for a few minutes. She'd been surprised by how keen he had been to get up and help her. A lot of kids would just want to lie in bed listening to their music or playing computer games. He seemed grateful as a puppy to her for taking him in and came down for breakfast like a shot every morning as soon as Dan had gone out of the door. He avoided Dan, as if he knew it was only by Lynn's grace that he was tolerated, although Dan had made himself perfectly charming towards him in public. When she and Dan were alone, Dan complained continually about Imogen's presence, making Lynn feel guilty for bringing him. Dan felt invaded. He was used to having Lynn entirely to himself.

Lynn could understand this. The free and easy way they'd

always had of being around each other, touching, undressing, initiating sex or cuddles whenever they felt like it, had been curtailed.

Imogen had taken to staying in his room when Dan was home. He was a sensitive boy, everything about him told Lynn that, how he anticipated their moods and made every effort not to be a nuisance. Sensitive in more ways than one? she wondered. The hairs still prickled on her neck when she thought back to that first evening when he'd seen someone on the stairs, someone who'd had no business to be there. She'd convinced him that it had been herself he'd glimpsed. There had been no more appearances and Lynn had almost managed to dismiss the visions as tricks of the imagination. Out here in the open thoughts of ghosts seemed such foolishness.

In the week he'd been at the farm, Lynn had spent more time with Imogen than she'd spent with Dan for months. He'd helped her put the final touches to the cottage and they'd been shopping in Ormskirk several times. They'd spent the long evenings together watching television and playing cards or Scrabble, while Dan was working late at the university.

The boy was determined not to return to Scotland or to Birmingham for that matter, but Lynn was hopeful that she could eventually persuade him. She hadn't pushed him so far, treading water, letting him settle, develop trust in her while she found out what kind of person he was. She liked what she saw and she was going to do her best to help him get settled somewhere. She would feel guilty if she didn't, no matter what Dan thought. She watched him now, digging clumsily, one of Dan's old sweatshirts flapping round his thin body. He was safe for the time being.

'Okay, you're qualified.' She grinned. 'See you in the middle.' She went off to her own end and took up her spade. There should be a ceremony, she thought, a ribbon to cut or something. The ground was soft from the rain and the spade sank through the grass roots. She turned the soil and piled it at the back of the hole, then dug into the same place again. The spade still went down effortlessly and the same black soil came up. This was going to be easier than she had expected.

At first her movements were awkward. Her muscles cramped and complained but within a few minutes she was in a rhythm with the spade and the earth, and all her worries were gone: Dan, Imogen, the faculty social she was dreading. Everything disappeared, except the black line of soil behind her and the white post that marked the middle spot where she could stop digging and rest.

The noise of a vehicle coming down the lane disturbed her and she straightened up, stretching her back as Annie Chapman's white van went past and stopped at the cottage. Behind it Ramsbottom's red truck pulled into the farm yard. Lynn was surprised to see Con Worrall get out. She drove the spade into the ground and walked to meet him.

'I didn't know you were working at the yard.'

'Lucky to get it,' Con said. 'Not much work about in the winter.'

'Oh. No, I suppose not.' Lynn thought of her plan to speak to Imogen about going home. He would never find work if he stopped at the farm. She would talk to him when they had their coffee. 'I expect you're glad to be outdoors.'

'Lot of it's in the shop.' He undid the sides of the truck and started loosening the ties on the fence panels.

Lynn felt awkward. His look was scornful. She felt he resented her being here, as if he, not she, belonged here.

'Would you like a coffee before you start?' She really wanted to get back to her digging. She was glad when he refused.

'Better get on. I only drink tea anyway.' He followed her over to the marked-out patch and burst out laughing when he saw her fresh-dug line and Imogen's inept figure at the other end.

'You're never going to dig all this?' He gestured at the former side lawn. 'Haven't you got a Rotavator?'

'I prefer to dig,' Lynn mumbled.

Con scratched his head. He looked at her as if she were crazy.

'You should get someone to turn it over with a tractor. A Fergie's small enough to do it. Pilling's got one. I heard you were letting the fields out to him.'

'Maybe.' Lynn reached for her spade. 'He's coming to see Dan at the weekend.'

'He's a good farmer,' Con said grudgingly. 'This is good land.'

'I wanted to ask you about the ditches.'

'What about them?'

'If we need to get them cleared. Annie Chapman said they'll

flood the fields, if we don't. She told me to check them, but I don't know what to look for.'

'Do you think I'd sell you the land without making sure it were in order?' His eyes flashed anger.

'Oh, I didn't mean – ' Lynn's face burned. 'It was just that I didn't know what she was talking about.'

'Aye, well the land will flood if the ditches aren't maintained. You'll need to do them next winter, just make sure the bottoms are clear of rubbish, weeds and so on. I used to do them soon as New Year were over, but I suppose you weren't to know.'

He peered at the trench Lynn had dug. 'Two feet down before you hit the peat. It's still there you know, six foot of it.'

'What?'

'The peat. Most of it's been taken out round here. Haven't you noticed how the land drops six foot at the edge of the side field? That's why this place is called New Cut Farm. It marks the start of the peat cutting on a commercial scale. Used to be a peat works further down, opposite Holmes farm. They took it all out. Before my time. Soil down that end's worth nowt now.'

Lynn felt stupid. How could she not have noticed a six foot drop? It all looked so empty. She saw that if she wanted to live here, live with the land, she would have to learn more of its history.

'Mr Dougan told me it used to be a lake.'

'Barney's been down here?' He laughed. 'He'll blind you with his fancy talk but it's true, it were a lake. Big one, six miles square. Must have been a sight to see. Have you been to Martin Mere yet? It's a wildfowl trust, but it's just a pond compared to the original Mere.'

Lynn shook her head. 'I've been too busy. Dan's been away and I've had to get the cottage ready.' She bit her lip, remembering how it had been Con's mother's home.

They both looked at the cottage where Andrew Chapman was negotiating the drive in a motorised wheelchair. They watched as he manoeuvred it close to his mother's van. Even from the distance they could see his irritation with Annie's attempts to help him into the passenger seat.

'Terrible thing. That poor boy. I don't know how he's going to manage in that cottage.'

'It's handy for Holmes.'

'I know but it'd be so much easier for him in something specially adapted, like one of those bungalows the council have.'

'He can walk a bit with crutches.'

'It's not going to give him much independence though, is it? He must need a lot of help. His mother's been running up and down, since he moved in on Monday. She must be worn out.'

'He wants to be on the land.'

Lynn looked down at the fresh earth. She turned back to her spade. Imogen gave her a wave. He was almost half way to the marker. Con followed her gaze.

'He's a family friend,' she lied. 'Just here for a few days.'

'I remember going to Andy Chapman's christening,' Con said, squinting at Imogen. 'I were twenty-one. Me mam was his godmother. He should never have gone away.'

'I don't know why we're in this war,' Lynn said. 'It seems so futile; it just goes on and on.'

'There's always war. My great-grandfather were killed in 1917. And his son Philip were gassed. My grandfather Douglas Askin inherited the farm. It were him as built the cottage, for Philip's widow to live in.'

'Your family's been here all that time?'

'Longer than that. 1880 the first Askin built the place. Joseph, my great-great-grandfather.'

'Did he come from Aughton? I've been researching the name in Ormskirk library. You know I had a relation called Askin; Lavinia. She lived in Aughton.'

'Never heard of anyone of that name. I don't know where Joseph come from.'

'I found records of your family, your mother and her brothers and sister.'

'My mother were all that were left. One brother died as a baby, and the other died in the Second World War. I'm the last, except for some cousins in Canada.'

'And you've no children?'

'No.' He clenched his teeth and looked away from her, out across the garden to the fields.

She felt his resentment. She was prying into his life, looking up his family records, quizzing him about children. She and Dan had taken his home, his land, his heritage. Her pleasure in the day, in the digging, disappeared. Suddenly she felt all the aches of muscles unused to physical labour. The white marker looked further away than it had before. Imogen was nearly up to his side of it.

'I'd better get on with this.' She turned her face away from Con and tried to focus her mind on the garden. It was hers now, her home, not his.

'Don't let the wicks get in there.' Con nodded his head at the trench.

'Wicks?' She turned back, curious.

'Couch grass roots. This patch were always kept as lawn. Them wicks'll run riot through it once it's dug.' He walked away and began unloading the fence panels from the truck. Lynn started digging again but this time the easy rhythm wouldn't come. Her whole body complained and the thought kept running through her mind that she was an usurper.

She tried to push it away but in its place came worries about Andrew Chapman. She'd hesitated to go and welcome him, see if he needed help. She'd been afraid of patronising him but now she determined she would go and see him later, after she'd pinned Imogen down about his future plans and before it was time to get ready for the faculty social that evening. So much for Valentine's Day. She and Dan had exchanged cards that morning then he'd rushed off after giving her a quick peck on the cheek.

The marker wasn't far away now but Lynn was so exhausted she felt like bursting into tears. Imogen had finished his side and was carrying on to hers.

'You're doing really well,' she called.

'I'm getting into the swing of it now,' he answered without breaking his movements. He had discarded the sweatshirt and the Darth Vader tattoo moved about on his arm as his muscles flexed. 'Why don't ye go inside and rest, I'll finish this off.'

She pulled her gloves off gratefully and went into the house. Con wouldn't come in for his tea when it was ready, but took his mug out to the truck. Lynn was glad. She felt uncomfortable with him and anyway she wanted to talk to Imogen.

She watched the boy wash his hands. He picked at a blister that was forming on his palm, despite the work gloves she'd given him.

'Soft,' he said. 'My hands are soft now, from doing no work for a while. I'll soon toughen up. It's good exercise. Great to be out in the open air.'

She brought the coffee and some biscuits, waited till he was sitting at the table.

'Imogen, you know you can't stay here permanently. We need to talk about your plans for the future.'

His face clouded. 'I like it here. I've nowhere else to go.'

'But your family. They must be wondering where you are.'

'They dinna care.' He scowled at her and she was taken aback.

'It might feel like that but I'm sure it's not true. If I had a son –'

'You haven't, so you dinna know. Do you no want any children?'

'It's not that,' Lynn stammered. 'We're not ready yet.'

'No ready? My sister had a bairn when she was seventeen. How old are you?'

'Thirty-four.' His questions were so direct, she answered blindly, flayed by his ability to cut to the heart of her pain. Ready? She'd been ready for years but how could she tell this, betray herself and Dan by revealing their failure to conceive? It would be admitting that there was something wrong with one or both of them, they were incomplete, faulty, in a way that even doctors couldn't discover.

It was better that people thought them selfish. No one must know how she longed for a child, how she kept hoping secretly, although on the surface she rarely thought about it any more. Thirty-four was late, so late. She realised with a start how quickly those years had passed. Soon any chance would be gone forever. If Dan had been willing they could have tried IVF, even gone for adoption but Dan had skilfully talked her out of these options whenever she'd suggested them.

Imogen was staring at her, his eyes huge and soft. She realised with horror that, for him, her thoughts were written all over her, he was reading her as Dan would read a seminar paper. She felt naked but instinctively she knew he meant her no harm. He was absorbing her feelings, probably didn't even know what he was doing, but still it frightened her. She looked away and broke the connection.

'Never mind about me. We're talking about you.'

'I've phoned my maw. She knows I'm okay. They don't care. I told you.'

Lynn wanted to believe him but surely no parent could be so callous?

'I'm no going back. They don't want me.'

'But you've no money.'

'I'll go and sign on at the Jobcentre. Ormskirk, is it? If ye'll lend me the bus fare. Maybe I can get a job. I'll go this afternoon.'

He looked woebegone and her first instinct was to let it go, tell him it didn't matter but she thought of Dan's tight mouth each time he came home and the false smile he put on at mealtimes when the three of them were together.

'That'll be a start,' she said, 'but I still think you should talk to your family. You must miss your home, the city. There's nothing for young people to do here.'

'I like it. It's peaceful.' He grinned at her. He was gaining confidence and he looked much healthier than when he'd arrived. His skin glowed from the cold air and the exercise and his khaki combat pants and tee shirt suited his complexion.

She thought of the students she'd taught, the boys smirking together in corners, all wet mouths, fervid eyes and dirty laughter that had suddenly stopped as she passed them in the corridor. She'd watched them watching the girls unconsciously. But she'd seen them in love too, sweetly worshipping the girls they were with.

'But there's no work here.' She thought of Con Worrall. 'You've no friends here, no one. You'll be lonely.'

'I've no friends anyway. Except you.'

Lynn's resolve crumpled. He was such a strange boy. Dan was so cynical about him, but then it was true they knew nothing at all about him. It didn't seem fair but he would have to stand on his own two feet.

The doorbell rang. Lynn answered it to find a pretty young girl on the step with a sheaf of red roses. A van marked 'Pilling's Flowers' was parked by Ramsbottom's truck.

'Mrs Waters?' The girl held out the bouquet.

Lynn flushed with pleasure. 'What a fantastic job you have, delivering all these flowers.' She smelled the roses but they were virtually scentless. There was no message on the card, except one word, 'Later.'

'Wow!' Imogen said as she walked into the kitchen. 'They must have cost a fortune.'

'What about you? Have you sent any cards? Didn't you leave a girlfriend behind in Scotland?'

'No,' he said shortly, getting up to rinse his mug at the sink. She rummaged in the cupboards for a vase large enough to take the roses.

'Nice-looking boy like you?'

'Aye, well, I've had a few,' he muttered.

She wondered about his world, where girls had babies at seventeen. When she reached to swing the tap over to the second sink, their hands touched for a second. Lynn blushed and hid her face in the roses. What was she thinking of? He was a child, barely out of school. She turned away, jammed the blooms into the vase.

'Better get back to work.' She marched to the door without turning back to look at him.

Con Worrall's empty mug was standing outside the kitchen door. Lynn looked across to the vegetable patch, where he was hammering a fence post into the ground. She saw how the muscles of his thighs braced each time he swung the lump hammer and she sensed the mechanical joy of the body parts working together to place the hammer in the exact right spot with every blow; the same joy she had felt when she was digging. It took her mind away from the scene in the kitchen with Imogen.

She didn't notice the woman with the baby approaching Con until she stopped at the line of posts he had already put in. The baby was sprawled face down across her breast and the woman rubbed its back and kissed the top of its head as she watched Con. Lynn could hear her singing softly to the child and something tightened in her stomach, made her arms and legs tingle. She was suddenly conscious of Imogen standing behind her.

Con seemed oblivious to the woman. His energetic movements continued their rhythm as the three of them watched. It seemed like ages that they all stood there, then the woman turned and walked back to the farmhouse, passing a few yards from Lynn and Imogen.

Lynn struggled with everything that was wrong about her; the clothes that looked not quite right, from another time, like the vintage fashions in the trendy retro shops in Birmingham. She was wearing a straight skirt that just skimmed her bare knees, a flowery blouse and a v-necked jumper and a pair of ancient black Wellingtons. The baby's clothes too were wrong. A terry nappy poked out of the leg of what was it called – Lynn struggled to think of it – a romper suit? The child looked about three months old. Neither of them wore coats despite the cold and their heads were bare.

The woman turned and looked at her as she passed. She was about Lynn's age with long dark hair, there was even a superficial resemblance between them but she was much thinner than Lynn, and wiry. The look she gave Lynn was questioning, almost mocking, but there was something demanding in her face. Lynn shrank back but the woman turned away and went out of the yard and down the lane to the cottage. Annie Chapman's white van had gone. The woman turned and looked back at them, hefting the baby on her hip, before opening the cottage door and going in.

'Who's that?' Imogen asked.

***

You were tiny, when you were born. Little Con, we used to call you. Look at you now. No one would believe you were only four-and-a-half-pound birthweight. I had to stay in the hospital with you till you got over five pounds and although I were glad of the rest I were itching to get home. Hospitals are places for people to die in.

I couldn't wait to get back to the farm, practise being a mother, even though I were a bit scared. It were something I never done before, but then I thought it can't be so hard, it comes to everybody. Except you Con, it never come to you and Christine.

It were May when I brought you home and it were like the whole world were in tune with us, new life pushing out of the soil everywhere. That were the best time for me. I didn't have to work for a while and your dad treated me like a queen. Even my father mellowed when he held you in his hands and Mother were in heaven. The land were alive, growing, making life and I were part of it. I could feel it when I held you close, when you pulled on my breast.

You was a greedy child, you had to be to build yourself up, but you've always loved your food Con. Life on the land makes you down to earth but it can be your downfall. You're a man of basic needs. That's how Diane's managed to hook you and look where you've ended up. It breaks my heart to see you here, skivvying for someone else and I can see you're hurting too but it's too late.

So that's what it were all about, all that painting and primping with new curtains. Annie Chapman's boy, sitting by my window, farting in my bathroom. I never thought I'd see the day strangers come living on the farm, but now even my own home's invaded without a thought for me.

Her with all her talk about keeping the place for her relatives and that Annie Chapman, couldn't wait to come sneaking round, talking her into putting Andrew in here. Not that I'm not sorry for the lad. It's a cruel shame to be maimed like that at twenty-four, crippled for life. What woman's going to look at him? What's he going to do with himself? These people who start these wars. They don't think of all the young men and women whose lives will be blighted. Look at our Thomas, my own grandfather and the uncle I never saw. All water under the bridge now and who even knows what them wars were really all about?

No thought for me. It's like reliving those years with our Thomas stumping about after he come back with never a kind word for nobody. Everyone always in his way, always moaning and shouting, or else miserable as sin. Same age as this lad now, just the same except nowadays there's gadgets to help them, make them a bit more independent. He's got a special bed and a chair that helps you stand up. Next thing you know, he'll be wanting to knock the walls down, make bigger doorways so he can get in and out with that fancy wheelchair.

I feel sorry for him, watching him struggling round the place on two sticks, or pulling himself along the furniture, but what about me? Pushed from pillar to post, there's nowhere I can take my rest what with them two up at the farm and him down here in my own house. Damn the lot of them, they'll get no good of chasing an old woman out of her family home.

Five generations of Askins have farmed this land, struggling through sun and rain, water and mud to make it profitable. My dad gave it order, made it flower and fruit, bent it to his will before it come to me, although it were only ever mine by proxy. It were like Dad were punishing me for being a girl when he left the farm to Albert.

He were delighted when you were born, Con. It might have brought him out of his coldness if he'd lived longer, seen you grow up. Thank the Lord he can't see what's happening now. Five generations of Askins and you're the last, Con, bearing the disgrace of coming back here, cap in hand, working for these townies. How can you do that? I could have spit in her face, watching her bring you a cup of tea, like you were some common workman, but maybe it's no more than what you deserve, selling your family down the river like you done.

If it didn't cut me to the bone, I'd laugh, especially at the way her and that lad was digging like a pair of crate-eggs. You can tell that boy's never held a spade in his life before and she's not much better. They'll have to do a sight more than that to master this land. She'll never get that patch dug over before the weed starts growing back where she started and then she'll have a job on her hands.

What are you thinking of, Con? Don't you know what you've thrown away? This used to be my vegetable plot. Do you remember, when you were a little lad, how you used to love helping me plant the seedlings in the spring, how wonderful it were to you when the things grew, when you could pick the peas and strawberries?

The farm were a marvellous world to you Con, when you was small. I did everything to make it good for you, because I remembered how my own childhood were blighted by Dad's bitterness, how I were always worked too hard to be able to enjoy childish things. I weren't going to let that happen to you, you were too precious.

You don't see me, Con, you're too blind to yourself but she sees me all right. She's staring at me now. You think you belong here but I don't think you've got it in you to take on this land. Happen you'll soon run back to your town, your shops and supermarkets.

You may well look at me like that, because you'll be seeing a lot more of me. This is my home and I won't be pushed out.

***

Lynn parked the car in the barn and set off down the lane. She'd left Imogen in Ormskirk, looking for work after they'd had a coffee. She'd done some shopping and planned to spend time researching in the library but she'd promised herself she'd call in on Andrew Chapman and she needed plenty of time to get ready for the evening. She was glad to see that Annie's van wasn't outside the cottage. At least if she made a fool of herself, there would be no witnesses.

She waited ages for him to answer the door. She could hear him dragging himself nearer and nearer and she had to resist the urge to run away.

'Who is it?' She thought she could hear him breathing behind the door.

'It's Lynn, from the farm. Mrs Waters.'

After a lot of fumbling the door creaked open. He had his mother's ice-blue eyes. He didn't speak, just stood there balancing on his crutches.

'I came to see if you're settled in okay, if there was anything you needed, if you're comfortable.'

'I'm fine.' His eyes were emotionless. He was a man, not a boy, with clear-cut features, an aquiline nose, a handsome man in an authoritative kind of way.

'Well, I just thought I'd stop by. We are neighbours.'

'I don't need anyone checking up on me. My mother does enough of that.'

'We are responsible for the tenancy. We want you to be happy here, to feel you can come to us if there's anything wrong.' She stopped at the bitter noise he made. Was it a laugh or an exclamation of contempt?

'I may be a cripple but there's nothing wrong with my mind. I'm quite capable of picking up the phone if I've got a problem.' With a sudden movement he slammed the door shut.

Lynn stood in shock for a moment. There was no sound on the other side. He was standing there waiting to see what she would do. After a few seconds, she turned away and went back up the lane to the farm.

***

Con resisted going into the Farmers' Arms at lunchtime. He was taking Diane to the Haywain that night so he had to stay sober but he was still seething from being sent to work on his own land, being treated like a hired hand. He bought a sandwich from the pie shop and took it back to the wood yard. Harry Ramsbottom was waiting for him.

'Need to get to the cash-and-carry, Con. Leaving you in charge. Job go okay?'

'Fine,' Con said. 'Should get it finished tomorrow morning.'

Harry looked him over. 'I can send Jim out instead.'

'No, it's fine.' Con turned his back and went to the tiny scullery to put the kettle on.

'Okay. I'll get off then. Should be back by four.'

Con ate his sandwich. The yard was empty. He felt the shop closing in on him, the shelves of screws and sundries, racks of wood stain and treatment compounds, sucking at him. That sense of belonging in his body without even thinking about it, the singing of his blood round and through his muscles and joints as he worked; that sense of everything being in tune like a sweet engine drained away in the shop. Here he shuffled among all these bits and pieces; his own body felt like separate parts, his head doing sums, his hands sorting and packing, the rest lost somewhere in between. Funny, he'd never been conscious of that feeling of body and mind working together until he felt the loss of it.

He hated it, hated the dry and tickling dusty air, the boring routines of till and computer, the enclosing walls. He felt like a puppet, this place was turning him into a lifeless body with just a waggling head, hands and feet at the edges of it. Even being a workman on his own land was better than this.

The shop bell jangled him back to the counter. Ralph Williams came in with a strong smell of horse muck.

'Just a box of five/sixty screws.' He helped himself from the shelf and put them on the counter. 'Bit of a change for you this, eh?'

'Yeah.' Con took his money, put a smile on his face.

'Never thought I'd see you give up the farm.'

Con turned his back, put the money in the till. 'Times change.' He handed Ralph his receipt and change. He waited till Ralph had driven out of the yard then nipped across the road to the Spar and bought a half-bottle of whisky.

***

Con made himself pass the open door of the Farmers' Arms as he walked home through the village. Diane would be furious if he was late. He took a pull from the whisky bottle instead, just a tiny one. Blondie looked forlornly at him from her post by the door as he passed. The twilight was blurred by the fine drizzle that had started up. He pulled his hood over his head and hurried on.

Diane was sitting at the dressing table, pinning her hair up. She was in her underwear, a tight black bodyshaper that cased her curves and showed off her golden skin but shouted 'hands off.'

Con went straight to the bathroom and cleaned his teeth.

'Hurry up,' Diane called. 'They won't keep the table if we're late.'

The image of his mother enjoying a single tot of brandy on her birthday came to his mind but he pushed it away.

He showered and went into the bedroom wrapped in a towel. He could see the tops of her breasts in the mirror, pushed up by the boned bodice. The knob of bone at the back of her neck was revealed as she swept her hair up into a French pleat. He bent and kissed it.

'You've been drinking,' Diane said. Her mouth was full of bristling hair grips.

'Only a quickie on the way home.'

'Honestly, Con.' She jabbed the pins into her hair. 'Couldn't you wait? Now I'll have to drive. Come on, get dressed.'

Con let the towel fall and went to the wardrobe. 'Do I have to wear a tie?'

'Shouldn't think so.' Diane patted the last pin in place, surveyed herself in the mirror and reached for her hairspray. 'But a nice sweater over your shirt. That blue cashmere I got you at Christmas.'

Con turned to see her stand and step into her dress. It took his breath away. Tight, tight midnight blue. It clung everywhere. It deepened her eyes to mystery.

'What do you think?' She posed for him, hands behind her back. The effect was instant.

He moved in close to her, his erection bumping between them. He tried to kiss her but she turned her head, laughing. 'You'll mess my lipstick.'

Her neck was the purest thing he'd ever seen. He put his hands on it, stroking down to her shoulders, and bent to touch his mouth to the soft space over her collarbone. The vibration from her laugh tingled his lips.

'Cock a doodle do!' she said reaching down between his legs and squeezing. He wanted to come right then, all over her new dress, but instead struggled to pull the fabric up over her thighs. She pushed his chest hard enough to make him stagger back.

'Later, Tiger, later,' she said smiling as she straightened her clothes.

***

He was uncomfortable in the Haywain. It was crowded, too formal with its silver-service and the waitresses looked down their noses at him even though they were just bits of kids. The cashmere sweater made him hot and already he was twitching for a stiff drink. He bought a double whisky for himself and a white wine spritzer for Diane while they waited to be seated.

'You never used to drink whisky so early.' Diane's eyebrows went up when he came back. Luckily the girl came to show them their table and he was saved from answering. The table was well away from the alcove where they had celebrated his mother's birthday but he couldn't help glancing round, looking for a familiar gesture or turn of head.

'A red rose for the lady.' The table waiter was young, blond and trendy. Diane shimmered at him, a slight blush on her cheeks as she took the flower.

Con read the menu, decided on a steak and forced himself to sip at the whisky while he looked round the room to see if the other men were admiring his gorgeous wife.

She was dazzling compared to the rest of the women at the tables. He couldn't get enough of looking at her, wanting to touch her. The farm, the wood yard, all the humiliations of the day retreated. She was worth it, worth everything he had given up. What had the farm been but a burden anyway?

He laughed to himself. Those two – the Waters. They'd bought a pig in a poke. He was the clever one, getting out of it. He had a nice, modern house, close to the shops and his job and he had Diane. That woman, Mrs Waters. 'Call me Lynn,' she'd said as if they were friends, as if he wasn't just there to do her bidding.

He felt sorry for Dan Waters, stuck with a fat frump like her and the farmhouse too. Well, good luck to the pair of them, he'd certainly got the best of the deal. Diane put her chin on her hand and smiled at him. Her eyes were soft and sexy and he forgot about the Waters, the farm, everything.

'Ready to order?' the blond waiter hovered at Diane's chair.

'What do you think about selling the Shogun?' Diane said as she picked over her prawn starter.

Con almost dropped his soup spoon. 'I don't think about it.' He looked at Diane. Her eyes had taken on a dark glitter that made him shiver.

'Things are getting tight. That job of yours doesn't bring much in and you walk to work, or use Harry's truck. We don't really need two cars.'

'But I've always had my own transport!' The thought of being carless, reliant on other people for getting around, translated in his head to an enormous feeling of helplessness.

He signalled the waiter, but Diane put her hand over his glass. 'No more whisky, Con. I want you in working order later.' She touched his knee under the table with her other hand.

'An orange juice for me,' she smiled at the waiter, 'and a Tiger beer for my husband.' She turned her gaze back to Con. 'Everything's getting so dear, fuel's going up all the time. There's no point in keeping a great gas-guzzler that nobody uses. You could buy yourself a moped.'

'But…' Con couldn't think of a reply. The whisky was going round his brain, softening everything up and he could only think of Diane's fingers on his knee.

'It's either that or you'll have to get a better job. Now you've got a bit of shop and office experience you could probably get something decent in I.T. You were always okay with the farm computer.'

The beer arrived and the plates were taken away. Con drank greedily, his mind reeling at the thought of working all day at a computer.

'Can't we talk about it some other time? It's Valentine's night.' He took her hand, rubbed his fingers over her engagement and wedding rings.

'But we never seem to get time to talk. You're always late home and we both get so tired.'

'Steak, sir?' The waiter placed the plate.

They ate in silence for a while. Con chewed woodenly. She was right, of course. He wasn't pulling his weight financially. It wasn't fair to expect her to keep him afloat from the salon's profits.

'I'll look for something else.'

'I know it's hard for you.' Diane was smiling again, her eyes had returned to that soft blue. 'It's just that we need to think about the future. Business at the salon isn't so good, everyone's tightening their belts. All this stuff on the news about money problems, even for banks, the government, it's frightening everyone. All this fighting in the Middle-East, people trying to come here as asylum seekers. I don't know where we're going.'

'Tell it to Andy Chapman.' Con remembered Chapman's frustration as he struggled to get into his mother's van. What was all that for? What kind of world had Chapman seen out in Iraq? The wet green fields of Lancashire had nothing in common with the bleak landscapes of the war zones that appeared nightly on TV like episodes from a Mad Max film. Con felt the world wobble around him. In the space of a few short months everything had changed. His life had been a fixed landscape, the contours of the farm and the matriarchal figure of his mother keeping it steady around him. Now everything was fluid. Diane didn't understand how his life had been rooted in the land. Change excited her but now she was all he had left to cling on to.

Only this landscape was real, only his life here and now with Diane, their own happiness. What else mattered or made sense? She squeezed his knee again and he forgot about it all. He would get another job, sell the car if she wanted him to. He would do anything for her, anything.

***

'I called in at the cottage, to see if Andrew Chapman was okay.

He was really rude, slammed the door in my face.'

'What did you say to him?' Dan came in from the bathroom, drying his wet hair as he walked.

'I didn't say anything. I didn't get the chance.' Lynn checked the seams of her stockings in her wardrobe mirror. 'I only wanted to introduce myself, see if he was having any problems settling in.'

'He's probably had enough of women fussing round him.' Dan began selecting clothes from his wardrobe.

'He had no need to be so rude.'

'Have you any idea what it's like for troops out there? We can't even begin to imagine the reality of it, and I don't suppose young men like Chapman can either, until they land in the middle of it. And then to come back disabled, having to come to terms with the fact that you're never going to be the man you were again. I'm not surprised he gets angry, listening to people whose only dilemmas are what colour to paint their bathrooms, or which brand of beefburgers to buy in the supermarket.'

Lynn bit her lip. She shouldn't have mentioned it. Dan was getting into lecture mode.

'I'll go down and have a word with him when I've a minute, he might respond better to another man. Anyway, let's forget about him. It's Valentine's night.'

He had his back to her, knotting his tie with movements that were familiar and dear to her. Relieved, she slipped the new dress over her head and struggled with the zip. It was tight. Surely she couldn't have put on that much weight since she'd bought it. She twisted and turned in front of the mirror, sweating with dismay. It had been a mistake to choose cream. Something darker would have slimmed her, but it had looked perfect when she'd tried it on, the colour contrasting with her hair and eyes.

It was easy to forget about appearances here on the farm where she hardly saw anyone. There was no reason to dress up and so much of her time had been taken up with decorating and gardening that it was becoming routine to slop around in jeans and sweaters. She'd been too busy to notice the extra inch or two.

Dan appeared behind her in the mirror. He was gorgeous in the mellow light from the bedroom lamps. The white shirt stood out against his skin. She wanted to pull it open, see the black hair on his chest curling stark against the fabric. She was lucky. A lot of academics didn't care what they looked like but Dan always looked immaculate.

He kissed her neck, his lips seeking out the tender spot under her ear. Delight shivered through her.

'Nice dress,' he murmured but she could feel his fingers probing the excess flesh round her waist and her pleasure at his touch shrank.

'I've got something for you.' He held up a small jewellery box. Lynn turned to take it. 'No, let me.' His fingers were gently skilful fastening the fine gold chain at the back of her neck. Her skin shivered at each touch.

'But the roses –' she sank back against him.

'This is something more lasting.' The single diamond nestled in the hollow of her throat. He dropped his head and bit her shoulder.

'Oh, Dan.' She turned and opened her mouth to his tongue, feeling her response liquid between her legs and up inside. His hands were hungry on the skin of her back above the dress.

She could feel the hardness of his muscles. All those squash sessions at the university gym. She was proud that he took such good care of himself. Right now she wanted to touch the soft skin inside his clothes, but his shirt fitted tightly. She pulled at it impatiently but he stopped kissing her and removed her hands, pulling away from her.

'Hey, come on, no time for that now.' He kissed the end of her nose. 'Later. It'll be even better, I promise.'

***

She thought about later as Dan led her into the crowded room of networking academics. She did the rounds being introduced to Dan's colleagues, forgetting the name of each one as she was presented to the next.

Already her face ached from smiling and she drank her glass of wine too quickly. Dan turned away to talk to someone and she was able to sink into a chair in a corner. They were in the original campus building, now surrounded by a collection of glass blocks of various dates from the 1960s up to the brand new post-millennium business centre that dominated the rear of the campus.

The room, once a refectory, still held the mellow atmosphere of old wood and ancient respectability, of the measured passage of time and many feet. Here the air smelled of polish and felt thicker, slower than normal, as if they had all slipped back to a time when the world ran at an easier pace.

'You must be Dan's wife. So nice to meet you.'

Lynn stared at the girl in front of her. She didn't look old enough to be a student, never mind being on the faculty. Ice-white hair cut short and sharp to draw out her fine boned features, rings through nose and eyebrows, black eye paint, black lipstick, black leather miniskirt and thigh boots, huge studded belt and a purple lace top with long flaring sleeves that must have come from one of the trendy city shops like Golgotha in Birmingham, the kind of place Lynn used to pass without going in. Strangely the girl wore an old fashioned perfume. Lynn had no trouble identifying it. Coty L'Aimant had always been one of her mother's favourites.

'Emma Cranton. I teach Women's Studies. Lovely dress.'

Lynn cringed. Next to Emma she felt like a carthorse. 'Nice to meet you too. Dan's told me so much about you all. It's great to be able to put faces to names.' She felt obliged to lie. She couldn't say that Dan hardly talked to her at all about his colleagues, only about his own progress and ambitions. He certainly hadn't mentioned Emma Cranton.

She looked round for Dan or Phil Eckersley who she knew vaguely but there was no escape. Emma Cranton seized her by the arm.

'Come over here, let's get another drink. Dan tells me you used to teach.'

'English F.E.' Lynn took a glass of orange juice from the table. 'I'm driving,' she explained to Emma's raised eyebrows.

'I did English A level at school.' Emma sipped her red wine. 'T.S. Eliot and Shakespeare. *King Lear*. Cordelia, now there's a girl after my own heart.'

'I specialise in Wordsworth, and the rest of the Lake poets of course.'

'Bit of a wild bunch weren't they? All that opium and free love. What was the name of that radical movement they started?'

'Pantisocracy,' Lynn mumbled.

'That's it. All high ideals and equality. Good in theory but turned out to be the usual story with the men loafing round writing poetry while the women did all the chores, brought up the kids and struggled to make ends meet.'

'What are you doing over here?' Dan appeared and grabbed her elbow. 'I need you to come and meet the Dean. Sorry Emma,' he flashed a smile as he drew Lynn away.

The Dean was polite, trying to engage her in small talk but he soon moved on to someone more interesting with Dan in tow. Lynn tagged along, feeling more and more like a spare part. She let her mind wander to her vegetable patch and the next day's digging. If only the rain would hold off. This seemed more important than the discussions going on around her. The physical work had energised her and now she was surprised to find that she was bored in this atmosphere of intellectual sparring.

At last the Dean invited them all to the buffet table. She and Dan filled their plates and sat down at one of the tables. She was glad to have something to do but would have preferred a romantic dinner for two at Raj's. She pictured Dan presenting her with champagne and another red rose, then later –

'Are you thinking of returning to teaching?' The man next to her, who looked like Dylan from the Magic Roundabout, looked at her enquiringly. She struggled to remember his name. He munched on a mini-quiche and looked expectantly at her.

'Er, maybe. I'm just so busy at the moment, settling into the new house and everything. You know how it is, lots of decorating and stuff to do.' Peter, yes that was it, Peter Shaw.

'Yes, but you don't want to lose touch. Especially as you're in a new area where no one really knows you. An intelligent woman like you shouldn't be hiding herself away. It's good to take a break but you'll get bored after a while.

'There's a sixth-form college in Ormskirk and there are always the schools of course. You might get an opening in the English Department here. Dan tells me you're interested in doing some research on the Lake poets. They're keen on research here and if you can get an associate lectureship you might get funding for your PhD. I'm sure you'd be welcomed if Dan puts in a word for you. Just don't leave it too long. Things change, move on. You don't want to get left behind.'

'Mmm. I'll think about it.' Lynn felt pushed. Peter's enthusiasm excited her for a moment but the thought of the cut and thrust of academic competition, the constant changes in departmental policy and staffing, not to mention the work and dedication involved in the years it would take to complete a PhD, terrified her. If she went down that path there would be no time for her garden or for her family research. She turned to Dan but he was deep in conversation with the man on his left. He bit into a piece of bread roll and she thought of his teeth on her shoulder.

Emma Cranton took the seat opposite Peter Shaw. Her body was lithe in her tight fitting clothes as she leaned forward to pour a glass of water. Lynn noted the well-developed muscles in her arms and shoulders. She looked like someone who kept fit, someone who might play a lot of squash in the university gym.

It couldn't be. Lynn thought of earlier, how Dan had been hungry for her, she could tell by his touch, by his kiss. Her fingers went to the diamond at her throat. It was just her imagination, but she glanced at Emma again and caught her looking at Dan. Lynn knew that look, it was much the same as her own way of looking at Dan in the privacy of their bedroom. Her heart thumped.

Emma moved her head slightly. Her eyes fixed on Lynn as if she were prey, as if her fate were already sealed. Her black lips widened in a lazy cat smile and she stretched her arms slowly before picking up her fork and starting to eat.

Lynn pushed the food round her plate. This couldn't be real. She was imagining it, being stupidly jealous. Dan was hers. She tried to concentrate on '*later.*'

'Do you plan to keep animals on the farm?' Peter demanded her attention.

'No. We're going to let the fields.' *But it's only her, only her looking at him. She might want him but she can't have him.*

'Will that bring in a good income? I thought people usually sell the land off.'

'We thought about it but we've decided to keep it, for the time being, anyway.' *It's not Dan. She's just a groupie. It happens all the time. Admit it, it's happened before.*

The woman on Peter's right began to talk to him. Lynn was saved from further conversation.

'All right?' Dan patted her hand. Lynn nodded. He turned to

the man on his left. She watched Emma Cranton but she had joined in the conversation between Peter and the woman next to him, laughing carelessly as if she hadn't stared at Lynn just a moment ago like a hunting tigress, like something so superior in strength and cunning that poor little Lynn didn't stand a chance.

But Dan loves me, she thought, remembering the red whorls of the roses hiding their secret inner folds. Her fingers went again to the diamond. It felt warm and heavy.

Emma Cranton looked up and for a second her face was naked as emotions flowed across it. Lynn flinched; each expression was like a slap: disdain, dislike, envy, hatred even. At once Lynn knew the woman was ruthless, without a shred of loyalty or thought for others. She should have realised from her comments about the Lake poets that she had no concept of beauty or romance, only a practical concern for her own desires that would be sated at all costs. She turned away but felt herself compelled to look again. Emma was smiling sweetly as she lifted her fork to her mouth.

Lynn nursed her glass, the food on her plate untouched as all these people chattered around her. She was back in the past, remembering all the times she'd had this feeling, these suspicions. Back in Birmingham there had been the occasional wafts of perfume blowing in with Dan when he came home from working late. And there were all those late night meetings and seminars, the clusters of pretty girls in the corridor outside Dan's room, not to mention the super-intelligent PhD student from Macclesfield with the enormous breasts and crazy red hair who always seemed to be having a one-to-one supervision with him every time she popped in. There were the student nights out, dances and drinks parties that Dan felt obliged to attend, coming home at four or five in the morning, worn out and smelling of wildness.

She glanced at him and froze, followed his gaze to Emma Cranton. They were connected, their eyes fixed on each other as information passed between them like a telepathic beam. Lynn could feel it singeing the air as it passed her by and her whole being faltered as she realised that for Dan and Emma there would also be a *'later.'*

Chapter Seven

Friday February 15th 2008

Lynn couldn't settle to her digging. The scene was the same as the day before; Con Worrall was putting in the last of the fence posts, Imogen was digging his way back to her from the other side of the plot, but everything had changed. All she could think about was the way Emma Cranton had looked at Dan and the way he had responded to her.

Dan was smooth, he had given nothing away on the surface but Lynn knew she was right. He hadn't been able to stop himself flicking glances at Emma and it was there in the deliberate way he'd avoided being near her, how he'd pulled Lynn away from talking to her.

Back home, he'd made love to her possessively but she'd been unable to enjoy it. It was as if her orgasm had been forced from her and afterwards, when she'd looked at Dan lying next to her, she'd seen a monster. How could he want them both?

She saw Emma Cranton's smug smile as she drove the spade into the soil, anger making her use excessive energy with each thrust. The metal chinked on something and turned up a bit of blue and white china. She picked it up, turned it over on her palm. How many generations had lived their lives here before her? What pains and passions had they suffered? Had they struggled with the same infidelities, deceptions? She sensed them watching, waiting, as if she mattered, as if she were part of their story, or were they simply laughing at her, malevolent spirits like the ghosts she'd seen? She still hadn't mentioned them to Dan for fear of being scoffed at. If it wasn't for the fact that Imogen had seen them too, she would have thought she was going mad but that last appearance in front of Con Worrall had convinced her of their reality. What did they want? It seemed as if everything was against her, Emma Cranton, Dan, the house with its rejecting ghosts, even the land she stood on.

She looked around the blank landscape. What was she doing

here? The lines of her relationship with Dan were wavering, she felt as if she were going under, losing her own identity in this strange place but she was sure about one thing, she wasn't going to be pushed out by any rival, living or dead. She'd done nothing to deserve this. She pushed the spade into the soil and stumped off to the house to make coffee.

In the kitchen she brushed away tears. Her face was on fire. How could Dan do this to her? Anger rose up her throat so that she coughed and gagged as she fumbled with the kettle. Imogen came in, the grin dying on his face as he saw her.

'What's the matter? Have I done something wrong?'

She shook her head, unable to speak for the rage trying to squeeze out of her. She pulled open the cupboard to reach for mugs and knocked one on to the floor. The sound of it shattering broke her control and she let out a strangled scream.

'I'll get it.' Imogen rushed to pick up the pieces. She was shaking. Her whole body was nothing but fury. If Emma Cranton had been in front of her now, she would have killed her.

'Come on, sit down. I'll make the coffee.'

She couldn't move. Imogen took her hand, pulled her gently. 'Come on.'

She took a step forward, then she was leaning against him. She could feel the warmth of his body, the muscles of his chest. She could smell the sweat of his exertions. His arms enfolded her like balm. Her head fitted under his chin. 'It's Dan,' she mumbled, tears and saliva soaking into his tee shirt.

'Shhhh.' He patted her head. 'It's okay.'

She wanted to sink into him, let her bones dissolve, but there was danger. She tore herself away and sat down at the table, covering her face with her hands. Her fingers were cold, they cooled her burning eyes, her hot dry skin.

'Are ye sure you're not over-reacting?' he asked when she'd finished recounting the previous night's events.

'Do you think I don't know my own husband?' She was calmer now, regretting showing her weakness.

'Do ye no want a biscuit?' He pushed the packet across to her.

'No, you eat them.' The anger was fading but its residue, a niggling annoyance was targeting Imogen. She would have liked to have been alone. She watched him eat.

'So what will ye do?'

'Nothing. It won't come to anything. It's happened before. Dan's successful, good-looking, popular. Students are always running after him.'

'I thought ye said she's a lecturer?'

'Yes,' Lynn's voice quavered. It was true, Emma Cranton was no immature student groupie; she had everything that Lynn lacked.

'If it were me, I'd have it out with him. I'd be too angry to keep it in.'

'That would be a mistake. Dan thrives on confrontation, it's like a game of chess to him, he makes sure he never loses.' He would annihilate her. Her emotions would rule her tongue and she might say things that would force Dan's hand, turn him against her.

'Ye're too good for him.' The softness of his tone made her look up. He reached across the table and took her hands. She flushed. How could a nineteen-year-old be so sensitive? She wanted to hold on to him like a lifeline but her stomach quivered in alarm, her legs wanted to get up and run. She pulled her hands away.

'Let's get out of here, I need a change of scene.'

'Where to?' Imogen got up and rinsed their mugs.

'Oh, I don't know. Ormskirk or Southport maybe.'

'I could go back to the Jobcentre.'

'I feel like doing something different, take my mind off all this. Let's go and visit that Martin Mere place, it's only down the road.'

Outside, Con Worrall was packing up the truck. The fencing was finished, neat and starkly new against the ancient landscape.

'Should be okay. Any problems, just call at the yard.' He nodded to Imogen as he swung himself up into the cab. Before he could pull out, Annie Chapman's van pulled into the yard. Andrew was sitting in the passenger seat.

'Andrew wants to apologise for his rudeness yesterday,' Annie called through her open window.

Andrew looked mutinously at Lynn. 'Sorry,' he muttered.

'It's okay.' Lynn couldn't think of anything to say that wouldn't be patronising.

'It's not okay.' Annie glared at her son. 'You've no right to take out your temper on other people.'

'You haven't met Imogen,' Lynn hastened to defuse the situation. 'He's staying with us for a while.'

Annie and Andrew looked Imogen up and down.

'Ye've been in Iraq?' Imogen said. 'Bet that was exciting.'

'Yeah. Never a dull moment.'

Lynn cringed but the sarcasm was lost on Imogen. He laughed. 'I'd like to hear about it sometime.'

'I don't like to talk about it.' Andrew turned his head away and stared in front of him.

'It'd be nice for you to have some young company, Andy,' Annie dug him in the ribs.

'You can call round if you want,' Andrew said carelessly, without moving his head.

'That's settled then, come round any time.' Annie beamed. 'We'd best be off. Andrew's got a hospital appointment.'

***

Con turned the 'CLOSED' sign on the shop door with relief at one o'clock. He'd hoped that the fencing job would last out the morning but he'd been finished by eleven. He hadn't enjoyed being there anyway. Nothing in his body was working properly and his head had echoed each nail he'd hammered.

The quarter-bottle of whisky he'd bought that morning had helped to dull the hangover but it couldn't stop him remembering with horror that he'd promised Diane he'd look for an office job the night before.

He tried not to think about it as he locked the till and put on his jacket, tried to think about the sex they'd had instead but he couldn't remember anything except lying on the bed watching Diane strip off her bodyshaper, her breasts round as apples, the black thong pinpointing her sex, defining her buttocks. After that was blank until he'd woken at three in the morning in his armchair in front of the television, dried spittle down his chin and an empty whisky bottle in his lap.

He hesitated to throw the empty bottle in the bin, put it in his pocket instead to dispose of outside. The whisky was getting to be a habit he ought to stop. He'd certainly never drunk in the morning before. Diane would kill him if she found out. Still, it was only a one-off for medicinal purposes. He couldn't work effectively with a raging hangover. He would definitely stick to beer in future.

In the Farmers' Arms he was surprised to see Andrew Chapman sitting at a table near the bar television, watching the one o'clock news playing scenes of a soldier's funeral.

'No Jackie today?' Con asked Chris, the landlord, as he ordered a pint of bitter and a steak pie. Con always looked forward to a bit of banter with Jackie. He'd known her since they were at school together in Chapel Lane.

'Gone to Paris with that boyfriend of hers.'

'Oh, that's right. She told me about it, I'd forgotten. No Barney either?'

'Dunno where he's got to. He'll be in sooner or later.'

Con nodded and went over to Chapman. 'Mind if I join you?'

Andrew leaned over and shifted his crutches from the chair next to him.

'Have to warn you I'm getting pissed, fast as I can before my mother comes back and drags me off home.'

'I'm surprised she let you in here in the first place.' Con knew Annie's views on drink. It had long been a joke in their family how Jim Chapman had to sneak out for an occasional pint.

'She wanted to leave me in May's caff while she's visiting some friend of hers, for fuck's sake. I was in charge of men in Iraq, taking life or death decisions, but trying to deal with a woman, especially your mother, is something else.'

'Tell me about it.' Con thought about Diane's demands that he find a better job. As soon as he gave in to her over one thing, there was something else.

'Let me buy you a drink, only you'll have to go and get it.' Andrew tossed a five-pound note on the table. Con realised his glass was almost empty already.

'Thanks.' He took the glasses and refilled them. 'So how's it going in the cottage?'

'It's hard. I can't say it's not, but it's better than being at home with Mum fussing all the time and anything's better than being in hospital.'

'How long have you been back now, four months? Must be a

hell of an adjustment, even if you come back in one piece.'

Chapman nodded. 'It's another world.' His mouth twisted.

'What are you going to do?'

'Dunno. No one's got around to talking about that yet. It depends on how much improvement I get in my legs. They say it takes a long time. It already seems like forever.'

Con saw the impatience in his face. He remembered Andrew stomping round the Holmes farmyard in mud-covered Wellingtons, swinging himself up on the tractor, his legs long and muscular in tight jeans.

'I suppose I could train for something in IT, maybe work from home.' He emptied his glass and reached into his jeans pocket.

'No, let me.' Con got up and ordered two more pints. 'Diane wants me to work with computers.' He picked at his congealing pie. He'd come in here for some lively chat, wanting to forget about his problems.

'You're working in Ramsbottom's aren't you?'

'It's not bringing in enough.'

'Why'd you give the farm up Con?'

'Why'd you join the army?'

Chapman's face clouded. 'You think I don't ask myself that, every day? It was a gap thing, you know? I wanted to try something different, see the world for a few years. I knew Dad would want me to take over the farm when he retires.'

'Didn't you want that?'

'Yes and no. I knew it was there for me but I wanted something else, something more, adventure I suppose. When you're young it seems so dull, same thing year in year out. I were bored stiff. Mud, pests, the weather, nothing to talk about except the price of spuds. I could just see myself ending up like our Penny, married with a couple of kids, never going anywhere, stuck in the family business.'

Con had never felt like that. Sure, he'd liked going into Liverpool or Wigan to the clubs as a lad in the eighties but he'd always felt more at home in the village pubs among farming people. His heart had always lifted at the sight of the farmhouse as he came home. The day his mother had signed the farm over to him he'd been too emotional even to thank her.

'Now it seems like I've thrown everything away. I'd give

anything, anything to be able to go out on the fields like I used to.' Chapman stared into his glass. 'Let's have something stronger. She'll be here soon to take me back. Get two double scotches.'

Con looked at his watch. It was already two-fifteen. What the hell. Ramsbottom had left for the day at twelve. If anyone came to the shop they could come and find him.

Andrew downed his whisky in one gulp. 'I don't know what's going to happen when Dad goes. I'm the only son. Our Penny's okay in the shop but she couldn't run the farm and that husband of hers is only a pen-pusher. He wouldn't have a clue. Mum's not getting any younger; she wouldn't be able to manage it by herself.'

'How old's your dad now?' Con tried to sip the whisky but habit sent most of it down his throat in one swallow.

'Fifty-eight. He'll go on for years yet, but he says he'd like to take it easier, have a few holidays. And here I am, useless.'

'You said yourself you might get better.'

'Not that much better.'

'You could still be a partner, take on a manager. Someone who knows the ropes.'

'Someone like yourself, Con?' They both laughed uneasily. 'Wouldn't be the same, would it? And it'd cost a fortune.' He tapped his empty glass on the table.

'The car's outside, time to go.' Con looked up to see Annie standing over them, the smile dying on her face as she took in the clutter of glasses on the table.

'Andrew!'

'I'm pissed as a fart, Mother. Sorry and all that.' Andrew tried to lift himself out of the seat by pulling on the table. Con shot his hand out in time to stop it going over.

'I don't know what you're thinking of, Con Worrall, letting him get in a state like this.' Her eyes blazed at him.

Con mumbled an apology and helped her get Andrew on his feet and onto his crutches.

Andrew grinned stupidly. 'Come round the cottage and bring a bottle.'

'He'll do no such thing,' Annie hissed. 'Help me get him to the car.'

The door opened and two of the girls from Diane's Den came in and headed for the bar. 'Sorry, I have to get back to work.' Con edged to the door, keeping his back to them.

Barney Dougan was tying Blondie to the rail outside. 'I wouldn't go in there for a few minutes, if I were you,' Con said as he made his escape.

***

If she hadn't known about the original lake, Lynn might have been impressed with Martin Mere. They walked round the formal area with its landscaped pens of waterfowl species but it was the more natural wetland area that she really wanted to see.

'It's only a puddle,' she said to Imogen.

'Looks big to me.' He laughed. The atmosphere between them had lightened now they were away from the farm. Lynn felt more relaxed, though thoughts of Dan and Emma Cranton still simmered at the back of her mind.

In the spring-like sunshine, the water was smooth and clear. The land spread level beyond it across to faint hills drawn against the sky. The expanse of land and sky made the lake seem smaller than it was. Lynn had been expecting something huge and implacable. Honks and quacks filled the air and the water was alive, white with crowds of swans and geese, interspersed with the busy doings of small, dark ducks.

Lynn turned, trying to orientate herself. In front of her the land stretched towards Rufford, to her left Southport, Tarleton more to the north and Preston to the east maybe? The lake had once reached almost to Tarleton and to Aughton in the other direction, where Lavinia Askin had gone to Sunday school. She still hadn't traced her ancestor. The birth date in the Bible had to be wrong, she hadn't been able to find anything in that year. She'd neglected the research while the weather had been fine for gardening but she resolved to spend the first rainy day in the library.

They ate lunch in the café and wandered around hides looking at the birds. The lake was too small to support the numbers of waterfowl on it and as they watched, a keeper came out with a bucket of feed, throwing it down on the water's edge and immediately causing an excited cacophony as the birds gravitated to the bank.

The wide open space and the breeze that drove unchecked across the flat ground cleared Lynn's head and swept away her emotions leaving her dry and empty but as the afternoon light began to fail, mist started to gather over the surface of the water and wisp into the atmosphere. The lake was transforming before their eyes into a ghostly glimmer. The shapes of the birds were barely discernible and their honking echoed eerily through the thickening air, creating a sense of melancholy.

The drive back restored normality. It had been good to get out and do something different. She'd almost forgotten Emma Cranton but as they neared the farm, her fears rose up again to haunt her. She was surprised to see Dan's car in the yard when they got back. It was only four-thirty.

Imogen went straight up to his room and Lynn went into the kitchen to begin preparing the evening meal. Dan was sitting at the table eating a sandwich and working on his laptop.

'Where have you been?' He carried on typing.

'Martin Mere, the Wildfowl Trust. I felt like a change.'

'Don't spoil that boy. We'll never get rid of him.'

'I was glad of his company.'

Dan looked up at the angry note in her voice. 'I can't help having to work. Someone round here has to earn something, especially now we're taking in waifs and strays.'

'You're home early.' She sat down opposite him, refusing to respond to his gibe.

'I forgot some papers I need for tonight, so I had to come back.'

'Tonight?'

'I've a meeting at six-thirty. Don't know how long it'll go on so don't make supper for me. I've had this sandwich and I'll grab something at uni. Don't look like that, it can't be helped.'

She couldn't speak. She stared as he drank the last of his coffee and snapped the laptop shut. 'Have to go. Don't wait up for me if I'm late.'

He came behind her, bent to kiss her neck. The fragrance of Coty L'Aimant wafted from his jacket. Lynn's eyes burned and misted. She listened to his footsteps on the stone floor, the slam of the car door, the growl of the engine receding. Her whole body was icy, stiff and solid like a rock carving.

She got up and climbed the stairs, her eyes fixed on the

sanctuary of her room. She fell on the bed, face down. She could smell Dan on the pillow and she clutched it to her for comfort. A howl was gathering inside her but she wouldn't let it out. Something touched her shoulder, gentle, tentative. She turned. Imogen was sitting on the side of the bed.

'Don't,' he said rubbing her shoulder. He was looking at her as if she were an injured animal. She heaved herself upright beside him. Tears dripped off the end of her nose. She wiped them away with her hand and laid her head on his shoulder. He began to stroke her hair. His hands were inept, like a child's, but gentle and as she did nothing, his touch became more confident, setting up a rhythm that soothed her, gradually stilling her sobs.

They sat in silence. At last she turned to face him. His mouth, close to hers, was tender and full like a baby's. 'Thank you,' she said and kissed him. It was a child's kiss but she felt the prickle of adult bristle above the softness. She pulled away. His hand dropped to her neck, then she was kissing him fiercely, feeling the answering pressure of his lips. Desire scalded through her. His hand fumbled at her breast and she tore her shirt open for him, dragging her bra up over her breasts to let him suckle there.

She was falling into sweetness then she was lying on top of him, breasts pressed against his chest, pulling up his tee shirt to feel skin on skin. Buttons and zips on his trousers dug into her flesh and she felt his erection poking at her belly, searching for her. He groaned as she shucked her jeans, undid his zip and took out his penis.

She tried to slow herself, he was only a boy. For a second she remembered her responsibility towards him, her seniority and she could have stopped, but then he slid his hand down between her legs and she thought of Dan touching Emma Cranton there. She raised herself up and mounted him, wanting to ride him, to teach him delight but he suddenly rolled her over and with three quick thrusts came into her and collapsed with a cry.

She was cheated, but it was glorious honest sex. He had wanted her so much he couldn't wait. She was still throbbing, rubbing herself against his thigh as she rolled him onto his back and slid down to take him in her mouth. Patiently she fondled with her lips and tongue, the movements of her jaw feather-gentle till she felt a response, heard him gasp and felt his hands tangle in her hair. He pulled her up, let her climb over him. She braced herself on her arms, pushing deeply onto him. His hips rose to meet her but he let her set her own pace and she was slow and gentle until the orgasm began to tug at the root of her belly like a plant being pulled, till it began to thunder in her blood, in her ears, till she forgot about the boy beneath her, bucking and screaming in the flood she had become.

It receded and she looked down, the lines of his face firming as her vision steadied. He looked scared stiff, still hanging on to her as if she were a windswept kite. They both began to laugh. She flopped onto the bed beside him. Juices trickled out of her onto the duvet. His face was soft in the gloom. It was almost dark. Shadows were forming in the corners. She curled against his warmth and slept.

***

I saw, I saw everything. You wouldn't have dreamt it, her going round looking so prim and proper and carrying on like that when her husband's back's turned. Not that he's any better I don't suppose. Still, carrying on with a coloured, and him nobbut a boy at that. This is how people are nowadays, no respect for right and wrong.

I wouldn't never have thought of doing the dirty on Bert and no more would he on me. We fitted together like a pair of gloves in that way. I'm not saying it's only city people as acts that way though. I've seen plenty of goings on out in the fields, especially round Spring planting and harvest times. And when the war were on, there were all sorts of shenanigans with soldiers and Yanks from the airbase passing through, even women turning to women while their men were away, but that were a time of desperation.

I were only a child, most of it went over my head but even I knew that endless doing without and drabness, knew how everyone seized on opportunities to have a little fun. We were all so full of uncertainty as to what was going to become of us, even the grown-ups, for all they tried to gloss it over. Once you've known that uncertainty, it never leaves you. The one thing you can cling to is the land, because although it changes with the seasons, it's always there.

I were brought up to believe marriage is for life and one man were good enough for me. Anyways, when we were first married Bert showed me the shotgun and says to me, 'Don't ever let me catch you with another man.' But people nowadays with their divorces and their new partners aren't no happier. Look at our Con, his life's ruined with running after that Diane.

There'll be high jinks if her husband finds out what she's up to. I felt sorry for her when she realised he's got another woman but any one could see he likes to have women on a string and getting her own back by sleeping with this bit of a kid isn't going to help her. If there's one thing that's sure about her, it's that she loves her husband. It's him she really wants, no matter how much of a rat he is. She won't settle easy with what she's done.

***

Lynn lay in bed, waiting. The house was quiet. She'd changed the bedding, soaked herself in the bath but she couldn't get the smell of sex out of her nostrils.

Imogen had gone to his room. She wondered if he too lay awake, if he was thinking of her. Could she trust him not to say anything in front of Dan? And how was she going to face Dan, pretend that nothing had happened? He knew her inside out, surely he would be able to tell, sniff out her secret even before it had a chance to become one?

She would never have believed she could be unfaithful to Dan, but then it wasn't really like that. It hadn't been a conscious decision, or even desire. She didn't love Imogen. It was a momentary thing, a reaction, revenge even. In reality, she'd used Imogen to get back at Dan. How could she have done that to someone young and vulnerable, who'd come to her for help?

She tossed under the covers, hot with guilt. The easy sleep of a few hours ago evaded her now as the implications of what she had done multiplied. It had been so good, even now, she didn't really regret it. Maybe Imogen had been right, maybe she should have it out with Dan, confess what had happened, encourage him to admit his affair with Emma Cranton, then they could start afresh. But maybe Dan hadn't gone that far, maybe he hadn't slept with Emma yet. Even if he had, he'd turn her own confession against her and admit nothing. No, it was better to keep quiet. It was a one-off moment, not worth risking her marriage for. She would make sure it never happened again.

The bedside clock glowed at her. Eleven-thirty. Why didn't Dan come? And yet she dreaded him coming. Shadows stirred in the corner. She sat bolt upright, skin tingling with fear and snapped the light on. The old woman was standing there in a grey crimplene frock, her lips drawn back in an evil grin that showed an even row of yellow false teeth. Lynn was caught rabbit-like in her gaze and watched helplessly as the woman wagged a finger at her in a 'naughty girl' gesture. Something was coming up the stairs, rattling the bedroom door. Lynn screamed as Dan burst into the room.

'Jesus, Lynn, what's the matter? You look like you've seen a ghost.'

She clapped a hand to her chest. 'You frightened me.'

'Who did you think it was, the boggart of the moss?' He pulled a horrid face at her clawing his hands in the air. 'I told you this place is getting to you, you need to get out more, stop listening to village gossip. Just going to get a shower.' He disappeared to the bathroom.

Lynn looked back at the corner. The woman had gone. She'd been watching, Lynn thought, blood rushing to her face. She'd seen everything. She remembered her greed, how she'd given herself up to her desire, and she cringed under the bedclothes. She listened to the sounds of running water, Dan's singing as he washed Emma Cranton's perfume off his body. She switched off the light when she heard his footsteps coming back, turned away as she felt his weight press into the bed and pretended to be asleep for the first time in their married life.

***

Thank God Saturday was a half-day, Con thought as he left the woodyard. He hurried past the Farmers' Arms. Diane was expecting him home for lunch and after that they planned to go shopping in Southport. Maybe they would stay late and have a Chinese.

Diane was talking on the phone as he came in. Milly ran round his ankles as he hung up his coat. 'Hello ragbag,' he said and picked her up, scratching her ears as he waited for Diane to end her call, but Diane carried on giggling down the line with her back to him. He put the dog down, went to the bathroom and had a shower. Diane was making a salad when he came back.

'That was Alex. Justin's there. Alex is bringing him tonight.'

'I thought he were coming tomorrow.' Con fought to stop irritation seeping into his voice.

'Alex's plans have changed. He has to go to London tomorrow.'

'What about our plans?'

'Don't sulk.' Diane turned and dangled a morsel of chicken in front of his face. He opened his mouth dutifully, catching her round the waist to feel the taut muscles of her back. 'We can still go to Southport, as long as we get back for about half-four. I've invited Alex for supper.'

The afternoon was ruined for Con, thinking about having to sit at the same table and make conversation with Diane's ex. Diane made him stand around umpteen clothes shops and then rushed him round Sainsbury's while she picked out delicacies for Alex and Justin.

A miserable rain began to fall around three o'clock, matching Con's mood. He wanted a drink but had to settle for a coffee before they returned home. It was dark when they got back. Con helped Diane unpack the shopping then took Rolo's lead from the coat-rack.

'I thought you were going to help me with the meal?'

'Rolo's been stuck in all day. He needs a run.'

'I don't know why you keep that dog; he really doesn't fit in with our lifestyle now. Maybe the Waters would take him. He'd be much happier on the farm and we'd still have Milly. She's a good guard dog.'

Con watched her laying places at the table. He could hear Milly barking in the garden, teasing Rolo in his compound. His hands balled into fists and he kept them shoved in his pockets so Diane wouldn't see. 'Don't even think it,' he said softly.

Diane looked up at the hint of menace in his voice. She put a smile on her face.

'Well, don't be late back. Alex wants to talk to you about a job. I mentioned this morning that you were looking for something else. His brother Jack has a big computer business in Liverpool. Alex says he'll speak to him about you.'

Con was beyond speech. He went out almost senseless with rage and fumbled blindly to open Rolo's compound. Milly yapped round his feet and he kicked her away, venting the anger that made bile rise violently into his mouth. He could barely trust himself not to go back in the house and shake Diane so he set off quickly, Rolo frisking beside him. He headed automatically for the canal and the path to the farm but he stopped at the corner shop on the way.

***

Lynn ushered Peter Ramsbottom out of the back door. There were no faults in the double glazing. That should have been a relief but why was the house so cold? She thought of the old woman grinning at her and shivered.

'These old houses can be very chilly. It's the stone floors. They're not like town properties. Country people were never used to mollycoddling.' He looked pityingly at her.

He annoyed her with his patronising manner but she'd been glad of his arrival. It had broken up the uneasy threesome of herself, Dan and Imogen at the breakfast table.

While Dan had seemed oblivious to everything but his newspaper, Lynn had been unable to eat, agonising in case Imogen gave something away with his conspiratorial glances and sidelong smiles.

Normally she would have been delighted to have Dan at home for the whole day; they would have slopped around in jeans and sweatshirts, watching football on TV with their feet up. Today she couldn't face it. She wanted to go out, anywhere away from them both but she was afraid to leave Imogen alone with Dan.

She waited till Ramsbottom had driven off before going upstairs to make the already tidy bed. Although the sky was overcast and looked set for rain, there was nothing ghostly about the bedroom this morning, with its bright bedding and cushions. The window framed a vee-shaped flight of geese, trailing across the sky like a carelessly stitched embroidery.

Someone was behind her. She felt a presence, a wave of cold on her back. She didn't want to look round, but her feet seemed to turn of their own accord. She cried out at the shape in the doorway till she recognised the Darth Vader tattoo, the camouflage trousers.

'Last night – I cannae stop thinking about it.'

'Shhh! Dan might hear.' Fear chased round her body. He came into the room. She could tell he wanted to take her in his arms and she made herself rigid. 'Don't, please don't,' she prayed under her breath as she edged past him.

'You're no sorry, are ye?' He stopped uncertainly.

She reached the doorway, looked over the landing. Dan was in the hall looking through the post. 'I have to go out,' she said loudly. 'Why don't you go and see Andrew Chapman? He'll be glad of some company.' She rushed down the stairs before he could respond and began gathering her research folders into a book bag.

'I'm going to the library. I'll be back for lunch.'

Dan looked up. 'Why don't I come and meet you? We could have lunch in Ormskirk, on our own. Maybe have a look round the shops.'

'Great. One o'clock.' She had to get out, right now. She went to her car, gulping the fresh air. She could only hope that Imogen would keep his mouth shut.

***

The library was peaceful upstairs, away from the children's section. Lynn immediately felt calmer. The assistant helped her set up the microfilm viewer and left her alone. There were so many records; births, marriages, deaths and all in different parishes. After an hour of peering, Lynn's eyes were sore. She'd covered 1860 – 1865 without result. She closed her eyes for a moment and when she opened them again a name jumped out from the close written text. 'Blackmore, Reuben, born 3rd April 1865.'

Surely Blackmore had been one of the names on their family tree? Excitement made Lynn flush with energy. She was almost certain Lavinia Askin had married someone called Blackmore. She forgot her smarting eyes, changed the reel to twenty years ahead and scanned page after page of records.

Suddenly it was there. She sat back, reading it over and over again to make sure she wasn't mistaken. Daniel Blackmore, farmer, of Blackmoss Farm, Aughton born in 1865 had married Lavinia Askin, spinster, of Yew Cottage, Aughton, born in 1868, on 14th January 1887. There couldn't be more than one Lavinia Askin, could there? And the dates fitted the Sunday school date. Lavinia would have been seven years old in 1875. The birth date in their family Bible had looked like 1863, but it had been blurred. No wonder she hadn't found it earlier. She wrote the details down and began scanning later records for the births of their children.

'Lynn, I've been waiting outside for ages.' Dan's voice broke in on her, echoing round the quiet area. The librarian looked up from her desk with a frown. Lynn stared at him stupidly. She'd been in another world.

She clutched his arm. 'Look Dan, I found her. Lavinia, she's real.' She flashed back through the film.

'Of course she's real. It's no big thing.' Dan inspected the record. 'Yeah, well done. It's interesting, but it doesn't tell you very much does it?'

'It's a starting point.' Lynn rewound the film, put her papers away. Her back was aching and she was glad to stop even though part of her wanted to go on. The sight of Dan brought her guilt flooding back. He seemed perfectly normal and she relaxed a little. It would all blow over. If only she could undo what she had done, but it was too late for that. She would put it behind her, get on with her life, make it up to Dan. She would try harder and Dan would forget about Emma Cranton.

'I'm sorry I was late, I just got so excited.' She reached up to kiss him. 'Let's go and eat, I'm starving.'

**

The black lad answered the door. Con was taken aback. 'Andy told me to come round.'

'Me too.' The kid grinned. His eyes had a vague, vacant look. Con guessed he'd been drinking. He tied Rolo to the gate and squeezed in past Chapman's wheelchair.

The cottage living room was heavy with the smell of beer and the tang of marijuana. Chapman leaned back in his recliner, puffing on a joint. Football played silently on the huge television. It was a bit different from Con's mother's day. He coughed, pulled the whisky bottle out of his pocket and set it on the glass coffee table among the litter of rolling gear.

'I had a few nips out of it on the way over.'

Chapman offered him the joint. Con shook his head. 'I'll stick to the booze.'

'Get some glasses.' Chapman waved Imogen towards the kitchen. 'And what brings you here on a Saturday afternoon?'

Con's temper had cooled. He never talked about Diane, knowing how gossip spreads in a small village. He never criticised her to anyone outside his own head, but the threat to Rolo had hit him like a kick in the balls. His tongue loosened as a large whisky went down and his anger kindled all over again.

Andrew laughed softly as Con recounted the story. 'Bloody women eh?'

'And she expects me to sit down with her ex tonight while he interviews me for a job like I were some useless relation.'

'You need to get on top, man.' Chapman squinted through a cloud of smoke and leaned forward to stub the joint out in the cluttered ashtray. 'Show her who's boss.'

'Listen who's talking.' Con reached for the bottle again, poured three shots. 'Bet you didn't get that stuff out shopping with your mam.'

'I've still got friends.' Andrew tapped his nose. 'What she doesn't know won't hurt her.'

'You'll look sick if she comes round and catches you.'

'She's away at the shop all day. She won't get round to checking up on me till late. Anyway, it's different for me. You think I'd put up with her bossing me about for one minute if I didn't have to? Soon as I get back on my feet, I'll be away. Women, they'll bury you if you let them. Stand up for yourself, mate, that's my advice.'

Con flushed. 'I don't need you to tell me how to run my marriage.' He half-rose out of the chair.

'All right, calm down. It's okay.' Chapman leaned forward, filled Con's glass again, started to roll another joint. 'What about you?' he turned to Imogen. 'You let girls give you the runaround?'

'No way.' Imogen gulped at his drink. 'This is good whisky.'

'Suppose you'd know, where you come from. Get it from your

mother's tit, don't you?'

Imogen snickered uncertainly.

'You fucked a girl yet? You don't look old enough?'

Con looked up. Chapman's voice had a sneering edge. 'Lay off the kid, eh, Andy?'

'Course I have.' Imogen blushed faintly.

'What are they like, Scottish women? I've had girls from all nations, but I never sampled Scotch pussy.'

Imogen took the proffered joint and sucked the smoke down, saving him from answering. Con felt uneasy. He should have just gone for a walk by himself. He would finish his drink and go, but then he would have to leave the whisky bottle behind.

'You won't find the local lasses so easy. Bet you've had no luck there.'

Imogen giggled. 'That's where you're wrong.' He knocked back his whisky and wiped his mouth.

'Come on then, who is it?' Chapman's eyes gleamed. 'One of the girls from the village? Does she do this for you?' He pulled a glossy magazine from under the cushion of his chair and threw it on to the table. It was open on a full face shot, the girl's red mouth stretched round a huge, veiny cock.

Imogen looked startled then began to laugh. Con laughed too but alarm surged through him. What had got into Chapman? Yesterday he had been the old Andrew Con had always known, except for the despair he was trying to hide. Con had felt sorry for him but today with all his laces undone, he was showing a new, unpleasant side. And why take it out on the boy? He was going too far with him; the atmosphere was getting out of control.

'Hope you're using protection. You never know what you might catch.' Imogen looked stupidly at him.

'You're not, are you?' Andrew smacked his forehead. 'Christ! What a wally! Here, look in the sideboard drawer. There's a box of army issue ones there. I got no use for them now.'

'You mean you can't – ?' Con's hand instinctively covered his crotch.

The smile wiped off Chapman's face. 'Well and truly fucked.' His face twisted and he forced a grin. 'It'll come back. They say it will come back.' His eyes were desperate. Con looked away, down into his glass.

'So you get a fucking glove on it, mate, before you start putting it round or you'll end up with a kid and a pile of debt before you even hit twenty-one, that's if you don't catch AIDS or the clap.'

'Leave him alone, for fuck's sake,' Con burst out. He drained his glass. 'It's bloody cold in here.'

'It's that old woman. She left the door open,' Imogen said.

Con's hand froze on the glass. He looked up the hall. The front door was shut.

'Old woman?' Chapman looked befuddled. 'What old woman?'

'She just came in and went up the stairs.'

Con shot out of his seat and ran up the stairs to his mother's bedroom. It was empty, the neat bed obviously unused. He ran to the other room where Chapman must sleep.

'There's no one there.' He came down the stairs feeling the cold at his back.

'You're fucking nuts,' Chapman said to Imogen. 'Seeing things.'

'Too much to drink.' He was only a kid, Con thought, couldn't handle it.

'Yeah. No more ganga for you.'

Imogen looked dazed, near to tears. 'I'll take him home when I go,' Con thought. He remembered Diane, looked at his watch. 'Jesus, it's seven o'clock. I'm supposed to be home.'

'Ah have another one,' Chapman poured the last of the whisky, slopping it on the table. 'Don't be a fucking old woman.'

***

Look at these three, in my house, in my own living room, looking at filthy pictures, talking smut, turning my home into a den of drugs and drink. Annie Chapman's lad were never like this afore he went away. It's not just his foul mouth and bad habits brought back from the army and foreign countries. There's something hard and cruel in him now like he's lost touch with himself.

I seen our Con going past and I followed him here, I could see how unhappy he were. He'll never settle in that new place. I were up at the farm, enjoying having the place to myself for once, even though it made me sad going from room to room, reliving all our family's life, me and Joan as young girls, Mam and Dad, young and strong, then older, me and Bert full of life and energy when we first got the farm. It were like I could still hear their voices in the walls, see their shadows slipping away round the corners, as if the shades of the old rooms themselves were still there for all the new paint and furniture.

It would have been better if I'd stayed there, than coming here to see my home desecrated and our Con taking part in it. He might as well have slapped me in the face.

I'm getting to the point of disowning you, Con. I can't forgive the things you're doing and I can't stand to watch you go down this way. You don't see me, but that boy does all right, a stranger. All you see is that woman and she's making you blind, to your family, your own mother, even to yourself.

***

'I couldn't believe it when I found them.' Lynn was delighted when her mother rang,

'It's fantastic news. Did you find anything else?'

'I couldn't find any children, but I didn't have much time left. Dan came to take me to lunch.'

'Well there must be some.' Her mother's laugh trickled through the mobile.

'I'll bet there's a connection to these Askins who lived here. I can feel it in my bones.'

'That place is getting to you. You might be right, though it'll take a lot of digging. Are you sure you have time for all this?'

'It makes a change from the house and garden. It is a bit isolated here, but I love it. Except – ' she hesitated.

'What?'

'Oh, I know it sounds silly but sometimes, there's a strange atmosphere – I've had these really weird dreams – and I've seen – '

'What?'

'I don't know – these women.'

'Women?'

'Just glimpses, then there's nothing there.'

'You mean ghosts? You think the place is haunted?'

'I don't believe in ghosts. But I've seen them, here in the house, out at the cottage. They just watch me.'

'Listen Lynn, moving into an old place often feels like that. You've always lived in modern properties before. When your dad and I bought this house, I used to feel as if people were watching me, people who'd lived here before me. It went away once I got to think of the house as my own. That's all it is, you'll see, once you settle in.'

'They seem so real, and frightening. It's as if they don't want us here.'

'I don't suppose Dan has seen them?'

'No, but Imogen has.'

'He's probably on drugs, ready to see anything you suggest. I don't know what you were thinking of taking that boy in. You've more to fear from him than any ghost. You always were one for taking in waifs and strays – all those injured birds when you were a girl and remember that flea-bitten hedgehog? Typical Pisces. Honestly, love, you're over-reacting. The country is full of funny noises, creaks and rustlings, especially in old houses.'

'You are still coming to stay in the spring?'

'Your father's scheduled a week off especially for it. It's a pity we can't make it for your birthday. Has Dan got anything special planned?'

'Not as far as I know,' Lynn said brightly, thinking that Dan had too many other things on his mind to think about her birthday.

'We can't wait to see you. Take more than a few ghosts to put us off. Don't worry, we'll frighten them away for you.'

As soon as her mother had gone, Lynn was aware of the silence in the house. Dan was a long time at Raj's, getting a takeaway for their supper, but it was Saturday, the busiest night. She switched on the television where a wife was castigating her husband for his infidelity. Lynn wondered what her mother would think if she knew she'd been unfaithful to Dan. There was no one she could confide in. All her fears flooded back and she let tears well up and spill out on the sofa cushion where she lay.

She heard the back door open and struggled to compose herself. Dan mustn't see her like this, but it was Imogen listing and lurching into the lounge. She could smell the drink on him as soon as he came in.

'Look at the state of you!' She was horrified. How had he got so drunk?

He dropped onto the sofa, trapping her legs. 'I'm no so bad, just a few bevvies. Con Worrall brought a drop of whisky round to Andy's.'

She struggled to sit up but his weight held her down. His breath stank of whisky and smoke. He laid his head on her chest and his hand sneaked under her sweater. Her body instantly responded then reason took over. Dan might walk in at any moment. Fear lent her strength. She pushed up hard and Imogen tipped onto the floor.

'Whassamatter wi ye?' He began to laugh.

'It's not funny, Imogen. Dan's only gone to the takeaway.'

'So? He doesna care anyway. I care. I'll take care of ye.'

'Don't be stupid. I love Dan.'

'Ye loved me last night. Dinna tell me I'm wrong.'

Her face blazed red. She had to stop him before Dan came in and heard him.

'Come on, let's get you upstairs.' She pulled him to his feet.

'Good idea. Are ye coming with me?' He groped her buttocks as she supported him up the stairs but she ignored it in her panic to get him out of sight. She manoeuvred him into his room and shut the door.

'Imogen – last night – it shouldn't have happened.'

'Ye liked it well enough.' He looked sulky.

'I can't deny that, but it wasn't right.'

'Dinna worry, look I got these.' He pulled a handful of condoms out of his pocket.

Lynn stared at them. 'Where did they come from?' Her heart felt squeezed.

'Andy gied them to me.'

The blood drained out of her head and body. It was all in her feet, weighing them down on the floor as if she would never move again.

'You told Andrew Chapman about us?'

'Ah no, it wasna like that.'

'And Con Worrall was there too?'

'Come on now, they didna know it was you.'

Her head cleared to the single picture of the three of them drunkenly discussing her. Movement came suddenly and she flew at him, punching out with balled fists. He laughed, caught her easily and pinned her against the wall. She twisted her head and his kiss slobbered down her cheek.

'Get off me!' Rage powered her and her push knocked him backwards so he fell on the bed. She stood over him, bracing her legs. 'Get this straight. Last night was a mistake, a one-off. It was my fault, I shouldn't have let you – '

She bit her lip. His eyes reminded her of a cow's, huge and uncomprehending. 'Forget it Imogen. I don't love you, I don't want you. I love Dan, he's my husband. Just forget it ever happened.'

The tension was gone from the room. She sat down on the edge of the bed, spent, her legs trembling. He curled in a foetal ball, back turned.

'I'm sorry.' She touched his shoulder.

He jerked away. 'Dinna fash yersel, ye scabby cunt. You and your man deserve each other.'

The words struck her like pebbles. She got up, stiff with hurt. 'I'm going to have a bath. You sleep it off and we won't mention it any more.'

She went out and ran the bath. The noises of running water drowned out the sounds of Imogen blundering around his room. Why didn't he just go to sleep? What if he was still carrying on when Dan got back?

Where was Dan, anyway? For once she was glad he was late. At last there was silence but even the hot water failed to relax her. Her mind twisted and knotted with despair. She had brought all this on herself with her own pride at playing the Good Samaritan, thinking she could make life right for Imogen. Instead, she'd made it worse. Would he ever trust a woman again?

She sank under the surface, letting her hair float around her like water weed. After a while she sat up and soaped her body vigorously. However much she tried to turn away from the decision she knew he would have to go. They made a volatile triangle and it was only a matter of time before Imogen would let it all out. He was too young to control himself. Pain penetrated her thoughts. She looked down at the loofah in her hands. The skin of her breasts and belly was chafed raw.

'You in there, Lynn?' Dan knocked at the bathroom door.

Lynn stood up, reaching for a towel. 'Come in. You've been a long time.' He brought the smell of Indian spices with him.

'I met Con Worrall. He was pissed, insisted on buying me a pint in the Farmers'. I didn't like to refuse. That mad Irishman was in there too. I had the devil of a job to get out again.'

Lynn's heart almost stopped but Dan was smiling, his eyes clear and friendly, so Con couldn't have known, or had kept quiet if he did. She had to get over this, she couldn't spend her days worrying about whether the whole village was gossiping about her.

'Where was the kid going?'

Her head jerked up in surprise. 'Imogen?'

'I passed him on the road, going the opposite way. Looked like he had a full backpack.'

Lynn pushed past Dan. Imogen's bedroom door stood ajar. She stopped with her hand on the doorknob, called his name, but she already knew she would find the room empty, all his belongings gone.

Chapter Eight

April 2008

Lynn sat in the summerhouse at the top of the garden at Dove Cottage, looking out over the houses to the polished steel surface of Grasmere and the tawny-red rise of Loughrigg Fell. The Wordsworths had sat here, also Coleridge and the Hutchinson sisters. The sense of their presence, of the continuity from past to present, comforted her. Fragments of their poetry drifted through her mind and she felt calmer. The turmoil of driving up the motorway with the blood pounding in her ears was fading, likewise the sick feeling that had lodged in the pit of her stomach when she'd done the test that morning.

Had it been joy or horror that she'd felt? She still didn't know. She'd only known that she couldn't think in the familiar environment of the farm, especially with her parents visiting, expecting her to make small talk. Even though she'd half-expected the result, she'd refused to think about it before so the shock had been such that she had to get away and this was the first place she'd thought of to find sanctuary.

The day was warm and lazy, perfect for the Lakes. Spring flowers and the last of the famed daffodils poked out from the grass, the occasional bee buzzing round. Because it was only ten-thirty there were few tourists in the cottage and its garden, not enough to interrupt Lynn's thoughts.

Pregnant – after all these years, her hopes finally justified. It had to be the move to the land, a more natural way of life. The doctors had told them to relax, stop worrying. There was no reason why they should not conceive. She tried to convince herself, but the dreaded alternative kept rearing its head with the repeated refrain, what if, what if, what if the baby were Imogen's? All this time, she and Dan had made fruitless love, then after a one night stand with a stranger she'd conceived. Wasn't it highly likely to be Imogen's child? No, it was unthinkable, a one in a million chance. The child could equally well be Dan's. Could she contemplate destroying Dan's child? Could she think of abortion in any case, no matter whose child it was?

As she sat with her arms folded round her stomach, staring across the lake, these thoughts chased round her head. Wordsworth had sat here composing. She thought of him writing here and lines flowed into her head.

> *'Like a shipwrecked sailor tost*
> *By rough waves on a perilous coast,*
> *Lies the Babe, in helplessness*
> *And in tenderest nakedness,*
> *Flung by labouring Nature forth*
> *Upon the mercies of the earth.*
> *Can its eyes beseech?-no more*
> *Than the hands are free to implore:*
> *Voice but serves for one brief cry.'*

The soothing rhythm, the sentiments, calmed her racing mind. She thought of the infants and young children loved and lost, buried in the Grasmere churchyard and peace enfolded her. The decision was made. Whatever the outcome she had a single purpose from now on and nothing would move her from it.

***

They was building the new school in Chapel Lane when I found out I were pregnant. I remember going past it when I come out of Dr Medlock's surgery. 'That's where my boy'll go to school,' I thought. It were right next to the old one where Bert and me went, although the headmistress Miss Brennan had retired years ago. There were a headmaster there by the time Con went to school, but I can't recall his name.

I were floating on air that day, after all the years of waiting, well not even waiting really. Me and Bert had given up by then, we thought we weren't meant to have no children but all of a sudden there it were growing in my belly. For weeks my thoughts and hopes skipped round it; I tried to ignore it, push it away, but for all that I never thought of nothing else the whole time till Dr Medlock made it real for me and I could tell Bert, Dad and

Mother, the whole world. I knew right away it would be a boy.

That's when the fear started, of all the things that might go wrong. He were such a little thing floating in there and when he got bigger and I could feel him pushing and struggling to turn himself inside me, I were afeared there'd be something wrong with him when he did come out, like Peggy, Mrs Allsop's mongol daughter: or that I might die in childbirth, after all I were old to be having a first child at thirty-two.

And when he were born and I seen how helpless he were it were even worse, what with all the talk on TV about the Russians and the Americans with their nuclear bombs. I were convinced we were all going to die.

I could remember the last war, how we used to see the glow in the sky at night as the docks burned in Liverpool. In the day when we went about our work, the land were solid, familiar, everything as it always was, but at night the fields sank into the dark and that fiery light shivered our spines. Not far away, hell was breaking loose. How long before it came creeping closer, came to us, the dreaded wave of invasion, to shatter our lives? We lived in fear of the burning, the destruction of our crops, the sound of booted feet, the blowing apart of our very landscape as if our whole world might disappear.

But in 1962, it weren't like that. There wouldn't be no watching, no hoping to be passed over, saved or rescued. These new bombs would destroy the whole world. If you was lucky you'd be instant ash, otherwise you'd get the lingering sickness, your own land blasted and poisoned, no one left to nurse or care for you.

I used to pick Con up and hold him tight, wondering what would become of us, thinking me and Bert had done a terrible thing bringing him into this world. What could I do to protect him? It were like a radioactive cloud were hanging over me already. It were only in the moment of keeping up with the cabbage planter, or the potato picker, in the race to get the barley in before it rained, that I truly forgot. Even in bed with Bert, if I lost myself for a few moments, as soon as it were over I were thinking what if we had conceived another child to be brought forward for destruction?

But it didn't turn out like that. Somehow all that fear got lost in amongst everything else that were going on. New things seemed to come fast and furious, the Beatles, flowers and music, miniskirts, new cars, bingo halls. Not that we saw much of them, only on the telly and there were precious little time for watching that. But we felt the atmosphere of good times and more money, even in our village. We worked hard and made a good living. By the time things turned bad in the seventies, we'd forgot the threat of nuclear war. We was too busy trying to make ends meet with prices rising like rockets. Little Con grew big and strong and me and Albert were content even though no more babies come along. All we ever wanted were to keep on doing what we'd always done.

Everything's different now. These modern wars seem smaller and further away, so you don't really notice what's going on. I could never keep track of them or understand what were happening or why. It all looks the same on TV. It were easier just to forget about it. It's only seeing Annie Chapman's boy that's brought it back to me how our Thomas were; how people are changed by war, not just governments or countries.

Now there's to be a babby on the farm again. That makes a difference. It tore me apart to see Con with no children, the last of our line. It's hard to accept this Lynn taking over my land, my home, but now I see her with that glow about her she reminds me of myself. There's a new confidence about her that makes me think she may be some use here after all.

I were here this morning when she were doing one of them newfangled tests and I watched her take off in a right flummox. She doesn't know which one of them it belongs to. I tried to tell her not to worry, there's many a child doesn't know its own father, although if it comes out coloured there won't be no doubts. It's a hard choice once you admit there is a choice, but there is no choice as far as I can see. I hope she makes the right decision. A child's a child no matter who its father be and if she's right and she is related to our family that means her child will carry on our line, the rightful heir to New Cut farm. And that changes everything.

***

'I think I might be pregnant.' The tremulous joy that sang in

Lynn's body quivered in her voice. Even though she'd slept on her decision, she still felt uncertain. It was such an enormous event, so unexpected, that she could only approach it by qualifying it.

'Don't you know?' Her mother, ever practical, stared at her. She put down the magazine she'd been reading. There was a moment's silence as they looked at each other, broken only by the humming of a large bumble bee that was exploring the tulips by the back door.

It was an effort for Lynn to take a deep breath and say, 'Yes.' As she did so, she felt another flood of joy but also a deep calm, as if the affirmation made it concrete; as if the tiny thing inside knew it was accepted, given an identity, was already loved.

'Darling. When?' Her mother got up from the picnic table, came to her and kissed her cheek.

'Around the end of November, I think.' Lynn thought back to that time in February, then pushed the pictures that crowded into her mind away. 'I haven't told Dan yet.' She stared across the yard. Matt Pilling's tractor was ploughing the far field.

She watched as the ploughshare lifted. It glinted in the sunlight like a guillotine as Pilling turned the tractor, ready for the next furrow. Black earth spurted up from the huge wheels. The tractor set off down the field again, turning rich slices of soil like chocolate cake to lie against the previous year's vegetation.

'You're telling me before you've told your husband?'

Lynn shifted on the bench. 'I'm just waiting for the right moment. I only did the test yesterday. Dan got home so late last night, then he was in his study. I was asleep by the time he came up.'

'We'd begun to think you weren't going to have any children.' Her mother's voice was hesitant. 'Of course, we didn't want to pry. Your dad will be pleased as punch.'

'Don't tell him yet. Not till I've told Dan. I'll speak to him tonight.' The prospect loomed before her like a dreaded task instead of joyful news. She was not sure Dan would share her delight. That seemed a dreadful thing to think but nowadays Dan was becoming a stranger, his world spinning away from hers. He was always away for weekends at conferences, supposedly worked late most nights and spent most of his time at home on the computer in his study. Often she thought she could smell Emma Cranton's perfume when he came in, but it was never strong enough for her to be sure. It was a far cry from the dreams she'd had when they'd moved here. He'd resisted every attempt she'd made to involve him in the house and garden but now things would be different. The news might come as a shock but he would come round. They loved each other. How could he fail to love their child?

But what if – ? She cut off the little voice before it could get started, drained the last of the cold coffee from her cup and stood up. 'I'd better get on with these.' She picked up the tray of pansies and her trowel.

'Take it easy now,' her mother advised. 'You need to be a bit careful at first, just for a few weeks.'

For a moment, Lynn felt uncertain again. It was not yet a baby then, just a tentative, burrowing ball of cells, that might be easily dislodged, flushed out, an unknown, a never-was.

No, her mother was wrong. Already it was there, formed, clinging tightly to her for life. She sensed its determination, making itself known to her body, declaring itself.

'I'm fine.' She grinned. 'Anyway, Barney's coming to help with the garden.'

'That Irishman's a complete reprobate.' Her mother's voice was sharp, but a smile crossed her face.

'I just love the way he garbles the Lake poets. His versions even sound better sometimes. Just what I need, a postmodern Irishman. At least we have something in common and he's a good worker. I need the help, now Imogen's gone.'

Just saying his name conjured up guilt. What would he say if he knew? But there's nothing for him to know, she told herself.

'Have you heard anything from him?'

'Not a word.'

'I wonder what made him take off like that. I thought you said he was happy here?'

'It was right after he got drunk with Andrew Chapman and Con Worrall. Maybe it was something they said to him.'

'I shouldn't worry.' Her mother stood up. 'It was good of you to take him in in the first place. You were there when he needed someone.'

Lynn felt her face flooding red. If she kept quiet maybe her mother would shut up or talk about something else.

Her mother slipped her arms into the sleeves of her cardigan. 'These young people today don't think about others, about letting people know that they're safe. It's all this mobility, backpacking and gap years. They think wandering about is perfectly okay. At least he didn't make off with your valuables.'

'No,' Lynn said vaguely. She held the tray of pansies in one hand. The other hand folded over her stomach. Pilling's tractor had divided the field neatly into two halves, one black, one grey-green.

'Have you seen the doctor yet?'

'No.'

'You need to do it soon. Make sure everything's all right and get your hospital bed booked.'

Her mother gathered her glasses and magazine. 'I'd better get ready. We're going into Liverpool to see what they're doing for the Capital of Culture year. Your dad says we'd better take the opportunity while we're here.'

'Dan says they're still building, I don't know if the new part is open yet.'

'You haven't been?' Her mother looked incredulous.

'Not since February.' The day she'd collected Imogen from the station.

'Come with us today. I don't know why you didn't wait for your father and I yesterday instead of dashing off by yourself. We would have enjoyed a day at the Lakes.'

'I'm sorry. I just needed some time alone to think. The thought of starting a family scared me; it's a huge change after all these years.'

'Well, surely you could have confided in your own mother? Come on, why not get ready and join us? It'll be nice to spend the day together, just the three of us. That Irishman can sort the flowers out.'

'I don't know,' Lynn wavered. 'I really want to do them myself, and I planned to make something nice for tonight, make dinner a special occasion if I'm going to tell Dan this evening. I don't want to be rushing around, I want to feel relaxed.'

'Of course.' Her mother leaned over, touched her hand. 'Don't cook for us tonight. Your dad and I will eat out. And we'll sneak in quietly. We won't disturb you.'

After her parents had driven off, Lynn got ready to fill the planters for the pansies with compost. She turned to pick up her trowel and saw the woman standing by the back door. It was the same woman she'd seen with the baby a few weeks ago, but now she was heavily pregnant, one hand holding up the weight of her belly.

Lynn gaped. The woman smiled at her. Suddenly Blondie ran into the yard and stopped by the back door, whining softly and thumping her tail. She was looking up, straight at the pregnant woman.

Barney Dougan stumped into the yard. 'Fine morning, Mrs Waters, fine morning and that's a great batch of pansies you're planting there. Here Blondie, stop that. Where's your manners now?'

Blondie ignored him, she sat up and begged by the door. Lynn stared as the woman stooped to stroke the dog's head. Barney grabbed Blondie by the collar and pulled her to his side.

'Give over there, Blondie. It's the divvil himself got into her today, Missus, I'm sure.'

'This used to be her home?' She watched as the dog struggled to get out of Barney's grip.

'Aye, she can still sense the old woman about the place, I dare say.' He looked around the farmyard in every direction except for the spot where the woman was standing. She was smiling conspiratorially at Lynn now. Lynn felt the corners of her own mouth twitch.

'Alice.' Lynn looked at the woman. The woman smiled again. Lynn sat down heavily on the bench by the door. It was the same woman. All the women she had seen were the same one, the old lady, the new mother, this pregnant woman, they were all Alice Worrall, at different stages of her life. Con's mother. She remembered Diane had said that any ghost appearing would be Con's mother, coming back to haunt her. But the sense of menace Lynn remembered from her last appearance had gone. The way Alice was holding her belly and smiling made her think she knew that Lynn too was pregnant, and that she was glad.

The yellow pansies shone in the sun, their heads waving in the breeze. When she looked back, the woman had gone. Blondie was sniffing the ground by the door. Everything looked normal, just an ordinary bright spring day. The only thing moving on the landscape was Pilling's tractor, the noise of it a faint whine across the land.

Barney lit his roll-up and puffed a stream of smoke. 'Well now, I'd best be getting started, while the weather's fine.

'Come sweet April, whom all men praise,
Bring your pansies up to the Raise.'

Lynn burst out laughing.

Barney grinned. 'The daffodils come too early now to fit the poem. Anyways, what is it I'm to be doing today?'

'I have to go down to Holmes.' Lynn got up again. She looked around for Alice but there was no sign of her. 'I've left some bundles of cabbage and sprout plants out that Mr Pilling brought me. Maybe you could put those in. It's already limed, I did it myself last week. And then maybe you could start on the potato trenches.'

'Aye, diggin' potato trenches is no work for a woman as's not used to it.' Barney squinted at the heap of manure waiting at the side of the vegetable plot. 'And the weed needs keeping down, it'll be out of hand in no time with this sunshine on top of the rain.'

'I'll try to get it hoed over.' Lynn was only just beginning to realise the amount of work that would be needed to keep the vegetable plot clean, work that she probably wouldn't be able to manage.

'Do you think you could come for a few more hours a week?'

'I'll see what I can do, but I've other jobs beside this one, and I'm not so young as I was. No sign of that lad coming back to help you?'

'No.' Lynn picked up her trowel and the empty plant trays. 'No, he won't be back.' She went inside and made Barney some tea. She'd tried to contact Imogen several times right after he left but there'd been no answer, the phone in her hand like a dead thing, the number ringing out into space, no one there, as if Imogen had never existed in the first place. She'd tried to forget about him after that until she'd missed her period. Yesterday, she'd agonised over whether to try again but what was the point? The child would be hers, hers and Dan's. It was nothing to do with Imogen. But if it were black, indisputably Imogen's, how would Dan react? It didn't matter. She would deal with it when the time came. The child was hers and she would raise it alone if necessary. She finished making the tea and took a shopping bag from behind the kitchen door, ready to set off for Holmes to buy vegetables for their supper.

Halfway down the road a blue van shot past her and swung into the entrance to Holmes farm.

The van was brand new. She could smell the newness when she came into the yard and got close to it, before the shouting drove it from her mind.

'I'm going and that's all there is to it.'

'One of us will have to go with you. You can't manage.'

'I'm going on my own. Stop trying to treat me like a fucking baby, Mam.'

'Don't you speak to me like that. I can't let you go on your own. I'd be worried sick.'

'You don't have a choice. You don't know what – '

The voices broke off as they both saw Lynn hovering uncertainly by the van. Annie Chapman came to the shop door.

'Come in, come in. We were just – '

She waved Lynn inside. Her face was even redder than usual. 'We'll have to talk about this later,' she hissed at her son.

'There's nothing to talk about.' He turned the wheelchair savagely, almost running over Lynn's foot. He glared at her as she held the door open for him and shot out into the concrete yard.

'Don't you have to help him?' Lynn watched as he fumbled with the keys to the van.

'Heaven forbid.' Annie picked up a crate of cabbages and banged it down on an empty display shelf. 'This new van's specially adapted. He only got it yesterday. There's no living with him already.'

'But it'll give him independence?'

'It's too much, too soon.' She turned her direct gaze on Lynn, but her blue eyes looked watery. 'He needs to get used to it. He wants to go to Liverpool at the weekend, wants to go on his own to see Everton play. He's not ready. I'm not ready. I'm terrified for him. I can't help it. You read all these terrible things in the papers.'

She lifted the cabbages out one by one, arranging them in neat rows on the plastic grass that covered the shelf. 'Anyway, enough of me. How are you?'

'I'm fine.' She longed to tell Annie, tell everybody. Holding it in was cruelty when it longed to burst out, fill the whole world. She looked out of the window. Andrew's wheelchair was gliding up the ramp into the van. The pleasure withered inside her. Imagine something like that happening to your child. At least he was alive. She thought again of the pitiful children's graves at Grasmere and her heart twisted with fear.

She turned away. Annie was looking curiously at her. Was it possible that she suspected? People said you got an aura when you were newly pregnant. That's just how it felt, Lynn thought, forgetting about Andrew, like your whole body was lit up from inside, shining out for all to see.

'I've come for some vegetables for supper. It's a special occasion, well sort of.' She laughed. 'Any time Dan's home for supper lately seems to be an occasion for celebration.'

Annie's expression was quizzical, her curious eyes on Lynn's.

Why had she said that, letting Annie know her business? 'He works so hard,' she added, trying to dispel any suggestion of disloyalty.

'Let's have a coffee.' Annie took the empty crate into the back of the shop and switched the kettle on. 'I see you've got Barney Dougan helping out.' She spooned coffee into two mugs.

'It's too much for me on my own. Dan's too busy to help.'

'What happened to that boy you had working for you?' Annie passed her a mug.

'Oh, he wasn't really working for us. He was just staying a while, an old family friend. He moved on, went back to Scotland.' The lies dropped easily, now she had told the story so many times.

'Are you okay?' Annie pointed to the kitchen chair by the tiny table. 'Here, sit down. You look a bit peaky.'

Lynn realised she was clutching her stomach. She put her mug down on the table and sat on the chair. 'No, I'm fine,' she insisted. 'Mr Pilling's started ploughing. Thanks for putting him on to us. Dan gets on with him really well.'

'That's what neighbours are for.' Annie leaned against the sink. 'It's good to see the land being worked again. We're just hoping that with all these price rises, people will turn back to local produce. We've been getting a few more customers in lately and the Ormskirk shop and the market stalls are doing well. People are starting to count their pennies. Maybe they'll stop buying all that exotic stuff at the supermarkets, go back to basics. So, you're settled in now, definitely stopping?'

The question took Lynn by surprise. If Annie had asked this a few weeks ago when the ghost had first started appearing, she might not have been so sure but Alice no longer seemed frightening; today she'd appeared quite benign.

She laughed. 'We love it. The garden's under way. Con Worrall did the fences.'

'He always were a good worker. Mind you, he won't be doing much of that now.'

'What do you mean?'

'He's left the woodyard. Didn't you know? He's got a job working in one of them big computer shops, PC World or somewhere down in Liverpool.'

'No, you're joking!'

'Must pay well, he's a company car now. Not that I know, I never seen him for weeks, but that's what they're saying in the village.'

Lynn thought of Con swinging the hammer as he worked on her fence, his ownership of himself and of the land and the way he'd looked scornfully at her, as if she were an intruder. Surely it would be deadly for him to work in a sterile place like a computer shop. But then, it wasn't her fault that Con had given up his land.

'What would you do if you had to sell this place?'

Annie stared at her. Her whole body stiffened and she burst out laughing.

'Sell our land? Never. I never thought of such a thing, nor Jim neither. Jim's family's been here almost as long as Askins and my family still farms across the moss at Lathom. We'll be here even if we has to live on bread and water. But Andrew –' her eyes clouded over. 'I don't know about when we're gone. Our Penny and her husband won't want it. We'd always expected that Andrew would take it over but now, I don't know what will happen. It's a worry.'

'I feel guilty sometimes.' Lynn hesitated. 'You know, we're

strangers here, coming from the Midlands, taking someone else's land, someone whose family's always lived here.'

'Don't be so daft.' Annie's eyes rounded with surprise. 'It's nowt to do with you. It's true Alice Worrall would swing for Con if she could see what he's done, but he's only got what he deserved. It were his choice to sell the farm. Not your problem, girl. It's yours now and all that matters is that you look after it.'

Yes, Lynn thought, it's a stewardship. The responsibility was a justification, taking her guilt away. Maybe Alice was there to make sure she accepted it, not to scare her away as she'd previously thought, or maybe her attitude had changed, because of the baby.

***

Con ripped off his tie the minute he got in the car. He sat there for a few moments with the windows open, letting the build up of heat escape. The sun was fading fast now, but it had been a scorcher for April, a fine day for raking the soil, ready for sowing the first of the season's carrots.

He undid the top button of his shirt, feeling uncomfortable all over. His legs itched inside his trousers, his feet hurt and the shirt felt clammy and sweaty against his back. He reached into the glove compartment for the half-bottle of whisky he kept there. He took a nip, just a little one, before he started the engine and joined the queue of cars waiting to leave the retail park.

Six weeks he'd been at Computerland and it felt like six years. The move from Ramsbottom's had happened so quickly he hadn't had time to think about it. Looking back, he felt sure that Diane had known about it even before she brought the idea of changing jobs up, back in February. He didn't want to think about the way Diane was so friendly with Alex. It didn't seem right. How would she feel if he were forever chatting to Christine on the phone? She'd even gone out to dinner with him when Justin was home for half-term. 'He is Justin's father,' she'd said. 'It's just a family thing, Con.'

But she hadn't invited him. And there it was again, the children thing, rubbing his nose in his childlessness. But then she'd put her arms round his neck, run her fingers through his hair and pulled his face to hers and between the touch of her hot mouth and the smell of her warm body, his thoughts had scattered. No matter what, he had her now, the real living Diane. He was the winner, not Alex, it was him she came home to.

The car crawled past Aintree racecourse. He tried to work out how long it would take him to get to the Farmers' Arms. At this rate it might be over an hour. His hand went to the glove compartment again but he stopped himself. It wouldn't do to be over the limit, not here in the city and in a company car. He could stop halfway home at the Fox and Goose for a quick half. Out in the country it would be safer and a small one would be okay.

The pub was bright and noisy when all Con wanted was cool and quiet. It smelled of hot food and grease and the tables were filled with people eating. He sat on a stool at the bar. There was no one to talk to, the bar staff were all young kids and they were busy taking orders. He didn't know anyone. The first glass of beer was empty in five minutes.

He opened the folder he'd brought from work and checked his sales figures. He might just make the month's targets with a bit of luck but it wasn't easy, putting up with the customers, flattering them and pushing them to buy. It took the patience of a saint and money was getting tight. He wasn't used to selling. It was okay for the others, the young ones with their snappy suits, even the older ones looked the same. They all had the gift of the gab, like Aspinwall, the estate agent. It was a game to them, they enjoyed it. They thought he was slow, he'd seen them laughing behind his back. And tomorrow he had a training day. That meant being trapped in a room full of people and computers all day, playing silly games about how to relate to your workmates, how to be part of the team. The second glass was empty. He hesitated a moment before ordering a third.

He couldn't believe it was ten o'clock when he got up to leave. He sat in the car, looking at the massed tree shapes on the flat land behind the car park. Now it was cold and quiet but his forehead felt hot. He rested it on the steering wheel, the dark landscape still printed behind his closed eyes.

He thought of that other landscape, its lines so familiar, the outlines of the elder bushes along the ditch fronting the farm. Witch trees, his mother had called them. They walked at night, she used to say and Con remembered how this had frightened him when he was small, how he used to hide under the bedclothes in his room, imagining he could hear the elders whispering outside his window, tapping on the glass with twiggy fingers. He would pull the curtains in the mornings to see the bushes back at their stations, crane to see if there was any change in their positions, but they were crafty, they always returned to the same places.

He awoke to a light shining in his eyes. Something was tapping at the window. He wound it down, shivering as the night air rushed in.

'Closing up now, sir. You can't stay here.'

'Uh?' Con lifted his head, peered at the shining torch beam. He couldn't see the man's face.

'You're not going to drive, are you? Why don't you call a taxi?'

Con felt in his pockets for his phone. A dog jumped up barking, pushed its nose against the window. It was a border collie.

'Wha' time's it?' He struggled to look at his watch. He had forgotten about Rolo. He just hoped Diane had fed him and let him out.

'Time you were home. Look, I'll ring for a cab. Where do you live? Come on, sir, out you come. Lock the car up. You can pick it up in the morning.'

Con salvaged the whisky bottle. There were a few dregs in it still. He shielded his eyes against the lights of the taxi as it turned into the car park. On the way home, he dozed in between worrying about facing Diane when he got back, but as he paid the cab driver, he could see that the house was in darkness. Milly barked as he opened the door but stayed in her basket. He stumbled through all the rooms, hoping Diane was already asleep in bed, but she wasn't there.

Outside he felt better, the air was clearer, colder. He was sick of being cooped up inside. Rolo jumped up as he approached. Con could see the whites of his eyes rolling in the dark as he wriggled with excitement at the prospect of being released.

There was food and water in the dog's dishes. Con let him out. The sound of the lead snapping on Rolo's collar cracked in the still night. Down on the canal bank it was black and silent. Con felt his head clearing. The temperature was barely above freezing.

This time last year he would have been worrying about frost on the early brassicas. His breath misted round him. Where was Diane?

It was past midnight. There were still lights on in the Turk's Head, but the doors were closed. He walked away into the blackness. The village lights were a glow in the sky round the bend but here it was like the grave, except for the faint slap of water against the canal bank and the scurryings of small creatures disturbed by Rolo's poking nose.

Con sat down on a bench and took a can of Special Brew from his pocket. There were two more left in the fridge at home for later. The black ribbon of water curved back towards the farm. He thought again of his mother's tales of the walking trees and the hawthorn bushes on the opposite bank shook their leaves at him. 'Where's Diane? Where's Diane?' they whispered.

Where could she be, after midnight? There was nowhere open, pubs, restaurants, all were closed up. His mind ran riot, imagining her pulling someone else close, some faceless man, not Alex, please let it not be Alex.

Once, soon after they'd married, he'd had her up against the wall under the canal bridge. A cold, dark night like this, but there'd been a moon, a bright moon that even in the shadows under the old stonework had cast light on the sweep of her eyelashes as they closed, on the dim redness inside her half-open mouth. He remembered the muscular feel of her legs clasped round his waist, the weight of her hanging from his shoulders and her buttocks working in his hands. The noises they'd made when they'd come had frightened all the other creatures into terrified silence. He opened his eyes, found the empty can crushed in his hand. A tear burned at the edge of his eye and he wiped it away, looking round but there was no one there. He got up, calling softly to Rolo.

When he got back to the house, the lounge lights were on. His fingers shook as he locked Rolo's compound. His whole body was churning with rage as he envisaged the confrontation ahead.

Through the open lounge door he could see the flickering light of the TV screen. He went straight up to the bathroom and urinated. The shower cubicle ran with water droplets and the room was damp with hot steam. He sniffed the towel she had dried her body on, folding it against him and looked at her discarded clothes in the linen hamper, blue jeans and a pink fluffy sweater, purple bra and thong.

When he came down, she was lying on the sofa wrapped in a bathrobe, drinking a mug of hot chocolate. He could smell the sweetness of it over the scent of her damp hair as he got close. Milly raised her head from under Diane's arm and looked at him questioningly. Diane ignored him, pretending to watch the screen.

'What time do you call this?' She clicked the remote, flicking through the channels.

'I was here before. You weren't in.' His voice came out threatening, louder than he'd meant it to.

'No point in being in, is there? You're never here.' She turned her head to stare at him. Her eyes were lizard-like. Milly cocked her head, all attention.

'Where were you?' He stood over her, clenching his hands in his pockets.

'Where were you?' She sat up suddenly, swinging her legs down and putting her mug on the coffee table in one smooth motion. Her jaw pointed up at him. 'Where's the car?'

'I left it at the pub,' he muttered. The question caught him off-guard and all he could think of was to retaliate.

'Fucking hell, Di, where've you been? It was after midnight when I got back.' He moved to sit beside her but she jumped up, warding him off. Milly leaped down, barking. She bared her teeth at Con and stood defensively in front of her mistress.

'Don't you dare question me!' Diane spat, 'When you're out night after night, coming home pissed all the time. What are you doing Con? What's it all about?'

'I can't take this Di.' Even as he looked at her he was thinking about the Special Brew in the fridge. 'Fucking Computerland, kowtowing to Alex's fucking brother, listening to idiots all day long, being shut in – I can't take it and as if that's not enough, I have to start worrying about where my wife is at night and what she's doing.' There was a tearing sound as Milly attacked his trouser leg and he felt a nip from her needle teeth. 'Fucking hell!' He picked the dog up and threw her out into the hall, shutting the door on her.

The blow on his cheek was the last thing he expected and he

staggered back, shaking his head. She followed him, her eyes like blue fire now.

'You bastard!' she hissed. He looked on like a stranger as the skin of her face stretched tight across the bones of her skull, pulling her mouth into an obscene horror.

'You can't take it! I can't take it. I didn't marry you to come home to an empty house every night after working all day, nor to put up with a total pisshead, because that's what you are Con, you're pathetic.' In the hall Milly barked furiously, throwing herself against the closed door.

Con's face smarted. He kept his fists in his pockets while he looked at the red blotches rising on Diane's neck. It was a slender neck with fine bones that would snap like a bird's if you squeezed it too hard.

What was he thinking? The anger sank inside him. He couldn't stay in the room with her any more. In the hall, Milly snarled at him before running in to Diane. He went to the kitchen and got the beer out of the fridge, squeezing its cold, hard sides even as he popped the tab and poured the liquid down his throat. Diane was at the foot of the stairs watching, cuddling the dog close to her breasts.

'Don't think you're coming to bed with me,' she sneered. 'Don't think I want some pawing drunk slobbering all over me.' Even her back looked disgusted as she climbed the stairs, Milly peering smugly over her shoulder

Con threw the empty can in the bin, got the last one and lay down on the sofa that was still warm from Diane's body. She still hadn't told him where she'd been.

***

Lynn rang Dan's mobile at eight o'clock when he still hadn't arrived home.

'I'm nearly there. What's the big deal? I'm driving, for God's sake.'

The phone went dead. She checked her image in the hall mirror. Her skin was flushed with the heat of the kitchen. It glowed against her black dress. She turned sideways, smoothing the skirt over her stomach. There was nothing to indicate the activity, the rampant growth going on inside her, only she could sense the fizzing energy.

She went into the kitchen, checked the fillet steak wasn't drying out under its tinfoil wrap. Why couldn't Dan get home on time for once? He'd been cross when she'd rung in the first place.

'I've got work to finish here. What's the problem, is something wrong?'

'I just thought I'd make a special dinner. Have a romantic evening for a change.'

'Well, I don't know. It could be after nine by the time I'm through.'

'No Dan. Leave it for once. Come on, we've hardly seen each other for weeks.'

'Oh all right, I suppose it can wait. I'll try to make seven-thirty. Have to go, just going into a lecture.'

Headlight beams flashed through the windows as his car rolled into the yard and Lynn sighed with relief. She picked a fallen petal from the vase of tulips on the table and went to greet him at the door.

'God, what a day!' Dan rushed in with a blast of cold air, dumping his briefcase by the back door. 'Wow! What's all this?' He stood back, took in her dress, her hair piled up the way he liked it. He leaned forward and kissed her nose. He smelled of the heated air of the car, of air freshener and a jaded undertone of stale aftershave. There was no hint of Coty L'Aimant.

'Five minutes.' He ran up the stairs. She went back to the kitchen and put the onion soup under the grill, feeling her mood lift. She'd been afraid that he would be in a bad temper after having to change his plans for the evening. Maybe he'd had to break a date with Emma Cranton. The thought made her smile with satisfaction.

He came behind her, reached under her arms and fondled her breasts as she juggled dishes at the worktop. He smelled fresh and lemony, his skin warm and damp.

'Stop it,' she giggled. 'You'll make me drop everything.'

'Your tits are amazing.' His breath was hot on her neck. 'Getting bigger. It's not that time of the month is it?'

'No.' She pulled away, laughing and carried the hot soup bowls to the table.

'Where are Malc and Jennie?'

'They've gone out to eat.'

'Have I forgotten something?' He looked apprehensively at the candles, the tulips, the wine goblets. 'You've had your birthday. It's not our anniversary?' He sat down, dug his spoon into the cheese crusted dish. 'You made my favourite soup.'

'Because I love you.' She watched how appreciatively he ate, quickly but neatly, his long fingers deftly wielding the spoon and fork, tearing up the soggy toast and dunking it in the onion broth. 'No one makes this better than you, not even the French.' He clattered the spoon into the empty bowl.

'You've had other women make it for you?' she teased, pushing the bread around in her own bowl. The cheese was making her feel nauseous. She poured wine for Dan, water for herself.

'Only the finest chefs in Paris. Not a patch on this.' He sat back and tickled her legs under the table with his bare toes. 'Drinking water instead of wine? What's got into you?'

'My stomach's a bit queasy.' She shrugged. 'How was work?' She got up to fetch the steak.

'Don't ask.' He followed her, bringing the empty soup bowls and stacking them in the dishwasher. He leaned against the worktop sipping his wine. 'Trying to co-ordinate all the different courses into a cohesive department is a nightmare. Bloody Women's Studies is the worst. They seem to think every man is out to attack them. You can't work with them.'

Lynn kept her face averted. She could imagine the fireworks that went on between Dan and Emma Cranton, but she didn't want to know. All that would have to stop. She was going to make sure of it.

'Garlic and mushroom sauce?' She put the sauce boat on the table. 'Something's going on,' Dan said, staring at the slices of steak in the serving dish. 'Come on Lynn, what's it all about?'

'I told you. I just wanted us to have a romantic evening. What's wrong with that?' She didn't want to reveal the news yet, not amongst the smells of food and dirty plates. Later, when they were both relaxed, that's when she would tell him.

'Nothing,' Dan said, reaching for the steak. 'This looks fantastic.'

After the meal, Dan cleared the dishes. Lynn made coffee while he talked about his staff, the students, the continual policy updates and new developments on the campus. She took the coffee into the lounge, put Dan's favourite Oasis album on the stereo and turned it down to background noise level.

'You were right, I really needed to relax like this.' Dan's voice nuzzled her ear as they lay on the sofa, curve tucked to curve, his arms possessively circling her waist. 'I've been working like the clappers ever since I started this job.'

'Maybe you've been trying too hard.' Lynn was drowsy with the heat of his body behind her but excitement and apprehension twined inside her.

His hands wandered over her stomach. 'You're putting more weight on. All this gardening isn't doing the trick.'

Now, the time was now. She took a deep breath, opened her mouth.

'You know, we've been here what – four months? I expected you'd be thinking about going back to work by now.'

She lifted her head, surprised. 'But you said I didn't need to.'

'I know I did. You don't need to. It's not the money. Aren't you getting bored, messing about here day after day? Surely you miss having some mental stimulation. You'll end up like that Dougan if you're not careful, reciting poetry to the field mice.'

'You mean I'm getting boring?' Lynn stiffened herself against him.

'No, but you have changed. We used to be able to talk about work together, we shared the same goals. It doesn't seem to be like that any more. This place – it feels like you're married to this place more than you are to me.'

Lynn compared herself to Emma Cranton in Dan's eyes. It was easy to pick the winner. 'You know that's not true but I do like it here and I don't miss college at all. And after all it was you who made me leave my job in the first place to come here.'

'I didn't make you do anything. It was only for something better. You deserve more than sixth-form tutor in some second-rate college catering for secondary school drop-outs. There's a place coming up in the English department here. I'll put a word in for you, it'll be a doddle, you'll see. You'd be able to get funding for research, do your PhD.'

'That's what you want for me, to spend my life in a department full of institutional politics and backstabbing, targets and constant training? You just said yourself, it's a nightmare.'

'You'd rather be here, grubbing about in the muck, like that Chapman woman? You think she could make a meal like you've just done? You think she knows the first thing about literature, poetry? You want to end up with rough hands and a red face? You want to be – '

He stopped.

'Go on,' Lynn's voice rose. 'Say it. Fat and ugly. That's what you meant, isn't it? Dan, I'm tired of trying to live up to your image. I'm not one of your sexy colleagues, your teenage students. And I'm not putting on weight because I'm lazy or I eat too much. I'm pregnant Dan. We're going to have a baby.'

'Pregnant?' It was as if she had hit him. His whole body jerked and she would have fallen off the sofa if his arms hadn't been clutching her. 'How?'

'How do you think?' She turned and fitted herself against him, trying to push her softness into his rigid muscles.

'But all these years – '

She looked into his face and her stomach lurched. He looked stricken. She thought of Imogen, saw herself putting a black baby into Dan's arms and resolutely pushed the picture away.

She took his hand in hers, twined her fingers round his. 'Maybe it's the change of lifestyle. Who knows? You know deep down, I've always wanted a child.'

'Yes, but it doesn't seem possible.' He pushed up, forcing her to sit up with him, then got up and walked to the window, rubbing the back of his head as if something had come loose inside it. He turned back to her. 'When? How long have you known?' He glared at her as if she'd committed a crime.

'Valentine's night?' She hazarded a smile. The number of possible occasions could be counted on one hand. 'I took a home test yesterday.'

'Maybe it's wrong.' Dan's eyes lit up. 'You'd better get to the doctor's tomorrow.'

'Dan, I know it's a bit of a shock, but aren't you pleased? It's the right time now, before we get too old and set in our ways.'

'It's not a good time,' Dan said through gritted teeth. 'I've got too many responsibilities.'

'When will be a good time, Dan? Five years, ten years, never?

You sound like you think I've done this deliberately.'

'It should be a conscious choice, a responsible joint decision. A child needs consideration, planning, not this –' he shook his head, – 'this – accident.'

She folded her hands over her stomach. If he mentions abortion, she thought, I'll leave here and now.

'It's out of our hands, Dan,' she pleaded. 'Aren't you glad, just a little bit?'

His hands fell to his sides and he looked at her, really looked into her eyes. His face softened and he pulled her into his arms. 'Yes, of course,' he murmured against her hair. Her mouth wobbled and she squeezed her eyes shut to try and stop the tears coming out.

'Don't,' he whispered. 'Don't cry. It'll be all right. It's just so unexpected.'

He pulled away from her and began taking the pins out of her hair, one by one. She stood trembling, trying to stop crying as the long locks fell round her shoulders.

Silently, Dan led her to the bedroom, undid her dress and slipped it off, then sat her down on the bed and lifted her legs up onto it. He kissed her feet, rolled her stockings off, then took up her hairbrush and sat down behind her, brushing her hair out over and over.

Gradually the tide of her emotion turned and the trembling left her. She let the weight of her upper body lean against Dan's support. The repeated brush strokes soothed her, took away her thoughts and left her mind clear and empty, waiting only for the brush to return after each sweep, for the scrape of the bristles on her scalp, for the touch of Dan's fingers as he separated each section of hair. Over and over, the brush returned, and into the calm it produced a thought came floating. It would be all right, the thought whispered to her. The baby was Dan's. It had to be.

He shifted behind her. She heard the thud of the brush as he laid it down on the bedside table, then his breath whispered along her neck as his hands slid under her breasts, weighing them, his fingers exploring her enlarged nipples.

Warmth washed her as he laid her back on the bed, opened her legs and lifting her buttocks, brought his mouth to the wet place in the middle. He sought out the pleasure spot as Lynn groaned and whimpered. Everything in her opened, relaxed as his tongue stroked her over and over, like a cat licking its kitten, sweet and slow.

Her flesh rose up to meet each caress, hungry for the joy of it. Even though she was pregnant, the purpose of sex fulfilled, this was for love, not the violent rush of desire, but a slow fire building delight that surrendered every cell to him. She sank into the depths of herself, going under then the orgasm rolled through her and Dan turned her, slipping into her from behind, her spasms coaxing his own orgasm almost immediately.

Still shuddering, she lay against him, enjoying their shared dampness, and thought of that exquisite pleasure flooding herself and the child, a wordless expression of joy, of love, claiming the child and welding the three of them into a shared identity, a family.

Chapter Nine

May 2008

'Sorry I'm late.' Con rushed into the office, took off his jacket and checked that his name badge was pinned to his shirt pocket.

'Three days in a row.' Shaun Maxwell looked up from his computer.

'It's only ten minutes.' Con dragged his tie straight.

Shaun got up and came round the desk to face him, hiking one chubby buttock up on the wooden surface.

'You should be setting an example to the others. You're going to be a manager.'

'Yeah, okay,' Con said through gritted teeth. He wished Shaun would go out into the shop so that he could get a nip of whisky from his desk drawer. 'It's the traffic. I set out early enough.'

'You look like you've been up all night.'

Con rubbed a hand over the stubble on his jaw. There had been no time to shave but it was fashionable anyway, wasn't it? He looked in the tiny mirror on the back of the office door. Bloodshot eyes stared back at him.

'Anyway,' Shaun got up and peered through the glass compartment at the sales assistants who were unlocking their tills. 'I've left the staff rotas for you to do for the next month. John Dawson's coming in later. He'll probably want a chat to see how you're getting on.'

'Okay.' Con hated the office as much as being in the shop but at least he wouldn't have to talk to anyone and he would be able to get at his desk drawer, if Shaun ever went out. The thought of Alex's brother coming to chat made him more desperate than ever for a drink. As if on cue, the phone on Shaun's desk rang, calling him out to deal with some problem elsewhere.

Con watched as he disappeared into the huge acreage of Computerland before turning on his own computer. He bent down and unlocked his desk drawer. The whisky bottle gleamed at him. There was no time to savour the screw of the cap, the way his lips fitted the neck of the bottle. He couldn't wait for the delicious fire of the spirit to run down his throat, deep into his body. Immediately he felt better. His head cleared as he straightened up. Now he would be set up for the day.

He turned at the noise of the office door opening, too startled to hide the bottle in his hand.

'Oh – ' it was the general office assistant, Jan. 'I wondered if you wanted sandwiches from the supermarket?'

Con grinned. 'Hair of the dog.' He tried to sound confident, jaunty. 'Big night out last night. Mum's the word, eh?' He nodded his head towards the shop floor where Shaun and one of the sales team were huddled over a till.

'Yes, sure.' Jan's eyes were like saucers. She was trying not to laugh as she backed out of the office.

'Shit!' Con slammed a fist on the desk. He took another long slug from the bottle and put it away in the drawer. He sat down at the desk, took a pack of mints from his pocket and ate one after another, biting hard into them as he stared blankly at his computer screen. By ten-thirty he'd finished the rotas. Shaun hadn't come back and he had begun to relax. He took the rotas to the staff room and pinned them up. Jan was in there, drinking coffee with two of the lads, the ones who worked on the accessories counter.

He could feel them looking at his back as he made himself a cup of tea, could almost hear their thoughts in the silence that fell as he walked in. He dreaded turning round. He didn't know what to say to them. The longer the silence lasted, the harder it was to break.

He'd never been one for making friends easily, even as a child, and these people seemed like creatures from another planet. All they talked about were clothes and music Con had never heard. There was football of course, but Con had never been that interested in football, never really kept up with the scene.

Well, he was a manager anyway, he didn't have to talk to them, it was good that there should be some distance between them and himself. He gave them a brusque nod and marched out with his tea. There were whispers that he couldn't catch and someone giggled as he closed the door.

He should have gone out onto the shop floor. He was

supposed to be learning the ropes in Customer Services in between office duties, but instead he sat at his desk and sipped his tea. His stomach growled. He'd been too late to eat breakfast that morning. The whisky bottle was empty. There was over an hour to go before he could escape for lunch. He cast his eyes over the row of screens that monitored the shop to see where Shaun was and found him gesticulating at someone in Deliveries.

He looked idly at the customers wandering through the store, the neatly dressed assistants, zombies each and every one. His gaze stopped at a middle-aged couple waiting at the service desk. The woman bore a vague resemblance to his mother as she had looked twenty years ago.

He put his feet up on the desk, nursing his mug of tea and watched them. The thought of his mother in Computerland made him chuckle then immediately he felt a tug of grief. Twenty years ago his mother had been a tall straight woman, fit and strong, still capable of doing a full day's work as well as any man. He could remember when they'd first moved into the farmhouse when he was fourteen, after his grandfather had died.

It had seemed like God was teaching him a lesson about life and death those few years between when he stopped being a little boy and when he had to leave school and think about a grown up life.

Nana had died first and that was the worst because although he'd seen animals die on the farm, he didn't really know death. The reality of his nana disappearing, reappearing hidden in a wooden box like a magic trick and then the emptiness where she used to be, had all been new. That reality hadn't matched up with the sun rising and setting every day, the reliable round of school terms and holidays, Christmases and Easters, planting and harvests, the ground dying down every winter and sprouting out every spring.

He'd kept waiting for her to come back and he still hadn't got used to it when Granddad died two years later. His grandfather was a funny bugger, Dad used to say, but he'd taken the time to show Con things like where the toads hid under the pipes in the glasshouse in the winter, how to make a decent hoe out of all the old clobber in the yard or how to pop a warble fly maggot out of a cow's back, just like squeezing a pimple.

His grandfather never had much to say, but he was always there, until that hot, hot summer of 1976 when the sun, so welcome at first, had shrivelled the land like a nuclear blast. It had lain on them like a suffocating blanket, and they'd all been helpless creatures before its strength, all of them constantly scanning the spotless sky for specks of cloud.

He remembered that day as the hottest of all. He'd been loitering in the relative cool of the farmhouse kitchen dragging out the task of filling flasks for the workers when they'd brought his granddad in from the fields, Barney Dougan and the other men carrying him on a stretcher made from sacks and hoes. His dad had shooed Con out of the way down to the cottage, where his mother was doing the washing. They'd taken Granddad to the hospital and Con had been taken to see him but it wasn't the person he knew, lying in the stiff white bed, all clean and combed, being run by machines. His real grandfather had already done the magic trick. Con used to lie awake thinking about his own heart thudding with a life of its own and wondering if it might just stop, today or tomorrow and how that would feel.

He had liked living in the farmhouse. It was lighter than the cottage and his room was bigger but it was as if his whole world had changed, even though everything went on the same, school, homework, working in the fields, feeding the animals. Then the pony died too. Somehow that was the worst of all. Granddad had bought him the pony for his tenth birthday. She had been white, fat with a round belly and slightly splayed legs but he'd loved her. Grief welled up in him as he stared at the monitor screens without seeing anything. It was still there, raw as ever. He closed his eyes. When he opened them again, John Dawson was standing in front of him.

Con jerked his feet off the desk, tipping his mug over in his hands. Dregs of tea soaked into his shirt, the cold trickles matching the sweat that sprang from his armpits.

'What's all this, Con?' Dawson's face was smooth, not even surprised.

Con fussed with his shirt. 'Sorry John. Not feeling too good. Think I'm coming down with something.'

'You've been drinking. I can smell it.'

He was lying. He had a smooth liar's face, like his brother. He couldn't smell it. It was half an hour at least since he'd drained the bottle. That cow had talked.

'Jan,' he said. 'So much for team loyalty.'

'It's not just Jan,' Dawson said. 'Do you think no one's noticed? Think you can cover it up by crunching mints? Everyone knows. Shaun's tried to keep it quiet, but everyone's talking about you. Team loyalty means loyalty to the team, to the efficiency and well-being of the team, not to shoring up your drinking habit. How can you be a team leader, a manager, if you're a laughing stock?'

The words cut into Con but Dawson only looked mildly annoyed, like he was used to making this kind of attack. He was just like his brother, no feelings, all they thought about was business, making money. That's why Alex couldn't keep Diane; she was too much for him, too sensual. That's why he had Diane now and Alex had lost her for all his business success. He glared at John. If he didn't shut up, he'd hit him, boss or no boss. He got up to face him, keeping his hands at his sides, his fists lightly clenched.

'I'm trying to help you here. Alex asked me to give you a start for Diane's sake. The least you could do is make an effort. Shaun's concerned about you. You're not pulling your weight. We need people to be enthusiastic here, part of the team.'

He sat down, gestured Con to sit. Con stood stony-faced, irresolute, then sat back in his chair, letting his eyes roam over the monitor screens to avoid looking at his tormentor.

'Con, I know it's hard for you. I know you're used to being outdoors, in open space. It must be difficult coming to work in this kind of set up; you probably feel like you're in over your head, but you're a capable man. You ran that farm single handed for years, managed all the admin work that went with it. Don't let yourself down like this. Don't let me down. I've put myself out for you.'

'For Alex,' Con said bitterly.

'Okay, yes. For Alex, for Diane, for all of you. It makes me look stupid if you can't do the job.'

'I can do the job.'

'I know you can. But you've got to shape up. They're not a bad crowd here. You have to learn to fit in, but Con, I can't have you drinking on the premises, or drinking in working hours.'

'It was just a hair of the dog.'

'No, it's not. You're smelling of whisky all the time.'

'You've been spying on me.'

'It's not like that. People notice, people talk and it spreads. If it were anyone else, they'd have been out of the door already.'

'You want me to go now?' Con jumped up, leaned over Dawson. The man was soft like a slug and unnaturally tanned.

John Dawson pushed his chair back. 'No, I'm giving you another chance. I promised Alex and Diane you'd get a good start. But you've got to pull yourself together. Let me get one customer complaint and you're out. No more booze. I don't know if it's just the change of lifestyle or if there's something deeper going on, but if you have to drown your sorrows, do it at home. If you take my advice, you'll get some help.'

***

'Congratulations,' Dr Wilson beamed. 'You're a fine healthy specimen. It's a little late for a first child but I don't foresee any problems. Don't hesitate to come and see me if you've any worries. Approximate birth date will be – ' she paused and turned to her computer ' – 15th November, but the hospital will check that for you.'

The smile split Lynn's face. She felt as if a special light were pouring down on her head, almost like Pentecostal fire. 'Do you have a family?'

'Two boys,' Dr Wilson laughed. 'Five and eight. Absolute terrors.' She turned back to the screen. 'Let's get the paperwork sorted. Any illnesses or conditions in your family? Yourself? Your parents, siblings?' She ran through a long list of possible dangers. Lynn shook her head to each one.

'What about your husband?'

'No.' Lynn shook her head again. 'At least, I don't think so.'

'I'll give you a tick list to take home. You can get him to fill it in and drop it into the surgery.'

Lynn bit her lip while Dr Wilson tapped her keyboard. A printer whirred into action. She ought to speak. She opened her mouth but her tongue refused to move.

'Have to make sure,' Dr Wilson handed her the sheet.

Lynn made a decision. Her baby was more important than her reputation.

'Um – there's a possibility that the baby isn't his.' The words rushed out and her mouth shut with a snap. Fear churned round her body as she waited for the doctor to look up.

Dr Wilson's eyes flickered but her expression didn't change. 'I'd better print another sheet then.'

Lynn shrank in her chair. How could she say she didn't know where Imogen was? She took the extra tick sheet.

'You'll get an appointment direct from the hospital. They'll go through your history, book your bed, give you some routine blood tests.'

'Blood tests? I hate needles.' Lynn shuddered.

'For your own benefit, you must realise that?' The doctor smiled. 'They have to check for underlying conditions and things like HIV and Hep B.'

'HIV?' Lynn's eyes bulged. Did the doctor think she was promiscuous, carrying on with anybody? It was only Imogen, he couldn't possibly be – she remembered Dan and her mother's suspicions.

'It's just a standard test. Everyone has it. But at the end of the day, it's your choice. You can refuse if you really don't want it.'

'What if it's positive?'

The doctor put down her pen. 'Do you have reason to think it might be?'

'No. But if it was?'

'Your partners would need to be tested, and you would need to think about the implications of continuing with the pregnancy.'

'You're talking about abortion.' Lynn's hand flew to her belly.

'Please don't alarm yourself. It's just a standard test and surely if you do think there's a chance you might be positive, then you need to know.'

'I'm not getting rid of it. It's a baby, a living thing. I've waited years for it.' Her mind whirled with fear. Imogen had been clean, she was sure of it, he was so young and innocent. But could she risk it, jeopardise her baby's health? And what would she do if she were positive, destroy her child and any chance of having another? How could she have been so stupid in the first place?

'Would you like me to arrange for you to see a counsellor? Maybe it would help to talk this out?'

'No! I'll be fine.' She tried to make her voice sound positive, to re-assure the doctor.

Dr Wilson turned away, tapped at her keyboard. She concentrated on her computer screen while Lynn sat before her, her mind a muddy pond of fear and uncertainty.

'I'll see you again in six weeks, but any problems with nausea or anything else, do come in and see me. Here are some leaflets about your pregnancy. Get plenty of rest but balance it with gentle exercise, walking or swimming.' She turned on a professional smile.

Lynn took the bundle of leaflets from the doctor's hand. She held out until she reached the waiting room before burning tears began to drip down her face, blinding her to the curious stares of the people in the waiting area.

***

I were so loved when I were pregnant with our Con. That's what I remember most about those early days. Albert couldn't do enough for me, like I were the most special person in the world. Not that he didn't love me before that, there were always love between us from beginning to end; it almost overrode my feelings about Dad leaving him the farm, but this were such a tender time. It were the thing that made all the fears of what might happen, to us, to our baby, bearable.

My mother too, treated me like someone special, cooking little treats for me when I come in at dinnertime and even Dad give me lighter work to do round the yard instead of hauling sacks and manure and digging like a man.

I used to love those times when I stayed in the house with me mam and Gran, doing the baking or washing together, while Dad and Bert were out in the fields. Mam'd tell me how it were for her the first time, with my brother Thomas, how scared she were with only Gran and the midwife from the village to help her. By the time she had me though, it were easy for her and my coming soaked up some of the grief of losing Will, the brother I never saw.

My Gran told me the story about how my mother had been born in the very same room, how she'd laboured for hours so that both her and the midwife had thought the child would never come out alive. Gran said that first angry cry of the newborn is the most wonderful thing you can ever hear.

'Stop it Mam, you'll fricken the girl to death,' Mam said, but I were watching Gran's hands kneading the bread as she talked, like they had a life of their own, like they knew everything about the mixing of flour, water, yeast and air, her whole body working the dough with easy grace.

I were thinking how we all had this kind of knowledge in our hands, in our whole bodies and all having the same fear too of the struggle to give birth; me, me mam, me gran, her mam before her, all doing the same things, going back and back into the past.

Gran used to say it were bad luck to be frickened by something when you were expecting. 'Watch out for black cats, them's the worst. You get frickened by a black cat, your baby'll be born with the mark of it for sure, and not in some place you can't see, but out on its hands or worst of all its face.

'Look at Joan Carter, her as used to live by the canal. A stoat run in front of her when she were pregnant and didn't Nellie have the mark of it on the back on her neck, clear as day when she were born?'

'Don't talk nonsense, Mother,' Mam said. 'Take no notice of her, Alice.'

But it were true Nellie Carter did have a birthmark on her neck, though whether it looked like a stoat, I couldn't rightly remember. I had more realistic things to worry about, like nuclear bombs and how much a baby were going to cost, but I couldn't put the thought of Nellie Carter's birthmark out of my mind and all the time I were pregnant I were looking out for black cats and stoats.

One time, I were about seven months gone, I were hoeing tatties when I disturbed a pheasant sitting on her nest and she flew up right in my face. I dreamed of a feathered baby and when Con were born I couldn't wait to check him all over, but he were beautiful, unblemished like a perfect apple.

Let's hope Lynn's baby will be the same, yet she's not easy in herself and a baby senses your mood both before and after it's born. She's a dark and quiet one, like all our family. Happen there's more of Askins in her than shows in her face.

Aye, I know what it is to hold a secret, one that's never been told, one that no one ever knew, only the land, the farm, as saw all things, but since I'm one with the soil of this place, the bricks of the house, the cottage, my secret's always safe.

Maybe hers will be too, only time will tell. It's funny to see that husband of hers so cocksure, thinking he's in control, playing away with his fancy woman. He's too full of himself to see he's been cuckolded behind his own front door. Happen he'll get his comeuppance in the end. I thought her a fool, but a pregnant woman soon learns to look out for herself. It's instinct to put your child before anything or anyone else.

I should be more worried about our Con. I see him sneaking around the fields at night instead of going back to that place he calls home now. I see him coming out of the Turk's, drunk as a lord, and he cuts a lonely figure creeping about in the dark and the rain. Can't be much of a welcome he's got at home to keep him wandering around like that. At least he's keeping away from Andrew Chapman. He's turned out to be a bad influence and no mistake. I daren't even go down to the cottage any more I get so angry when I see what he's doing in there.

I've walked alongside Con many a night, all along the footpaths almost to Lathom. I've seen the torment in his head, how he longs to be back on the land, but it's too late now. I were angry with him when he done it, selling the farm soon as my back were turned, but God knows he's my only child and to see him in this state, it's like a knife in my belly. He's always alone, except for the dog and even though I've been right up close to him, put my hand on his arm to comfort him, he don't see me and there's nothing I can do to help him. He turned his back on the land and he'll have to sink or swim. The land is unforgiving. It don't forget.

***

'You're very quiet.' Lynn's mother looked up from setting the supper table.

'I'm a bit tired.' Lynn summoned a smile.

'No more ghosts? I certainly haven't seen any.'

'No.' She ought to make a joke, but she felt so dispirited. Dread of the HIV test left no room for other thoughts.

'Sit down, put your feet up. Dr Wilson told you to rest.'

'I'm okay, really. I'm just finishing this sauce.'

'Leave it. I'll do it.' Her mother shooed her to the chair by the fireplace. 'I hope Dan's not going to be late tonight. It's our last evening together so we wanted to make it a bit special.' She poured the sauce over the chicken pieces and put the casserole to keep warm in the oven as Lynn's father came in with a bottle of champagne.

'Our turn to celebrate the good news tonight.' He grinned and Lynn suddenly realised how much older he was getting, how they had both aged since retirement. Their fierce joy at the news of the pregnancy made her sad. All these years they must have waited for grandchildren, too polite or diplomatic to say anything, to question the years of childlessness. How would they feel if they knew the truth? Lynn longed to confide in her mother but she knew how she often sided with Dan. She had lived all her life in the traditional female role, supporting her husband. She would be unable to comprehend how Lynn could have seduced Imogen, let alone collude with her plans to deceive Dan.

Yesterday that joy had enveloped all three of them but now Lynn struggled to play the part of the happy mother-to-be. She watched her mother fussing round the table and wondered how she would react to a black grandchild or worse still, a diseased one.

She sat obediently and put her feet up on the old wooden footstool her mother had found in the outhouse. 'This is silly. I'm perfectly all right.'

'Do as your mother tells you. You know how bossy she is.' Her father ducked as her mother swiped a tea towel at him. Lynn looked at her for signs of softness. Perhaps she would understand or at least would be able to waive her judgemental attitudes for the sake of the much-desired baby.

A movement by the range caught her eye. Alice was watching her, this time manifesting as around the age of Lynn's own mother, still strong and capable, dark mixed in the grey bun of her hair. Her eyes were eloquent, offering solace, sanctuary. Lynn felt no shock or fear. She looked at her mother. Alice seemed more welcoming; she was obviously invisible to the others. Lynn was glad, it made the relationship between them special.

The clatter of china distracted her as her mother fetched plates to the table, She moved to help and when she looked back the corner was empty. She stifled a sense of abandonment and began setting the places. Despite the undercurrent of loss, she felt comforted. Alice knew her secret yet still accepted her. She had an ally.

The sound of Dan's car rolling into the yard was a signal for Lynn's mother to start putting the hot dishes out on the table. 'Just in time,' she said as Dan rushed in, bringing the smell of outdoors with him. And something else, Lynn thought as he bent to kiss her; the cloying scent of Coty L'Aimant hung about him, so faint that she kept persuading herself that she imagined it, even though each time she smelled it, her senses instantly took her back to Valentine's night and to Emma Cranton's cat-like smile.

They sat down to eat. Stars were beginning to show in the darkening sky.

'Might be a touch of frost tonight,' her father said, 'you'll have to watch those cauliflowers you just put in.'

'Barney's fleeced them.' Lynn watched her father's practised hands flip the champagne cork out. He filled their glasses to a round of applause.

'To all three of you,' he toasted and for a moment Lynn was caught up in the family gaiety. Even Dan seemed exuberant, his face slightly flushed, his eyes glittering.

'It's wonderful news, absolutely. We're delighted.' Lynn's mother put her hand on Dan's arm. 'Congratulations, both of you.'

Dan grinned and raised his glass. 'To Lynn. I know she's going to be a fantastic mother, just like her own mother. You know, Jennie,' he patted Lynn's mother's arm, 'it was a hell of a shock when she told me, completely out of the blue, totally unexpected, but now I'm getting used to the idea. Just think, I'm going to be a dad.'

Lynn said nothing. She sipped her champagne, covered the glass with her hand when Dan tried to refill it.

'Ooops, no, of course, you have to take it easy.' Dan laughed too loudly, refilling his own glass.

'You'll have to take good care of her now, Dan.' Jennie's voice was light but there was a serious look on her face. 'We won't be here to help out after tomorrow.'

Dan looked up quickly. 'Tomorrow? God, that's gone over so quickly. Can't you stop a bit longer? I have to go away at the weekend.'

Lynn began serving the chicken. She saw her mother's mouth tighten as she spooned vegetables onto her plate.

'No, I'm afraid we can't. Malcolm's still on the hospital board you know. He has to attend a conference on Saturday.'

'Lynn's going to need you, Dan, need your support.' Malcolm fiddled with the stem of his glass, gave Dan an 'old boys' smile. 'Yes, work's important, but not as important as your family. You need to make time to spend at home.'

'Tell that to the faculty.' Dan's face turned sulky. Lynn knew how he hated being criticised in public. 'You should know how it is Malcolm. It's not like being a shop assistant, I can't just take a day off when I feel like it. This conference at Milton Keynes is important to me. Lynn, you've known about it for ages.' He glared at her as if he thought she had been complaining to her parents.

'You can always come back with us for a few days, Lynn. Be nice to have you at home for a bit.' Jennie looked pleadingly at her daughter. Lynn looked away, spooned sauce onto Dan's plate. 'It's kind of you, Mum but I need to be here. There's so much to do in the garden, I need to be around to organise Barney.'

Malcolm snorted. 'That man was working this land before you were born. He could do that patch with his eyes shut.'

'But I want to make sure he does it the way I want it.'

'I still think you should be home.' Jennie turned her pleading on Dan. Lynn could tell by the set of his shoulders that Dan was irritated.

'Maybe we should get an au pair. We can afford one now and it would solve the problem.' He looked defiantly round the table.

Malcolm frowned and looked into his glass. Jennie pushed a potato round on her plate. Lynn felt she must do something to rescue the situation. She changed the subject to her family history research and the conversation moved onto memoirs of family members. Dan seemed relieved to be off the hook and regaled them with tales of his uncle Bill's corner shop in Salford. The atmosphere lightened again, although Lynn could still see her father looking thoughtfully at Dan and knew he was planning to have a word with him alone later.

'I've been thinking, maybe I could do some research at our end,' her mother said as they cleared the dishes. 'Wouldn't it be odd if these Askins here turned out to be relatives? What did you say the old lady's name was who died?'

'Alice. Her married name was Worrall.' Lynn thought of the woman's appearance earlier. Something had flowed between Alice and herself, a bond that went beyond shared motherhood. The idea that there was a family tie gained strength in her mind but beyond that was another tie, their shared love of the land. It was the first time she'd given the thought concrete expression, but immediately she knew it was true. She felt the knowledge warm and strong bonding her together with Alice, the farmhouse, the fields and the cottage, all protecting herself and the child.

After her parents had gone to finish their packing, Lynn ventured into Dan's study. His face looked pinched and tired in the glare of the computer screen.

'Your dad's been giving me a lecture in family responsibilities.' He swung round in his chair and patted his knee for her to sit.

'They just worry about me, I'm the baby of the family you know.' She laid her head against his chest, relaxing as his arms went round her. She could no longer smell anything but Dan's own warm musk mixed with a faint scent of the lemony soap he always used. She'd imagined she could smell Emma Cranton on him earlier. Pregnant women were known to be fanciful, weren't they?

'I am pleased about the baby, honestly. It was just such a surprise.' He ran a hand over her stomach. 'Your dad made me feel like I've been neglecting you.'

'He's just old-fashioned,' Lynn said. 'I know you have to work. I'm fine, really, I am.'

She felt reassured leaning against Dan. Everything would be all right. She was going to have a healthy baby who would be the image of Dan. The house seemed to fold round her, keeping them all safe.

'I love you.' She reached up to kiss him. He put his hand into her dress and pulled out her breast, taking his mouth from hers to suckle her nipple. She moaned and squirmed on his lap, feeling him stiffen under her then he separated himself from her, tucking her breast away, pushing her gently to her feet.

'I'd like to take you upstairs right now and shag you soft and slow, but I have to finish this – ' he waved at the columns of figures on his screen, 'so get thee hence and get ready for me. I won't keep you waiting long.'

Lynn wandered through the kitchen and the lounge. She couldn't settle to watch TV. She went upstairs and lay on the bed, listening to the rhythms of her body. She turned on her side with her hands clamped between her legs to contain the melting heat that Dan had started. Could the baby feel it too, that racing desire beating round her body, filling every cell with anticipation?

How big was it now? It must be a frenzy of heat, action and reaction, the anticipation of growth, of birth. It was wanted, it was loved. She pushed away the thought of Dr Wilson and her tests. Everything would be all right.

She got up and went to the window where stars shone in their accustomed places. She put her face against the glass and saw something move outside, separating itself from the uniform darkness of the fields. It was going along the perimeter of the garden, something low and patched with white. The white marks showed up in the moonlight, although the shape was unclear in the distance. An animal of some sort, she thought, with its nose to the ground, then she recognised the border collie and lagging behind it the figure of Con Worrall came pacing slowly along the border.

The hairs on the back of her neck rose as she watched him pass by the house and move on along the edge of the back field. He seemed to be looking up at the windows and she ducked down in case he saw her.

When he got to the corner of the field, he turned to look back, it seemed directly at her. She felt a thrill of fright, seeing this solitary apparition melting into the black landscape. What was he doing, patrolling her land as if he still owned it?

She saw him gesture to the dog. It ran to him then they both walked on. She watched until he turned at the edge of the far field, along the drop where the peat had once been then his figure became indistinct in the distance, against the bushes that gathered there. The dog's white patches continued to gleam here and there until they too disappeared.

She lay down again and pulled the duvet over her, feeling too cold now to get undressed. She didn't want Con Worrall wandering around the farm at night; his presence threatened her. Maybe she could ask Dan to speak to him, but Dan was going to be away and she would be at the mercy of Con Worrall or anyone else who felt like coming by.

She was being foolish. She knew Con meant her no harm. She wished Dan would come up to bed. The stars shone through the window casting strange shadows. She would not be afraid now if Alice appeared, but there was no sign of her.

Her body began to warm again and she lay cradling her belly, thinking of the child and listening to the squeaks and cries of nocturnal creatures outside. Suddenly rain began to batter the window and she thought of Con and his dog out on the moss, exposed to the elements. The rain slackened to a steady rhythm that lulled her, she was warm and so comfortable then she was on a white bed in a white room with a light shining in her eyes. People in green were murmuring round her but she couldn't hear what they were saying for the noise of rain beating on the windows. There was a terrible pain and a horrible need to push everything out of her then a feeling of flood and all her insides falling, emptying out into waiting hands.

Everything fell silent, the voices, the rain, but the silence was strained, a silence of concentration, of desperation, of censure, finally of pity.

'Here's your baby,' a nurse said handing her a bundle and she turned back the blanket to see the head covered with running sores, angry yellow eyes glaring at her through crusted lashes. It opened its scabbed lips and cried, a weak, sickly, blaming sound, 'Wh-y-y-y-?' She could see white fungoid patches inside its mouth, coating its tongue, its throat.

She woke suddenly, fighting back nausea as Dan came in and turned on the light. She rushed past him to the toilet and vomited up everything she had eaten. When she came out, they were all standing there: Dan, her mother and father in their nightclothes.

'Thought you were supposed to be sick in the mornings,' she joked weakly. 'Please, don't fuss. Just let me go to bed.'

She got undressed quickly and lay down. She could hear Dan making tea downstairs, hear her parents whispering to him. Their voices reminded her of the people in her dream. She looked out of the window. The rain had stopped. There was no sign of Con Worrall or his collie.

***

Con drove past the Hen and Chickens on his way home. He knew that if he stopped, he would be there all night and what he really wanted was to get home, take Diane out and get drunk with her, forget the whole shitty day.

His jaw ached from clenching his teeth. All afternoon he'd smarted from the things John Dawson had said to him, from the huddled backs and whispers of the assistants, from Shaun Maxwell's over-friendliness and barely disguised contempt.

The car in front of him was driving too slowly. What was he playing at? Fucking idiot! Some old granddad, blind as a bat and senile. You could tell by the car, an S reg Fiesta, lovingly polished. Silly old bugger had nothing else to do all day. He could see two white heads nodding in their seats.

His hands gripped the steering wheel the way he'd been tempted to grip Dawson's ears, crash his forehead into his smooth liar's face. He pictured Dawson's expression of surprise as his nose exploded in a crimson burst and laughed to himself. That would have taught him what life was really about.

The driver in front braked unexpectedly. Con was too close. He swung out to overtake and saw Bill Bryant's tractor coming straight at him in the opposite direction. He swung the wheel instinctively and shot through the gap, seeing Bryant's head turn sharply in surprise.

He pulled over at the bus stop up the road. His heart was racing. The Fiesta passed him. 'Stupid bugger!' Con shouted. Their round faces stared at him then they were gone. 'Shouldn't be on the road,' he muttered, reaching into the glove compartment. There was an inch or so in the whisky bottle. He drained it in one gulp.

When he got to the village he stopped at the shop and picked up four cans of Special Brew and some chocolates for Diane.

'The usual is it?' Amir asked, turning to the shelves of spirits behind the counter. Con looked round at the queue behind him, checking there was no one he knew, no one who would report him to Diane, before nodding.

As he got back in the car, he saw Blondie tied outside the Farmers' Arms. He was tempted to have a quick one with Barney, but he was determined to get back to Diane. More than anything he wanted the comfort of holding her in his arms, knowing that he had her, a woman more special than any of those Computerland nerds would ever have. Even more than the whisky, he wanted the taste of her mouth, the pressure of her lips that would blow his brain, unite it with his body, bring him back to life and explode the persistent image of John Dawson's face.

Diane's car was not on the drive. Con frowned, focussed on his watch. It was a quarter-to-six. Maybe she'd had a late customer at the salon. But it was Wednesday. The salon was closed for the half-day.

Milly started barking even before he put his key in the lock. He could see her leaping behind the glass door panel. She ran round his legs, almost tripping him as he walked through the empty rooms.

'Shut up!' he snarled and she subsided into yaps, looking warily at him until he opened the back door and let her out.

There was a ready-meal chicken curry defrosting on the kitchen worktop next to the kettle and a note. 'Gone out for a meal. Back about ten.'

He put the chocolates down on the worktop and popped the tab on a can of beer. Gone out where? Who with? That slag Melanie from the salon, twice divorced and flashing her knickers at anyone who cared to look? He tipped the beer down his throat. It wasn't enough. He opened one of the new halves of whisky and poured a large glass. The other he hid in the meter cupboard.

Alex, maybe it was Alex. She'd been phoning him a lot, supposedly about him helping out with money for Justin's university course. Maybe there was more to it, maybe he was being taken for a fool by the pair of them, maybe that was why John Dawson looked so smug. Maybe he knew something Con didn't.

The sound of Rolo barking broke into his thoughts. Milly would be teasing him with her freedom. He went outside and picked the terrier up. She growled at him and showed her teeth but didn't dare to bite. 'Should set Rolo on you,' he muttered as he pushed her inside the back door and locked it after her.

Blondie was still outside the Farmers' Arms. There was an excited exchange of sniffs and wagging tails as Con tied Rolo beside her. Barney was in full swing, a half-drunk pint of Guinness on the bar beside him.

The snow hath retreated, there's joy in the mountains. The lambs are bleating and May is near. The ploughboy is whooping, – ah and here he is, once our jolly ploughboy, too good for the likes of us now in his fancy suit with his posh colleagues.' He bowed low as Con approached. The other men standing round the bar chuckled uneasily.

Con realised he was still wearing his hated suit. He dragged his tie off as Jackie Mack pulled him a pint. 'Just my luck. My one night on this week, and I have to put up with you two.' She winked as she pushed the pint across to Con and gave him a toothy smile.

'Give me a whisky chaser with that.' Con ignored the joke. 'Diane hasn't been in here has she?'

'Diane? She doesn't come in here. You know that. You lost her then?' Jackie Mack leaned over the bar and waited, playing with her bracelet. Con drained the whisky and pushed the glass back to Jackie for a refill. She raised her eyebrows and made a face at Barney.

'Aye, she won't come in here. We're plain and simple country folk in here.' Barney raised his glass.

Jackie Mack looked warningly at him, put the whisky down in front of Con. 'Tough day?' Her voice was sympathetic, but wheedling, fishing for information.

'Will you look at that now?' Barney pointed at the politician waffling on the large screen TV over the bar. 'Sure, if they're not putting up the price of petrol again. You must be feeling the pinch Con with all that travelling to the city and back.'

'It's a company car,' Con said. 'I get expenses. We sold the Shogun.' He felt better with the second whisky inside him.

'A company car? That must be grand, but you must miss your old life so, you must be glad to get back here of an evening. *The soft breeze can come to none more grateful than to me, escaped from the vast city.* The great man Wordsworth, himself.'

Con drank his pint while Barney rattled on. 'You wouldn't recognise the old place now and 'tis easy work for me, tending a few vegetables and helping Mrs Waters with all her fancy flower tubs and such. Makes a pretty sight though I have to say, all those pansies and so on, *tossing their heads in sprightly dance*. But then it's not the same as a working farm, not like the old days. What do you say, Con?'

'Pilling's on there, isn't he?'

'To be sure. It's a sight to see the land being worked properly again.'

'Leeks, is it?'

Con smarted afresh under the insinuation that he'd neglected the land but made no reply.

'A big contract I'm told but Pilling's the man to do it.'

Con emptied his glass. He could no longer stand there listening to Barney. He went outside and untied Rolo. It was getting cold and dark. Stars were beginning to show in the sky. The village was quiet although the convenience store and the chip shop cast pools of light. When he got back, Diane was still not home.

He switched on a lamp in the living room and sat down in front of the television, nursing his bottle of whisky. He awoke to the slamming of the front door and the sound of a car driving off outside. He opened his eyes to see John Dawson's face talking at him from the TV screen. He looked again, saw it was Gordon Brown and rubbed his eyes. Milly's barking pierced his brain.

He turned. Diane looked up from petting the dog. The smile died on her face.

'Just look at you.' She put Milly down, took off her jacket. She was wearing a sparkly red top. One strap had slipped off her shoulder.

'Where've you been?' he growled.

Some of her hair had fallen down from her French pleat. Her cheeks burned and her eyes looked feverish.

'What's it to you?' she said sullenly. 'What time did you get in?'

He stood up and tripped over the whisky bottle on the floor, almost knocking her over. Up close he could smell her, that woman smell that was exclusively hers. He reached out, pulled her to him. 'C'mere.'

'Get off, Con. You're drunk.' She struggled in his arms, more of her hair falling down. How he loved it. He dug his hands into it, pulling at the pins, then brought his mouth down hard but missed her lips as she turned her head away. The kiss slobbered in her ear.

'Get off!' She pushed him hard in the chest so he stepped back but kept his grip on her shoulders. He sniffed. There were other odours on her, smells of drink, the sweetness of Coke on her breath, the cold smell of outdoors and something else, something he recognised as male, a man's perfume.

'Where've you been? Tell me!' He shook her, stared into her face, felt satisfaction as her eyes rounded with alarm.

'Stop it.. You're hurting me.'

'I want to know. Why can't you tell me? You've been out somewhere you don't want me to know about. Clubbing with that tart from the shop? Or is it Alex?'

'Alex?' She looked amazed. 'Alex? You think I'd go out with Alex? Let go of me.' She squirmed away but he held her easily. She was like a doll, a beautiful, brittle little doll.

'You're lying.' Anger blazed up in him. 'Tell me where you've been.' His voice shouted out in her face, the strident sounds mixing with Milly's anxious barking. He felt a sharp nip at his ankle and kicked out. The dog ran, yelping.

'Oh you bastard! Get away from me. Your breath stinks.' Diane kicked at his other ankle but he held firm.

'You've been with a man, haven't you? I can smell him.' He put his face close up to hers, pushing into her space. He wouldn't let her get away from him.

'Well, I won't find one here.' She stared him out. 'Look at you. You're useless. I don't know why I married you.'

His head reared back. It was as if she had punched him in the face. Blood roared through his body, washed away his thoughts. His hands gripped her shoulders. John Dawson's face was in front of him, smooth, taunting, the smiling mouth masking the sneering derision in his eyes.

With a grunt of release Con flexed his thighs, brought his head forward like a hammer. There was a satisfying crunch of something breaking and then there was an awful silence.

For a second it wasn't real. It was something he had imagined, something he might have thought about but would never, ever have done then horror flooded him. He opened his eyes a fraction and saw blood splattered on the carpet. Diane was a crumpled heap on the floor, her hands over her face. She made a strange noise. Con turned, picked up the whisky bottle and went out without looking back.

He needed Rolo. The dog was still eager to walk. He didn't want to get in the car, but Con pushed him into the back seat, he needed to get away.

He didn't get far, the car wouldn't go where he wanted it to as he drove down the village street. It was dark and silent. He gave up and parked crookedly at the canal towpath. He couldn't think, couldn't see anything except John Dawson's hated face and the crumpled thing Diane had turned into.

She deserved it, something said in his head, but he knew this wasn't true. If only he could turn time back five, ten minutes, if only it was like on TV, or films, to be rewound and learned from. Maybe it hadn't been real, just a dream, something he'd imagined. His thoughts were muddied but the picture in his brain was all too clear.

There was nothing out here, only the black water, the skulking bushes made stark by the riding moon and the stars. Even the Turk's Head was dark and silent as he passed, but there were lights in his mother's cottage as he rounded the bend, and in the farmhouse too.

He should have listened to his mother. He looked up at the bedroom window of the cottage. He should never have left the farm then none of this would have happened. He went on, turned onto the footpath along the edge of the far field and passed the house. None of the curtains were drawn. He could see Dan Waters framed in one of the downstairs windows, intent on the unnatural glare of a computer screen and despair gripped him as he thought of having to return to Computerland and the sneers of his colleagues. He could see from the light upstairs that they had re-decorated the master bedroom. Instead of Diane's floral wallpaper, it was a soft, plain beige.

Diane. What had he done? His mother would have killed him if she'd seen him hit a woman. He had frightened himself. Never, never in all his life had he hit a woman before, not even a girl at school when he was a child.

His hands shook as he pulled out the bottle. He was well past the house now, out on the open land, walking the narrow strip between the fresh-ploughed fields. Elder bushes stalked alongside him and he looked ahead to make sure Rolo was still there to protect him. He remembered his grandmother's tales of boggarts and will o' the wisps.

It began to rain, a heavy batter of sharp needles that soon turned into a steady downpour. Con scarcely felt it. He shivered with shame and fear as he walked. He should have stayed with Diane, she might have needed to go to hospital. She might be dead. He might go back to find that broken heap still lying there, mute and cold. He stopped and vomited violently in the ditch. Water gleamed at the bottom, water that could rise swiftly, wash everything away. He could feel the water under his feet, sliding through the soil, wobbling his whole world, felt himself dissolving. He lifted his face to the rain as if it might wash him clean. The water ran down his neck and into his clothes till his jacket and trousers weighed him down like stone.

He didn't go back. He couldn't. The fear was a lead lump in his stomach, concrete boots on his feet. It was inside his head, pushing the bones of his skull apart. He drank and drank till the bottle was empty but still he couldn't shift the vision of John Dawson, couldn't stop replaying the reel of Diane coming into the house: the red top, her hair falling down, that look on her face like all the rest of them, her anger – and the tangled heap on the floor.

In the end it was Rolo that made him move. The dog came whining, poking his sodden nose into Con's hand. He got up from under a dripping tree and stumbled back along the canal to the car.

He couldn't face going home in the morning. When he woke in the car, he thought it wasn't true. He'd got drunk on the way home from work, slept in the car and had a bad dream, but then he saw Rolo looking sorrowful on the back seat, felt his clothes still damp and clammy and sank his head on the steering wheel. He should go back to the house but he couldn't.

Traffic was racing past on the main road. Con remembered he had to go to work. He got out of the car. Weak sunlight washed over him but it lacked warmth. He shivered in his wet clothes, waiting for his legs to strengthen, to take his weight after being cramped in the car all night. He went across to the shop, borrowed a dish from Amir for Rolo, bought some dog food and water and another half of whisky.

'You okay man? You look rough.' Amir looked strangely at him as he gave him his change.

'Mind your own business,' Con snapped, taking the carrier bag. Back at the car, he took a long slug of whisky and the world seemed brighter. The sun sparkled on the canal, slow wavelets from passing ducks glittering like fish scales. He fed and watered Rolo and put him back in the car, deciding against taking him home. He would be okay in the car and by the time he had finished work, Diane would have calmed down. He would be able to make it up to her, everything would be okay.

He shrugged off the fears of the night before, of Diane lying unconscious, maybe bleeding to death. He hadn't hit her that hard, it wouldn't be as bad as he'd thought and he hadn't meant to do it. She had provoked him, surely she would realise that?

Shaun Maxwell's eyebrows shot up as Con walked into the office. 'What the fuck?' He watched as Con fell into his chair and fumbled with the key to his desk drawer.

'Con – what happened to you?'

'I'm here. I'm on time.' Con couldn't keep his voice from slurring. His tongue didn't seem to be in the right place.

'You look like you slept under a bush.' He touched Con's jacket with distaste and backed away. 'You're all wet.'

Con laughed. 'I'm okay.' He gave up with the keys, banged them down on the desk. 'Can I bring my dog in?'

'Dog?' Shaun looked at him as if he'd gone mad. 'Look mate, you can't come to work like this.' He pulled Con up, showed him the bleary face in the mirror. 'Your clothes are soaking, you're covered in mud.'

Con looked down, surprised. It was true. His shoes, the bottoms of his trousers, were thick with the black mud of his land.

'I'll get a brush up.' He reached for the door handle.

'No, you won't. You can't come to work like this. You're not fit. You're drunk. It's only nine o clock and you're pissed as a fart. I suppose you drove here too, in the company vehicle.'

Con sat down again. He felt like he was going to cry and he mustn't, not in front of this condescending bastard.

'It's the end of the line, Con. I've tried to help you, cover for you but this is as far as it goes. You'd better stay here while I phone John Dawson. I'll get Jan to make you some coffee, then I'll find someone to take you home.'

'Fuck you!' Con stood up again. He towered over the fat little man. 'Fuck you and all your fucking computers.' He tore off his name badge and threw it on Maxwell's desk. Water had got inside the laminate coating and blurred Con's name into a soggy blot of ink.

'Con –' Maxwell backed away and held out a supplicating hand.

'Fuck off!' Con said and stalked out, grinning with satisfaction at Maxwell's stunned expression. In the car park he began to shake. It was his damp clothes. His waxed jacket was in the back of the car. He pulled it on, dragged off his tie and stuffed it in his pocket. They would expect him to leave the car here but why should he? How else was he going to get home? They could come and pick it up some time. He got in and drove off quickly in case John Dawson was already coming to relieve him of his keys.

It was late afternoon by the time he got back to the village. The whisky he'd bought earlier had long gone and he'd stopped off at the Hen and Chickens. He jerked the car to a halt outside Diane's Den, almost falling as he got out.

The shop door jangled unbearably. They were like cyborgs inside, the women reading magazines in their allotted seats while the hairdressers mauled their heads, the whole room soporific with heat and the scents of shampoos. They turned to look at him as one as he hung on the door. The customers' bland faces crinkled with alarm. Diane's girls tightened their mouths. Their eyes were hard and round.

'Diane?' he said.

'She's not here.' Mary, the senior stylist spoke from the reception desk. She kept one hand on the telephone.

'Where is she?'

'I don't know.' Her voice was like flint. 'Maybe she's at home.'

A sudden fear cut Con. Diane hadn't come to work. She was lying dead on the floor of the living room. No, the atmosphere here was solid ice. The girls all knew. It was in their eyes, the fear, the hatred. They would all club together against him to protect her.

'Fuck the lot of you,' he said and banged the door as he left.

Dread crawled up his throat and into his mouth as he got near the house. Diane's car wasn't there. He breathed a sigh of relief. She must be okay. He would take Rolo in, settle him down, get a hot shower and change his clothes, sober up and get some food inside him. He realised he hadn't eaten since the day before yesterday. He was going to start afresh, get a new job, make it all up to Diane. He would never let anything like this happen again.

He must be drunker than he'd realised. He couldn't fit the key in the lock. He tried over and over, tried all the keys in the bunch. He stood back, puzzled. The lock barrel winked at him in the sunshine. It was new and shiny. The bitch – she'd changed the locks.

Chapter Ten

May 2008

Lynn came out of Dr Wilson's surgery and floated down the village street. She felt as if she might fly up in the air like a kite. The sun had come out after the early rain and the buildings and pavements gleamed as if they'd been freshly washed.

Home and dry. The HIV test was clear and everything was fine with her pregnancy. She was going to have a perfectly healthy baby. She went into May Gorman's café and ordered a cappuccino and a cream slice to celebrate.

Andrew Chapman was in the corner by the window, the chairs moved to one side to accommodate his wheelchair. Lynn hesitated. She wanted to be alone to savour her good news, but she didn't want to seem churlish.

'Hi. May I join you?'

'Sure.' He indicated the chair opposite. Lynn noticed an empty cup opposite his. 'Is your mum with you?'

'She's gone to the florist's. She insists on coming out with me, as if I can't do things for myself.'

'You're her baby. She worries about you.'

He looked at her, the same direct gaze as his mother but there was something dead in his expression. 'But I'm not a baby. I'm a grown man.'

He turned his head and looked idly out of the window at the cars and the people on the busy street. He looked bored and angry. The lines of his face and body were stiff with tension, frustration.

'It must be hard for you, coming out of the army to this.' It was a platitude but what else was there to say?

'At least I'm alive. I should be glad. So everyone keeps telling me.' His voice was like acid, dissolving any response she might have made. She tried to imagine herself in a wheelchair, her body heavy and clumsy, having to be lifted and dragged everywhere, while the still quick mind fumed with impatience. Somehow it seemed it was her fault he had ended up like this, maimed in service of the country, the people of which she was a part. She listened to Dan's perspectives on the sociology of war often when the news was on, but most of it fell on deaf ears, it didn't seem real to her, in the way that this young man pushed his presence into her consciousness. He was spoiling her mood, all her joy dampened. Even as she recognised the resentment she felt towards him, shame overcame it. He was grinning, enjoying her discomfiture.

A loud bang made her jump, a car backfiring in the street. Andrew jerked the wheelchair away from the table. He hit the wall behind him. His face was rigid, his eyes blank. Lynn reached out a hand to him. It was like touching a statue.

'Are you okay?'

He began to shake harder and harder although his legs stayed motionless. He was still staring right through her as if he could see a different landscape. What should she do? There were no other people in the café and May Gorman had gone into the back room. She looked out of the window, hoping that Annie was coming back.

Andrew blinked, came back, stared at her. He was still seeing things she had never seen but now he knew they were in the past, now he was aware of sitting here with her.

'Sorry.' He looked embarrassed and still slightly confused.

'I'm going to have a baby.' She couldn't think of anything else to say.

'I know. Mum told me. When?'

'November.' She couldn't help looking at his legs. The chances were Andrew Chapman would never father a child. She bit into her cake to distract herself.

'Not Bonfire night, I hope?' He looked at her and smiled. His expression softened and he looked like his mother.

'Fifteenth, or thereabouts.' Under the table, her hand went to her stomach. There was still nothing to feel there, nothing to show but her breasts straining heavy at her tee shirt.

'Is it a boy or a girl?'

'I don't know. I don't want to know. I'm having a scan next week, I can't wait to see it, but I want the sex to be a surprise.'

'If it's a boy, don't let him join the army.'

'Even more so if it's a girl?' They both smiled.

Someone tapped at the window, a blonde girl of about eighteen. Lynn was relieved.

The girl made faces at Andrew through the glass. His eyes lit up. The girl came in.

'I've been looking for you. I saw your mum. A few of us are going to Southport for the day. You want to come? Your mum says she'll make her own way home.'

'Sounds good to me.' He was trying not to appear keen, Lynn thought.

'You don't mind if I steal him?' The girl stood possessively behind the wheelchair.

'Not at all.' Lynn watched as Andrew expertly manoeuvred the wheelchair away from the table. Now he seemed just like any other young man with a pretty girl.

'Nice seeing you,' he said dismissively. 'Hope everything goes well for you.'

'Thanks. Have a good day out.' Lynn lifted her cup.

She was glad to be alone. His reaction to the backfire had frightened her. He was so young, yet his face had the look of a man who had seen hard things, secret things he knew someone like her couldn't know, wouldn't want to know. She wondered what he had been called on to do, what dilemmas he had faced and how his experiences had tempered or changed him. She felt as if she herself had done nothing in comparison. How could she criticise his coldness, his bitter brusqueness, the drinking she knew went on at the cottage? The place was becoming a meeting place for all the no-hopers of the district. Annie was always going on about it.

Yet his short stubby blond eyelashes reminded her of a young animal, a calf. The sprinkle of freckles over his nose was childlike and the skin of his neck was soft, like Imogen's.

Imogen's lashes were black and sweeping; they should have been on a girl. Where was he now? What would she do if he suddenly re-appeared or rang her mobile? One part of her wanted to see him, to re-assure herself that he was okay. He could be the father of her child and he would never know. She'd already decided she would make no attempt to find him even if the baby was his and Dan deserted her. Even if her family ostracised her it wouldn't matter. She would have the child and Alice. Her place was on the farm.

She'd thought it over, time and again in the long evenings while she waited for Dan to come home. Alice had taken to sitting by her side. There was a harmony between them now that went beyond words so that even though they couldn't converse, Lynn felt Alice would support her no matter what she did as long as she stayed loyal to the farm. She knew it was the child that had caused Alice to change, that drew her to her. At first she'd been afraid that Alice somehow wanted to steal her baby but she no longer felt any threat from her. Alice was the only one who understood her love for the farm.

'Penny for them?'

She jumped as Annie Chapman put a bunch of carnations on the table and pushed a chair into the space Andrew had left.

'I was just thinking about the future, how things are going to change now, with the baby coming.'

'Long time since there were a child on the farm. Con were the last and he's what, must be forty-six now. And he were a long time coming.'

'Oh?' Lynn drank her cooling coffee.

'Thirteen years Bert and Alice was married before she fell pregnant. She used to tell me when I were a girl, she thought she'd never have a child. And of course Christine and Con never did.'

'How strange. Dan and I have been married for six years. I confess I'd begun to think we'd never have a family.'

'You know Con and Diane have split up?'

'No!' Lynn thought of the lonely but frightening figure Con made walking round the fields at night. She'd never spoken to him since the time he'd put her fences up. She was hardly surprised that Diane had left him, but she felt vaguely sorry for him. She didn't care for Diane Worrall either. She hadn't gone back to her salon even though it meant driving to Ormskirk to get her hair done.

'She threw him out, must be six weeks ago. He's living over the Farmers' Arms. Suits him fine, I should think, the way he's drinking now. Everybody's talking about it. I blame him for the way our Andrew's gone. He got worse after Con started hanging round the cottage.'

'Threw him out of his own house? How could she do that?'

'He hit her. Broke her cheekbone. Didn't you hear about it? The whole village was agog. She locked him out, got an injunction on him. He can't go near her, or near the house.'

'I don't know many people here yet, besides you. Barney hasn't said anything.'

'Well, he wouldn't would he? Protecting his mates. Even he can keep his mouth shut when it suits him.'

'What's she going to do? Do you think she'll take him back?'

'Not if she's got any sense. It weren't just a slap you know and one smack is one too many. Rumour has it she's seeing someone else, though no one knows who it is, so it can't be anyone from round here. I got no time for her, never have had, but I got no time for a man that hits a woman, neither.'

Lynn was stunned. She'd never have taken Con Worrall for a wife-beater, despite his odd behaviour. She couldn't help thinking it was something to do with her and Dan, with Con giving up the farm. She pushed the thoughts away. Nothing mattered now except her baby. She had to concentrate on that.

'I'd better be getting back. Jim'll be coming in for dinner. Shanks's pony for me now Andy's gone off with Helen Jameson and her pals. Do him good to get out with some young ones. They're a sensible bunch, they won't let him get drunk – I hope.'

'I'd offer you a lift, but I'm just going to the library to do some reading up,' Lynn said. 'I'm still trying to find out how the Askin in my family ended up in Somerset. I don't suppose you know anything about their family history?'

'Only as far back as Bert and Alice. I remember Alice's mam and dad, Anne and Doug, and her grandmother, but that's all. You'd be better asking Con.'

They left the café together but separated outside. Lynn went down towards the car park. She was thinking about asking Con Worrall for help with her research. As if on cue, she saw him come out of the Farmers' Arms on the opposite side of the road and stand looking towards Diane's Den. He looked terrible, with several days beard and his clothes all crumpled. She hurried away to her car and drove to Ormskirk library.

The librarian had got to know Lynn over the last few months.

'What period are you looking for today?'

'I want to look up the family that used to live in our farmhouse. I think we may have a relation in common from way back. I've looked at them before but I need to go further back, starting from the 1930s and working backwards.'

'You're best looking at the parish records, births, marriages, deaths. Do you know what church they might have attended, what religion they were?'

'I don't. All I know is they built the farmhouse around 1880 and they were there until quite recently when the last son sold it.'

'At that time most of the land belonged to Lord Derby, mostly still does belong to the estate. And there were still a lot of problems with flooding so people moved about a fair bit.'

'The Mere.' Lynn shuddered, remembering the horrible dream where she had floundered in the icy water.

The librarian showed her where the collection of computer discs was kept and left her to get on with it. She settled down, scrolling through endless names, endless repetitions as families reproduced themselves over generations.

She went back through the records from Alice born in 1930 and found her siblings, Joan, Thomas and the baby William who lived only two years. The records led her further back to Alice's father Douglas, his father, Con's great-grandfather, George who built New Cut farm.

Time flew by. Her stomach growled. It was way past lunchtime when she sat back in satisfaction. George Askin's father Joseph, born in 1852 was the younger brother of Walter Askin, Lavinia Askin's father. The two branches were related. Her neck and back were aching, but she was exultant. She logged off the computer and took the discs back to the librarian.

'Any luck? It's a slow job.'

'I found them. Their family is related to mine.' She couldn't keep the excitement out of her voice.

'Fantastic,' the librarian enthused. 'I always feel it justifies keeping the archive when people use it like this.'

'Now I need to find out how my branch got to Somerset, where I was born.'

'Try the local history section, there might be something. And you could look through the old newspapers, we have them all on microfilm going back to 1840. Fascinating reading, if you've got the time, and the eyesight. I'm afraid the print is tiny.'

'I've quite a bit of time at the moment,' Lynn said. 'I'm expecting a baby.'

'Better get it done now then,' the woman smiled. 'You won't have any once it arrives.'

Lynn went out thinking about the work of looking after a baby; the feeding, washing, the sleepless nights. She knew Dan would pride himself on doing his share but maybe he would stop harassing her now about going back to work. She didn't want to put her baby in a nursery and plunge into academic life with a lot of strangers, have her time taken up with lesson plans and objectives. She had got used to the rhythms of the days at the farm, to sitting out on the garden bench whenever the rain went off, daydreaming about her child. But Dan was so keen for her to keep up with him, sharpen her intellect. Was she leaving the way open for Emma Cranton? She thought not. The baby would settle Dan, make them a family, bring them together. Anyway, there were always Emma Crantons. She would soon be forgotten.

As she drove back through Burscough she saw Con Worrall and Diane arguing in the doorway of Diane's Den. Con looked dirty and unkempt next to Diane in her pristine overall. Both of them bristled with hostility.

***

'You're not supposed to come here, you know that. I can't have you frightening my customers, ruining my business. Just leave me alone, Con.'

'I only want to talk to you.' Con swayed forward. 'You're my wife, Di.'

Diane stepped back 'That's over. You know that. Stop doing this. I'm calling the police.' She stepped back into the salon, went to the reception desk, and picked up the phone.

Con looked at them all, the customers, the stylists, even the apprentice, all frozen like sculptures, staring at him. 'It's not over, Di. I still love you.'

'Go away Con. I mean it, I'm calling the police.' She punched numbers on the keypad, never taking her eyes off his face.

Con looked round again, grinned at them all and waved, then turned and walked away. He went back to the Farmers' Arms. Jackie Mack pulled him a pint.

'Here, get this down you.' She took a film-wrapped cheese sandwich from the glass dome on the counter and pushed it across to him.

'No Barney? Not like him to miss lunch time.'

'He's down at the farm, helping Pilling to plant the leeks. Pilling was here yesterday, looking for you to see if you wanted a couple of days' work, but you weren't around.'

'I were busy.' Con couldn't remember yesterday, couldn't remember anything any more except how he burned for Diane, how he was fired up with anger at being turned out of his own house and eaten up with jealous suspicions that Diane was seeing someone else. Now the whispers and silences he'd had to endure at Computerland were all around him in his own place, where he had lived all his life. Only Barney and Jackie Mack showed him any sympathy. It was only thanks to Jackie's intervention that he'd got the room upstairs.

He wanted Barney to come and keep him company. There were a few young ones in, workers from the paper mill down the road but they looked askance at him and kept to their end of the bar, watching the sports news on television.

'Nothing doing, then?' Jackie Mack was back, twiddling her earrings.

'What?'

'I saw you going in the Den. You're not supposed to go near there are you? Must be hard though, losing the farm and now the house, never mind Diane.'

'It's not lost. We'll have to sell it.' He didn't want to talk to Jackie, didn't want to tell her all his business. She was nosey, always had been but she had been kind to him over the last few weeks since his life had been turned upside down.

'I should make myself scarce for a bit if I were you.' Jackie nodded towards the street. 'She'll have called the police.'

'She won't really do that.'

'She got the injunction, didn't she?'

'That was just temper. Revenge. And because, because – ' he couldn't come out and say, 'because I hit her,' that would make it real and it was indefensible. He especially couldn't say it to another woman even though he was sure that Jackie Mack already knew all the details. Diane hadn't lost much time putting it all round the village. For a moment he felt that his mother was no longer there. He could never have faced her with the knowledge of what he had done. But then, if she had still been there, none of this would ever have happened. Maybe he'd feel better if he went for a walk. Barney wasn't coming and he couldn't stay here having everything he said probed and pulled apart so that Jackie could gossip about it with the regulars later.

He looked out of the window and saw a police car park outside the salon.

'See you later,' he told Jackie, putting the sandwich in his pocket and emptying his glass. There was no time to get Rolo from the yard. Outside he turned right and walked quickly away in the direction of the canal.

***

He's a good farmer is Pilling, good Lancashire stock. It's like the old days, seeing the land worked so well, the soil fine and soft despite all the rain and the leek slips row after row, their tips poking out of their holes in neat, straight lines, for as far as you can see, all three fields. Leeks is an easy crop compared to tatties or cabbage. They're not bothered by blight or eelworms, or root fly or caterpillars. Mildew and rust is all you has to watch for and sometimes white rot but you won't get that if the land's in good heart.

He's a good man too, Pilling, ready to give our Con a day's work even after he's sunk so low. I scarce recognise him even though he's my own son.

I've heard them whispering, Barney Dougan and the other casuals, the Harrison boys from out Newburgh. I couldn't credit my ears when I first heard what they were gossiping about but I know Barney Dougan. He's full of the blarney and tall tales, but he'd never lie about something like that.

Striking a woman. For shame, Con. If your father were here, he'd knock you into the middle of next week, for all Diane's a vixen and a strumpet too by all accounts. I always felt she were no good, right from the start but that don't excuse you. How could you bring shame on our family name like this?

I don't know Con now, don't know what he's become. I've seen him in the middle of the night, roaming the fields like a will o' the wisp, with the fires of hell in his eyes. There's nowt does for a man like drink once he's gone over to it. I don't mean the odd glass, there's not many as doesn't thirst for a cool pint of beer after a dusty day on the land. We always had beer or cider with our suppers at home, but there's drinking and drinking and Con's gone way past the limit.

And we had such dreams for him, me and Bert. Once we got the farm we knew one day it would be his and all the work, all the struggle to keep it up were worth it, because it were his inheritance.

But Bert never felt the way I did about the land. He were a newcomer, and his family were only ever farmhands, working in one place or another. It were a vanity to him, becoming Lord of the Manor so to speak, when Dad left the farm to him. Bert knew the land all right, loved it in his own way, but his way were to overcome it. He didn't see the land, only the money to be made from it. He weren't one with it the way I were – still am, and in the end that were his downfall.

Here comes Con now, sloping along the hedgerows like a baby with his bottle. He thinks no one is watching, but I see him, treading the edge of the Mere, watching Pilling doing the work he should be doing. I know he's thinking the same thoughts as me and when Pilling stops the planter and gets down from the tractor to speak to him, my heart lifts.

Pilling will give him a start and if he gets back on the land, maybe even now it won't be too late but I know my son. I can see pride in the set of his legs, in the way he rears his head back to answer Pilling and I know he's going to turn down even this chance and there's nothing I can do to save him from himself.

Chapter Eleven

October 2008

There had been a farmers' association of sorts in the district of West Lancashire since 1865 but from the coverage in the old newspapers it seemed that it had been largely controlled by the landowners, replicating the traditional master-servant relationship: an opportunity for the owners to secure and consolidate the loyalty of the tenants.

Lynn rubbed her belly. She was in 1893, peering at the tiny newsprint on the microfilm reel. She was reading a report on the meeting of the Farmers' Club where a request for a rent reduction in view of hardship had been turned down by the estate's trustees.

The farmers complained of agricultural depression, of cheap foreign produce being brought in, undercutting prices. Nothing changes, Lynn thought, visualising the shelves of produce from all round the world sitting on supermarket shelves, while the good arable land of the district lay fallow, or was used for grazing horses or storing caravans. And now, large pieces of local farmland were being sold off for industrial building. Within the last few months, a huge distribution centre had sprung up on the flat landscape, close to the motorway that cut through the area.

She sat back to relieve her spine. She and Dan were as guilty as any, thoughtlessly filling their shopping trolley with out of season foods from Spain, Holland or South Africa.

She read on. The landlords had pointed out the superb fertility of the best drained land, the rich soil of the Mere bed. The farmers had rejoined with complaints about the difficulties of keeping the land adequately drained and the poor soils that resulted on those fields most prone to flooding. Constant battle and expense was needed to keep the land sweet.

These were solid, respectable men, not the powerless day labourers whose hand-to-mouth existence depended on them. Yet the gulf between them and the estate owners, with their shooting parties and their town and country homes, was enormous in those days before economic changes and the machines of war sounded a death knell for that way of life. The meeting had ended bitterly.

Letters went to and fro in the correspondence columns of the local papers. Individual farmers took sides, some putting their trust in the estate bailiffs, others speaking out against the landowners, accusing them of failing to recognise farmers' needs. The agents retaliated by claiming agitators were at work, attempting to set tenants against landlords and they sounded a rallying call to tenant farmers to show solidarity with the landlords in the common cause of husbandry.

And here was the agitator. Lynn's interest focussed on the letter from 'an Aughton farmer', decrying the move to expel Reuben Blackmore from the Farmers' Club because of his attempt to organise a protest of tenant farmers in the matter of rent reductions. She followed the responses that flew back and forth in successive issues of the Advertiser. These increased in ire and accusations until in August the news broke that Blackmore had been evicted from his farm and had left the district.

Lynn scanned the pages with mounting excitement. A letter from the agent claimed that the notice to quit was nothing to do with Blackmore's abilities as a farmer but had been issued as a result of his own expressions of dissatisfaction with his farm. She read between the lines, imagining the harsh words that must have passed between the two men, Blackmore dissatisfied not with his farm, but with the landlord's handling of his tenancy. He must have found himself in an impossible position. She knew nothing about the man, yet she felt a familial pride and admiration at his courageous stance.

After his departure, correspondence on the subject gradually tailed off, until a final letter from Blackmore himself. Lynn read it carefully, imagining her ancestor scratching the lines with a stick pen and rusty ink.

> *Sir,*
> *The tyranny of landlords in the West Lancashire locality is now rampant. They have tried to terrify and crush me and to corrupt farmers wholesale. Recently a dismal story has been*

> *told of how one such farmer, as agent of the trustees was sent round to all the other farmers in the district asking them to sign a petition to expel me from the Farmers' Club and to repudiate and condemn all that I have said and done.*
> *Other farmers have signed this against their will only because they were afraid not to do so.*
> *From this you will perceive how such intimidation is debasing men who wish only to be virtuous. Clearly there is no longer any place for honest farmers in the district and it is for this reason alone that I have felt constrained to give up my farm and remove myself and my family to other parts where a man may farm at peace with his conscience.*
> *Yours respectfully*
> *Reuben Blackmore,*
> *Chawleigh, Devon.*

Chawleigh was less than thirty miles from her parents' home.

The child inside her somersaulted as she checked over her notes. Dan was going to love this. She couldn't wait to tell him. She would drive up to the uni now, catch him for lunch. She tried to ring his mobile but it went to voicemail. She would just have to wait for him to finish the class if he were teaching.

She was stuck behind a tractor for most of the journey. The grain fields were shaved stubble but sprouts and cabbages still greened the land. The tractor trailer carried a load of potatoes, dropping a few each time it went round a corner. At home, Pilling had harvested the early leeks.

She felt completely comfortable now in this rural world. It seemed a lifetime ago that she had trotted along college corridors, spent her time on lesson plans and marking. It was as if she were floating away from Dan and his world of education, his rush of work, reading, keeping up with the intellectual scene. He was hoping she would change once the baby was born, that she would want to get back to work, become the companion he wanted but it was Dan who would have to change, even though he didn't yet realise it.

Maybe she would return to work one day, but for now she was content to be on the farm. They were enjoying the first fruits from the garden, fresh picked vegetables. Barney was doing the work she could no longer manage. It was home, the right place to wait for her child to be born, but she shared it more with Alice than with Dan.

Alice was everywhere, in the house, on the land. Lynn wondered if she appeared to Andrew in the cottage but she had never dared to ask him or Annie after the way Diane had laughed at her when she'd told her about the haunting and Andrew was so cynical and bitter. He wouldn't be one to believe in ghosts either. It was as if Alice belonged solely to her. Lynn felt her benign presence watching over her, helping her to learn the ways of the land.

Things were going to change soon. She knew Dan would want to spend more time at home once the baby arrived. She would test the water, ask him today about taking paternity leave, after she'd told him the news about Reuben Blackmore.

Parked cars cluttered the road on the approach to the campus. Eventually Lynn found a space. She made her way through throngs of chatting students across the square in front of the main building and entered the wing where Dan's department was housed.

There was no one around, but she could hear noises coming from Dan's room. She would just pop her head round the door, let him know she was there.

There was a sound from inside as she knocked, a sound that she recognised, a sound she had often made herself and instantly she was aware of intense cold shocking her body, all except for the tips of her ears burning, blazing as her hand turned the door knob before she could stop it and the door swung open.

Dan turned towards her as he pulled himself out of the woman bent over the desk. His features were a mismatched jumble like an abstract painting as he struggled to shove his cock back into his jeans.

Lynn looked at the woman's white buttocks, the wet cunt glistening. She took in the hiked black skirt, the ice-white hair. Emma Cranton turned her head and looked at her. Her green eyes were dreamy with pleasure. She smiled her cruel hunting-cat smile. Lynn turned and walked away, planting her feet one after the other. Her baby was a huge stone in her belly. The corridor was endless.

***

Con saw the Porsche parked outside Diane's Den when he came out of the shop. It was black and highly polished. The autumn sunshine glinted off its surfaces. A man came out and jumped in the driver's seat and then Diane followed, in jeans and a tight red top, Milly tucked under her arm. Her hair, loose on her shoulders, was yellow in the sunlight.

So, it was true. He flattened himself against the wall, but she didn't notice him. She only had eyes for her new lover. He wasn't local, that was for sure. He looked young, dark and lean, younger than Con, much younger than Alex, and rich. Con laughed to himself. He would have to be rich. Diane had taken Alex for half of everything he had and now she was fighting for half of Con's inheritance and this would be the next poor sucker.

Maybe he was just a toy boy, someone she'd soon tire of. Then she would realise what she had lost, come running back to him, but he wouldn't look at her, not even if she begged, not after what she'd done to him.

The car roared away. He saw Diane laughing then they were gone. He crossed the road back to the pub, the two flat half-bottles of whisky weighing down the pockets of his jacket. He couldn't face the bar without Barney and lately Barney always seemed to be working up at New Cut. The cheek of Pilling, trying to get Con working as a casual on his own land. He wasn't that desperate yet. He'd told him where to get off all right.

Jackie Mack was in a corner chatting to some women who were eating lunchtime sandwiches with their glasses of lager. They were like a coven of witches, watching him as he went through to the staircase and up to his room.

The divorce papers were still on the dressing table where he had left them but the cleaner had been in. His bed was made and the bedside table had been wiped clean. It would be all round the village before nightfall. No wonder those old bats downstairs had stared at him like that.

He opened one of the bottles and drank straight from it. Phrases from the divorce petition floated through his mind. *Irretrievable breakdown, intolerable behaviour, intoxicated, violent, assault, injunction.*

His mother had been right all along. Diane was no good. She'd warned him that Diane would ruin him and he'd laughed, told her not to be jealous, but she'd been right. Diane was a townie and her gods were money and possessions. But he still wanted her. Despite everything, if she came to him now he wouldn't be able to say no.

The pain of wanting her stung him and he drank more to blur it all away, looking out of the window at the shadows that grew as the sun's power waned. Time meant nothing as he waited for the Porsche to bring her back.

The sound of footsteps along the corridor to his room roused him. His head had sunk on his chest and a string of spittle ran from his mouth to the top button of his shirt.

'It's only me,' Jackie Mack shouted from the other side of the door. 'Can I come in?' She entered before he could answer. 'Brought you some toast and a coffee. You okay, hon?'

He grunted, rubbing his eyes against the low sun that now glared into the room. He tried to look at Jackie, but she was just a black silhouette after the bright light.

'Look at the state of you.' She clicked her tongue against her teeth and put the coffee and toast down on top of the papers on the dressing table. She went into the tiny bathroom, came back with a wet tissue and wiped his face.

She was big and smothering, bending over him like that and the smell of her perfume mixed faintly with sweat, caught in his throat but he could feel the warmth of her. His hands went to her breasts, touching the flesh that bulged out of her low top and she pulled his face up to hers. Her long fingernails dug into his cheeks and her lipsticky mouth opened to the pressure of his tongue.

He would show her, that Diane, show them all what kind of man he was. They laughed at him, but they would see. He'd give Jackie Mack something to gossip about.

He pulled her breasts roughly out of her bra, listened to her groan as he fastened his mouth round her nipple. Her hand was on his leg, reaching up to his crotch, feeling how stiff he was then she pulled away.

'There are condoms in the dispenser downstairs.'

When he came back, she was naked. He stared at the expanses

of her bared flesh as she lay on the bed, leaning on her elbows and grinning at him, waiting.

'What about your boyfriend?' The last thing Con needed was trouble with another woman.

'He went back to his wife.' She shrugged, making her bosom heave.

Without her clothes, her flesh was everywhere. Her breasts were huge, twice the size of Diane's. They flopped on her chest and her hips spread across the bed as she raised dimpled thighs to meet him. He was on her before he had time to think about it, burrowing into her warmth, burying his head in the great mounds of her breasts.

For a moment he was making love to Diane, her small round tits bouncing, her slender waist arched under him, his hands clamping her tight little arse, then he opened his eyes, looked down, felt himself wilt.

It was no use. The more she worked, the more he turned off. He was humiliated by her efforts. Her hands expertly massaged him. Her strawberry lips made red rings round his limp penis. At last she gave up, got up and went into the bathroom.

He rolled over and buried his face in the pillow. He didn't care, hadn't wanted her in the first place. Who had asked her to come up here and force herself on him, the fat old cow? He couldn't wait for her to go so he could get in the shower and wash the sweaty stink of her off his body.

Nothing was said. At last he heard the click of the door as she left, then the sound of her moving down the corridor. He got up and fetched the whisky bottle, ignoring the cold toast and scummy coffee that sat on top of the divorce petition.

***

Lynn wanted only to get home. Despite the heat of the sun, her bones ached with cold. She couldn't stop shivering as she drove. She wanted to hide in the house, where no one could see her, no one but Alice. She barely looked where she was going. All she could see was Dan's face, smeared with sex and shock, as his office door had opened. She had never seen him so emotionally naked before.

She was almost at the farmhouse when she noticed the clutter of vehicles on the verge of the driveway. She stared, puzzled, dragging herself away from the vision of Dan and Emma Cranton to the question of the present. None of the cars were familiar. One was a BBC film unit van. What was going on? Alarm fizzed through her as she drove past them into the yard.

Two men with cameras slung round their necks were smoking by the outhouses. They stopped talking when they saw her and before she could get out they were at the car door.

'Mrs Waters?'

'What is it?' She shielded her face as they snapped her. 'What's happened? Who are you?'

'Liverpool Echo. They've dug something up,' one of them said. He had a broad Liverpool accent. 'A body.'

'A body?' Lynn repeated. Her stomach pulsed and the child turned. She put one hand over it. 'What are you talking about?'

She followed their gaze. She hadn't noticed the gaggle of people on the edge of the far field. She'd been too busy re-visiting the nightmare scene with Dan. They were huddled in a circle like some strange pagan gathering while Pilling's tractor sat behind them, the lifted ploughshare glinting in the sunlight. Other machines cluttered the field, pumps and generators.

She followed the camera men, her mind blank with horror. A body – on her land. Who? How? Why?

Barney Dougan and Pilling separated themselves from the group and clumped along the footpath to meet her.

'What is it? What's happened?' she gasped. The child turned and turned and she stopped to steady herself, catch her breath. Any moment she was going to be sick.

'It's okay now; it's nothing for you to be worrying yourself about. Come on.' Barney took her arm, led her towards the edge of the field. His eyes gleamed with excitement. He was grinning at her. Grinning! She must be going mad. She turned back to the two men but they had already disappeared into the crowd.

'They said there's a body?'

'Aye, we hit it this morning, not long after you'd gone out.' Pilling pushed his cap off his forehead. 'We'd just started ploughing over where the leeks had been when I felt this almighty thump. Thought it were a bog oak, they're common round here.'

'Bog oak?' She didn't understand, didn't understand anything. The whole world had shifted on the turn of a door knob and Pilling's mouth opened and closed without anything meaningful coming out.

'You know this land were under the Mere?'

She nodded because it seemed expected of her, although his words seemed to be rolling down a tunnel from somewhere far away.

'In dry times, the Mere'd shrink and trees'd grow round the edge, then when it flooded again, the trees would drown and fall in the lake. Over the centuries they turn black and hard as hell. Bloody nuisance, I can tell you, when you hit one, ruins the ploughshare.

'Anyway, I jumps down and looks at it, careful, didn't try to pull it clear, because you know, years ago, when I were a nipper, my dad hit one but it turned out to be a log boat, prehistoric, it's in the museum at Churchtown now.'

'But they said it was a body?' Lynn was bewildered.

'Aye. First thing I seen when I looked down were a great lump of peat. It were only when I got down off the tractor that I saw the hand. It were black like twigs all stuck together but for all that and for all the muck on it, I could tell it were human.'

'We're going to be on the telly,' Barney said. 'Six o'clock news.'

Why was he so excited? He seemed pleased, yet it was horrible. Someone had died on her land and no one had known. How long had he or she lain there, in the silent darkness of the soil? What would happen now? Would there be police, questions? Was it something to do with Con Worrall, or with Alice? Who were all those people?

She looked around but Alice was nowhere to be seen.

'Have the police been?'

'They were here this morning, but it's not a case for them. It's a bog body.'

Pilling smiled, his teeth white against his sunburned face.

Lynn shaped the words with her lips. Bog body. They meant nothing to her. She looked at him questioningly.

'Over a thousand years old. Mummified in the peat. There's quite a few been dug up round the country in different mosses. You'll be famous. Come and see. The university people are working on getting it out.'

Lynn stumbled over the furrows, Barney Dougan holding her arm. 'Careful does it now, Mrs Waters, you don't want to be bringing on a mishap.' He stopped to pat Blondie who was sitting on the path waiting patiently.

Barney ushered Lynn past the camera men and the film crew. In a fair-sized hole a team of people were carefully scraping at a bed of rusty brown peat. Lighter patches of something stood out here and there, wood or maybe it was leather. Two more men were securing slings round it which they proceeded to inflate.

'They're from the university at Liverpool,' Pilling said. 'You don't mind me letting them on to your land? I didn't know how to get hold of you or your husband.'

'Of course not,' Lynn said. She peered into the hole as the men on top began pulling on the ropes while the two in the hole supported the slings. Slowly the chunk of peat rose to the surface.

Lynn laughed out loud. 'It's just a tree,' she turned to Pilling. Relief washed over her.

'Look,' Pilling whispered. 'Look again.'

The thing was dark and ancient against the bright yellow slings. It was peat and yet not peat. She recoiled when she saw the outstretched hand, like the claw of a bird. But how could that flattened, wooden thing be a human being? It was no more than an inch or two thick, curved and twisted like a gnarled branch and it was impossible to tell where peat ended and flesh began. With a thrill of horror, she saw a face, flat and elongated, the cheekbones drawn up and out, the eye sockets stretched, an oriental caricature of a face with its mouth perfectly formed and pulled into an over-wide smile. It looked like something conjured up for a science-fiction film, or a piece of innovative wood sculpture not quite released from its origins. Its body was curved and its legs fused like a monstrous merman. It seemed essentially male, although Lynn could see no means of identifying its sex. Suddenly she remembered the awful nightmare she'd had when they first came to the farm, where the mere had returned black and evil, grasping her thighs and a foul thing had floated just under the surface, something that had looked like this.

The landscape that she'd thought of as her own seemed frozen round her. She was temporary, meaningless to it and this thought so terrified her that she wanted to turn and run but there was nowhere to go. Almost at once, Alice was beside her, as if she was trying to tell her something. She grasped for it but it was elusive. Her sense of her own importance, of her baby's priority, kept filling her mind while Alice's message had something to do with integration and harmony, just as the long-dead man before them was part and yet not part of the block of peat in which he was embedded.

A sombreness seemed to invade the air as they all stood looking. The sun suddenly faded and dwindled behind grey clouds and a solitary bird flew overhead. Lynn heard the rhythmic beat of its wings as it passed low and she shuddered at the melancholy whisper of the sound. The bog man silenced them all, presenting his mortality.

It was like a moment of respect then Barney broke the silence.

'Lord have mercy, look at its neck.' He crossed himself and muttered a prayer.

'It's like all the others,' Pilling said.

'What? What do you mean?' Lynn craned her neck. 'What can you see?'

A girl had climbed out of the hole and was wiping muddy hands on her white boiler suit. 'It's a ligature. Look, round his neck. See how tight it was tied. He was murdered, garrotted.'

'But why?' Lynn looked closer, horrified but fascinated. She could smell the damp peaty reek of the earth and the lingering oniony smell of the recently harvested leeks.

'Who knows?' the girl shrugged. 'We think it's some kind of ritual. We've seen it before. They've been dug up all over the country and they're all the same. It's thought to be some kind of sacrifice.'

The baby squirmed and Lynn felt faint. The sun came out again but she was chilled and the ground seemed to quiver beneath her. She could feel water in the yielding softness of the soil. She trod backwards until she felt the firm texture of the grass path. What was this place she had come to, a place of ghosts, of ritual sacrifice, neither land nor water and yet a place where somehow she belonged?

She stared across the fields where the land met the sky, smooth and impassive. Clouds were piling up in the west. Soon it would rain. She turned and Alice turned with her. Today she was middle-aged, a scarf covering her short salt-and-pepper hair. She looked at Lynn and her expression was cunning, complicit. It was as if she and Lynn were bound together in something that Lynn didn't yet fully understand.

'Excuse me, I'm from the BBC. Mrs Waters? Could I ask you a few questions for the six o'clock news?'

Lynn looked at the young man in his neat suit. He didn't belong here, any more than the rest of his crew. She saw Alice cock her head towards the farmhouse where Dan was running along the footpath. Lynn saw the swinging door, Emma Cranton's naked buttocks, her taunting smile, Dan's expression. She looked down at the twisted face of the bog man.

'Maybe you'd better talk to my husband.' She turned away.

***

What kind of omen is this that the land's given up, this twisted thing like the dark places of the human mind? The bog man – on my land.

I've seen them on TV but I never seen one real before and it's a scary thing, but pitiful too, with its bent body and that hand reaching out for help, or to curse, pointing its finger.

Look at that face now, it's like the land itself that lives unchanging, or changing so slow that the likes of us don't see it, a face that doesn't know us or care about us. It's lain there all them years, centuries, under the water of the mere, sleeping in the dark mud, shifting round in the earth layers, waiting for the day, the right moment for Pilling's plough to bring it up into our lives, into our thoughts. Why this time, this day, the bog man puts in his appearance isn't for us to know.

It's an omen all right, with the strangling cord round its neck, a mark of birth and death together in one sign. Murder will out. They say the Mere's full of secrets never told.

It pulls. I can feel it. Those old stories my Gran used to tell, the tales we'd giggle over when I were a young girl, about boggarts and Jenny Greenteeth, they were only shadows of the power that streams from this woody, human, earth shape.

We're in its circle, all of us here; the TV camera draws the eye of the world to this spot, this moment. She's here, and here comes her husband, summoned, running to the unknown, to a place he can never find in his schoolbook learning. Now, only one is missing, but I sense the drawing. I know he hears it calling. Con is coming. The time comes for stories to be told, secrets revealed, but I'm afeared for my boy and for Lynn. Why now, why this moment, with her so near her time?

***

'What do you want me to do? Do you want me to go?' Dan put his head in his hands. The lines of his body despaired.

Lynn was too exhausted to think. She lay on the sofa behind the huge bulk of her belly. 'Go where? Off with that tramp?'

'You know she means nothing.' Dan looked at her through his fingers.

'You said that last time. Remember the PhD student, Judith something?'

'But it's true. I never meant it to happen. It's just been hard, the new house, new job, and then the baby. You know Lynn, we haven't had sex in months. My defences were down, it was just one of those things.'

Lynn hesitated. Maybe she should confess her own moment of weakness. Maybe now was a good time, but she held back. He was weaker than her for all his arrogance, she saw that now. He wouldn't cope with her confession the way she'd coped with her suspicions about Emma Cranton. He wouldn't be able to see it was his fault anyway. If she hadn't been smarting over his affair with Emma she would never have bedded Imogen.

Did she want him to go? He was her husband, she still loved him and she had lived through his infidelities before but somehow it didn't seem that important. It was all part of a larger picture involving the imminent birth of her child, her relationship with Alice, and the farm. Events were rolling to an unseen conclusion beyond her control and she would accept what came. Her only fear was for her child. The newsman had told her the history of the bog men, how they died a triple death of strangulation, head injury and stab wounds, thought to be of ritual significance. The finding of the remains on her land at this moment seemed propitious, a harbinger of sacrifice to the earth. But who was to be the new victim? She was certain of one thing, she would never let it be her baby. She looked at Dan's pleading eyes. Could they still be a happy family, the three of them, after what she'd seen in his office?

The actual sight of the act, Dan's glistening penis, Emma Cranton's vagina dribbling juices, was burned on her brain. In the nine hours that had elapsed since the event, she had walked through that door hundreds of times. She couldn't stop doing it. She didn't think she ever would.

'I need a drink.' He got up and went to the kitchen. 'You want one?'

She shook her head as he turned to her in the doorway. If he went, they would have to sell the farm. She would be forced back to work, would have to put her baby in a nursery. She would have to return to the city, maybe even move in with her parents for a while. It was unthinkable. Her place was here. She looked at Alice sitting in the chair by the window. She was nodding, waiting while Lynn thought out the implications, examined her choices.

Dan returned with a large brandy. That hangdog expression was one he knew she'd always fallen for. Despite all his treachery, under all the hurt, she still felt love for him. As if he sensed her softening, he came to her, knelt beside the sofa, took her hand and stroked her fingers.

'I don't want to go.' She offered no resistance and he put his head in the curve below her belly at the top of her thighs. 'I can hear the baby,' he murmured. His hands ran over the distended flesh and the child stilled as tremors ran round Lynn's body.

'I don't want you to go.' She stroked his hair and he groaned. She felt his shiver of relief. It mirrored her own calmness once she'd made the decision.

They stayed in silence, each with their own thoughts. At last Dan said, 'It won't happen again.'

'No,' she sighed, letting his hair slide through her fingers. 'It has to stop.'

He kissed the underside of her belly through her thin smock. All her sexual parts tingled. She saw herself opening his office door and pushed the picture away.

'I was coming to tell you, I found some stuff about Lavinia's husband. I was so excited I couldn't wait for you to come home. I thought, I thought we could have some lunch together.'

'I'm sorry.' Dan's voice was low, broken, but it had lost its urgency, now that he knew she was ready to forgive him.

'I thought you'd be so interested, it was all about the early collectivisation of farmers against local landlords. He was evicted from his farm, they said he was an agitator.' Her voice talked on but all the time she was thinking, thinking of what lay ahead and watching Dan's reactions like a hawk with a mouse. She could feel Alice beside her, watching, waiting.

'Yeah?' Dan didn't stir. He really must feel bad, Lynn thought. Under normal circumstances he'd have jumped up and demanded to see her notes.

'He went to live in Devon, a few miles away from our family home. That's how our family came to be in the area.'

'Are you sure you checked your facts properly? You need to research from the Somerset end too. Maybe we could go and stay with your parents for a bit, after the baby's born.'

She smiled. He was always the social scientist. 'We'll see.' She had no intention of leaving the farm.

'I know it's keeping your mind active, but, like I've said before, maybe you shouldn't get too hung up on all this stuff.'

'What do you mean?'

'I don't know. It's just, you've changed since we came here. You're not interested in the uni, in my work, you don't want to go back to teaching. I hoped it was just a pregnancy symptom but you seem to be getting more and more like the people round here, never going anywhere, listening to local gossip.'

'I like it here. I feel like I belong. I thought the idea was that we would both spend more time at home. Is that why you took up with Emma, because you find me too boring?'

'This isn't like you. It's just your hormones. There's something funny here, I'll give you that. This afternoon, after you left, I came after you. I couldn't think straight. You'd gone by the time I got to the car park. I rushed back here and then, when all I wanted was to talk to you, put things right, there was that thing in the ground, pointing like some kind of doom bearer.

'I mean, from a scientific point of view it's a marvellous discovery, a fascinating piece of history, but seeing it there all covered in mud, those sightless eyes – it gave me the shivers.'

It wasn't like Dan to admit to feelings that couldn't be rationally explained but she remembered the horror and that paid him back in her mind for the pleasure on his face when she discovered him with Emma. She thought of the shock he must have felt, the turmoil in his mind as he chased after her, leaving him open to the impact of the bog man, silently rising from the depths of the earth. She smiled to herself.

'There's something weird about this place. If I didn't know better, I'd think it was haunted.' He hesitated. 'Maybe I should look for another post.'

The words jolted through her body. She sat up, tipping him off her belly. The drink in his hand spilled on the carpet.

'But we've only just got here.'

'Steady on, it was just a thought. After the baby's born. Might do us good to make a fresh start.'

***

Con was waiting till he felt sure that Jackie Mack would have finished work and gone home, but the whisky was all gone and he had to have more. It was starting to get dark already. He checked the radio alarm by his bed. It was twenty-past-five.

He looked out of the window at Diane's Den. There was no sign of the Porsche but a white van was parked outside and the sound of hammering came faintly through the glass. He opened the window to let the cool air come in. A man was fixing a sign into position over the door of the shop.

Con's throat closed over. He shut the window and threw on his coat. He was at the bottom of the stairs before he remembered Jackie Mack. She was still there. Her eyes bored into him as he crossed the bar and he couldn't stop himself from glancing over at her.

Her mouth twisted, then she turned on a taunting little smile and muttered something to the landlady who was polishing glasses beside her. They both laughed as he went out of the door. His face burned as he remembered his earlier performance, or rather the lack of it. 'Brewer's droop,' Diane used to say with that same taunting smile. He felt sick with shame. What was wrong with him? He couldn't even screw Jackie Mack properly. But it wasn't that. He'd got it up okay, hadn't he? It was her fault, she was too fat and flabby.

He stopped opposite the salon. The man was climbing down the ladder. The FOR SALE sign rattled in the breeze. Village Estates, Aspinwall's firm. So much for sympathy with farmers. Aspinwall was just another snake-in-the-grass. He'd be happily flogging the house he'd not long sold them in the next few weeks. Diane's solicitors had sent a letter asking Con to sign permission for the sale.

He'd already decided to let it all go through, the sale, the divorce, everything. She wasn't going to come back to him, he knew that, and now her selling the business put a final stamp on the end of their marriage. It meant she was going to move away, disappear from his life altogether. What was the point of fighting? He had lost everything that meant anything to him. He walked back to the shop to buy two more bottles of whisky.

'Heard the news?' Amir took his twenty.

'The salon's up for sale? I've just seen the sign.'

'I didn't know that.' Amir looked sympathetic. 'No, I meant about the body. They found a body on your farm.'

'A body? Who?' Con forgot everything.

'Oh, it's old, hundreds of years old, prehistoric it said on the news.'

'A bog man?'

'Yeah, that's what they called it. Preserved in the peat, they said. A tractor dug it up this morning. Barney was on the telly and some professor from Liverpool University.'

'Trust Barney,' Con said. He took his change. Through the window he saw Jackie Mack come out of the pub and walk towards Ramsbottom's. He went back through the bar and fetched Rolo from the yard, then turned left on the street and walked towards the end of the village.

In the cul-de-sac where he used to live, the Porsche sat outside his house. Con felt his face fire up again. The night was coming on fast and lights shone in the windows, upstairs and down. The master bedroom curtains were drawn.

Con watched for a long time but he didn't see anything. When the first bottle was empty and no one had come out, he pulled on

Rolo's lead and walked back up the street to the chip shop. He bought a meat pie and chips and sat down on the bench by the canal towpath to eat, but after a few bites, he gagged and put the food down for the dog.

It was dark now and the water lay silently between its stone banks. Cars still roared over the bridge and lights from the road were reflected in the black canal. Con went back to the shop and bought four cans of Special Brew, then started walking along the towpath.

He wondered about the bog body, if it was still there. He had seen one once, in the museum in Liverpool when he was a young man. It had been a touring exhibition, something about farming and he had gone on a Young Farmers' day out. He remembered how creepy and scary it had looked with its wizened form and empty face. A sacrifice, the curator had told them, but to what no one knew.

Like himself, a sacrifice to Diane. Now he was finished, it was all over. Birds flew into sleeping quarters in the privet hedge along the path. He thought of Jackie Mack, lying on the bed, beckoning him, the great hairy bush between her legs waiting to gobble him up and he began to laugh, then felt tears running down his face.

Just ahead, the lights of the Turk's Head broke the darkness, chased away the spectres. Blondie was tied up outside. Con stopped, irresolute. Should he cross the bridge and go in? He wanted a drink, the warmth of human company, but Dottie Martin cleaned there as well as at the Farmers'. They would all know every detail of the divorce petition by now, his sexual failure would have been discussed minutely along with his penchant for violence. He couldn't face the way they would break off their conversations when he went in, act as if they knew nothing. He would have to go along with the pretence and Barney would be boasting about his part in finding the bog body.

Con popped a can of beer and walked on. Pictures jumbled through his brain; Jackie Mack's sneering smile, Diane taunting him, the way she'd laughed with the guy in the Porsche, John Dawson's tight-lipped mug, Alex, Aspinwall, all of them, all of them out to screw him one way or another.

He came to the farm, turned up the path where the bog man's

burial site had been taped round and covered over with a tarpaulin. He squatted down and peered underneath. There was nothing to see, only the empty hole like the socket of a tooth. There was a bare sliver of moon to see by, the stars were hidden by slow rolling clouds and as Con hunkered there, he heard the patter of rain against the cloth cover. 'Dark as the hobs of hell,' he seemed to hear his mother's voice and he turned towards the lighted cottage.

Everything was gone, his home, his family. There were strangers on his land, in his house and the most precious thing he had gambled on, his possession of Diane, was also gone.

This land he stood on was the same land he had always walked. He belonged here, just like the bog man, just like his mother had always told him. If only he had listened. The tears kept rolling down his face and he felt in his pocket for the second bottle of whisky. Something snaked in his hand and he pulled it out. It was the tie he'd ripped off that last day at Computerland.

The rain was coming down heavily. He looked round for Rolo but the dog was nowhere to be seen. He walked back to the road, whistling, then set off for the shelter of the small copse of trees that hid Holmes farm. He climbed the stile onto the footpath that bordered the small wood and walked alongside the ditch at the edge of the field. The ditch glimmered, almost full of dark water, its surface patterned by the driving rain. He sat down under the shelter of a great silver birch, his back against its trunk. He stared at the lights of the village in the distance while he emptied the beer cans one by one, then started on the second whisky bottle.

***

Now it's time to tell what I never wanted to tell, what I never did tell before, what I never even thought about again once it were done. I wouldn't tell it now but I need to show her the way. Nineteen years me and Bert had the farm after Dad died and for fifteen of them we were happy enough working side by side. We never had no money to speak of. What we had went into making sure Con had all he needed at school and later, helping him and Christine when they got married.

But them last four years, Bert's chest got worse and worse.

What with the cough at night when he lay down and the spitting when he got up in the morning, I could tell it wouldn't be long till he would have to let Con take over the farm. I looked forward to it, a time when we could take a little rest, sit in the sunshine, maybe grow a few flowers and just enough veg for ourselves.

But Bert had other ideas. It were a complete shock to me when he said he wanted to sell up the farm and buy a retirement flat in St Annes-on-Sea. I were gobsmacked. He might as well have suggested moving to the end of the world.

I should have seen it coming, but I didn't. Bert's sister Nellie had bought one of them flats when they were built the year before and she come to us at Christmas, giving out about how wonderful it were but I never thought Bert would be one to want to move away. Didn't he tell me when Dad left him the farm that it would still belong to me and to Con?

I never paid no mind at first. I thought it were just another of them crazy ideas he'd soon forget about, like the time he were going to buy an acre of glasshouses, but he kept going on about it. Then, in the winter of '95, he took bad just after Christmas and I were kept busy day and night, running up and down the stairs with hot drinks and medicines and rubbing his chest and his back. The thanks I got were him telling me he'd made up his mind to sell the place, whether I agreed to it or not.

'It's for the best Alice, you might not think so now, but we'll be much happier away from here. It's too much for us now.'

'I'm not for going,' I said. 'This is my family home. Let Con take the farm. We can live in the cottage, give Barney Dougan notice.' He were struggling for breath.

'Listen,' he leaned up to whisper. His voice were thin and papery. 'If we sell up we'll have money for a nice place, not that damp rathole. We'll be able to go places, have holidays. Sea air will do me good.'

He sank back and started coughing. I lifted him up and plumped up the pillows. He were my husband and I'd loved him these forty-seven years but he were wrong. If he loved me he wouldn't go against me now.

I thought he'd forgot about it but the next day when he were a little stronger, he said his mind were made up.

'Soon as I'm well enough to get up, I'll ring the estate agent.

You needn't look at me like that, Alice, I know what's best. My name's on the deeds and what I say goes. You'll see I'm right, once it's done, once we're away.'

I saw the land meant nothing to him, only money. Did he think I'd slaved like I had all them years, just for the bit of money it brought in? I never realised my husband were a fool before, but surely anyone could see I worked on the land the way I did for love, only for love?

I went on doing what a wife should do, dressing him, washing him, making his favourite meals, giving him his medicine but all the time I were wondering how he could do this to me. How could he think himself the owner of the farm when all along it had belonged to my family, to me and rightfully to Con?

And then it seemed he were getting stronger each day. Each day the fear of him getting up, picking up the phone, putting the farm up for sale, haunted me so I could think of nowt else.

I got this same bad feeling now that I had that day, that feeling that something dreadful is coming and there's nothing I can do to stop it. It were just the same that night too, the wind rattling the windows in their frames, rain stinging the panes, drowning out the sounds of Bert coughing in his sleep.

She's coming now, Lynn. I can hear her footsteps on the stairs and I don't want this to happen, but I have to let it come. There's something else, something outside, somewhere else I need to be. I have to go, but I can't, she's coming in the door. I'm torn in two; there's something terrible happening here.

***

Lynn went up to bed early. She told Dan she was tired and that was true, but the thought of selling the farm had hit her hard and she needed to be alone to think.

As soon as she turned the door handle a strange smell hit her, a smell of sickness, a smell of warm, unwashed body, tinged with stale urine. She stood with her hand on the light switch, a thrill creeping along the back of her neck. This was worse, much worse than the vision of Dan and Emma Cranton that had haunted her all day; some uncanny, evil scene that she was being plunged into against her will.

She clicked the switch. An old man lay in her bed, his white hair barely visible against the pillow. Lynn gasped. It was not her bed, but one of those old fashioned wooden frames, with a walnut headboard.

Alice was standing against the wall by the window. Rain hammered on the glass. She stared at Lynn then very deliberately leaned over and opened the window as wide as it would go. Freezing air rushed in, throwing sheets of water into the room. The curtains billowed. The roar of the wind filled the room. Suddenly Lynn understood.

'No,' she cried as Alice grimly pulled the blankets off the bed. She tried to pull them back but her hands closed on nothing. The old man coughed but didn't wake. He was wearing only a pyjama jacket and Lynn turned her eyes away from his skinny legs and withered genitals.

Alice glared at her across the bed and still rain came into the room, blowing onto the form on the bed. He coughed again, shifted and opened his eyes briefly. Lynn moved to wake him but again her hands felt nothing but empty air. She didn't even feel the rain, although the room was bitterly cold. She ran to the window, but Alice was in her way. Lynn had to squeeze against her but there was no sense of contact, no warmth of touch, just a fizzle like electricity as she pushed by Alice's manifestation.

The baby kicked violently but she ignored it, intent only on closing the window. The handle was unexpectedly solid, cold in her hands but the wind tugged it away from her, swinging the window back against the wall. A fierce gust blew icy rain in her face and soaked her clothes. She fell back and half turned to see the rosy light of her pink silk lampshades, her own brass bed. It was empty, the duvet turned down, her nightdress laid out ready. There was no sign of Alice.

Lynn sobbed with horror as she leaned out to catch hold of the window frame. Something was scratching and scraping down in the yard. Eyes glowed up at her and she stepped back with a cry. Frantic barking started up and she looked down again, recognised Con Worrall's collie dog.

She ran down the stairs and opened the back door. The dog's eyes blazed at her, looking enormous in its sodden face. Its fur clung to its skin, making it look like an emaciated ghost.

Immediately it started barking, running to and fro, wanting her to follow.

She glanced over her shoulder. Dan was asleep with the empty brandy glass balanced on his chest. A football commentary blared from the TV.

She pulled on her waxed jacket and took the torch from its hook. Something must have happened to Con. She hesitated as she stepped into the downpour outside but the dog was frantic, running to her and pushing its wet nose against her, then running off in the direction of the road.

After only a few yards, her clothes were saturated, her skirt slapping against her legs as she picked her way with the torch, following the white patches on the dog as it ran ahead of her.

This is stupid, she told herself. She should have woken Dan instead of coming out in this, endangering her child. She would turn back in a minute if she didn't find Con, go home, phone the police.

Suddenly Alice was beside her and her fear was like nothing Lynn had ever seen on a human face. She was the same as she had been in the bedroom, early sixties, same polyester slacks and jumper, impervious to the rain.

Lynn's mind went blank, ravaged by the terror that was pouring from Alice. The old woman was running after the dog and Lynn did her best to keep up, flailing along through great puddles, her belly and breasts bouncing and knocking the breath out of her. She was sodden; water streamed from her hair, ran through her clothes till she felt as if she were made of water, had always been one with the water. Her shoes sank in the mud as she slopped after Alice and the dog into the copse of trees just before Annie Chapman's farm.

The dog stopped, howled and whined and Lynn looked up to see something swinging from a large silver birch. She made out the dog lead dangling from a branch and under it something floated in the ditch where Alice capered, up to her thighs in the black water. The light of the torch caught a flash of colour, something red sunk so deep in Con Worrall's neck that it could barely be seen. A tie, she thought vaguely as she looked at his face, eyes bulging, his mouth pulled open in an over-wide smile from which his tongue hung like a lump of liver as he floated face up in the overflowing ditch.

There was a tiny tug in her belly. She closed her eyes and opened them again but Con was still there. He seemed to be laughing at her, as if he had beaten everything in death.

Alice was grabbing at the body in the water, her mouth an elongated scream, but Lynn could see her hands pass through it. The tug came again. Lynn folded her arms over her belly. Her legs trembled, her feet slid in the mire. She saw a light bobbing along the road towards them.

'Dan,' she cried as she sank down into the dark, soft mud.

***

'What were you thinking of? Why didn't you wake me?' Dan was rubbing her hands in the ambulance. She couldn't stop shivering. She was wrapped in a red blanket, like Father Christmas. Someone was wiping her face.

'The dog,' she said and slipped down again.

They'd given her something. Time came and went, in between smelling that hospital smell, seeing Dan's anxious face. She saw Imogen spitting angry words, Con Worrall laughing the soundless death laugh, Emma Cranton grinning like the Cheshire Cat, Alice's grim face as she dragged the bedding off her dying husband, the strangulated bog man with his frozen smile.

The tugging and dragging in her belly became real pain, ebbing and flowing. There were bright lights. The pain crept closer, receded, came nearer again, grew strong and hard, insistent. Cold things pressed on her belly, voices muttered round her. There were the smells of strangers, swishing fabrics, voices chatting, laughing, everyday sounds, then at last, the unendurable pain, the uncontrollable pushing and a voice from nowhere, from somewhere above, like God, 'Easy now, easy, don't push.'

She heard whispers, something was wrong. A hand gripped hers. It was Dan's, she could tell without looking. The voice boomed over her.

'The cord's round baby's neck. We just need to loosen it. You need to hold still, try to relax.' Her whole being was a great lump of fear. Her eyes focussed. The midwife stood between her legs, not meeting her gaze. She saw the scabbed child of her dream, the bog man with the cord round his neck and Con with the red tie sunk in his throat.

There was a scream, her own and a great rush as the child squeezed out of her. She saw the midwife raise the bloody bundle and move away out of her sight. Something else flooded out of her but she was straining, straining to see, seconds were hours. Dan's nails dug into her hand, then at last, the wonderful sound of the child's first terrified cry.

A scream of triumph rose to her lips, but instead she started to laugh. There was a flurry of activity round the constant reassuring wails coming from her baby. Dan kissed her forehead.

'Here's your little boy. Absolutely perfect.' A nurse laid the baby on her chest. Its damp nakedness, its squirming warmth were the first things she felt. Flesh of my flesh, she thought and opened her eyes. The delight on Dan's face wavered and dissolved. His face seemed to melt. She watched his eyes change colour, lose focus and turn inwards. He shook his head, turned a confused look on her, the grin slipping, his jaw loosening, letting his mouth hang open. His skin lost its colour, became yellowish white then suddenly flushed a deep turkey red.

The baby was black. She held him, registering the soft stickiness of his skin. He had stopped crying, his mouth opened and closed making little slurping noises but his eyes stayed squeezed shut. Lynn felt his arms and legs, checked his fingers and toes. Dan stared without speaking; he seemed to shrivel as if collapsing from inside. He got up and walked out without a word.

Chapter Twelve

November 2008

Lynn took Carr off her breast. He was asleep, his mouth slackly open, a dribble of milk running down the dimple in his chin. His head hung back across her arm. The warm weight of him filled her with satisfaction. Every cell of her, all the space that could not be pinned down and classified, was awash with love. She ran a finger over the birthmark on his shoulder. It stood out darker than the rest of his skin, shaped like a tiny fish, or maybe a merman. She thought of Imogen, the tattoo of Darth Vadar, a strong champion, emblazoned on his shoulder.

His letter had arrived two days earlier, out of the blue. She'd felt settled in her mind about her decision not to try to make contact, justified by the fact that she had no means of doing so but the letter had changed that. She'd wondered at the unfamiliar writing on the envelope but she'd half-known and her fingers had shaken as she opened it. Who else would be writing to her in a round, almost childish hand?

> *Dear Lynn*
> *Bet you wondered what happened to me. I'm sorry I went off like that. It seemed the best thing to do. I couldn't handle it. I wanted to ring you lots of times but thought it was better not to after you said it should never have happened, what we did. I'm not sorry it happened though even if you are. I went back to Glasgow but it was no good. I've joined the army and I'm in training, learning catering. It's better than making barrels and I feel like I belong here now. I expect we'll get shipped out to Iraq but I won't be in the firing line, I hope. I just wanted to thank you for everything and to let you know it's turned out okay in the end.*

There was no return address but it was a closure of sorts. For a while Lynn considered making an attempt to find him. He had a future now, a career, but he might end up like Andrew Chapman, might even be killed without ever knowing he had a son. In the end she decided against it. Carr was hers and hers alone. She pushed away the odd twinge of guilt when she looked into Carr's face and saw Imogen there. That would pass. She wanted only to go on like this forever, ensconced in the warmth of the house with the child and Alice, her land a protective barrier around her.

Alice sat in the chair by the fire. Rolo lay asleep at her feet. The room was warm, filled with a benign peace. The baby's body jerked in his sleep. He gave a little snort, just the way her grandfather had used to when he slept in his chair after Sunday lunch. His upper lip wobbled. There was a tiny blister on it caused by the intensity of his sucking.

What must it be like to be so hungry? Lynn wondered. The memory of his greed, Carr's physical demands, ran through her in a flurry of sensation that made her nipples tighten and leak but she was getting used to this journal of the body. She couldn't remember when she hadn't been governed by its insistent story. It overrode her worries about Dan coming back.

She'd been totally oblivious to his pain; everything had been subsumed under the overwhelming sensations of motherhood. The anger and recriminations he'd spat down the phone had no effect on her at first, but once she'd settled to life with Carr, become sure of the flow of love between herself and the child, their endless exclusive satisfaction with each other; once she'd got over her fear of Carr's fragility, of her own ineptness, her confidence grew and as she relaxed, she'd gradually become aware of Dan's suffering.

Her parents wanted her to take him back. They were scandalised at her behaviour, although her father had been slightly more forgiving than her mother, but they'd soon been won over by the baby's charms. Lynn was glad they'd gone home. She wanted to be alone with her son and their constant exhortations to let Dan back into her life had begun to wear her down.

She went to the window holding the baby close against her chest while she rubbed his back gently. It had been raining for days; unrelenting heavy showers that sheened the empty field where the bog man had lain. In the top field the late leeks stood in the puddles waiting for Pilling to come along and take their lives. The rain was their reprieve. Her garden now contained mostly empty patches of used land with only a few stalks of sprouts and some winter leeks still standing.

It was good to be inside, in the warmth, looking out, cosy with the baby. The light was fading. The dark trees shielding Holmes farm loomed in the distance. Once part of the everyday landscape, they now bore a sinister significance that took her back to that terrible night each time she saw them. But that too would pass. She kissed the top of Carr's head, his hair feather-light on her lips then laid him down in his crib. She pulled the curtains on the approaching darkness, just as the telephone began to ring.

'It's me.'

'Yes?'

'Are Malcolm and Jennie still there?'

'They went back yesterday. Dad had to go to a banking conference.'

'How are you managing?'

'Fine, I'm fine. Fe's coming next week.'

'Can I come and see you?'

'And Carr?'

'Of course, I meant Carr as well.'

'Are you still with your mum and dad?'

'It's not working out too well. I miss you – and the baby.'

She stayed silent. Her emotions tugged so she didn't trust herself to speak.

'Have you thought any more about letting me come back?'

It barely sounded like Dan at all, his voice was so uncertain.

'I – haven't decided.'

'What's there to decide? We still love each other, don't we?'

'Are you back at work?' She thought briefly of Emma Cranton but it didn't really matter any more.

'I'm still on paternity leave. They think I'm living at home.'

'Playing happy families?'

'Lynn, I'm trying hard here.'

'Don't try to make me feel guilty, Dan.'

'I'm not. I don't want to fight. I've thought and thought about it. I'll accept the baby. I don't care if people talk. I still love you, despite everything.'

Her lip curled but she didn't speak. After all that had happened, she still wanted the old Dan, the sweet and tender Dan she thought she'd married. Maybe it would still work, if they both tried hard enough, but he would have to come on her terms.

'I don't know.'

'Let me come round. We can't talk properly on the phone.'

Lynn looked at Carr in his crib. He was her first priority but maybe Dan should be given a chance. 'Okay, but only for an hour – and it doesn't mean I've changed my mind.'

She put the phone down and turned to the crib. Alice looked up from watching over the baby. She smiled at Lynn but her eyes were full of foreboding.

***

I never thought the day would come when I'd want to leave but after I seen our Con floating in the ditch like a bundle of rags with all the life drained out of him and not a thing any of us could do about it, I wanted to follow my bones into the ground and sleep. All my life passed before me, the good years of love and work with Albert, the joy of Con's birth. Thank God then I couldn't see what was to come. All my family's gone, Joanie, my brothers, Mum and Dad, all shades of the past and now Con too. Even as I looked at the shape of him blurred in the water I thought, this is my punishment for my crime, the greatest pain that could be inflicted on me, and I'm to be kept here to suffer it for eternity, but gradually the pain eased and I remembered it were my own choice to be here. All along I knew in my heart that Con were doomed from the day he sold the farm.

The need to care for the land has always driven me. Love is the only name for it, but its fire is waning, I can feel myself weakening, the power passing from me to her. Yet there's still work to be done. The land always provides and there's another marked to take Con's place, Lynn's child Carr, born with the sign of the bog man on his shoulder.

She's strong for him but she's wavering over that man of hers and he's not to be trusted. She's got a mother's fierce love for the child but she's just pure emotion right now and that makes her soft. He knows how to search for the weak spot and he'll attack without mercy to get his own way. She has to see that. Lynn and Carr are the last of my family and I'll stop at nothing to make sure they stay where they belong.

***

'Can't we make a fresh start? Go away somewhere, where no one knows us? There'd be no one to ask questions.'

Lynn stared at Dan. How could he even suggest such a thing? Didn't he realise she was rooted here? 'We could pretend we adopted a black baby?' Her own venom surprised her.

'Don't, please. You don't know how I've struggled over this. In the end, through it all, only one thing came clear. I love you. I always have. You know that, don't you?'

'Yes.' She did know it; it was in his voice, in his eyes. She had always known he would stay with her despite all his sexual adventures, but she hadn't realised the depth of the pride he'd had in her. She had taken this away from him. His speech was clotted with tears. Dan was actually crying. Her throat dried up. She wanted desperately to take him back but there was more at stake than her own feelings.

'And Carr?'

'He's our son.' He spoke without hesitation. 'But what if the boy comes back? Have you tried to trace him, tell him about the baby?'

Lynn almost smiled at the way Dan couldn't bring himself to name Imogen. It was as if Imogen was some remote, faceless figure but she realised that even for her, Imogen had moved into a different world. She wouldn't tell Dan about the letter.

'Carr's mine.' It was out before she could stop it; that unshared belief that she could choose the father of her child, even choose whether he should have a father at all.

'Don't you mean ours?' Dan got up and looked in the crib and Lynn saw Alice move protectively towards the child. 'Can I hold him?'

Alice jumped up to get between Dan and the crib but Lynn nodded. She went to the bassinet, picked Carr up, ignoring Alice's fluttering hands and handed him carefully to Dan. 'Watch his head,' she said protectively but Dan was a natural. He cradled Carr expertly and the baby stirred only to shift his position to fit Dan's arms, one leg dangling bonelessly in total comfort.

A smile of innocent delight spread over Dan's face. It was so unlike his usual impassiveness that Lynn was instantly pierced, the defences she'd erected against him breached. She began to cry.

'Don't.' His voice wavered. 'It'll be okay. We'll be all right. Let me come home.'

Alice was capering and grimacing but Lynn took no notice of her. 'Yes,' she said, sobbing freely now.

He laid the baby back in his crib and came to her, enfolding her tightly. It was so good to fit her head under his chin, breathe in his clean, lemony smell. He kissed her, stroking her hair over and over. His hand went to her breast but she stopped him. She was conscious of Alice hovering over the baby, glaring at them. She would have to get used to Dan. Couldn't she see he was a different person, now that she herself had the upper hand?

She leaned in closer, fitting herself against him, making them a ball of ragged emotion, each soaking up the other's feelings. There was no need for speech.

'It's this place,' he said suddenly. She drew back, sensing his need to blame something. 'There's something wrong here, I've felt it all along. We can't stay here, Lynn, not after that horrible thing they dug up in the field and then finding Con Worrall like that. I've never believed in ghosts, evil, stuff like that before but there's something about this place. It's going to destroy us if we don't get away.'

'No.' Lynn pulled out of his embrace. Her hands went to the slack of her belly. She'd totally misjudged the situation; Dan was still angling for power. To him, the farm was a rival for her affection as well as a constant reminder of her infidelity with Imogen, just as Carr too would be. She hurried to the crib. Alice shot her a smile of triumph.

'Lynn, this place has got a hold on you. I know you're not the unfaithful type and you started acting strange right after we got here, even before you got pregnant; all that stuff about being related to the Askins and your obsession with the land. It's not healthy. You need to see that for both our sakes, and for the baby's sake. There's a possibility of a job in Manchester, or if you'd rather, I'll look for something near Somerset. Malcolm and Jennie would be delighted and you'd have someone to help you with Carr. Oh, I know we'd have to take a loss on the farm to get a quick sale. It'll be difficult with the way the housing market's collapsed but it doesn't matter. What matters is us, our family. I want us to be happy again. You'll see I'm right. You'll feel better once we're away from this place.'

'No, Dan, if that's what you're thinking you can forget about coming back.' She looked to Alice for support, felt strengthened by her smile.

'If I don't come back, you won't be able to stay here anyway. I've been staying with my parents for free but if I have to find my own place, I won't be able to carry on paying the mortgage here.'

'I'll get a job.' Lynn felt the ground dissolving under her feet.

'You couldn't earn enough, you know that. You'd still have to depend on me. Don't forget I'm the injured party here.'

'What about Emma Cranton?'

'That's hardly the same level as trying to pass off another man's child as mine, is it? Don't get me wrong, I'm willing to accept responsibility for Carr but I don't have to. There's not a court in the land would expect it.'

Lynn felt nothing but the invisible cord that connected her to Carr. It thrummed with power energising all the cells of her flesh The sound of the rain running down the window swelled in the absence of voices. Alice stood beside her but as power flowed into Lynn, so Alice seemed to weaken and shrivel. Lynn felt herself growing, the energy seemed to come from everywhere, not just from Carr but from the farm, the ground under her feet, the very bricks of the walls. Her body, arms and legs extended, unfolded, inflated.

She was huge, she floated above them all. She could see everything, how the house had lived through generations, how the land changed and reformed, waiting, the water suspended within it, always trying to spread, transform the ground back to the lake it ought to be. It had to be worked with, handled with love.

There was no room for carelessness or compunction. Alice's vision entered her, the full meaning of the scene in her bedroom exploded on her brain, how Alice was so joined to the land that her desire for it meant more than the laws and conventions of her world, more than her love for her husband, and ultimately more than his life. This was why Alice was still here now, why Lynn herself had been drawn to New Cut farm, so that the last of the Askins, her son Carr, should receive his inheritance.

'Lynn?' he was watching her, the impassive face back now, masking his real thoughts but she had seen him, knew him once and for all. 'I'm sorry. I don't mean to hurt you. I just want the best for us.'

'I'm not moving, Dan.'

'Forget about that for now. Let me come home. I promise you won't regret it.'

'All right.' She looked at Alice. Alice was trying to say something, pulling at her arm but it was only the touch of a feather, a whisper in the roar of strength in Lynn's blood. Lynn shook her off. Puzzled, she stared into Alice's eyes; really she should be happy that at last Lynn understood it all, knew what she would have to do. She couldn't read Alice's expression, her features were blurring and fading.

She turned to Dan with a smile. Elation showed in his face, his movements. He pulled her into his arms.

'Lynn, we're going to be so happy, the three of us.'

'Yes.' She let him hold her but kept herself apart.

***

There's many a way to die, none of them pleasant but some is better than others. Slipping away in hospital with nurses looking after you, deadening your pain, your family sitting round, happen that's one of the best, though Lord knows all I wanted were to be back in my own bed.

Accidents now, they're another kettle of fish, depending on the circumstances. Some don't bear thinking about, like my Uncle Philip, caught in the thresher. Dad used to say he never forgot the screams. All his life they came haunting him round harvest time. But something quiet, something so sudden you don't even have time to think about it maybe wouldn't be so bad.

And accidents are common enough on farms. Them ditches can be over five-foot deep. Look what happened to Con. Happen if he'd fallen on the ground when the noose broke, he'd still be alive to tell the tale. Coroner said he'd actually drowned. There were an old farmer in Banks as fell down in one and couldn't get out. Had a heart attack and drownded in the water afore anyone knew he were there. There's many a chap taken a tumble in the canal too, coming out of the pub with a skinful. Most gets themselves back on the bank, or their pals pulls them out but Tommy Martin were unlucky. The night he fell in, there were no one around and he were only found the next morning when one of Holmses' hands cycled up the footpath to work. I were only a slip of a girl but I remember it right enough. We all run out to see Tommy, his upper body floating on the surface, his hair black and slimy, his legs invisible, trapped below the water under an old bicycle someone had threw in. There were a bit of a fuss but Tommy were known for a drinker and he couldn't swim. It's painful to think on, that picture of Con that terrible night, but it makes what happens now so important.

Farmers commit suicide too, especially nowadays with how hard it is to make ends meet. Faced with having to leave your land, go and live in the world of towns, cut off from the soil, who can blame them? Look what happened to Con. And just look at it the other way around, suppose you come here, a complete stranger, you've always lived in a city, knowing nothing about the land, the local people? You don't fit in, you work too hard at your job, trying to make a name for yourself. You're carrying on with another woman, maybe she's getting at you, trying to make you leave your wife, then you find out your wife's been unfaithful, she's carrying another man's child and the man you bought the farm from kills himself on your land, like you're responsible for his death. Wouldn't that be enough to turn your mind, tip you into doing something out of character?

***

Lynn waited patiently for Dan's return. He might yet save himself if he agreed to stay with her on the farm but in her heart she knew he would never settle. And she would never leave. There was no need to think or plan, she only had to let events unfurl. The right thing to do would present itself when the time came.

The doorbell rang. Lynn and Alice froze. Rolo lifted his head from his paws and listened. Carr jerked, startled; his eyes opened and wandered vacantly till they fixed on Alice. Lynn forgot Dan. 'He can see you,' she breathed. It wasn't possible at three weeks, surely, but she could swear there was understanding there. She felt stung that Alice, not herself, should receive this first recognition, but the baby's eyes wavered to her with the same examining look.

Alice inclined her head towards the door. The bell rang again, insistently. Carr opened his mouth and wailed. His skin flushed instantly, the miracle of it's fine strength revealing the network of veins beneath it. Lynn picked him up, felt his damp bottom. She carried him to the door trying to comfort him, Rolo padding behind her.

Annie Chapman stood on the step. 'Sorry to call so late. I only just got back from Ormskirk. Have you got time for a word?'

Lynn stood back for her to enter. It was the first time she'd seen Annie since Carr's birth. She'd supposed Annie had been too embarrassed by the village gossip to come and see her. She closed the door, brought Carr back to the lounge and placed him on the table on his changing mat. He was crying hard now, working himself up for a howling session.

'I've kept meaning to call, but with everything that's happened...' she kept peeking at the baby and looking away.

Lynn nodded, her hands deftly removing Carr's nappy, cleaning his bottom as he screamed, his fists waving with anger. She'd expected ostracism from the villagers once Barney Dougan's wagging tongue had spread the gossip around. His open easy manner with her had changed, once he'd set eyes on Carr after she'd come home. It didn't mean anything to her, she barely knew any of them anyway but she'd expected a bit more understanding from Annie; she was the nearest thing to a friend that Lynn had in the area.

'You know Jim had a stroke?'

Lynn turned, her face red as Carr's. 'No – I didn't know. I haven't seen anyone, except Barney and he doesn't have much to say to me nowadays. My parents have been here – and – well you know how it is with a new baby. I'm so sorry. I would have got in touch if I'd known. How did it happen?'

'It were only a minor one, luckily, not long after you went in hospital. I were going to come and see you but the shock of Con and everything and then, poor Jim, he just got up one morning, went in the bathroom and collapsed. He were in hospital himself for a week but he got better right quick. You wouldn't know he'd had a stroke now, just a bit of weakness in his left arm, a little bit of slowness when you ask him a question, but they reckon that'll disappear if he takes care.'

Lynn finished changing Carr, picked him up and held him. She was sorry for his anger, but it was funny, such a tiny, puny little thing, such a terrible demonstration of fury. His whole body showed the conviction of his own strength, his own importance. His head bumped against her chest, searching for her breast. He screamed even harder.

'I'll have to feed him. Do you mind?'

'Course not. He's a bonny lad.' Annie watched as the baby clamped his mouth on Lynn's nipple, his movements quick and practised already.

'Nine-and- a-half pounds,' Lynn bloomed with pride.

'What made you choose Carr? It's such an unusual name.'

Lynn smiled. 'It means "from the marsh". You know, like the bog? It just seemed right.'

Annie smiled uneasily. 'It suits him though', she said at last. 'I kept saying to Jim, I'd have to get up to see you, but he still needed looking after when he come home and what with our Andrew as well. You must have thought I were – '

'Ignoring me like the rest of the village?' Lynn sighed. 'I'm not bothered. I'm glad you came though.'

She rocked herself slightly in time with Carr's rhythmic sucking. It pushed thought to the back of her mind. There was only the connection between Carr's body and her own, the milk pulled from her breast, the powerful action of the baby's jaws tugging her breasts, belly, legs and pumping through her brain. Nothing else mattered. The only sound in the room was of muffled gulping when one of them shifted and the seal of gum to nipple was breached, letting air rush in.

The other women watched. Lynn could see in both their eyes their own memories of suckling their children. Pain cramped her bowels as she thought of Alice's son floating like a log in the ditch and Andrew Chapman, blasted and bitter, forever damaged. Carr pulled away from the breast and cried. She was holding him too tightly, almost squeezing him. She sat him up and winded him, his head lolling comically as his eyes rolled from Alice to Annie.

'I have come for a reason,' Annie turned her direct gaze on Lynn. 'Andrew's coming back to live at home. I come to give you a month's notice.'

'Oh.' Lynn's first reaction was of dismay. The rent from the cottage was something she might have to rely on in the future. She looked at Alice but she was grinning.

'It's been a warning signal to Jim, this stroke. He's realised he ought to take things easier, we're both agreed on that. It's made Andrew take a look at himself too. Jim wants him to take over all the admin stuff for the farm and the shops. We're thinking of taking on more labourers and employing Andrew as manager. He knows the farm business backwards, it would be better for us than getting in some college kid. He won't be able to do the physical stuff but there's nothing wrong with his brain.'

'Will he never get better, walk normally?' Lynn put Carr to her other breast. His sucking was less demanding now, but still gratifying.

'Who knows? The doctors can't say for sure. I suppose so much depends on his will, he's been in such a bad state mentally, but he seems to be picking up a bit now.' Annie twisted her hands in her lap. 'In a way Jim's having this stroke opened up a way for Andrew. He were so bitter and frustrated. I were worried sick over him, the drinking and everything. We couldn't lift him out of those black moods of his; we couldn't even speak to him half the time without him flying off the handle. We didn't know how to help him, I mean look what happened with Con.'

Lynn glanced at Alice, there was no way of sparing her from painful memories but Alice's face gave nothing away. She was staring intently at the back of Carr's head.

'I'd better be going anyway,' Annie stood up. 'I still don't like to be away from Jim for too long. How are things with you, then?' She looked down at the baby. 'I suppose you'll be moving on now?'

Lynn jerked in surprise, disturbing Carr. He waved a fumbling fist as if trying to restrain her, take possession of the breast. 'I've no plans to go anywhere.'

'Oh,' Annie flushed. 'I didn't mean to pry.' Her knowledge of the village gossip about Carr's colour and Dan's expulsion was making her feel awkward.

'I belong here, I'm the last of the Askins, remember?' Lynn tried to make her voice light. 'Dan's still around anyway. I'm expecting him any minute.'

Annie's eyes rounded. 'I'd better be going then.'

'No need to rush.' Time seemed endless for her. She could just sit forever with Carr emptying her breast. His sucking was sporadic now, his eyes drooping then suddenly opening again, his mouth slackening then tightening again, attacking her nipple with fresh ferocity for a few moments before sliding back towards sleep again.

'No, I have to go. I've supper to get and I need to check on Andrew. I will come again, or you could walk up with the baby.'

Lynn lay back in her chair after Annie had gone, Carr asleep on her breast. Gently she detached him, his mouth giving her up with a plop. She waited for Dan, watching the flickering light of the fire. There would be more gossip but it didn't matter, it would die down and she would be left alone to fulfil her task.

Rain rattled the window panes.

She got up, cradling Carr in one arm and drew back the curtain. Water streamed down the glass, blurring the view. Outside all was water rippling reflected moonlight in the dark, the fields inundated like a practice run for the return of the mere. The ditches must be full. She could just make out the copse where Con had died. The rain made a music that accompanied her vision of that awful night, the first night of her baby's life.

Rain garbled the silvery lake that lay over the bog man's only grave. He would be examined, stared at by millions of eyes, forever separated from his native soil. Desperate attempts would be made to keep him from the disintegration that must come to them all but there would come a time when even he would return to the earth. She and Dan, even Carr would become dust, there would be no more Askins, no more stories, only the land returning to its rhythm, a composition of earth and water.

She carried Carr back to his crib and laid him down. What did he know of this? Did he feel these rhythms that would be lost once he gained the illusion of thought, of language, these wordless spaces to be found again only in dreams or moments of poetry or love? Whatever she did would be to protect this.

***

So we wait, the Mere and its secrets outside, warmth and new life inside. We are made of water, my mam told me once, the cells of our bodies pull with the tides of the sea, the pull of the moon, the ripples of wind on the lake. This comes before everything; the water and land from which we spring.

Her husband don't know this yet. He doesn't know how his life hangs on a single choice, how he thinks of the land, whether he can feel the water within himself. He is coming now, bent with his hopes and his fears. He knows less than this infant sleeping between us. She thinks he could learn but leopards don't change their spots.

His key is in the lock. She turns to look at me. It is time. I am not afraid. Whatever happens, we will never leave here.

Bibliography

All poetry quotes originally taken from The Lake Poets (1980, 1985) Dalesman Publishing Company Ltd and The Complete Works of William Wordsworth, edited by Charles Kennett Burrow (Collins' Clear Type Press)

Barney quotes, and sometimes misquotes, from the following texts:

Southey, Robert *Skiddaw and Derwentwater*

Keats, John *Castlerigg*

North, Christopher *Helm Crag*

North, Christopher *Loughrigg Farm*

Coleridge S.T. *Small and Silent*

Wordsworth, William *Aira Force*

Budworth, Joseph *Windermere in November*

Wordsworth, William *Grasmere*

Rawnsley, HD (misquotes from) *A Song of Spring*

Wordsworth, William *Intimations of Immortality* (Burrow)

Wordsworth, Wordsworth, *To_Upon The Birth of Her First-Born Child* (Burrow)

Rawnsley, H.D. (misquotes from) *A Song of Spring*

Wordsworth, William *A Dale in March* (Burrow)

Rawnsley, H.D *Song of Spring*

Wordsworth, William *Untitled verse*

Wordsworth, William *Daffodils* (Burrow)

About the Author

Carol Fenlon is a Lancashire novelist whose writing is heavily influenced by place. Her novels and short stories are set in the landscapes of West Lancashire where she lives but also feature the contexts of Liverpool and North Wales. Carol's first novel *Consider The Lilies* won the Impress Novel Prize in 2007 and many of her published short stories are to be found in the collections, *Triple Death* and *Plotlands*. When she is not writing fiction, Carol is a keen gardener and local historian.

More Books From ThunderPoint Publishing Ltd.

The Oystercatcher Girl
Gabrielle Barnby
ISBN: 978-1-910946-17-6 (eBook)
ISBN: 978-1-910946-15-2 (Paperback)

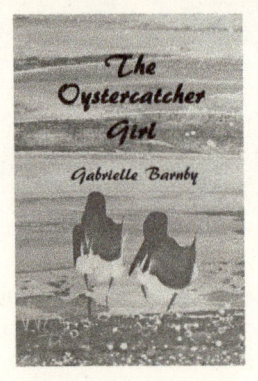

In the medieval splendour of St Magnus Cathedral, three women gather to mourn the untimely passing of Robbie: Robbie's widow, Tessa; Tessa's old childhood friend, Christine, and Christine's unstable and unreliable sister, Lindsay.

But all is not as it seems: what is the relationship between the three women, and Robbie? What secrets do they hide? And who has really betrayed who?

Set amidst the spectacular scenery of the Orkney Islands, Gabrielle Barnby's skilfully plotted first novel is a beautifully understated story of deception and forgiveness, love and redemption.

With poetic and precise language Barnby draws you in to the lives, loves and losses of the characters till you feel a part of the story.

'The Oystercatcher Girl is a wonderfully evocative and deftly woven story' – Sara Bailey

The House with the Lilac Shutters
Gabrielle Barnby
ISBN: 978-1-910946-02-2 (eBook)
ISBN: 978-0-9929768-8-0 (Paperback)

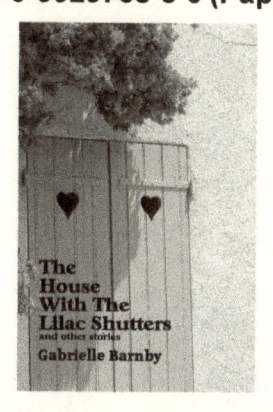

Irma Lagrasse has taught piano to three generations of villagers, whilst slowly twisting the knife of vengeance; Nico knows a secret; and M. Lenoir has discovered a suppressed and dangerous passion.

Revolving around the Café Rose, opposite The House with the Lilac Shutters, this collection of contemporary short stories links a small town in France with a small town in England, traces the unexpected connections between the people of both places and explores the unpredictable influences that the past can have on the present.

Characters weave in and out of each other's stories, secrets are concealed and new connections are made.

With a keenly observant eye, Barnby illustrates the everyday tragedies, sorrows, hopes and joys of ordinary people in this vividly understated and unsentimental collection.

'The more I read, and the more descriptions I encountered, the more I was put in mind of one of my all time favourite texts – Dylan Thomas' Under Milk Wood' – lindasbookbag.com

Over Here
Jane Taylor
ISBN: 978-0-9929768-3-5 (eBook)
ISBN: 978-0-9929768-2-8 (Paperback)

It's coming up to twenty-four hours since the boy stepped down from the big passenger liner – it must be, he reckons foggily – because morning has come around once more with the awful irrevocability of time destined to lead nowhere in this worrying new situation. His temporary minder on board – last spotted heading for the bar some while before the lumbering process of docking got underway – seems to have vanished for good. Where does that leave him now? All on his own in a new country: that's where it leaves him. He is just nine years old.

An eloquently written novel tracing the social transformations of a century where possibilities were opened up by two world wars that saw millions of men move around the world to fight, and mass migration to the new worlds of Canada and Australia by tens of thousands of people looking for a better life.

Through the eyes of three generations of women, the tragic story of the nine year old boy on Liverpool docks is brought to life in saddeningly evocative prose.

'…a sweeping haunting first novel that spans four generations and two continents…' – Cristina Odone/Catholic Herald

The False Men
Mhairead MacLeod
ISBN: 978-1-910946-27-5 (eBook)
ISBN: 978-1-910946-25-1 (Paperback)

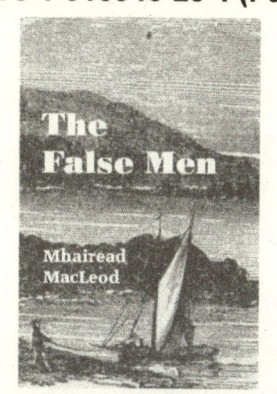

North Uist, Outer Hebrides, 1848

Jess MacKay has led a privileged life as the daughter of a local landowner, sheltered from the harsher aspects of life. Courted by the eligible Patrick Cooper, the Laird's new commissioner, Jess's future is mapped out, until Lachlan Macdonald arrives on North Uist, amid rumours of forced evictions on islands just to the south.

As the uncompromising brutality of the Clearances reaches the islands, and Jess sees her friends ripped from their homes, she must decide where her heart, and her loyalties, truly lie.

Set against the evocative backdrop of the Hebrides and inspired by a true story, *The False Men* is a compelling tale of love in a turbulent past that resonates with the upheavals of the modern world.

> **'...an engaging tale of powerlessness, love and disillusionment in the context of the type of injustice that, sadly, continues to this day' – Anne Goodwin**

In The Shadow Of The Hill
Helen Forbes
ISBN: 978-0-9929768-1-1 (eBook)
ISBN: 978-0-9929768-0-4 (Paperback)

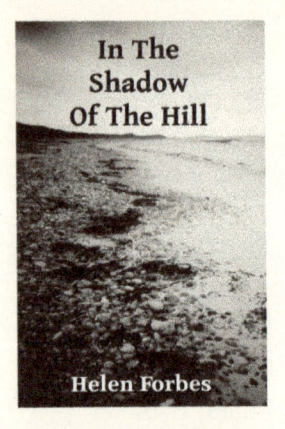

An elderly woman is found battered to death in the common stairwell of an Inverness block of flats.

Detective Sergeant Joe Galbraith starts what seems like one more depressing investigation of the untimely death of a poor unfortunate who was in the wrong place, at the wrong time.

As the investigation spreads across Scotland it reaches into a past that Joe has tried to forget, and takes him back to the Hebridean island of Harris, where he spent his childhood.

Among the mountains and the stunning landscape of religiously conservative Harris, in the shadow of Ceapabhal, long buried events and a tragic story are slowly uncovered, and the investigation takes on an altogether more sinister aspect.

In The Shadow Of The Hill skilfully captures the intricacies and malevolence of the underbelly of Highland and Island life, bringing tragedy and vengeance to the magical beauty of the Outer Hebrides.

'...our first real home-grown sample of modern Highland noir' – Roger Hutchinson; West Highland Free Press

Madness Lies
Helen Forbes
ISBN: 978-1-910946-31-2 (eBook)
ISBN: 978-1-910946-30-5 (Paperback)

When an Inverness Councillor is murdered in broad daylight in the middle of town, Detective Sergeant Joe Galbraith sees a familiar figure running from the scene.

According to everyone who knows him, the Councillor had no enemies, but someone clearly wanted him dead.

The victim's high profile means the police want a quick resolution to the case, but no one seems to know anything. Or if they do, they're not prepared to say.

This second novel of Highland Noir from Helen Forbes continues the series with a crime thriller that moves between Inverness, North Uist and London, reaching a terrifying denouement at the notorious Black Rock Gorge.

'Gritty and ominous, Forbes's brand of 'Highland Noir' is shaping up to be a good series' – Sunday Herald

Changed Times
Ethyl Smith
ISBN: 978-1-910946-09-1 (eBook)
ISBN: 978-1-910946-08-4 (Paperback)

1679 – The Killing Times: Charles II is on the throne, the Episcopacy has been restored, and southern Scotland is in ferment.

The King is demanding superiority over all things spiritual and temporal and rebellious Ministers are being ousted from their parishes for refusing to bend the knee.

When John Steel steps in to help one such Minister in his home village of Lesmahagow he finds himself caught up in events that reverberate not just through the parish, but throughout the whole of southern Scotland.

From the Battle of Drumclog to the Battle of Bothwell Bridge, John's platoon of farmers and villagers find themselves in the heart of the action over that fateful summer where the people fight the King for their religion, their freedom, and their lives.

Set amid the tumult and intrigue of Scotland's Killing Times, John Steele's story powerfully reflects the changes that took place across 17th century Scotland, and stunningly brings this period of history to life.

'Smith writes with a fine ear for Scots speech, and with a sensitive awareness to the different ways in which history intrudes upon the lives of men and women, soldiers and civilians, adults and children'
– James Robertson

Dark Times
Ethyl Smith
ISBN: 978-1-910946-26-8 (eBook)
ISBN: 978-1-910946-24-4 (Paperback)

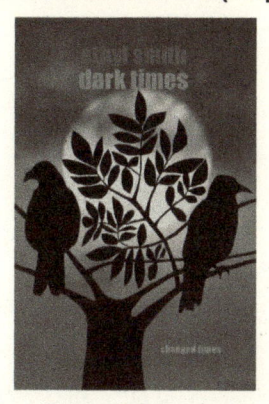

The summer of 1679 is a dark one for the Covenanters, routed by government troops at the Battle of Bothwell Brig. John Steel is on the run, hunted for his part in the battle by the vindictive Earl of Airlie. And life is no easier for the hapless Sandy Gillon, curate of Lesmahagow Kirk, in the Earl's sights for aiding John Steel's escape.

Outlawed and hounded, the surviving rebels have no choice but to take to the hills and moors to evade capture and deportation. And as a hard winter approaches, Marion Steel discovers she's pregnant with her third child.

Dark Times is the second part of Ethyl Smith's sweeping *Times* series that follows the lives of ordinary people in extraordinary times.

'What really sets Smith's novel apart, however, is her superb use of Scots dialogue. From the educated Scots of the gentry and nobility to the broader brogues of everyday folk, the dialogue sparkles and demands to be read out loud.' – Shirley Whiteside (The National)

Dead Cat Bounce
Kevin Scott
ISBN: 978-1-910946-17-6 (eBook)
ISBN: 978-1-910946-15-2 (Paperback)

"Well, either way, you'll have to speak to your brother today because...unless I get my money by tomorrow morning there's not going to be a funeral."

When your 11 year old brother has been tragically killed in a car accident, you might think that organising his funeral would take priority. But when Nicky's coffin, complete with Nicky's body, goes missing, deadbeat loser Matt has only 26 hours in which to find the £20,000 he owes a Glasgow gangster or explain to his grieving mother why there's not going to be a funeral.

Enter middle brother, Pete, successful City trader with an expensive wife, expensive children, and an expensive villa in Tuscany. Pete's watches cost £20,000, but he has his own problems, and Matt doesn't want his help anyway.

Seething with old resentments, the betrayals of the past and the double-dealings of the present, the two brothers must find a way to work together to retrieve Nicky's body, discovering along the way that they are not so different after all.

'Underplaying the comic potential to highlight the troubled relationship between the equally flawed brothers. It's one of those books that keep the reader hooked right to the end' – The Herald

The Wrong Box
Andrew C Ferguson
ISBN: 978-1-910946-14-5 (Paperback)
ISBN: 978-1-910946-16-9 (eBook)

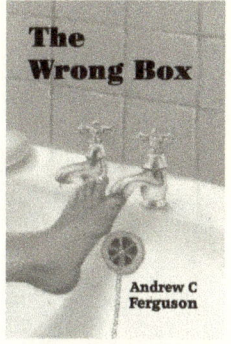

All I know is, I'm in exile in Scotland, and there's a dead Scouser businessman in my bath. With his toe up the tap.

Meet Simon English, corporate lawyer, heavy drinker and Scotophobe, banished from London after being caught misbehaving with one of the young associates on the corporate desk. As if that wasn't bad enough, English finds himself acting for a spiralling money laundering racket that could put not just his career, but his life, on the line.

Enter Karen Clamp, an 18 stone, well-read wann be couturier from the Auchendrossan sink estate, with an encyclopedic knowledge of Council misdeeds and 19th century Scottish fiction. With no one to trust but each other, this mismatched pair must work together to investigate a series of apparently unrelated frauds and discover how everything connects to the mysterious Wrong Box.

Manically funny, *The Wrong Box* is a chaotic story of lust, money, power and greed, and the importance of being able to sew a really good hem.

'…the makings of a new Caledonian Comic Noir genre: Rebus with jokes, Val McDiarmid with buddha belly laughs, or Trainspotting for the professional classes'

Toxic
Jackie McLean
Shortlisted for the Yeovil Book Prize 2011
ISBN: 978-0-9575689-8-3 (eBook)
ISBN: 978-0-9575689-9-0 (Paperback)

The recklessly brilliant DI Donna Davenport, struggling to hide a secret from police colleagues and get over the break-up with her partner, has been suspended from duty for a fiery and inappropriate outburst to the press.

DI Evanton, an old-fashioned, hard-living misogynistic copper has been newly demoted for thumping a suspect, and transferred to Dundee with a final warning ringing in his ears and a reputation that precedes him.

And in the peaceful, rolling Tayside farmland a deadly store of MIC, the toxin that devastated Bhopal, is being illegally stored by a criminal gang smuggling the valuable substance necessary for making cheap pesticides.

An anonymous tip-off starts a desperate search for the MIC that is complicated by the uneasy partnership between Davenport and Evanton and their growing mistrust of each others actions.

Compelling and authentic, Toxic is a tense and fast paced crime thriller.

'...a humdinger of a plot that is as realistic as it is frightening' – crimefictionlover.com

Shadows
Jackie McLean
ISBN: 978-0-9575689-8-3 (eBook)
ISBN: 978-0-9575689-9-0 (Paperback)

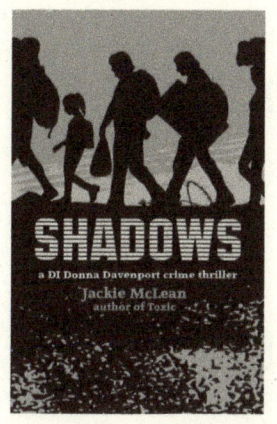

When DI Donna Davenport is called out to investigate a body washed up on Arbroath beach, it looks like a routine murder inquiry. But then the enquiry takes on a more sinister form.

There are similarities with a previous murder, and now a woman connected to them both has also gone missing.

For Donna, this is becoming personal, and with the added pressure of feeling watched at every turn, she is convinced that Jonas Evanton has returned to seek his revenge on her for his downfall.

Fearing they may be looking for a serial killer, Donna and her new team are taken in a horrifying and unexpected direction. Because it's not a serial killer – it's worse.

Moving from Dundee to the south coast of Turkey and the Syrian border, this is a fast paced novel about those who live their lives in the shadows, and those who exploit them.

'...a frank and unapologetic depiction of the ways human trafficking affects societies worldwide' – The Lesbiam Review

The Bogeyman Chronicles
Craig Watson
ISBN: 978-1-910946-11-4 (eBook)
ISBN: 978-1-910946-10-7 (Paperback)

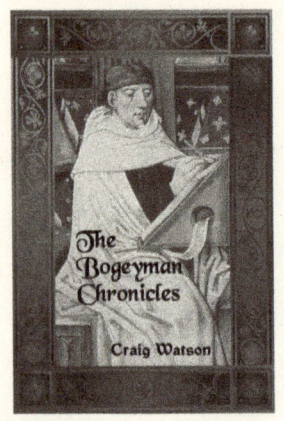

In 14th Century Scotland, amidst the wars of independence, hatred, murder and betrayal are commonplace. People are driven to extraordinary lengths to survive, whilst those with power exercise it with cruel pleasure.

Royal Prince Alexander Stewart, son of King Robert II and plagued by rumours of his illegitimacy, becomes infamous as the Wolf of Badenoch, while young Andrew Christie commits an unforgivable sin and lay Brother Brodie Affleck in the Restenneth Priory pieces together the mystery that links them all together.

From the horror of the times and the changing fortunes of the characters, the legend of the Bogeyman is born and Craig Watson cleverly weaves together the disparate lives of the characters into a compelling historical mystery that will keep you gripped throughout.

Over 80 years the lives of three men are inextricably entwined, and through their hatreds, murders and betrayals the legend of Christie Cleek, the bogeyman, is born.

'The Bogeyman Chronicles haunted our imagination long after we finished it' – iScot Magazine

Mule Train
Huw Francis
ISBN: 978-0-9575689-0-7 (eBook)
ISBN: 978-0-9575689-1-4 (Paperback)

Annie MacDonald is fed up and stuck in a dead-end job in London, where she recently lost out on a promotion to someone with old-school connections. What better way to kick-start her life than resigning her job, taking the legacy left by her grandfather, and heading to his beloved Pakistan looking for adventure?

When four lives come together in the remote and spectacular mountains bordering Afghanistan, a deadly cocktail of treachery, betrayal and violence explodes, with devastating consequences.

Written with a deep love of Pakistan and the Pakistani people, Mule Train will sweep you from Karachi in the south to the Shandur Pass in the north, through the dangerous borderland alongside Afghanistan, in an adventure that will keep you gripped throughout.

'Stunningly captures the feel of Pakistan, from Karachi to the hills' – tripfiction.com

QueerBashing
Tim Morrison
ISBN: 978-1-910946-06-0 (eBook)
ISBN: 978-0-9929768-9-7 (Paperback)

The first queerbasher McGillivray ever met was in the mirror.

From the revivalist churches of Orkney in the 1970s, to the gay bars of London and Northern England in the 90s, via the divinity school at Aberdeen, this is the story of McGillivray, a self-centred, promiscuous hypocrite, failed Church of Scotland minister, and his own worst enemy.

Determined to live life on his own terms, McGillivray's grasp on reality slides into psychosis and a sense of his own invulnerability, resulting in a brutal attack ending life as he knows it.

Raw and uncompromising, this is a viciously funny but ultimately moving account of one man's desire to come to terms with himself and live his life as he sees fit.

'...an arresting novel of pain and self-discovery' – Alastair Mabbott (The Herald)

A Good Death
Helen Davis
ISBN: 978-0-9575689-7-6 (eBook)
ISBN: 978-0-9575689-6-9 (Paperback)

'*A good death is better than a bad conscience,*' said Sophie.
1983 – Georgie, Theo, Sophie and Helena, four disparate young Cambridge undergraduates, set out to scale Ausangate, one of the highest and most sacred peaks in the Andes.

Seduced into employing the handsome and enigmatic Wamani as a guide, the four women are initiated into the mystically dangerous side of Peru, Wamani and themselves as they travel from Cuzco to the mountain, a journey that will shape their lives forever.

2013 – though the women are still close, the secrets and betrayals of Ausangate chafe at the friendship.

A girls' weekend at a lonely Fenland farmhouse descends into conflict with the insensitive inclusion of an overbearing young academic toyboy brought along by Theo. Sparked by his unexpected presence, pent up petty jealousies, recriminations and bitterness finally explode the truth of Ausangate, setting the women on a new and dangerous path.

Sharply observant and darkly comic, Helen Davis's début novel is an elegant tale of murder, seduction, vengeance, and the value of a good friendship.

'The prose is crisp, adept, and emotionally evocative' – Lesbrary.com

The Birds That Never Flew
Margot McCuaig
Shortlisted for the Dundee International Book Prize 2012
Longlisted for the Polari First Book Prize 2014
ISBN: 978-0-9929768-5-9 (eBook)
ISBN: 978-0-9929768-4-2 (Paperback)

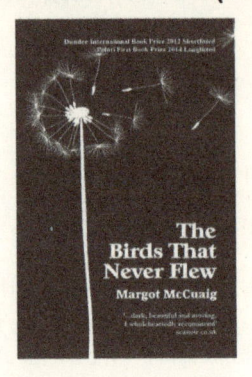

'Have you got a light hen? I'm totally gaspin.'

Battered and bruised, Elizabeth has taken her daughter and left her abusive husband Patrick. Again. In the bleak and impersonal Glasgow housing office Elizabeth meets the provocatively intriguing drug addict Sadie, who is desperate to get her own life back on track.

The two women forge a fierce and interdependent relationship as they try to rebuild their shattered lives, but despite their bold, and sometimes illegal attempts it seems impossible to escape from the abuse they have always known, and tragedy strikes.

More than a decade later Elizabeth has started to implement her perfect revenge – until a surreal Glaswegian Virgin Mary steps in with imperfect timing and a less than divine attitude to stick a spoke in the wheel of retribution.

Tragic, darkly funny and irreverent, *The Birds That Never Flew* ushers in a new and vibrant voice in Scottish literature.

'...dark, beautiful and moving, I wholeheartedly recommend' scanoir.co.uk

The Bonnie Road
Suzanne d'Corsey
ISBN: 978-1-910946-01-5 (eBook)
ISBN: 978-0-9929768-6-6 (Paperback)

My grandmother passed me in transit. She was leaving, I was coming into this world, our spirits meeting at the door to my mother's womb, as she bent over the bed to close the thin crinkled lids of her own mother's eyes.

The women of Morag's family have been the keepers of tradition for generations, their skills and knowledge passed down from woman to woman, kept close and hidden from public view, official condemnation and religious suppression.

In late 1970s St. Andrews, demand for Morag's services are still there, but requested as stealthily as ever, for even in 20th century Scotland witchcraft is a dangerous Art to practise.

When newly widowed Rosalind arrives from California to tend her ailing uncle, she is drawn unsuspecting into a new world she never knew existed, one in which everyone seems to have a secret, but that offers greater opportunities than she dreamt of – if she only has the courage to open her heart to it.

Richly detailed, dark and compelling, d'Corsey magically transposes the old ways of Scotland into the 20th Century and brings to life the ancient traditions and beliefs that still dance just below the surface of the modern world.

'...successfully portrays rich characters in compelling plots, interwoven with atmospheric Scottish settings & history and coloured with witchcraft & romance' – poppypeacockpens.com